When Somebody Loves You Back

Also by Mary B. Morrison

Nothing Has Ever Felt Like This

Somebody's Gotta Be on Top

He's Just a Friend

Never Again Once More

Soul Mates Dissipate

Who's Making Love

Justice Just Us Just Me

Coauthored with Carl Weber

She Ain't the One

Copresented with Lou Richie

Diverse Stories: From the Imaginations of Sixth Graders

(An anthology of fiction by Lou Richie's sixth grade class)

When Somebody Loves You Back

MARY B. MORRISON

KENSINGTON BOOKS
www.kensingtonbooks.com

DAFINA BOOKS are published by

Kensington Publishing Corp.
850 Third Avenue
New York, NY 10022

ISBN: 0-7582-0730-1

Printed in the United States of America

This book is dedicated to the man I am most proud of:

Jesse Bernard Byrd, Jr., my son

ACKNOWLEDGMENTS

I thank God for blessing me and I thank God for each of you, praying your lives are filled with joy and prosperity.

To all of the Hurricane Katrina victims, many of whom are my family and friends, stay strong; hold on to God's unchanging hand. Although I cannot relate firsthand, I do know home (New Orleans) will never be the same for me, especially for you. Wherever you are, keep love and faith in your heart, and get every dime you deserve from the government. In my opinion, no amount is too much, because the government hasn't done nearly enough to compensate you. Never give up hope. There is a brighter day ahead.

To my fans, writing the series was an enjoyable but not easy journey. After five novels, you've anxiously awaited number six, *When Somebody Loves You Back*, eager to find out what happens to Darius. All I can say is, "You are awesome!" I know many of you are still recommending *Soul Mates Dissipate*, and I cannot thank you enough for supporting my works.

To my deceased parents, I've never written a book without expressing gratitude, and I never will. In loving memory of my biological parents, Joseph Henry Morrison and Elester Noel. To my great-aunt and uncle who reared me, Willie Frinkle and Ella Beatrice Turner, I am eternally grateful.

To my loving son, Jesse Byrd, Jr., anything worth having is worth working for. Continue doing your best at all times. Take the bitter with the sweet. Visualize your success. As Chris Farr tells you, "Prepare for war in time of peace." I know you can make it into the NBA if you bring your A game every single time. Adversity and success are teachers of life but only when you learn the lessons. Always respect yourself, respect others, and surround yourself with positive people who are good individuals. Stay humble. I'm proud of you, sweetie. You are truly a wonderful young man with great character and you are Mommy's most cherished gift from God.

A special shout-out to Jason "JG" Grisby, a wonderful young man beginning college. Jason, your strength comes from within. You've overcome more mental and physical challenges than the average teenager and I've never heard you complain. Jason, you have a quiet sense of confidence that some, but not all, of us understand. Progressing to the next level, you need to step it up and verbalize your confidence. I'm not suggesting you become arrogant. It's not what you say but how you say it. The key is to speak up, speak out, respectfully so, especially when communicating with coaches.

With mad love for my recently adopted godson, Robert "Chew" Owens, you have made Mama proud. You earned your number-one ranking in the Oakland Athletic League. A wise man, Mr. Al Cason, once told me, "You must always help someone. But when you choose that person, you've chosen wrong." Mr. Cason made it clear that I could never help someone who didn't want help. Chew, when I looked into your eyes, I felt your sincerity for wanting help. In many ways, I'm the one blessed because you've helped me to grow too. As you begin your first year of college, I want you to know, the thing I admire most about you, Chew, is your determination to succeed. No matter how challenging college becomes, hold on to your winning spirit. A man only fails when he fails to try. I will continue to be one of your catalysts. More importantly, I want you, on your road to success, to remember that you must help someone less fortunate. But when you choose that person, you've chosen wrong.

I've got nothin' but love for the Oakland/San Francisco Bay Area college basketballers with game: Jesse Byrd, Jr., Antonio Kellog, James Morgan, Manny Quezada, Armondo Surratt, and Alan Wiggins, Jr., at the University of San Francisco; Timothy Kees at Menlo College; Diamon Simpson at St. Mary's College; Larry Gurganious at Gonzaga University; DeMarcus Nelson at Duke University; Quinton Thomas at North Carolina Universisty, Jason Grisby, and Robert Owens, college bound seniors. Stay focused and I look forward to witnessing all of you play professionally.

To my siblings, you're the greatest! I love Wayne, Derrick, Andrea, and Regina Morrison, Margie Rickerson, Debra Noel, and Brian Turner.

To my Sweeter than Honey sisterhood group, author Rachelle Chase, Onie Simpson, and Malissa Walton, I appreciate your love, respect, and wisdom, as we continue to support and empower one another in achieving our personal and professional goals. Let's attain our group goal of becoming serial daters traveling around the world.

Yolanda Parks of TV One, Michael Baisden, Cherisse Gage, Lissa Woodson, Jeremy "JL" Woodson, Barbara Cooper, Carmen Polk, Shannette Slaughter, Larry Addison, Gloria Mallette, E. Lynn Harris, Lou Richie, Jessie Evans, Chris Farr, Brian Shaw, Phil Doherty, Bill Johnson, Pete Morales, Carl Weber, Victoria Christopher Murray, Ruth and Howard Kees, Vanessa Ibanitoru (my friend since third grade), Brenda and Aaron Clark, and my McDonogh No. 35 Roneagles family, thanks for your continued support.

To my entire Kensington family, Joan, Jessica, Mary, Maureen, Nicole, Steven Zacharius, and Barbara Bennett, I am grateful for all you do.

I love my editor, Karen Thomas. Karen, you have a magnificent head on your shoulders. You're a powerful and brilliant woman operating the most successful African-American imprint, Dafina Books.

To Claudia Menza, my agent, although we've separated, I still love and respect you. When all of the contractual obligations are fulfilled, we will have presented eleven books.

Last, but damn sure nuff not least, Felicia Polk, you are forever my best friend and the world's greatest publicist. May God bless you beyond measure. Thanks for believing in me.

The acknowledgments for my next book are dedicated to book

clubs and bookstore owners and managers. I appreciate your love and support.

I have so many more people to acknowledge, but I also have other books to write, so if I didn't mention you this time, forgive me now, remind me later.

PREFACE

Soul Mates Dissipate, Never Again Once More, He's Just a Friend, Some-body's Gotta Be on Top, Nothing Has Ever Felt Like This, and *When Somebody Loves You Back* are intertwined. I recommend reading the series in the order listed above. You can preview an excerpt of each novel at www.MaryMorrison.com and www.SweeterThanHoney.net.

Next is my *Sweeter than Honey* series. Pussy is sweeter than honey and more valuable than money. Women everywhere, after reading this series, will become sexually, spiritually, and emotionally em-powered, learning, that is, if they don't already know, women are a triple threat—possessing power, passion, and all the pussy in the world. Fellas, just when you thought it couldn't get any sweeter for the ladies, more women are earning good salaries and/or owning and operating businesses. Therefore, men who are liabilities can kiss a *Sweeter than Honey* asset good-bye.

Sweeter than Honey women worship themselves. They don't hesi-tate to sit on a man's face, give him a taste, and ultimately do him right, but only if he comes correct. *Sweeter than Honey* women de-mand respect. I know what you guys are thinking . . . what about the women who disrespect men? Most women respond to the way they are treated. So don't undermine a woman's intelligence, ex-pecting her to accept your chauvinistic behavior (i.e., infidelity, lies, control tactics, abuse, etc.). When you genuinely love your woman, she'll truly love you, but it's going to cost you. *Sweeter than Honey* women never give their sweetness away for free.

My *Dicktation* series is also forthcoming. *Dicktation* is set in my hometown of New Orleans, which was virtually destroyed by Hurricane Katrina. Having grown up in, as we say, Nawlins, I'd like to bring the "City that Care Forgot," back to life and create visuals for those of you who'd planned on but hadn't visited New Orleans.

For those of you who've left your stamp or stench on The Big Easy by being oh so sleazy, and you know you were off the mutha-fuckin' chain—one step away from starring in a Snoop Dog *Gone Wild* video—if the *natives* called you *cheese-zy ba-ba* you are going to love the series. For y'all, *Dicktation* will reignite fond memories of—Essence, Mardi Gras, Jazz Fest, the French Quarters, Bayou Classic, Bourbon Street, Harrah's Casino, Comic View, 7140, Second Lines, and all the shit you can't tell nobody, probably 'cause your ass couldn't remember, but couldn't wait to do again.

New Orleans will forever be a city like no other, especially after the city is rebuilt, but it'll never be the same. Therefore, I must do justice to both the before and the after depictions. *Dicktation* will arise and arouse like no other work I've done . . . until then, enjoy *Sweeter than Honey,* and remember you are what you eat, so stay sweet.

PROLOGUE

A black woman did it all . . . because she had to.
She did it all and she did it well, caring for others while ne-
glecting herself. Four hundred and fifty years of birthing babies
for white masters and black slaves sold off to the highest bidder,
leaving her to raise her children all alone. Four hundred fifty–plus
years struggling for freedom, while black men died, for what they
seemingly couldn't live with today, dignity.

Whose fault was that?

If only a man could teach a boy how to become a man, then the
question would be rhetorical. If the black woman birthed the black
man, raised the black man, loved the black man she gave life to, then
when did the black man begin disrespecting the black woman, replacing her birth name with bitch?

Bitch. Bastard. Incontestably the black man could win at one
thing: throwing a boomerang. The black man's life would forever
remain incomplete until he learned how to love and respect the
black woman. Good or bad—what he believed was golden—a dick
didn't mean shit when the black man chose not to give back to the
black woman what she'd freely given to him. Unconditional love.
Respect. Devotion.

Freedom came with a price, and now that the black woman
could choose her mate, her fate was the same, leaving her to take

on more responsibility than she should, but not more than she could, so she carried on doing all she could do, the best she knew how. It's been proven that if one tried to do everything, one would risk doing nothing well.

After dropping off the kids, working nine-to-five and then sometimes five-to-nine, picking up the kids, cooking dinner, changing diapers, checking homework, and lying down for a four—should be eight—hours' rest, did the black woman have any quantitative time to invest in her children's future? If she made time, did she have any qualitative time for herself? If the mother was unhealthy, the children were unhealthy too.

When the alarm clock sounded, the next day was a replica of yesterday, and it seemed like the groundhog saw its shadow every day because each tomorrow for the next eighteen-years-plus brought sorrows that would make demands of the black woman to carry on, humming the same old hymn . . . "I won't complain."

Who would take care of the black woman while she sacrificed to rear her kids, pay the bills, and all too often, sleep alone at night, wondering if her direct deposit would post in time to keep the lights on, or balance her checkbook the day before payday to re-stock the refrigerator before emptying the cabinets, or feed her children the last few slices of bread while she watched them eat?

The black woman didn't need anybody's empathy. She was a survivor by nature. The Mother of Jesus, many denied the undeniable, but what the black woman fell short of was an epiphany: a lesson in how to love herself first. How to stop stressing about not knowing if her baby daddy—daddies—would ever show up at his children's events, parent-teacher conferences, if he'd ever pay her child support, and ultimately to stop worrying about whom he had sex with when he wasn't loving her, that is, if he'd ever loved her.

Love or the lack thereof, based on his mother's mistakes, Darius reluctantly admitted to himself, what most men at some point in their lives experienced; he was terrified of two things: falling in love and failure. No one had taught him how to attain one while avoiding the other. Either, or would render him vulnerable. Destroy his character. Ultimately strip him of his manhood.

A man in love was weak for his woman. Would do anything for

his woman. The more he gave, the more control she wanted. Darius didn't want to be hard on women; he had to be. The cold, callous, careless, arrogant, inconsiderate, selfish person ruling his existence, primarily with his dick, wasn't him. But if Darius didn't protect his heart, who would? Surely not the women who'd emotionally broken him down. Like the one blabbering on the other end of his cell phone wasting his time, burning up his daytime minutes.

Sitting in the white Hummer limousine, next to his fiancée, Darius regretted answering his phone. If it were up to him, he would've ignored the call, but no, Fancy had to insist, "Answer, it." Translation, "Put that bitch in check so I won't have to."

Darius was stuck again between the old and the new pussies.

Ashlee cried in his ear, "I'm sorry." No, she wasn't. "I never wanted to hurt you." Yes, she did. Otherwise she wouldn't have phoned. "And no matter what, I love you." That was probably the one truth.

No woman could resist Darius's six-foot-eleven, 240-pound muscular caramel frame with six percent body fat, his lustrous shoulder-length locks, chiseled chin, hazel eyes, perfect white teeth, his millions of dollars, or his big eight-inch dick and the fact that he knew how to sling Slugger and eat pussy oh so sweet that the strongest women submitted to him.

Ashlee continued, "But you need to know."

Exhaling, Darius conceded, "Then tell me."

Crying, like most women did when they wanted sympathy for something that was their fault, Ashlee said, "Our son, Darius Junior, died from HIV complications."

Whoa, that was some cold-blooded shit to drop on a brotha on his wedding day. Hell, any day. "And you?" Darius whispered.

Sniffling, Ashlee said, "Positive."

The numbness in Darius's body caused the phone to slip from between his fingers.

Picking up the phone, Fancy questioned Ashlee. "What did you tell him?" Fancy looked at the phone, then said, "Hello? Hello?" Staring at Darius, Fancy began crying along with him. She muttered, "She hung up. Please tell me. What did she say?"

If Fancy had kept her damn mouth shut, he wouldn't be trippin' over Ashlee's bullshit. Why in the fuck did he have to answer his phone?

"Move! From now on, don't tell me what to do."

"Don't you dare turn this on me! Fine, forget I asked. You think you can handle everything by yourself. In here," Fancy scolded, pressing her finger into Darius's temple. "Well, you can't. And I'm not marrying a man who doesn't need, trust, or value my opinions."

Softly, Darius said, "It's not like that. I do respect you." Her opinion was what he didn't care for. Darius pressed a button, lowering the divider window, then instructed the driver, "Man, take me straight home."

"Oakland or Los Angeles?"

That's how Darius wanted his life, clear cut. Black or white. A or B. Gray areas were like women, ambiguous and complicated. Darius answered, "Los Angeles."

Banging his face against the limo window, Darius worried, was his HIV test, taken years ago, a false negative? How many women had he possibly infected? Darius could start with the one sitting next to him.

CHAPTER 1

Candice

Alone, Candice sat in Jada's guest bedroom by the large bay window, enjoying the second-floor view. Inside the cozy space, a plush queen-size bed with a red satin button-hole headboard rested catty-corner facing the door. The sparkling fuchsia duvet adorned a dozen tasseled pillows. A pink leather bench perched adjacent to the footboard.

The glass-top computer desk faced outside, snug beneath the redwood window frame. Candice's fingers skated along the keyboard, sixty, seventy words a minute:

> *I had a dilemma many married women shared: Should I divorce my impotent husband or not? I'd instantly trade in a broken car I couldn't fix or sell a run-down house that cost more to maintain than its value. My husband wasn't a thing; he was a human being. A cheating man, who'd fucked around for over twenty years, with the same woman.*

Candice paused, gazing at the rolling green hillside resembling the peaks and valleys of their friendship. Jada was Candice's girl, her best friend, her right hand. They'd partied together, laughed, cried, double-dated. Met their husbands the same night at Cityscape in San Francisco at a Will Downing, Rachelle Farrell concert.

That was BM, before marriage, those were the good old days.

Jada met Wellington. Candice met Terrell. Wellington fucked up, Jada married Lawrence. Terrell fucked up, Candice married Terrell. They both relocated from Oakland to L.A but not together. Jada moved to get away from Wellington. Candice would've moved anywhere in the world to be with Terrell, who lived in Los Angeles.

Terrell was five years younger, an international model, and, so she'd thought, wealthy until she married him, realizing Terrell lived well above his means. He owned a huge house with a waterfall, bought her an expensive wedding ring. The first sign of financial trouble was when Terrell purchased matching his-and-hers Mercedes Benzes, with her money.

Accepting Terrell's ring, Candice felt obligated to get married. What if she didn't get another chance to meet a man like him? If Candice had remained single, and Jada had gotten married, they wouldn't have stayed friends. Not close friends.

Assuming their wives weren't intelligent enough to think, insecure married men objected to their spouses kickin' it with single girlfriends. A selfish man could ruin a good friendship. Hoping she and her girl would stay close, Candice said, "I do," shortly after Jada called off her engagement to Wellington.

The main thing Candice tried to avoid happened. Thanks to Terrell's controlling ways, Candice lost touch with her best friend. For years. Without a friend and time on her hands, Candice wrote and sold a screenplay about Jada's life. Putting Jada's business on the big screen got Candice a not so warming house visit. After Jada got over being pissed, they were friends again. How long would their friendship last this time, considering Candice was temporarily living in Jada's house, secretly writing part two of Jada's life? Tapping the keys, Candice continued:

The empty twenty-count blue Viagra tablets he'd hid in his office drawer weren't used for my womanly pleasure. He'd found the sexual stamina to stick his dick in another woman, but he couldn't, or wouldn't, make love to me. He was eager to sign the divorce papers until the doctor told him his prostate cancer had spread and they had to operate immediately. What's my obligation to stay with a two-timer? I'm clear. I have none. But I do have a conscience. I won't leave him while he's down, but after the surgery, she can have him.

Candice sighed. "This is too boring. I'ma have to throw in some cussing to sell this one. Let's see," she said, backspacing, then revising:

That muthafucka emptied a twenty—you hear me?—a twenty-count of Viagra on that stank-ass bitch. If his sorry ass wasn't dying I swear I'd kill that dead-dick bastard! Twice!

Anger was better, Candice thought, mesmerized by the fading sunrays.

Jada always had one man on her arm and another on her charm bracelet dangling from her wrist. The ten years she was married to Lawrence, Wellington was in the background. Once Jada married Wellington, Lawrence disappeared and Darryl bopped side to side, doo-wopping as backup, waiting to sing lead in her chorus.

One man at a time was Candice's style. Terrell wasn't that bad in the beginning. They'd still be married if she'd been woman enough not to let him change her. Candice never found peace with wanting but not having a child. Terrell didn't want kids. Too late now, premenopause and a baby who'd stare at her for crying, yelling, snapping, swearing, and forgetting things would drive Candice crazy.

Not so long ago, Candice remembered her husband was her life. In many ways, having Terrell was like having a child and an over-protective father. At first marriage was kinda cute, him telling her what to do. That chauvinistic shit got real old, really quick, but she hung in there till they damn near hanged one another with misery. Candice thought when, he left her, she'd fall apart. Wrong. She didn't lift him up to put herself down. Surprisingly the second his shadow walked out the door, the sun seemed brighter. So was her spirit. Like before she'd gotten married, Candice felt stress-free. The days of him telling her how to dress, "Cover your breasts. Take off that skirt. You're not leaving this house looking like that," were gone.

Like what? A sexy male magnet? The way she used to dress when he met her, wearing a peach minidress. But he could bare his masculine chest or muscular thighs whenever he desired, saying, "You know, baby, it's different for a man." And he had no problem being admired by women. Because of her, he'd made a great career move after their divorce that guaranteed him access to more pussy than he could eat. Terrell went from modeling to acting; she'd bartered with the casting company and secured him a supporting role in Soul Mates Dissipate.

Candice was happy for her ex, happier for herself. Thankful that over the years she'd respected her body by exercising, eating healthy foods, sleeping six to eight hours a day. She'd aged gracefully. Single, available, with no intentions of remarrying, she knew she was sexy and thanks to her girlfriend's never-a-boring-moment life, she had an eight-figure bank account and the waterfall house to cushion her divorce. Nice landing.

Tap, tap.

The finger mouse centered on the dash. *Click.* The screen faded to black. Candice minimized her document, closed the laptop, picked up *The Guide to Becoming a Sensuous Black Woman* by Miss T, then answered, "Come, in."

Peeping her head through the door, Jada asked, "What are you doing?"

"Just reading this book on how to seduce a man. Nothing you'd be interested in," Candice said, parting the pages.

Smiling, Jada moved closer. Slyly Candice propped her elbow on her laptop.

Glancing at the book, Jada said, "You right. I need one on how to unseduce your husband. Do you mind going to the store? Wellington wants some more snacks."

Candice stood. "Sit down for a while."

Massaging Jada's neck and shoulders, Candice said, "You are tense."

Jada rotated her head, neck, and shoulders. "Um, that feels so good. Thanks, girl."

"How's he doing?" Candice asked, not giving a damn because

Wellington's sorry ass didn't want Jada to leave his side for more than five minutes at a time.

Candice gave up on investing her energy into finding a faithful man who was honest, considerate, loving, good-looking, and wealthy. If a man had three good qualities, she'd take him for what he was worth. How long he stayed with her depended upon when or if he became useless. Candice pressed her thumbs into Jada's muscles.

Jada sighed. "Not good. He's in a lot of pain. I'm glad he's checking into the hospital soon, because he's wearing me out and not the way I'd like. All he wants to do is watch television, kiss me to death, and rub on my titties like he's doing something."

"Like this," Candice said, groping her hands on Jada's shoulders.

Laughing, Jada said, "Exactly. He works me all up for nothing because he doesn't want to lick my pussy, and I'm tired of playing with her to entertain him. Girlfriend, I'm too young for this sexual frustration. There's nothing wrong with my pussy."

Candice thought, *First it was beer, now snacks. Couldn't he make a list?* replying, "You know how I feel. Get some dick lined up on the side. You'll be well within your right, and ain't shit he can do from a hospital bed."

Standing, Jada said, "I can't be like him. I can't cheat on my husband for the sake of having sex. I have to love the man I'm with."

"You're delirious. That's why I'm here. For you." To write all this shit down so next time Jada got a man, probably Darryl, she wouldn't forget.

Jada lived a fairy-tale kind of life, suppressing reality to suit her beliefs. Jada could watch her screwed-up life on the big screen and think it was somebody else's, claiming, "I could never do . . ."

Candice continued, "Whatever you need me to do, just tell me. And I want you to know, being here has helped me get over Terrell," she lied, then told the truth, "and I am going to help you get over Wellington." Candice had emotionally divorced Terrell years before he'd left.

Shaking her head, Jada said, "I shouldn't complain. I'm not trying to get over Wellington."

Damnit, Jada, stop lying to yourself! Whenever Candice tried to get

Jada to leave Wellington, Jada defended Wellington every single time. "I should stop off at Darius's house and see if any wedding gifts arrived. They may be sitting outside."

"Huh, what? Oh yeah. Good idea. The keys are on the key rack in the kitchen."

"If Wellington thinks of anything else, call me, girl." Candice supported Jada, not Wellington, and no matter how many errands Wellington sent her on, she'd go, and she'd return. At least he couldn't accuse her of cock-blocking.

Waiting for Jada to leave, then watching her walk away in Betty Boop pj's with red eyes that were half closed, Candice wondered, why had her girlfriend stayed with Wellington after his affair? Closing the bedroom door, Candice input the information Jada had given her.

"Oh," Jada said, reentering the room, "I almost forgot. Darius is on his way home so you don't have to go to his house."

Shit, she didn't knock. Next time Candice had to lock the door. *The hell I don't,* Candice thought. Darius's life was ten times more exciting than Jada's, and this might be her only opportunity to have access to his dirt. Quickly saving the new chapter before removing her memory stick, Candice powered off her laptop, slipped into a pink sweatsuit, laced her tennis shoes, then skipped out the front door jiggling Darius's keys.

One press of a button on her remote and the engine of her red-hot convertible Benz roared. Candice sped to the neighborhood grocery store, tossed chips, pretzels, peanuts, cashews, beef jerky, Snickers bars, and red vines in the handbasket. "That'll do." Waiting in the "ten items or less" checkout line, Candice tapped her foot, sighed; as she shifted the basket to the opposite hip her toes froze in midair. A KEYS MADE sign was near the entrance. Leaving the junk food on the conveyor, she darted to the counter, extended Darius's keys to the tall, bald-headed man, and said, "One set please. Make that two."

Spiraling her copies on her chain, Candice said, "Keep the change."

Speeding to a nearby shopping center, she stood outside the electronics store and dialed Jada's number.

Jada answered, "You still at the store?"

"What does he want now?"

"Ice cream. Strawberry."

Along with the junk food she'd forgotten to pay for. "Girl, if I didn't love you . . . I'll pick it up later."

"I'm sorry, you called me," Jada said, yawning.

"I have to make a stop, but I'll get back ASAP," Candice said, hanging up.

Entering the crowded store, she approached the first blue-vested khaki-pants-wearing employee she saw. "Yes, I need ten, make that twenty, of those hidden clock cameras. And twenty one-gig memory cards."

"Twenty? Twenty? Why so many?" he questioned.

"Is that part of your duties? To get personal with me, young man?"

"Sorry, ma'am. I'll bring 'em to the register for you."

"Now we're communicating. And bring me two sets of binoculars."

Standing in line, Candice tapped her foot. Placing her items at the register, the employee said, "Have a nice day."

The cashier said, "I know you'd like to protect your devices. I recommend purchasing our additional warranty—"

"Stop wasting my time," Candice replied, signing, then handing the white paper to the cashier. Candice snatched the bags, running like a linebacker to her car, then broke every residential speed limit for a five block radius to Darius's house. Retrieving her keys, Candice entered Darius's home, then secured the inside latch.

Quickly she raced upstairs, hiding a camera in Darius's closet, aiming the motion detector toward his bed. "This is a sweet-ass setup. What's this button for?" Candice said, pressing the black dot. "Oh, shit!" Three hidden doors opened at once. A black leather sex swing rocked, bright red lights beamed on a stage with a dance pole, white stars and a crescent moon danced on the ceiling as R. Kelly played in the background. Squinting and walking over to a cavelike opening in the headboard, Candice stared in disbelief. Adult toys: vibrators, butt plugs, pearls, lingerie, pasties.

"Edible what! Piña colada dickalicious," she exhaled. "Let me get out of here. I see why women go crazy over his sexy ass. Hell, if he weren't my girlfriend's son, I'd wait right here to do him. Who would think of all this?"

R. Kelly switched to Luther right before a projector screen lowered from the ceiling, playing an X-rated video entitled *Bootylicious.* "No, he is not putting his big dick in her . . ." Candice said, pressing the black button. "My pussy is puckerin'." She was sure of one thing, the best was yet to cum.

Squinting, Candice moved closer, then stepped back, staring up at a red dot. "Oh, shit! I'm on his camera." Now she'd have to come back sooner than expected to find his recorder. Happy she had more material than she'd originally imagined, she was worried Darius might expose her first.

Swiftly planting cameras throughout the house, Candice noticed tiny red dots on every ceiling: the kitchen, living room, bathroom, garage, and five other rooms. The ten cameras she'd left in her car she'd place in Jada's bedroom, living room, kitchen, bathroom, Wellington's office, and a few other places.

Soon, Candice Jordan—screenwriter, novelist, producer, and director—would become a household name. Like before, in time, Jada's initial anger would subside. But if Darius found out, he'd kill her.

CHAPTER 2

Darius

"Los Angeles," Darius instructed the driver, then raised the divider and flopped against the backseat, loosening his onyx wing-tip collar. Why had he fucked Ashlee? Kimberly? Crystal? Desire? Maxine? Ciara? The others were pissed at him, probably for life, but that was their problem 'cause each of them had moved on. Ashlee was the only dumb one who'd gotten sprung on cum. Sure, he was thirty percent, give or take five, at fault, but he'd grown tired of Ashlee.

Holding her dangling curls away from her face, Fancy laid her cheek in his lap. Her lips kissed Slugger.

"Ow, Ladycat, oh my goodness." Darius's dick expanded four times its size.

"Heeyyy, this is a pleasant surprise," Fancy said, nibbling his head. "I thought you were too upset to get excited."

"Shid, never that upset," Darius said, nudging Fancy's head closer to his dick.

"Let me take your mind off your troubles. We can and will talk later." Gently she bit through his slacks.

Translation, she'd talk. He'd listen 'cause whatever conclusion Fancy conjured wouldn't matter. She was a woman. He was the man. His castle. Her home. Maybe. If she'd act right.

Fancy unzipped his pants. Wrapping her hand around the shaft, she freed Slugger, letting him go. The tip of her tongue chased, steadied, then licked the underside protruding main vein right in the triangular groove below his pee-hole. Fancy licked his second hottest spot—next to the span from his asshole up to his balls—again.

"Yes, indeed, there is a God. Ooouuu." Darius shivered.

Fancy cuddled his dick next to her cheek, closed her eyes, and sniffed.

"Ahhhhh." *That's my girl. Worship your master.*

Fancy's tongue wavered along his vein from his balls up to his hole. Gently licking his spot right before engulfing his head into her hot juicy mouth, she devoured him.

"Ummmm," Darius moaned, removing the diamond button-hole links on his white tuxedo shirt, "that feels so damn good. Suck this big-ass dick."

Precum seeped onto her succulent lips. Painting his semen like lipstick, his bulging head swayed corner to corner, covering Fancy's lips. Darius gripped Fancy's hair, commanding, "Don't you dare stop," desperately desiring to bust a nut or two.

Darius's asshole tightened on the upstroke, relaxed on the down. Uncontrollable sexual energy danced in his balls, possessing Darius to lock his fingers into Fancy's weave and thrust his shaft down her throat. He did. She gagged. Repeatedly heaving. Good for her if she regurgitated. What didn't kill . . . fattened. In the zone, too deep to stop, past her tonsils, beyond her reflux ability not to swallow, Darius banged Fancy's vocal cords.

"Oh my God, you just don't know, ba-bee." He pushed, knocking his nuts against her lips. "Ba-by, shit, yeah." He stroked deeper. "Uh-huh. Aw, damn. Here it comes, whoa!" Thick fluids gushed toward her stomach like water from a fire hydrant, releasing his backup. Quenching his thirst. Pushing Fancy away, Darius stroked his afterflow cum and her saliva onto his dick.

"You must be crazy if you think you're finished," Fancy protested, watching him shake his heads. "After all I endured, here, put him in while he's hard." Eagerly, Fancy lifted her gown.

That was his woman, no panties. A gold-laced thong.

Fancy spread her lips, granting him full access. Never having left a woman dissatisfied, Darius unbuckled his pants, shoved them to

his knees, popping the head into his pussy. But what if he had . . .
Fuck! Darius shouted in his mind, pulled up his boxers, then his
pants. Leaving them unbuckled and unzipped, he flopped on the
cool leather.

"What's wrong with you?"

"Nothing. Got a lotta shit on my mind, that's all. Go to sleep."
What the fuck was Slugger doing? He'd zoned out and . . . damn,
damn, goddamn. Darius removed his gold-trimmed black jacket,
balling the coat into a pillow.

"I bet you do have a lot bothering you. I'll give you a minute to
stop trippin', but I don't care how frustrated you are, when we get
home, you're giving up the dick."

As she stretched her feet across the seat, Fancy's gold train spilled
onto the floor. Her precious head weighed heavily on his thigh,
facing his stomach. Darius could tell she was tired. He was mentally exhausted knowing he'd disappoint her again once they got
home.

Darius wanted to sleep too, but all kinds of audiovisuals rewound
in his head. Especially when Ashlee had the audacity to say, "I love
you no matter what." *Liar.* Love didn't have shit to do with what
she'd said.

The driver was already cruising on Interstate 5 South, practically
a straight shot to L.A. but hours away. Moving his limp dick from
under Fancy's mouth, Darius closed his eyes, trying to understand
how a woman's need to be loved vastly differed from a man's desire to love a woman. How did anyone ever get married? Better
question, why? Should he marry Fancy, knowing that he might be
infected? To his grave, one way or another he had to lie.

Perhaps his mother's need for love or her desire to be adored
was the reason it took Darius Jones twenty years to discover her lie.
After a paternity test confirmed the truth, Darius took back—or
should he say claimed—his real name, and irrespective of whether
his mother was to blame he could never eradicate the pain or escape the shame of having to explain why, at twenty years of age,
he'd changed his last name. From Jones to Williams.

With the exception of not marrying Fancy and losing his firstborn, the day his mother told him who his biological father was

was the worst day of Darius's life. Darryl Williams. That was his real daddy's name, but how could Darius regain the years? Years lost. Not knowing the man he'd idolized growing up; his dad was a former NBA star. Darryl was his college basketball coach when Darius played at Georgetown.

Darius's mother knowingly sent him to Georgetown, knowingly allowed him to play an entire season coached by his father, knowingly attended all of his high school games but never attended one of his college games, and knowingly never said a fuckin' word until after she'd conned Darius into quitting the team, giving up his dream, to accept a six-figure executive vice president position at her company. To repay his mother, Darius fucked all four of her top-level executives the same way she'd screwed him, secretly. Man, he'd forgotten to add Heather, Miranda, Zen, and Ginger to the list.

Darius imagined what his mother might think now that four years had passed since her confession. "You still trippin' on that? I'm sorry I fucked up your life, sweetie. Get over it. Move on. Be a man about it. Okay, if you won't forgive me, then I'll just have to forgive myself and you'll have to get professional help."

Women.

Be a man about it! About what? Her emotional autopsy gutted his insides, ripped out his beating heart, then tagged his toe with "John Doe," like she'd done no harm. Like suddenly without cause he'd become a heartless stranger to her.

Women.

They always wanted men to forget their mistakes, especially after they'd told their cure-all truth. If a man lied to his woman, she'd nag the hell out of him, reminding him every chance she got. That's why a man had two choices: bury the lie and never tell the truth, or bury his soul for the rest of his life. A man in love eventually forgot his woman's lies, but his subconscious never forgave her. Ever.

A tear sat on his left eyelid as Darius struggled to disguise the bitterness in his voice. Lowering the divider, he instructed the limo driver, "Man, drive faster," then raised the window. The ride from Oakland back to Los Angeles seemed a lot longer than the trip going.

For a moment, Darius chuckled, flashing back on how neither Fancy nor he had showed up at their wedding in Los Angeles. Instead, both of them ended up at the pier in Berkeley—the first stop of their first date—forever their special place. Darius would never take another woman there. Most women he couldn't remember where he'd taken them. What he did know was Fancy had better not take another man there.

Yeah, Fancy was right. They were two of a kind. Over five hundred miles away from their matrimonial service, they'd stood on the planks next to Skates Restaurant, overlooking the Pacific Ocean. Undoubtedly Darius loved Fancy. Fancy excited him in every way imaginable. Challenged him. Confronted him on his lies.

In his heart, Darius also loved Ashlee. Only God knew how much he loved Ashlee. Ashlee, no matter what the circumstances, supported him. Every man needed a supportive woman. Ashlee shouldn't have had to carry his baby nine months without him. Bury their son without him. Now that Ashlee needed him, she shouldn't have to deal with her illness without him. He'd already failed her several times.

Glancing down at Fancy while she slept, Darius thought, *Stop trippin', dog. Your commitment isn't to Ashlee. You've got the finest woman in the world on your lap.*

Darius had already revealed more of his skeletons than he'd intended to Fancy, but how could he explain to his fiancée the phone call he'd received from Ashlee? He couldn't. Hopefully, things would work out and he wouldn't have to.

Not wanting to seem selfish—it was too late for Ashlee but hopefully not for him—silently Darius prayed, "God, I tried to pull out, but, but you know how good sex feels. Right? I'm not blaming You, Lord, we know the devil made me do it. Satan, I rebuke you. Lord, I know I'm on my second set of nine lives, but thanks to You I'm on a winning streak. I've rolled the dice again, please let's not crap out. Too many people would lose their lives." Darius leaned closer to Fancy, making sure she was asleep, and then he quietly dialed Ashlee's number.

"Hey, how are you?" Ashlee answered like she hadn't just given him the worst news of his life, next to the day she'd told him their son had died.

Angrily, Darius whispered, "How do you think I am? Were you serious about what you said earlier or trying to fuck up my wedding?"

"I was at your wedding. You weren't."

Darius's lips tightened. "So what you sayin'? You was gonna drop that shit on me in front of over a thousand people?"

"You mean like the way you dropped me?"

Darius became quiet, biting his bottom lip. His eyes automatically shifted to the corners whenever he lied or avoided telling the truth. He had no nonargumentative response, so he waited for Ashlee to say something.

"Darius, I need to see you."

"I don't think that's a good idea, right now, or ever," Darius replied, worrying how he'd feel about Ashlee if he did see her.

Firmly she asked, "Where are you?"

Darius whispered, "On my way home," checking on Fancy, praying she was still asleep. Fancy was motionless. Eyes closed. Lightly breathing.

"Which home?" Ashlee asked.

Lowering his voice more, Darius mumbled, "The Valley. Why? What's up with all the questions? You haven't called me in months."

"How close are you?"

Darius hissed, "Where are you?" then tightly ground his back teeth while flinching his jaw. Whenever his jaw tightened, Darius wanted to punch something or someone. Right now it was Ashlee.

"Close."

"To what? Ashlee, don't. Look, I can't ignore what you said earlier, but right now I gotta go. Don't call me. I'll call you later."

"I'm sick of being your fuckin' puppet!"

Widening his eyes, Darius felt his forehead tensing in disbelief, giving him an instant headache, as he continued listening when what he should've done was hang up on the bitch. He didn't mean to call her a bitch, but he hadn't realized how attached she was to stupidity.

"Ashlee, please move in with me. Ashlee, please don't leave me.

Ashlee, I need you to work for me. Let me lick your pussy. Ashlee, let me fuck you! Well, I'm tired of being fucked!"

At any time she could've simply said no. Wasn't like he'd held a gun to her head. Women. Was that why she'd fucked his brother?

"Doing every damn thing your damn way just to make you happy when you obviously don't give a shit! About me!"

Maybe she should've given a damn about herself, less about him, and neither one of them would've had to have this conversation.

Ashlee continued, "So I'ma tell you the fuck what!" Gasping heavily into his ear, she softly said, "Better yet, hurry your ass home. I'll talk to you when you get here."

Like the bull he was, quick sharp puffs of steam hot enough to form smoke balls escaped Darius's flaming nostrils as he shut his eyes, rolling his eyeballs to the top of the sockets. "Ashlee, you'd better not be at *my* house." Darius wanted to exceed her anger but instead he said, "Fancy's carrying my baby and she doesn't need to deal with your nonsense."

Darius could've simply said Fancy was with him, but Ashlee already knew that and that wouldn't have convinced Ashlee to stay away from him. Damn, did he trust Ashlee wasn't daring enough to trespass on his property that he hadn't changed the locks? Fuck! How ignorant of him.

"Our house. I love you, Darius. I'll see you when you get home. Bye, baby."

Smothering his voice, Darius hissed, "Ashlee. Ashlee. Damn it," then sucked in all the oxygen he could before blowing the hot air out of his mouth, fogging up the window.

A woman sure knew how to fuck with a man's head. Heads. Both of his were in pain: one from not getting enough pussy and the other from hearing too much bitchin'. Was any of the shit Ashlee said true? Or was Ashlee jealous of Fancy and willing to do anything to keep him from getting married? Women.

How could Darius tell Fancy he was sorry he came in her mouth and that he couldn't make love to her? Not today. Not tomorrow. Maybe never again. He definitely didn't want Fancy to hear the bad news from Ashlee. Why, of all days, had Ashlee called him on his wedding day to fuck with him?

Interrupting his mental monologue, the limo driver said, "Mr. Williams, you're home," cruising into the driveway.

Darius lowered the rear passenger-side tinted window, staring at his house.

Fancy opened her eyes. "What was that all about?"

The living room, dining room, and kitchen lights were on. Seconds later, all of the lights in his house went out.

Oh, shit, Darius thought. Holding his breath, he prayed for the best and prepared for the worst.

CHAPTER 3

Ashlee

Rocking little Darius in her arms, Ashlee kissed his lips, then laid him across the back car seat. The royal-blue baby blanket covered his lower body. Folding a pair of sweatpants into a makeshift pillow, Ashlee slightly propped his head, then fingered his thick curly hair. Six months had passed since the day she'd given birth. The same day he'd first and last seen his father. That would change when Darius got home.

Ashlee sang, "You light up my life, you give me strength to carry on . . . hum, hum, hum, hum . . . " until little Darius's round hazel eyes became heavy, heavier, then gently closed. Their son was the new love of her life. His golden-tanned complexion was a perfect blend of her pale and Darius's melt-in-her-mouth caramel-sugary skin. The shape and color of their son's eyes were an exact replica of Darius's mom's.

"Wait here, my precious baby," Ashlee said, rubbing his hand. "Mommy'll be back soon. This time with Daddy."

Leaving the black rental SUV in Darius's circular driveway, Ashlee grabbed her purse, quietly closing the car door. "Oh no." Reopening the door, she lowered the window a half inch, then reclosed the door.

A few steps toward the front entrance, Ashlee yelled, "Ooohh," then covered her mouth while shielding her eyes. Blinding lights beamed across the lawn. Kneeling on the GO AWAY mat, she rummaged inside her purse.

"Okay, wallet, credit card holder, lipstick. Shit!" The teeth of her comb lodged underneath her fingernail. Ashlee sucked her middle finger, then pulled out her keys.

"Please let this work." Boldly she shoved the silver metal ridges into the lock, twisting to the right.

Click.

"Yes!" Entering Darius's home through the front door, Ashlee stood in the foyer. An enormous topless painting of Fancy hung on the wall above. "Uuhhh. How disgusting!" Critiquing the image, Ashlee thought Fancy was as beautiful as the day she recalled meeting her for the first time at a fund-raiser Darius had taken Ashlee to. And while Ashlee would love to say the painting was airbrushed, she knew it wasn't. A woman that gorgeous, another woman never forgot.

Long breezy hair fluttered side to side with each sensuous sway of her shoulders. Immaculate glowing skin. Peachy, perky, gravity-defying breasts that stood alone separated by nature. Sexy engaging brown eyes with hypnotic lashes batting like she was taking snapshots of Darius. Darius had pretended not to notice Fancy's perfect size 7. Now he claimed she was carrying his baby. Fancy was probably the reason Darius had dropped Ashlee off in such a hurry, then left that night to return to the fund-raiser after-party.

Was that seventy-five-thousand-dollar check Darius donated and Ashlee had placed in Fancy's cotton-soft meticulously manicured hand for Fancy? Or Byron's philanthropic organization?

A man could easily pass another woman off as a friend or pretend she was a stranger, all along knowing he'd fucked her before, sometimes the night before. Ashlee had been that woman once when Darius had introduced her to Ciara. Had Darius fucked Fancy while Ashlee was living with him? What difference did that make now? Fancy had everything, including Darius.

More curious about Fancy than Darius, Ashlee roamed about Darius's home in search of what she didn't know. Anxiety, fear, and trepidation tripled-attacked her as she impatiently awaited his arrival. What would she say? How would she react if Darius was more concerned about Fancy's feelings? Ashlee was already on the edge, and any form of rejection would push her into insanity.

"Why can't I turn off the radio?" rang from her cell phone, indicating that Darius was calling. Hastily she answered, "Hey, how are you?"

Reclining on Darius's plush golden suede sofa, Ashlee entertained his pathetic attempt to control her again. Not this time. Terminating their conversation, she said, "I'll see you when you get home. Bye, baby," then ended the call.

She rose angrily from the couch, and then the beaded train on Ashlee's wedding gown traced her footsteps throughout the house. Cautiously entering Darius's weight room, Ashlee froze in front of the ceiling-to-floor mirror. Tension wrapped her chest and shoulders in an invisible harness. Disappointed, she scolded herself, "I shoulda made a beautiful bride. Coulda been the perfect wife. Woulda become a fantastic mother."

Mother, mother, mother, echoed in her mind. Fancy was carrying Darius's baby. Was it a girl? A boy?

Gripping the cold iron bar propped parallel above her head, Ashlee reflected on the first time—over a year ago—when Darius screwed her in the same room she now stood in feeling dejected. Tears flowed over her cinnamon lipstick into the crevices of her mouth.

That evening, a while back, Ashlee had entered his workout room. "Darius, Ciara is on the phone. She said it's important that she speaks with you right now." Ashlee handed Darius the cordless.

Darius coldheartedly answered, "I'm busy. Let me call you back," then tossed the phone to the floor.

When Ciara called back, Darius said to Ashlee, "Don't answer that. I'll call her when I'm done. Come here. Let me teach you how to work on your upper body."

"No, thanks. I have to get dressed. Maybe next time," Ashlee said, rejecting Darius's offer.

"It'll only take a minute. Hold on. Grab each side."

With the bar suspended above her head, Ashlee did as Darius had instructed.

Unexpectedly Darius cupped her breasts. Brushing her hair

aside, he pressed his lips gently against the nape of her neck. Then he whispered ever so seductively, "I want to make love to you, Ashlee."

How could she deny him? Darius was every woman's dream came true.

She remained silent. Her fingers loosened, but not wanting to sever his touch, she didn't release the bar. Her hips curved backward into Darius's thighs as Darius pressed his long hard dick into her spine.

"You won't regret it," Darius whispered. "I promise."

Lowering the spaghetti straps on her silk nightgown, exposing her breasts, Darius teased her pink nipples, then passionately made love to her from behind on the weight bench. Straddling his muscular thighs outside hers, Darius massaged her clit with his long fingers. The head of his dick navigated through her pussy as if he'd been there before. But he hadn't. He poked, then stroked, her deep, inside and out, until she came at his command. "Aw, damn. I'm cumming Ashlee. Cum with me." She had cum and somewhere along their blissful journey Darius detoured leaving her for another woman.

Staring in the mirror at her tattered image—dressed in all white—Ashlee knew if Darius had showed up at his wedding, he wouldn't have married Fancy. Ashlee had prepared her "if anyone knows why this man and woman should not be joined in holy matrimony let him speak now" speech. But no, Darius ruined her presentation. His limo never arrived.

Taking a brief intermission from the video replaying in her head, setting her purse on the floor, and picking up a twenty-pound dumbbell, Ashlee stepped back from the mirror, once, twice, three times, then resumed her thoughts. "I do," she would've said, entering through the church doors, posing in the back aisle with a veil hiding her face.

Every guest would've turned. Stared. And in unison would've said, "Aahhh." Then the mumbling would've started. At a snail's pace, she would've commanded their attention as she stepped, then paused. Stepped, then paused again all the way down that aisle, the aisle she should've graced instead of Fancy. Standing face-to-face with Darius, Ashlee would've politely uncovered her face and said, "This man is already married."

He was. To Ciara Monroe-Jones. Darius had married Ciara before changing his last name, but legally Ciara was his wife. For the longest time, Ashlee had no idea Darius had married Ciara, and he had no intentions of mentioning his little secret. Fortunately for Ciara, she discovered Darius's motivation, to gain control of her casting company, before it was too late. Darius needed Ciara's Hollywood contacts more than he needed her, but now that Darius didn't need Ciara anymore, he had moved on, letting his father Darryl take over his movie-production company while Darius prepared to play in the NBA. The most fearless cat wasn't luckier than Darius Jones-Williams.

Ashlee blamed herself for falling in love with Darius. Believing she was different. Special. And Darius would protect her, never disrespect her. Ashlee should've spared herself countless heartaches and left when she'd discovered the truth about Ciara. One day, Ciara had showed up unannounced at their front door at nine o'clock in the morning.

Bam! Bam! Bam!

Opening the door, Ashlee had asked, "Ciara? Is that you? Why are you knocking on our door so hard?"

Ciara bypassed her and entered the house. "Why are you here?"

"I live here. Well, at least until I find a place. But Darius isn't here. I don't know where he is."

Ciara said, "Don't lie to me," then stormed into Darius's bedroom and froze. Ashlee watched in amazement too.

"Ow, baby mama's cumming," a woman's voice muffled from underneath a pillowcase. The woman's hands pulled Darius's face closer to her pussy, and then she rotated her hips on his lips. As Ciara and Ashlee watched, Darius's face rose from between two chocolate thighs. His mouth looked like he'd been lapping in a bowl of milk.

Wiping his mouth with the sheet, Darius said, "What the hell are you doing coming to my house?"

On a return visit, Ciara threatened to kill Darius. Now Ashlee understood why: A woman's heart was a terrible thing to break.

Lifting her arm, Ashlee hurled the metal weight toward the mirror. "Ouch! Fuck! Oh my God!" Ashlee yelled, limping. "I think I broke my toe!"

The edge of the dumbbell had landed on her little toe. Removing her shoe, Ashlee wiggled all her toes. If she had the courage, she'd pull the stake out of her bleeding heart and return the favor to Darius. Ashlee would one day kill Darius. No, she wouldn't. She loved him too much. Her only true desire was for Darius to love her back. Was that too much to ask for?

"Owwww! Shit!" she cried, hopping on one foot, gown in one hand, shoe in the other.

Despite her heartbreak, the positive side was that Ashlee still had a chance to convince Darius not to marry Fancy. Ignoring the pain, Ashlee limped to Darius's room and rolled around in his lush king-size bed, ruffling the rich purple velvet duvet. Darius loved big things. Twelve hundred square feet, larger than most peoples' entire home, covered his whorish bedroom, complete with a stripper's stage, dance pole, sex swing, and moonlit ceiling engulfed with simulated stars.

Leaving the bed ruffled, Ashlee slowly opened the top dresser drawers. They were all filled with expensive imported lingerie sets: peach, pink, orange, banana, candy-apple red, plum.

"How dare he move her into my space!" Ashlee yanked and ripped until all the frilly dainty items were shredded, and then she politely tucked them back in the drawers, closing each one tight. Peeping in the bottom drawer, she saw a pink leather strap with flaming red embroidery that read *Pussy Whip*.

"I bet," Ashlee said, retreating to what used to be her room. Her chin dropped as she gasped, "Wow." Everything was exactly as she'd left it. Lime-green comforter, with matching pillows, and satin sheets. Removing her other shoe, Ashlee eased under the covers, careful not to tangle the train on her gown or smash her throbbing toe.

"Oh, shit." Ashlee jumped from the bed, hiked up her dress, then swiftly ran toward the door. Looking back, she yelled, "Goddammit!" watching her train hook the bedpost.

Wham!

Her face smashed against the floor. "Huuuhh." Ashlee sat in the hallway for a moment questioning her intentions. Maybe this was a sign for her to forget about Darius.

"No way." Ashlee stood, ripped her train from the bedpost. Beads fell to the floor. A patch of satiny material remained between the wood and the carpet. Barefoot, Ashlee dashed outside and parked the SUV one block away, grateful that little Darius was quiet. His eyes were open wide. "Here, sit in your car seat. Is that better? Daddy'll be home soon," Ashlee whispered, placing the blanket beside his head. "And when he gets home, Mommy'll come and get you right away. Okay?" she said, kissing him.

Her baby was sniffling, his mouth gapped open. Ashlee had seen that look before. That facial expression meant there was a matter of seconds before the sniffing would end and the wailing would begin. Remotely locking the doors, racing downhill, Ashlee tripped, rolled into a snowball, entangling herself in the train, thankful and sorry that the palm tree stopped her. "Shit!" Tussling with the satin, finally she freed herself, then hurried inside, locking herself in her bedroom.

She hadn't even broken the stupid mirror and she'd already started having bad luck. Glancing at her image, she saw her hair scattered about her head. A few stems and twigs intertwined in it. Her face was flushed with dirt on her left cheek. Ashlee nodded. "I look pretty tough."

Was she tough enough to move in? Darius's house was huge. If it weren't for the baby, she could live there without Darius knowing. Maybe she would. Nah, staying wasn't a good idea, but coming back was.

Ashlee removed the gown, threw it across the bed, went to the closet, and eased into a size 5 of her stretch-to-fit jeans. Scanning the neat cotton blouses, Ashlee shook her head. "No more prim and proper. I like this rough and rugged look. And no more being nice. Nice women always get fucked." Anally.

Marching back into Darius's room, Ashlee put on one of his wife-beaters, tied a do-rag over her head, and put on one of Darius's button-up shirts but didn't button it up. The shirt hung below her knees. Staring at the ruffled comforter, Ashlee smiled, removed her soiled white lace panties, slid them underneath the sheets toward the middle of the bed, pulled up the covers, and deviously smiled.

"Where in the hell is he? He said he was close."

Restless, Ashlee circled the living room, then preset the radio alarm on it highest volume to go off at six in the morning, which was only a few hours away. She programmed the television for six thirty. Just enough time for them to go back to bed and get cozy. Still bored, Ashlee stumbled to Darius's kitchen. Her toe ached again.

"Toughen up," Ashlee grunted, inspecting the contents inside the refrigerator. Juice, juice, and more juice: cranberry, aloe vera, Noni. "What's Fancy calling herself doing? Her ass is trying to turn my man into a vegan with all this crap. Darius doesn't like all this stuff."

The juice reminded Ashlee of what she'd almost forgot. Retrieving her purse from the exercise room, she returned to the kitchen, filled a glass with orange juice, downed two of the prescribed pills in her purse, then poured out all the beverages, placing the empty containers back in the refrigerator.

How could she forget to take her meds when that was the one thing that kept her sane? But the side effects often drove her insane. Lethargy. Memory loss. Severe mood swings.

Picking up a bottle of veggie tablets, Ashlee said, "CKLS. What's that?"

Slamming the refrigerator, she considered refilling the bottles with poison. What could she use? Ashlee searched below the kitchen sink.

"Let's see, bleach, ammonia, detergent. All of this stinks and probably would only make them sick to their stomachs. That was if they'd even take a swig. I know what, I could scare the hell out of them when they walk in all happy."

A smirk emerged while Ashlee's eyes widened. She went back to Darius's bedroom, continuing into his bathroom, opened the medicine cabinet, shook all the headache tablets into the toilet, and flushed. Ashlee removed the aspirin-looking abortion tablets she'd stolen from her doctor's office on her last visit when he said, "Ms.

Anderson, I'll be right back," before leaving her alone. Ashlee wasn't having sex, so she definitely wasn't having another baby. Didn't want to raise the one she had. At least not by herself. One at a time, she dropped all eight of the abortion pills into the empty red and white bottle.

"Perfect," she said, smiling.

Ashlee raced to the living room, opened, then quietly shut the heavy cherry-wood door. Darius's limo was creeping up the driveway. Ashlee's heart outraced her footsteps as she dashed to her bedroom, then locked herself in.

"No, that won't help me escape without being noticed."

Carrying her white shoes, Ashlee quickly turned off the lights, then hid in the garage.

CHAPTER 4

Candice

Less than a block from Darius's house, Candice's neck snapped in disbelief. "Not in this affluent neighborhood."

A car, with a driver wearing a veil shielding the face, zoomed by. Either they were an underaccomplished actor, an actress hiding from the paparazzi, a pissed-off bride, or a crazy person. Realistically, all or any of those characters could reside in The Valley.

Adjusting her rearview mirror in one fluid motion, Candice saw the car skid into Darius's driveway. Candice hit her brakes, rotated her steering wheel to the far left, stomped her clutch, and shifted into second gear, making a U while turning off her headlights.

Candice backed a few feet into Darius's driveway, prepared for a quick escape if necessary. Fumbling through her shopping bag, grateful she'd bought binoculars, she leaned between the driver and passenger seats, adjusted the magnifying lenses, then peeped through the holes thinking, *Why didn't I get a camcorder?*

The black SUV, license plate HH2, faced the house. Dim, dimmer, the headlights vanished. The driver's door opened. A woman, about five feet five, dressed in a wedding gown, got out of the car, in the car, then out of the car again. Tossing the veil inside, she definitely wasn't Fancy.

"This is great material for Act I of my screenplay. I've got to get closer."

Hanging her spy glasses around her neck, Candice tiptoed behind a pineapple-shaped tree. How many people had keys to Darius's house?

"Oh my gosh." Candice ducked when sensor lights beamed in the woman's face. Why was this woman entering like she lived there? Adjusting the binoculars, Candice gasped. "My goodness. It's Ashlee."

Candice hadn't seen Ashlee in years. The unmistakably creamy pale skin, straight dark hair, and small nose were definitely Ashlee Anderson. But why was she there? Ashlee was always a nice, polite, innocent little girl who'd grown up the same until she started working for, nah, make that fucking around with, Darius.

Waiting for the door to close, Candice continued squatting as she scurried closer to the SUV. Peeping through the driver's window, she saw the veil on the floor. Moving to the back window, "Oh God." Candice's heart thumped as she hoped what she saw wasn't true. "A baby!" A precious little baby was asleep on the backseat.

Sliding all eight of her fingers in the crack, Candice struggled to force down the window. The glass didn't budge. She shook hard. The baby's short arms stretched over its head, then covered the ears. Maybe Candice should call the police. Naw, that would ruin her chances of being the first one with the "breaking news." Forget it. She'd find another way to rescue the infant.

Lightly sprinting, Candice eased into her car. Scrolling her PDA, she entered the license plate number into her Palm Pilot. Shifting into second gear, she crept up the block at five miles an hour, headlights off, rubbing her palms, like she was preparing for a sneak attack on someone.

"Why am I still hiding?" She laughed, pressing the accelerator. "I can't wait to see the videos."

Candice wanted to stay, but Jada would soon wonder where Wellington's stuff was. She should crush sleeping pills in Wellington's food so Jada could get some rest. Poor thang.

Stopping a few blocks away, Candice reentered the convenience store, reluctantly purchasing the junk food and a pint of strawberry ice cream. Parking in Jada's driveway, Candice sat. Worrying. What if the baby was still in the car?

Candice circled, then exited Jada's driveway en route back to Darius's house. Wellington would have to get his sweet satisfaction elsewhere. Candice had a screenplay to develop. With the short distance between the homes, maybe she could make it back before the ice cream melted.

"Oh no." Looking in her rearview mirror, Candice noticed a limousine behind her, so she bypassed Darius's house, slowing to five miles an hour. When the limo cruised into Darius's driveway, Candice made a U-turn. This time she parked curbside, knelt beside her car, and adjusted her binoculars. The shrubs shielded her body.

The limo stopped. No one got out. Then all the lights in the house went out. Eagerly Candice mumbled, "No one would believe this if I told them."

"Believe what?"

"Ooowwww!" Candice screamed, raising her hands to her face. Her eyes widened to a blinding flashlight.

"Excuse me, miss, but what do you think you're doing?" he asked, standing over her dressed in a dark blue LAPD uniform.

If she had the balls, she'd punch him in his nuts. *Go do some real police work.* "Could you move that light out of my face? I thought I saw a puppy roaming in the bushes," Candice said, fumbling with the branches before she stood.

"Yeah, yeah. I've heard it all before. Unless it's your puppy, you're trespassing. You're a little too old to be one of Mr. Williams's groupies, wouldn't you say?" Stepping closer, the officer said, "Consider this a warning, lady. I will arrest you if I find you trespassing on Mr. Williams's property again."

Sorry-ass wannabe cop. Probably trying to earn free tickets. "My apologies, Officer," Candice said, looking at his badge, "Nero. I'll leave. If you find a dog, give it to Mr. Williams." Candice muffled, "So you can have an ass-kissing partner to cover your off shift."

"I heard that," he said.

Brushing off her sweatpants, Candice fingered her ponytail. He wasn't worth arguing with, but he succeeded in ending her stakeout. For the moment. "Shit!" Getting in her car, Candice squeezed the carton of ice cream.

"Great, now I have to go back." Stopping three blocks away, Candice entered the convenience store, exchanged the pint of strawberry, and headed toward Jada's via Darius's house.

Candice frowned. The black SUV was now parked on the street. Was it there before? Shaking her head, Candice doubled-parked. She peeped to see if the baby was still inside. Red and blue lights rotated behind her.

"Oh, great. This is incredible." Was Darius's house the only one on his beat? If he was doing his job he would've discovered the kid was in the car. Maybe the baby wasn't. But what if the child was? Nero wouldn't believe her. Candice would come back after Officer Nero's shift ended at seven o'clock in the morning.

Parking at Jada's, Candice entered the quiet house. Except for the foyer, all of the lights were off. "Hopefully they're asleep." Candice placed the snacks on the kitchen counter, the ice cream in the freezer, then strategically hid all except one of her clock cameras. She'd hide the last recorder in Jada's bedroom after Jada took Wellington to the hospital.

Returning to her guest room, alone, she sat by the large bay window. Her fingers tapped lightly against the keyboard, sixty, seventy words a minute.

See, that's why a brotha should never fuck his sister.

CHAPTER 5

Darius

Applying pressure to his misbehaving, naughty, out-of-control, hot-and-bothered dick, Darius glanced at Fancy's lips cushioned at the opening of his boxers. "Yeah." He had to feel his dick inside her. But how, without putting her and the baby at risk? Ashlee was lying. There was no risk. But not knowing what he knew could be true; next time he had to consider precautionary measures and use a condom. Right? Wrong?

He who was without sin was a liar. And since all sins were weighted equally, Darius was no different from the average man: selfish, self-centered, thinking with the, what Darius considered, right head. Suppose he tested positive and Fancy didn't. Darius didn't trust that love would convince Fancy to stay. Especially if she found out he knew beforehand. But if both of them were positive . . .

Man, what is your fuckin' problem? Your whole thought process is screwed up. HIV isn't as easy to contract as most people think. Hit it. Quit it. She won't get it.

Unless she was susceptible.

Ashlee explained that to him when Darius's ex-fiancée, Maxine, tested positive and he tested negative. Somethin' about a viral load in the first few days. Whatever. Hopefully his results would fare the same. If not, how many women had he blasted off in? He'd lost count. Wasn't his fault. They wanted what he'd given them—an opportunity to brag to their friends that Slugger was their best lover and how they'd fucked the shit out of a millionaire who was now an NBA-bound player.

Damn, reflecting on the pussies he'd stroked, there really were too many females to track, trace, or remember names of, let alone faces, places, pussylicious tastes. Darius's tongue got hard, sliding along his lips. "Umm." Fancy's honey-suckle milky soft pussy lingered as he inhaled. His mental palate always tasted her on his lips. Darius drew an imaginary outline along the bumpy tips of pretty Miss Kitty. "Um, um, um." Ever so sweet, better than the most decadent dessert.

Just use a condom, dawg. If Fancy questions why . . . lie. Better yet, don't answer her: You're the man, that's your pussy, and she has the rock on her finger to solidify. Fuck! I see why so many people are infected. I got it. You're a genius, man! Why didn't I think of this sooner? Fuck her in the ass. Condom necessary. Explanation unnecessary. Darius would legitimately protect everybody's best interest.

Knowing he could've been positive didn't give his morality a reality check. Darius had to die someday from something. Why not go out like a G, on top.

Sex wasn't everything. Sex was the only thing that mattered to Darius. To any man who was a real man. When Darius wasn't getting his head straight-up waxed, he thought about busting nuts like that Thoroughbred that got paid a half million a pop. His sperm was priceless. Wham! Bam! Gotta go! Who invented that cuddling nonsense? Pillow talk? If his woman was too busy to fulfill her duties, another woman of his liking would do if she'd let him bang her a time or two. Now that he was a professional player, Darius's new rule: a two-fuck maximum to minimize the drama.

Sex. Master or slave? So powerfully tempting, made his legs weak before, during, and after orgasms. *Don't fight the feeling. Go on. Succumb to the cum. Do her. One better. Do you.*

Flawless beauty graced Fancy's entire body. Perfect full lips. Supple, firm tits. Blemish-free skin. Tight phat ass. Unbeweavably long hair that tickled his dick. Great tone with the right amount of definition to accentuate her femininity. Other than his mother, Darius had never met a woman so obsessed with her appearance.

Fancy was highly intelligent. Owned a thriving real estate firm. Plus, she was a self-made millionaire like his mom. For the first time Darius realized why he loved Fancy. Her beauty and self-determination reminded him of all the things he admired about his mother. Only difference was, Fancy couldn't cook worth a damn. Thus, he'd have to hire a chef. Female, 'cause no nigga was hangin' around his woman when he wasn't home.

The train of her gold gown sparkled, covering the limousine floor. Her lips puckered fractions of an inch from his dick, making Slugger harden into an aching throb. Darius imagined Fancy sucking him again until he exploded all over her face before waking her. Badly he had to moisturize her pussy with his creamy sperms. Could he think of anything other than sex? No. Not really. Nothing felt better than cumming.

Lovingly massaging her scalp, Darius gently said, "Ladycat, we're home."

Sleepily opening her eyes, Fancy sat up, stretching her arms across his face. "What was all that about?"

"What?" Darius's eyes shifted to the corners.

"Don't play me for stupid. Who'd you call?"

"Call, who?"

Frowning, Fancy stared at the house, then at Darius. "Did the lights just go out?"

"No, I mean yes, it's the timer," Darius lied, feeling his dick slump between his shrinking balls. Exhaling, he said, "Wait right here." Any reason to escape Fancy's series of questions was welcome.

Zipping his pants, Darius left his belt unbuckled just in case he had to whup ass. Cautiously he entered his home. "Ashlee?" he whispered.

Darius searched the downstairs hallway, then trotted upstairs. Bypassing Ashlee's old bedroom, he stopped, backed up, then slowly opened the door and hissed, "Ashlee? What the hell?" A wedding gown was on the bed. Darius closed the door, locking it from the inside first. Fuck! Ashlee wasn't lying. That conniving crazy woman was somewhere in his house.

"Ashlee!" he yelled this time. "I'm not going to play games with you! If you're in my muthafuckin' house, I'ma beat your ass, then call the cops, and have you arrested for breaking and entering!"

The threat sounded good. No way in hell would Darius hit a woman. Ciara could've died from gashing her head after she pulled away from his embrace, slipped, then hit her head on the sharp edge of a table.

The house was eerily quiet. Darius heard himself breathing heavily.

Checking the remaining rooms, Darius returned to the limo. Hesitantly he escorted Fancy to the door. One hand braced her back, the other swooped under her legs as Darius carried his bride-to-be over the threshold, then kissed her lips before she opened her mouth. "I'll be back in a few hours. I have to go check on someone, I mean something. You know where everything is. Um, make yourself comfortable." Raising his voice, Darius continued, "I love you, Ladycat! I want you to stay here with me. Move in."

Fancy poked Darius's side, then hugged him. "You're so silly. I'm not deaf. Stop yelling." Pulling him down to her, she pressed her lips tenderly along his neck, then on his ear. Juices trickled off her wiggling tongue into his eardrum. Another hot spot. "And just because we didn't get married," she said pinching his nipple, "doesn't mean we can't have honeymoon sex. Me-ow." Fancy purred, licking from his chin to his cheek. "I wanna do the private dance I've practiced all month exclusively for my man."

Darius watched Fancy's hips grind the number eight into the air, then into his heads. Pushing her away, he said, "Later," then removed Fancy's hands from his sizzling nipples.

"Baby, this has been a long and hectic day, I need you to take the edge off Miss Kitty. And don't think I forgot about your conversation in the car."

"Okay, tell me, what did you hear?" Right now starting an argument was better than fucking.

Tilting her head down, batting her eyes up at him, Fancy pleaded, "I don't wanna argue. Make love to me. I need to feel your dick inside here." Massaging her clit, Fancy reached behind her back, then stood in the foyer peeling away her gown.

Swaying like a tree in a gusty wind, Fancy caressed her breasts. Darius's eye followed her hands' movement. Sucking her fingers, touching her navel, twirling her pubic hairs, then spreading her pussy lips wide, invitingly she swiped between her thighs. Darius bit his fist as Fancy pasted a mustache of sweetness under his nose, easing her scented fingers into his mouth alongside his knuckles. Lusting to lick her protruding nipples, suck her engorged shaft, bury his face in her pretty money bag with a dollar-sign-shaped bush, then cum deep enough inside her to impregnate her again, Darius said, "Later. Not now. I've got a lot on my mind." His love for Fancy refused to let him put her at risk ever again.

"Well, I do too. Come on. Don't make me take your magic stick," Fancy protested, palming Darius's stiff dick like a pitcher warming up on the mound.

"Oh, shit!" Spasms traveled from his feet to his head. Closing his eyes, Darius jerked his pelvis forward, then back, trembling on the verge of busting a nut in her hand. His legs weakened as he pleaded, "Baby, please."

"Uh-uh. No, you won't cum without me. Don't walk away, baby. I can see he wants me. Don't you?" Fancy pleaded, following Darius into the bedroom.

If she only knew he needed her more than he wanted her. "Not tonight. I've got a headache. In fact, get me some aspirin." Could headache medicine cure a dick-ache? Probably not but it couldn't hurt.

Entering the bedroom behind Darius, Fancy stopped in the doorway and pointed.

Ignoring Fancy, Darius entered the bathroom, pissed, scrubbed his hands clean, then retrieved the red and white bottle from the medicine cabinet. Antiinflammatory. Exactly what he needed.

Following him, Fancy stood in the bathroom doorway and asked, "Darius, why is your bed messed up?"

"I guess the maids didn't come."

Aligning the arrow on the top with the notch on the bottom, Darius shook two tablets into his palm, filled a mouthwash cup with faucet water, and swallowed the pills. Raising his hand, he slammed the medicine bottle on the counter and yelled, "Damn! Get off my ass! Fuck!" Before Fancy spoke another word, Darius brushed past her and said, "I love you," then stomped his way to the garage, got in his platinum Bentley, turned on his headlights, and backed his car into the driveway.

Reentering the garage, Darius hissed, "Ashlee, I know you're here somewhere. Where are you? Ashlee!" Tiptoeing to the wall, Darius retrieved a flashlight from the middle shelf. The bright light beamed in every corner. "I swear when I find you, you'll be sorry."

Settling into his car, Darius drove off, searching his neighborhood for Ashlee. Approaching a black SUV, license number HH2, Darius slowed down, lowered his window, peeping at the foggy passenger-side window. Raising his window, he mumbled, "This is ridiculous. She ain't worth my trouble."

Driving downhill thinking of women, where in the hell was Ciara's scheming ass? Asking him to help raise her son after his paternity test came back negative. Aimlessly cruising for an hour, Darius prayed that Ladycat was peacefully sleeping, because he had unfinished business that would preoccupy his time all night and well into the morning.

En route to his destination, he felt salty water clinging to his eyelids. Blinking repeatedly, Darius was tired of crying, but the tears overruled, siding with his depression. His deceased grandpa Robert's voice echoed in his mind, "Crying is for girls and sissies." Darius should've been celebrating his dreams come true of finally going pro, getting married, and being an expectant father, but the women in his life wreaked havoc. Worrying about Ashlee, Fancy, Ciara, his mother, their issues always superseded his problems. Why, deep inside his heart, did he care about each of them?

Darius refused to cry over some bullshit that wasn't his fault. Easier to discount his mother's lie as bullshit than to try to understand why, of all the women in his life, she'd lied. The more he prayed seeking the truth, the more he hated—not his mother— himself, because of what she'd done. Could a woman make a man hate himself? His mother was easier to forgive than the lie, but the pain she'd caused was impossible to forget. Because of her, his life was filled with endless disappointments and an underlying disregard for all women.

Was Darius one of the men whose actions toward women differed from his affection? He said he loved women but had a hard time showing them. Obviously he loved sex. But maybe sex was all he loved about women. Outside of being a sperm receptacle, being fruitful and multiplying, cleaning house, raising kids, women had no other purpose. Females were cute to look at too. Some of them.

None of his women could comprehend him. Perhaps because he didn't understand himself. Contradiction upon contradiction. Darius wanted to shed his tears on Fancy's shoulders. Instead he'd chosen a woman who'd best know his pain. A woman who wouldn't judge him.

Pow! Pow!

"What the hell?"

From seventy to zero, Darius's heart punched his chest from the inside out. Fighting with his steering wheel, Darius could hardly breathe. Spinning like a donut, Darius's car whirled in a circular cloud of smoke.

Honk! Honk!

Were the people around him so ingrained with their destiny they couldn't see he was dying? Speeding cars dodged his Bentley. Bright white lights blinded him. "Ma Dear?" he whispered. Soon his luck would end. Two bullets fired. Two shots sliced his head. His heart. Blood dripped from his subconscious as Darius navigated his way to the slow lane, then exited the freeway. His body slumped over the steering wheel. Inhale. Exhale. Inhale. He couldn't exhale.

A man couldn't take another man's life and go free. The day Darius pulled the trigger, killing Fancy's father, haunted him every day. How could he and Fancy pretend or ignore that Darius had single-handedly executed a death sentence? Unwanted mission accomplished. If Darius hadn't shot Thaddeus, Thaddeus would've raped, then killed Fancy. Darius cried long and hard, begging,

"Lord, please forgive me. When I try to do right, I do wrong. But I want to do what's right. Help me please."

A caring angel wing rested on his shoulder. "It's okay, baby. You did what most people do, you did what you thought was right. But I want you to know. God is a forgiving God."

Darius knew it was Ma Dear's spirit speaking to him before the bright light shrunk into a dot, then vanished. He exhaled, thankful he could see a glimmer of hope. Ma Dear was the only woman who'd never given up on him. He feared that somehow he'd failed his grandmother. Darius's mind had made his third deepest fear—abandonment—resurface. He didn't want to be lonely, or go to hell, or end up in purgatory for straddling a fence of women. One day Darius would give his life to God. Hopefully, before his last breath. Murder wasn't worth battling alone. Darius had visited Fancy's therapist once. At first he believed that therapy was for crazy people, but Mandy actually helped him. When Mandy's office opened, he'd call for another appointment. Like with his first visit, Darius wouldn't tell Fancy. Especially since Mandy refused to see Fancy after Fancy called her a bitch.

Drying his eyes, he glanced in his rearview mirror. Large brown eyes, a do-rag, and a pale face reflected back.

Ashlee whispered, "Hello, Darius."

"What the fuck!"

CHAPTER 6

Darius

Ashlee's, hopefully temporary, insanity was exactly the kind of underhanded immature feline foolishness that made Darius distrust women. Ashlee sat in the backseat of his car like he was her damn chauffer. Legs crossed. Head cocked to the side. Arms overlapped damn near under her neck. Darius cruised to the next public place and parked in the most visible space he could find, a hotel parking lot in Beverly Hills.

Turning to face Ashlee, he asked, "What the fuck are you doing? First you're trespassing in my house, now you're hiding in my car."

"Our house. Our car, Darius." Ashlee stared through him.

Banging his fist on the headrest, summoning her attention, Darius yelled, "It's not our house! It's my damn house!" then gestured toward Ashlee, asking, "And what the hell are you doing with my clothes on?"

"Our clothes," Ashlee calmly replied.

"Your ass is crazy. Get out of my car."

"Our car."

"Oh, you're acting so brand-new I don't know what's gotten into you," Darius said, shaking his head. "All right, Ashlee. Tell me. What do you want from me?"

Melancholy, she asked, "Why do you hate me?"

Her question fucked with his head as Darius stared into Ashlee's sad brown eyes. He didn't hate her. He loved her but didn't know how to be her friend without using or hurting her again. His hostility was meant to protect, not hurt, his women.

"Look, Ashlee. I don't hate you. It's just that..." His words trailed into thoughts. One woman couldn't satisfy all of his needs. Make that desires. A light bulb went off in his mind. But if Ashlee was infected, and there was a possibility he might be too, then why not? Hell, a good fuck was what she'd probably wanted, and deserved for stalking him.

Matter-of-factly, Ashlee said, "I don't want you to marry Fancy."

Darius opened his glove compartment. Yes! He had condoms. Quickly he rolled two into his palm.

"Let's get a room here. That way I can get some rest and you can have my undivided attention." Not giving Ashlee an option, Darius valet-parked his car, then said to Ashlee, "Let's go. You can get everything off your chest at once." So could he. Darius eased the condoms into his pocket.

Smiling at the woman behind the counter, Darius placed his American Express card in front of her. "One room, best available, one night."

"Aren't you, um, don't tell me," she said, bouncing her titties. Pausing to read his credit card, she continued, "Yeah, it is you. The guy who killed a man, then got drafted. How'd you get away with that, playa?" Waving her hand, she continued babbling, "Forget I said that. So"—she smiled wide—"who are you playing for?"

Best to ignore her kind. Darius looked at Ashlee, then turned to the clerk. His head involuntarily snapped back toward Ashlee, shaking side to side as he wished he'd made her wait in the car. Seeing Ashlee under the lobby's sparkling chandelier, he thought she looked horrible. Dark circles underneath both eyes. Smeared lipstick. Dirty face. White shoes? Debris tangled in the stringy matted hair sticking from underneath his do-rag.

"What the hell happened to you?"

Ashlee softly replied, "You."

Hopefully that wasn't the devastating effect Darius left on most women. Was it? "Fine, let's go." *Before anybody else sees me with you,* Darius thought.

Ashlee paced her dragging steps two feet behind him. Darius peeped over his shoulders every few seconds until he slid the key card into the slot and opened the door. Ashlee placed her tote bag on the computer desk, then sat on the edge of the king-size bed.

"Why are you still wearing your tuxedo?"

"Whooooa." Darius exhaled. Was the pussy worth all this? Popping the cork on two bottles of champagne splits from the minibar, Darius answered, "Didn't feel like changing."

Darius filled one glass, handed the bursting bubbles to Ashlee, then gulped his straight from the bottle as he sat beside her. A shower for both of them would be nice, but Darius hadn't planned on staying long after he'd gotten what he'd cum for. He watched Ashlee remove his button-up. Unzipping her jeans, she stepped out, left leg, then right, placing her denims over the back of the large cushioned chair. All that remained was his wife-beater T-shirt, no panties.

Damn. Darius hadn't seen the scars on Ashlee's thighs from the fire he'd rescued her from months back. That was his fault too. If he hadn't pissed off Ciara, Ciara would never have burned down his office with Ashlee inside.

Touching her thigh, Darius said, "So that's where they took the skin to reconstruct your face."

Ashlee nodded. "I have lots of scars, emotionally and physically, to remind me of you. How many scars do you have to remind you of me?"

Ciara had scars. Maxine. Kimberly too. Darius had none. Physically, that is. Emotionally. Two. Thaddeus and . . . the second one, not his HIV scare, was unmentionable. Darius wasn't even sorry that his past relationships didn't last.

"What happed to your toe?" Darius asked, reaching for Ashlee's foot. "It looks dead. You'd better get that checked out before it falls off."

Blocking his hand, Ashlee said, "I dropped your dumbbell on it."

"You had a field day going through my things, didn't you?" Before Ashlee answered, Darius held his hand up and said, "I know, our things."

"No, you're right. Those are your things. But can't you see I just want to be a part of your life? Like I used to be when we were kids, when we lived together, worked together, made love together." Hanging her head, Ashlee continued, "When you actually cared about me. We have a—" Ashlee sighed.

Darius held Ashlee's hands. "What?"

"Nothing."

"Ashlee, I do care about you." If she only knew how much. "But the things you're doing are only pushing me further away."

"Further?" Beet-red tearful eyes confronted him as Ashlee yelled, "This is not about you! It's about me! Why can't you care about anyone else! Why do you have to turn everything around? Nothing is ever your damn fault!"

Darius's eyes shifted away from Ashlee. She had no idea how awful he felt about abandoning her. Better to leave her before she would've left him. No need to mention the times he did try contacting her and she chose to ignore him. Defending his irresponsibility, Darius yelled, "But you were the one who fucked my brother!"

Ashlee covered her face, crying. "Here we go again. How many times am I going to have to say I'm sorry? I wanted to use Kevin to get back at you for all the things you'd done to me. I never loved Kevin."

She didn't? Although he'd refused to ask, he was relieved to know. That meant the only man she'd ever loved was him. Comforting Ashlee, Darius secured her in his embrace. "Let's forget about Kevin." But he'd never forgive or trust Ashlee or Kevin again.

Kevin's stealing ass was getting out of jail on a technicality. The embezzlement charges for the million dollars Kevin had stolen from Darius's company, Somebody's Gotta Be on Top, were dropped after Darius's father Darryl pleaded with Darius not put Kevin behind bars. The only reason Darius agreed was to please his father. Whatever, after Darius got what he wanted from Ashlee he'd leave her alone, for good this time.

When Ashlee raised her arms to hug him, the stench invaded his nostrils. "Make love to me, Darius. I need you."

"Whoa, didn't you tell me you were and I might be—" Darius said, backing away while covering his nose.

"I'm not sure about all that, but we can use protection because I can't remember what I did with my abortion pills. I keep condoms with me, though. I need you to love me."

"Well, personally, I need you to freshen up. Slugger won't, make that can't, get hard with that odor lingering." And if her underarms stunk up the place, Darius could only imagine that crevices of her pussy smelled like wolf.

Removing the do-rag and T-shirt, Ashlee said, "I'll be right out."

"Take your time. Please."

Waiting for Ashlee, Darius turned on the television. His cell phone rang. Glancing at the caller ID, he saw it was Fancy. Darius silenced the call and turned off the phone with one prolonged press of a button. Easier to lie and say his battery died. Placing his phone on the desk, Darius paused, staring at Ashlee's purse. He looked at the bathroom door, turned up the television, then rumbled through Ashlee's bag to retrieve all of her keys except the obviously tagged rental car key. "SUV? HH2 . . . that was her car?" Fumbling, grasping more keys, Darius dropped the keys from his hands inside the purse when he saw a worn picture of Ashlee, little Darius, and himself that was taken at the hospital the day his son was born. The edges were bent with lines creasing the middle, but that was his son. A lump, too big to swallow, formed in his throat. Darius frowned. "Stop trippin', dog. He's dead."

What type of man would Darius have raised his son to be?

"What are you doing?" Ashlee asked, standing behind Darius. Water dripped over her nipples. "Give me my purse."

"I was trying to get a head start. I was looking for your condoms. You lied. You don't have any."

Turning her back, then holding up a cosmetics case, Ashlee said, "I do."

Taking the condom pack, Darius unbuckled his pants, lowered them to his knees, rolled the condom halfway up his shaft before it stopped. Unrolling the condom, Darius dug in his pocket, removed a gold Magnum packet, and covered his dick.

Darius forced the image of his son out of his mind. "Turn around. I want to fuck you from behind." What he really wanted was not to look Ashlee in her eyes, or start conjuring feelings for her.

"No, Darius. I want you to look at me," Ashlee said, lying missionary style on the comforter.

Climbing on top of Ashlee, Darius raised her pelvis to his hips, penetrating his head inside a pussy. "Aw, you feel so good." Not knowing when he'd have sex again, he stoked her long, deep, and slow, pretending he didn't know her. "Your pussy is so warm, ah, so sweet, and damn so tight."

Ashlee whispered, "Your pussy. This is your pussy, Darius. Only yours."

The hell it is. Closing his eyes, Darius leaned his head back and pressed his dick as deep as he could inside her. Then he pulled out and commanded, "Turn over."

This time Ashlee didn't refuse. Reentering her from behind, Darius pounded his dick. Quick. Fast. Hard. Faster. Harder. "Aw, shit!" His hips smacked against her ass, which turned redder and redder. "Aw, shit! Cum with Daddy. Cum with me, La-dee—cum with me, damn it!" he yelled, slapping her ass hard so she'd be too busy cumming to question him, almost calling her Fancy's nickname.

Ashlee collapsed into the bed. "When was the last time you got some?"

"You a trip. You don't wanna know the answer to that," Darius said, shaking his heads. With his pants around his ankles, he took baby steps, entering the bathroom. Darius snapped off the condom, held it over the toilet, then threw up. "What the hell?" His stomach tightened. "Shit! Man, what kind of pussy was that? Is this payback? Fuck!" he yelled, bellowing champagne and particles from the partially digested tablets into the white porcelain bowl.

"Damn, I shouldn't have taken those tablets on an empty stomach." Darius's body weakened as he flushed the last of what he'd regurgitated.

Running warm water in the sink, Darius rinsed his mouth, splashed water on his face, dipped his dick, lathered, rinsed, quickly dried himself off, then exited into the bedroom before Ashlee thought of some more devious shit to do to him.

Darius pulled up his pants, stretched across the bed on his back, and laid Ashlee's head on his chest.

"I want you to get rid of her," Ashlee sleepily said.

When would she give up? Rolling his eyes under his lids, Darius felt slightly better but awfully nauseated. "It's not that simple." he kissed Ashlee's forehead.

"It was when you got rid of me."

"Give me some time. I've got a lotta things going on right now," Darius said, stroking Ashlee's hair. When she didn't respond, he looked down. Ashlee had fallen asleep. *Snooorrreee,* lightly whistled from her lips.

Easing from underneath Ashlee, Darius gently placed a pillow under her head. Digging in his pocket, he tossed five hundred dollars on the table, then quickly scribbled a note that read *Take a taxi back to your SUV and never contact me again.* Darius quietly fumbled through Ashlee's tote, removed all of her keys—except the rental car key. He took the family photo of them together, and then tiptoed out of the hotel room.

Some women never knew when to quit.

CHAPTER 7

Darius

"Oh, wee! A brotha's feelin' kinda nice," Darius said, holding his dick while waiting for the elevator. Mentally he'd willed himself back to health, focusing on the good stuff. "Come on, man before she wakes up."

Press. Press. Press.

Ding!

"It's about time." Darius touched the L button, admiring his handsome smiling face in the mirror.

The doors opened. "Oh, shit!" Lowering his head, Darius turned his face away from the registration desk. "That nosy chick is still working."

"Bye, Mr. Williams. It was my pleasure having you. Do come again," she said, laughing, returning to her conversation with her coworker. All Darius heard was, "Girrlll, let me tell you about him."

How in the fuck was she going to tell somebody about him when all she knew was what she'd read in the newspaper? Women like her were the reason Darius didn't share his dick with groupies. Retrieving his car from the valet attendant, he proceeded to his original destination before he had been abruptly sidetracked by Ashlee. He'd watch the videos recorded by his hidden cameras of her roaming throughout his house later. No, on second thought, he wouldn't. Ashlee wasn't worth him spending that much time tracing her steps, but he'd have every single lock in his home changed immediately. Now that he had her keys to his house and her house, Ashlee would never trespass on his property again.

Darius drove along the freeway, lowered his window, tossed out Ashlee's keys. She had no reason to see him again. None. Fucking Ashlee took a dead weight off his shoulders and his dick. Finally, Slugger was momentarily satisfied. In or out of the bedroom, Ashlee didn't compare to Fancy. Ashlee was his best friend and stepsister since they were kids, so conceivably they might never stop loving one another, but Darius wouldn't marry Ashlee if she were the only pussy on his jock. Yeah, he was spoiled but whose fault was that?

Reflecting on his upbringing, Darius thought his childhood was better than most kids'. His mom, Jada Diamond Tanner, was a self-made millionaire all of his life, making him a millionaire the second he was conceived. There was nothing that Darius wanted, didn't have, couldn't get, including women. But like most children, he'd taken his mother for granted. That she'd always be there for him no matter what he'd done. This time he'd committed the unthinkable, unimaginable, unbelievable. If God delivered him once, He shouldn't have to deliver him again. He could. But would He?

Powering on his cell phone, Darius listened to his messages. "Darius, call me—" Darius deleted the call when he heard Fancy inhale. "Darius, you bastard! Where the fuck are my keys!" Ashlee yelled. Darius turned off his phone, tossing it into the passenger seat. Women. His passion. Their problem.

Darius's time had come to grow up and become a man. A real man. This time was different because he actually *wanted* to do the right thing—things. If not now . . . when? Tired of hurting people, he questioned his purpose in life, rotating the ignition key counterclockwise, silencing his engine. The music continued playing.

"It's so good, loving somebody, when that somebody loves you back."

Who did he honestly love? Feeling his eyebrows draw into a unibrow, Darius listened to the lyrics while staring at her front door. He did love her. But not more than she loved him. Love was never fifty, fifty. But ninety, ten? That was below friendship level. Well, he had to confront her at some point, so Darius slowly opened his car door.

Thump.

The tan leather sole of his left shoe greeted the dark asphalt. The cool California before sunrise breeze invaded his cheeks, numbing his spirit. Los Angeles could be a cold place any time of the day or night.

Thump.

Or was his numbness the result of his eternal internal pain?

Thump.

A woman could make a man both numb and cold. The black leather square-toed shoes resounded up the driveway, stopping side by side at their destination. Fearful, Darius stood facing her solid oak double doors. In his deepest moment of needing her, why did she have to need him?

The palm of his hand covered his nose, his not knowing which was colder, sliding to his lips, then over his chin, casually flopping along his side. His full lips disappeared into his mouth. Tears swelled; he clenched his bottom lip between his perfect teeth, preventing the outpouring of depression drowning his heart.

Good looks didn't mean shit when he felt like shit on the inside. His chest tightened as he prayed the bad news he'd received from Ashlee wasn't true. Why didn't he demand more information from her at the hotel? His right foot crossed over his left. About-face, he pivoted. Today wasn't a good day. For him. Maybe he'd come back to console her, tomorrow.

Thump. Thump. Thump . . . screech.

Halfway to his car, Darius stopped, closed his eyes, exhaling, knowing she stood in the doorway staring at his back. Rubbing his hand over his shoulder-length locks, he paused.

"Hi, sweetheart" resonated from behind. He'd recognized her soothing voice all of his life. But he wasn't quite ready to face her.

Without turning around, Darius opened his eyes and answered, "I forgot something in my car, I'll be right in." He'd lied to her, hopefully for the last time.

Click. Her front door gently closed.

Bam . . . He shut his car door. Soft orange and red hues reached to the dark blue sky. The keys dangled from the ignition. He could leave before the break of dawn exposed him, but how long would he run away from his responsibility to her? Gripping the top of his steering wheel, he clung with his forearms to the cherry-wood circle. Both elbows indented his muscular thighs. Teddy Pendergrass's vocals strummed to the beat of Darius's heart . . . it was good loving someone . . . but how would she know? He'd never unconditionally loved her back.

"Why me, Lord? Why now? Why this? Just when I was trying to do the right thing and get married, why all the temptations?"

Sobbing not so sobering tears, Darius knew he hadn't treated most of the women in his life right, especially his mother, but he was working on it. Didn't he deserve some credit for trying? Instead he might be dying. What a fucked-up world to live in, when having an orgasm, something that felt so incredible, could mark the beginning of the end his life. Women were definitely more scandalous than men.

It wasn't his fault his wife, Ciara, hadn't signed the divorce papers so Darius had to cancel marrying Fancy; otherwise, he'd become a bigamist. Darius wasn't going back to jail for nobody, including Fancy. It wasn't his fault his mother caught her husband cheating again or that his mother's husband was diagnosed with prostate cancer.

Karma was a muthafucka.

Wellington got what he deserved. Who gave a damn if Wellington's dick didn't work anymore? Wellington brought that bullshit upon himself fucking that good-for-nothing, got-nothin'-to-lose, trifling-ass ho, Melanie. Nor was it Darius's fault his stepsister's newborn baby had died of complications. But if Ashlee's son was in fact his son, then perhaps he was to blame.

"Fuck!" Darius yelled, banging his head against his knuckles. "Why does this shit always fuckin' happen to me!"

Screech.

Sniffling, then holding his breath, he heard the door reopen. Shifting his eyes to the corners, he exhaled, seeing her slender sil-

CHAPTER 8

Fancy

*B*oom. *Ba-boom-boom. Boom!*
"Oh my gosh!"

Fancy wrestled with the purple duvet. The vibration reverberated, shaking the mattress. "Earthquake!" she screamed, rolling out of the bed. Her feet landed catlike on the floor, balancing her ass and shoulders until they were in alignment. The aftershock followed.

Boom! Throw your muthafuckin' hands up!

Racing into the hallway, Fancy flattened her palms over her ears, scurried downstairs, then darted into the living room, desperately searching for the source of the loudest noise she ever heard. With a hand covering her pounding heart, frantically she'd pressed the power button on the stereo. Her palm patted her breasts, then massaged her neck.

"Whew! My gosh," she said, stretching her eyes, rattling her head, breathing deeply. "Darius," she gasped, "where are you?" Fancy stood dazed in the middle of the floor trying to slow her accelerated heartbeat. "Darius."

Taking several steps toward the garage, Fancy started to check for Darius's car, instantly changing her mind. He hadn't answered her calls since he'd left. One minute his cell phone was on, the houette through his passenger window. *Oh my gosh,* he thought, seeing how much weight she'd lost. Ten, maybe fifteen pounds. *Okay, man. Pull yourself together. She needs you.* Lowering his head, leaning into the glove compartment, Darius retrieved a napkin, wiped his face, blew his nose, and then crumbled the tissue into his hand before dropping the white paper to the floor. Turning on his cell phone before slipping it into his pocket, he retraced his footsteps to her front door. Now would be a good time for Fancy to give him a reason to leave.

"Hi, Mom." He paused, noticing the swelling barely exposing her hazel eyes. He wanted to say, "Ma, you look terrible," but instead he whispered, "How are you?"

Silently, she hugged his waist, resting her head below his chest. Her hugs always comforted him. He towered six feet eleven inches in the air. She held him tight and didn't let go. Her face clung to his already soaked white button-up shirt, drenching it more. He wrapped his arms around her shoulders, his long fingers sprawling about the back of her head in his desire to comfort her.

Pulling her closer, he whispered with sorrow, "It's all right. Whateva it is, Ma, it's gonna be all right. I'm here for you." And for the first time, in his heart and soul, he meant it.

She muttered, "Wellington has to have surgery. Soon. Will you stay with me a few days and go with me to the hospital the day of his surgery? Please, baby. I need you."

As much as Darius hated the way Wellington misused him and his mother, he said, "Yeah, Ma, sure. Anything for you. I'll stay until it's time for his surgery and I'll go with you to the hospital." Tears flowed down his face, splattering onto his mother's head.

She didn't care about him messing up her hair. Darius didn't care either, about Wellington, that is. Darius had his own problems. So while his mother stood in the doorway crying about her husband, Darius cried too, praying the Lord would spare him once more from having HIV.

next, off. Player recognized game. Darius's tactics were lukewarm at best. She knew the schemes all too well. Fancy was a true diva who knew how to be a straight-up bitch. Nothing could hurt a man worse than a woman.

Tracking Darius's whereabouts was not how she wanted to start their lives together. "I'm not becoming an inspector, checking pants pockets, online cell phone histories, incoming or outgoing cell phone numbers, calling him fifty times a day or sniffing his ass to see if it's too clean or sour from having sex."

She'd leave that nonsense for insecure women like Ashlee. Fancy would give Darius all the rope he needed to hang himself with lies. She went into the bedroom and slammed the door, praying this wasn't a sign of how marriage to Darius would progress. Glancing at the digital clock she wondered, where had Darius gone at midnight and stayed over seven hours?

Sitting in the bed, Fancy checked her mental Rolodex. Who could she call to help take her mind off Darius? The three-hour time difference made it nine in the morning in Atlanta. Fancy thought about Desmond. A part of her missed him. His attentiveness. Kindness. Desmond was a good enough lover to satisfy her appetite but not adventurous enough to explore her curiosities or fulfill her fantasies. She hadn't heard his voice in months. Picking up the handset from the nightstand, Fancy dialed Desmond's number.

"Hey, you're gonna live a long time." Fancy could hear the smile in Desmond's voice. "I was just thinking about you." His tone was soothing. Seductive.

"Thinking about me? Or *thinking* about me?" Fancy asked, stroking her hot pussy.

"Both. I miss you. But shouldn't you be all hugged up honeymooning with your husband?"

"Yeah," she moaned, "I will be, in a minute. But he's not my husband."

Desmond's voice escalated. "What? You didn't marry him?"

"Somethin' like that," Fancy purred, slipping her middle finger inside her puckering pussy.

"I knew it! You know I'm the man for you."

"Ha, ha, ha." Sarcastic or otherwise, Desmond always made her laugh. When was the last time she'd laughed with Darius? With so much going on, Fancy couldn't remember. "Dez, you're my best friend. I shouldn't have called. Don't know why I did. Ummm."

"Yes, you do. What better man to marry than your best friend? You don't want to admit how you feel for me. Well, I'm not too proud to say I love you, Fancy. I'm doing well in law school. And I've got my own place now and you have an open invitation to visit. Or stay."

Spanking her clit, Fancy might have to take Dez up on his offer if Darius didn't get his act together. "What happened to Tanya?"

"Tanya is your friend. Her name is Trina."

"Whateva, what happened to her?"

"Couldn't do it. Haven't gotten over you. Besides, studying takes up all of my time."

"Dez." Fancy already knew, but didn't understand why, Desmond truly loved her. "I, I, I've gotta go. Bye."

No way could she be with Desmond. Any one of her other exes would've had her screaming and cumming so hard the phone would've been stuck inside her pussy. Not clueless Dez. But right now, Fancy was so horny, any dick would do, including a vibrator. Would using a vibrator harm her fetus? Fancy was excited about having Darius's baby and didn't want anything to interfere with her pregnancy.

Since Darius had lost his firstborn and she'd terminated her first pregnancy, their baby growing inside her would bring both of them happiness. Did he or she have eyes yet? If so, what color? How much longer before she'd feel the first flutter of life? "If it's a girl, I wanna name her Diamond." Not because of any sentimental attachment to Darius's mother's middle name. Diamond was the strongest, most precious gem known to man. That's how Fancy wanted to raise her daughter. Rubbing her flat stomach, she poked out her belly, then laughed. "Mommy loves you, precious.

"If it's a boy, I want to name him Thurston Williams." Fancy loved the strong tone of the name Thurston. But she'd raise him with a sensitive loving side and teach him how to treat a lady. Any woman less than a lady, she'd tell Thurston to leave her alone and never bring her home.

Wow, the thought of motherhood scared and excited Fancy. She visualized decorating the room, shopping for clothes, breast-feeding. First word. First step. She wanted to experience everything. No day care until their baby could speak complete sentences.

The risk of using a vibrator wasn't worth the orgasm, so Fancy eased out of her gold thong, tossed it to the floor, stretched across the bed, spread her legs, and allowed her fingers to bring her the pleasure Darius didn't.

"Ummm, yes," she moaned, imagining Darius's long dick entering her pussy. "You make me feel so good, Daddy. Go deeper," Fancy moaned, entangling herself in the silk sheets, envisioning Darius hitting her spot . . . until she heard a woman singing . . . "If I can't have you, I don't want nobody, baby."

"What the hell? Not the stereo again." This time Fancy took her time walking into the living room. She stared at an oldies commercial on the big-screen television.

"Darius has got to take these alarms off. This is driving me nuts."

Unable to sleep, Fancy picked up the cordless and dialed Darius's cell phone. No answer. She hit REDIAL. Voice mail. Fancy called the last person she honestly wanted to speak to—her mother, Caroline.

Fancy's relationship with her mother wasn't great. Therapy sessions with Mandy had helped Fancy to forgive her mother for never having been a mother. Fancy regretted calling Mandy a bitch. No more sessions. Mandy seriously refused to see her. Twenty-plus years it took for Fancy to stop crying over how she was the child who practically raised her mother, and to start trying to be a daughter. Stop insulting Caroline's obesity and start complimenting her accomplishments. Like Caroline earning her GED. A few more classes and her mother would have a diploma. Caroline, like everyone else who'd attended the wedding, had left numerous messages on Fancy's voice mail.

After several rings, Caroline answered, "Hi, honey. Are you okay? I've tried calling you. What happened to you guys? Everyone was at the wedding except you two. But it's probably best because you wouldn't believe that a crazy lady showed up in a limo with a veil over her face dressed in a white wedding gown. And since no one else was getting married, I figured she was waitin' to start some shit. Rolling down the window. Rolling up the window. Peeping every few minutes. Oh, she didn't think anyone saw her, but sho nuff, your mama stood outside long enough waiting for you and saw her. That's why I sat on the last pew, so I could check her ass at the do'."

"Mama."

"I'm sorry, baby. You know, considering I never got married, I wanted your wedding to be perfect. How's Darius?"

"Ma, it's okay. That was probably Ciara."

"Ciara? Who's Ciara?"

"Never mind. Where are you?"

"Never mind my foot. Who's Ciara?"

Fancy mumbled, "His wife."

"His what!"

"I shouldn't have told you. We couldn't get married because Ciara refuses to sign the divorce papers." Fancy told the truth and a lie at the same time because she'd had no idea before the wedding that Darius was legally married.

"Well, I'ma say my piece and I'm done. Move on."

"Ma, I'm grown. Let me make my own mistakes. Where are you?"

"In the Ritz enjoying the suite y'all paid for. I've got a massage scheduled in my room at noon. Can't wait. This baby been kickin' my stomach left and right all night."

"Speaking of a baby, Mama, I'm pregnant too."

"Baby, you need to slow down. Are you happy? Are you going to keep this one? You're not going to change your mind about raising my baby, are you? I sure hope not, 'cause I don't have no more energy to chase after no kid. Not even my own."

"Of course I'm keeping my baby. And yes, unlike you, I'm keeping my promise."

"Is it Darius's baby?"

"Ma, what kinda question is that?"

"Knowing you, a good one. What about Byron, and that child that followed you around like a sick in-love puppy? Desmond. So is it Darius's?"

"Bye, Ma," Fancy said, then hung up before Caroline asked any more probing questions.

Walking into Darius's closet, Fancy put on one of her jogging suits, laced up her tennis shoes, and tied a bandana over her pony-tail. Unlocking the front door, she jogged around the driveway, stretched, then trotted uphill. Running a few miles wouldn't take her mind off Darius, but afterward she'd feel better.

The sunrise was blinding and yellow and orange hues stretched across the sky. Once she and Darius married and moved to Atlanta, Fancy would be closer to Desmond. At least she'd have one friend in Atlanta.

Fancy stopped alongside a parked car. "Waaa. Waaa." Did she hear a baby crying? Peeping through the window, she saw the cutest lit-tle baby wailing back at her. Fancy's eyes bucked. "Oh my gosh! The poor kid is alone." The baby was lying back strapped in the car seat, its hazel eyes seeming to plead for help as if to say, "Don't just stand there, get me outta here!"

"Waaaaaaaaa!"

"Okay, okay, I'll be right back."

Racing downhill, into the house, Fancy dialed 9-1-1.

"Yes, there's a baby abandoned inside a vehicle near 12121 . . . the license plate number is HH2 and it's a black SUV."

The operator replied, "I'm sending help right away. What is the baby doing?"

"Crying like this," Fancy yelled into the receiver, "Waaaaaa!"

"Calm down, miss. What is the child doing now?"

"I don't know. I had to come home to call you."

The operator asked, "Can you go back to the car?"

"Yes, but I can't stay on the phone and go back."

"Okay, can you call us back from a cell phone?"

"Okay, bye."

Fancy grabbed her cell phone and headed back uphill. When Fancy saw the police car parked behind the SUV, she was relieved, went back inside, and flopped on the golden suede sofa.

"What crazy person would leave a child alone in a car?"

CHAPTER 9

Ashlee

"**D**arius," Ashlee called out, rolling over in the bed. There was no response, so she sat up and spoke louder. "Darius?"

Scrambling off the floral-print comforter, Ashlee flung open the bathroom door. "No," she cried, backing into the wall. Her knees buckled as she slid to the floor. She should've put the valet parking stub in her pants pocket. What good would that have done?

"You're the one who let yourself down, so pick yourself up," Ashlee said, standing tall. Wrapping her hand around the receiver, she pressed the Front Desk button.

"Yess?" the receptionist cheerfully answered. "I bet I know who you're looking for. Honey, he's gone and I tell you I've never seen anyone leave faster. I hope you got paid first, sista girl."

Soon as Ashlee said, "I am not a prostitute," she noticed money on the desk.

"It's your world, call it what you want, but in my world, you a hooker. Look, can you give Mr. Williams a message from me?"

"This is not a game! What idiot hired you? Don't make me come down there and have you fired!"

The receptionist said, "See, I was gonna tell you where he went."

Lowering her voice, Ashlee asked, "Where?"

The receptionist laughed, then said, "You must've been polishing your nails when God gave out common sense, 'cause you sure are naïve."

"I'm not naïve, I'm sick," Ashlee said, dropping the phone on the nightstand. "I hate this damn medication!" She sniffled, unscrewing the white cap from the yellow bottle. Pacing, Ashlee walked from the desk to the door and back. Picking up the note, she read *Take a taxi back to your SUV and never contact me again.*

"Fuck you, Darius!" Ashlee screamed, then cried, "Somebody heelllp meeee! I can't remember what I'm supposed to remember. I'm losing my mind. I don't deserve to be a . . . oh God! I'm the worst mother in the world."

Debating on whether to take two tablets or flush them all down the toilet, Ashlee picked up her glass of flat champagne, tossed the pills to the back of her throat, and swallowed. If anything happened to little Darius, she'd never forgive herself.

Postpartum depression had overtaken her body the second day after little Darius was born. Months later, her doctor claimed she hadn't recovered, reporting she'd gotten worse. What did he know about being a woman? A mother? All he did was write one addictive prescription after another that obviously hadn't cured her problem.

"Bastard!" Crumbling the five one-hundred-dollar bills individually, Ashlee pitched them into the trash can. "How dare you treat me like one of your whores? Your money can't buy me!"

Not true. He already had bought her. Her love, her body, all of her was willingly given to Darius in exchange for nothing but headaches. She'd freely dedicated her life to him, not realizing anything worth having was everything except free. Love had a price. Problem was, Ashlee didn't know her self-worth.

She hated taking her meds. Hated herself when she didn't take her meds. Either way, Ashlee's mental state was adversely progressing. One step away from going insane or committing suicide, she felt her brain like a time bomb. Tick. Tick. Tick. Boom! She could snap at any moment about anything. Darius was the only person who made her feel normal. Not her mother. Not her father. Darius. Why did bad things happen to sweet little innocent Ashlee?

Putting on his wife-beater, her jeans, his button-up, and her wedding shoes, Ashlee ran down the exit stairway to the front desk, panting. "Please, can someone get me a taxi, fast?"

"Girl, I told you. See, that's why I gets my money first before giving up my stuff to these athletes. I'ma personally call you—"

Slamming her hands on the counter, Ashlee leaned in the woman's face and screamed, "Shut! Up!" then ran outside to the valet. "Can someone pleeaaassse get me a taxi?"

Inserting his pinky fingers into the corners of his mouth, the valet blew three sharp times, then waved his hand in the air. "Lady, are you okay?" he asked, opening the back door.

"Thanks," Ashlee said, handing him five dollars. Settling into the backseat, she handed the driver a hundred-dollar bill. "Hurry to 12121 . . . it's an emergency. How could she have forgotten about little Darius? Actually she hadn't completely forgotten. One moment she remembered, the next moment she was distracted, all along thinking, *He's asleep. He's okay. I'll get to him soon*, before drifting into another thought.

As she replayed the sequence of events, Ashlee's eyes narrowed, her lips tightened. "There." She pointed. "Park alongside that black SUV."

When the taxi stopped, Ashlee heard her baby hollering. Remotely she unlocked the doors, sat in the back, unbuckled his car seat, then rocked him in her arms. "It's okay. Mommy's here. I didn't mean to leave you alone for so long. Mommy won't do it again. I promise, baby. Mommy loves you so much."

But it had happened before. Hopefully, it wouldn't happen again. Sirens blared, startling little Darius. "Waaaa!"

A Los Angeles police car parked behind her. *Whurrrup!* An officer marched to her car with his hand on his gun.

Ashlee's heart pounded. Quickly she pulled little Darius to her chest and uncovered her breast, placing her nipple next to his lips. Little Darius patted her as if to say, "What's this, Mommy?"

Knocking on the window, the officer asked, "Is everything okay, miss?"

Partially opening the back door, Ashlee said, "Yes, officer. We're fine. I'm just feeding my baby."

Holding the door open, the officer said, "Several people"—he looked at his notebook, then said—"reported an abandoned child in a black SUV, license HH2. . . ."

"Sorry, must've been a mistake. But thank you," Ashlee said, holding her titty in his view.

"Miss, did you leave your baby alone in the car, maybe to go inside?" the tall, young-looking officer asked. "Three calls can't be a mistake."

Annoyed, Ashlee replied, "I said thank you," then closed the door.

"Have a good day," he said, then walked away. Sitting in his car with a partner who never got out of the car, the officer was jotting down a few notes as if he was finishing up his report.

She waited for him to drive off. He didn't.

Little Darius's car seat was to wet to put him back in, so Ashlee sat behind the driver's wheel, propped her baby between two fresh blankets, strapped him into the passenger seat, then headed downhill. She decreased her speed as she drove past Darius's home. Tempted to revisit him, she drove slower. Almost to the corner, Ashlee heard *whurrrup!*

Exhaling, she thought, *Not him again.* Parking in the turning lane, Ashlee lowered her window. "How can I help you this time?"

"I just wanted to tell you your baby's blanket is hang—miss, you can't drive with your child in the front seat like that."

Little Darius had tumbled over the seat belt. "His car seat is wet," Ashlee said, raising her window.

It was midway up when the officer placed his hand atop the edge of the glass. "I'm going to have to issue you a ticket and you must put him back in the seat or I'm going to impound your vehicle."

Annoyed, Ashlee said, "Officer, let me see, Nero, badge number . . . you wouldn't."

"I will and I can have you arrested for child endangerment. What is your problem, lady? You're arguing with me about your child's safety. Are you crazy?"

Yes, Ashlee thought, quietly getting out of the car. She placed two blankets over the wet cushion, strapped little Darius in the car seat, and said, "I'm okay."

"Sign here," the officer said.

"Are you serious? Giving me a ticket for what? Or are you crazy?"

"Miss, don't push your luck. Obviously it's not good. Sign here, and please drive safely."

With so many things happening, Ashlee drove directly to the rental car return, left the charges on her credit card, and boarded the next flight back to Dallas with her son.

CHAPTER 10

Candice

Tossing, turning, Candice couldn't sleep. There were too many thoughts invading her mind. Getting out of bed at 9:00 a.m., she toured Jada's house removing and replacing the video cards in each camera except the one in Jada's bedroom.

Candice lounged by the bay window waiting for the sunrise. Whose baby was in Ashlee's car? Inserting a memory card into her laptop, Candice clicked PLAY. Ten minutes went by and nothing exciting had happened. Replacing the kitchen card with one from the living room, Candice laughed. "I see why my girl is sexually frustrated. I wouldn't dare put that scene in the script." Watching Wellington made Candice cringe. "That's the worst pussy massage imaginable." Round and around. "Jada's pubic hairs are probably tied in a knot by now. I guess they got tired of the bedroom. I'll check the rest of these later."

Picking up the phone, Candice dialed information, then pressed 1 to be connected to the number she'd received from the automated system. Opening her document, Candice positioned her fingers above the keyboard, prepared to type the conversation.

"Dallas Child Protective Services Agency, how may I help you?"

"Yes, I'd like to report a case of child abandonment."

"Let me transfer you to an intake specialist. Hold please."

Ashlee should've known better. Darius should've done better. But not to worry. Candice would gladly help them out.

A woman's voice answered, "Intake Department."

"Yes, I live in Los Angeles and would like to know if I can make a report."

"Does the child reside in Dallas or Los Angeles?"

"Dallas. At 2555 . . ."

"Then, yes, you can. Go ahead."

"A child was abandoned overnight in a black SUV, license . . . HH2. The mother's name is Ashlee Anderson. She left her child shortly after midnight. Her car was parked near 12121 . . . then she spent the night at a hotel in Beverly Hills with a man." Candice didn't want to give Darius's identity, fearing someone might leak her information. "She took a taxi back to the location where her car was, which was near 12121 . . . where her child stayed alone all night. Later that morning, around six thirty, LAPD Officer Nero questioned her, but she arrived back at her car exactly three minutes before Officer Nero. Long enough for her to get in the back of her car and pretend she was with the baby the entire time. After questioning her, Officer Nero let her go, then followed her because she put the baby on the front seat of the car. He did in fact issue her a ticket. I'm not sure what the ticket was for, but afterward she immediately went to LAX. That's the Los Angeles Airport. And that was the last time I saw her or the baby."

"This sounds personal. But since the child appears to be in an endangered environment we will send someone out to investigate."

Great! "Oh, and one more thing. I did report the abandonment to 9-1-1."

"What's your name?"

Candice continued giving her information to the intake specialist.

Tap, tap.

Jada always had bad timing. *Shit.* Candice yelled, "Just a minute! I'm getting dressed."

"What's your contact number?"

Candice responded, then said, "I've got to go. If you need more information, call me later," then ended the call. "Come in!"

Jada opened the door, scanning the room. "You got dressed fast."

"I know, girl. Come in. How are you?" Candice asked, hugging her best friend.

"Just mentally preparing to take Wellington to the hospital later."

"That's right. I'll go with you."

"You sure? You've done so much for us already."

"Oh, I'm sure. Call me when you're ready."

CHAPTER 11

Ashlee

A mistake was only a mistake when she didn't learn the lesson. Ashlee placed little Darius in his playpen. This time she left the door open so she could hear him stirring. At what point would Ashlee realize Darius wasn't the man for her? After the trip to Los Angeles, Ashlee vowed never to enter Darius's house again but couldn't convince herself to throw away the spare set of keys to his home.

Don't do it.

Whenever Ashlee wasn't talking to Darius, she thought about him. At this moment, sitting in her living room in Dallas miles away from Darius, Ashlee was lonely. Trying to escape reality, she struggled to bury the skeletons haunting her.

Don't do it. He's not worth it.

Zombielike, Ashlee strolled into her kitchen, stopping in front of the long black-handled knives. Her eyes roamed as she tried to decide which knife was sharpest. She didn't want to gnaw herself to death. Quick. Fast. One deep slice sharp enough to sever her veins and kill herself before her father or anyone else discovered her body.

She closed her eyes, Ashlee's fingers meandering, then clenching a medium-handled knife. "I don't wanna live without him," she whispered, gliding the edge over her middle finger. She didn't feel any pain. Opening her eyes, she watched the stream of blood flow into the crevice, then into her palm.

That's the one.

Ashlee's head rotated side to side. Faster. Faster. And even faster, wobbling her cheeks until she became dizzy, leaning her hips against the counter. Great, now she'd developed a migraine. Ashlee grabbed her ears, squeezed the knife, and screamed, "Stop it, Ashlee! Just stop it right now! Darius is out of your life! He doesn't love you anymore! He *is* going to marry Fancy! You do have to raise his baby!" Ashlee glanced out of the corners of her eyes to the left, then whispered, "Alone." The blood from her palm dripped from her wrist onto the floor, creating perfect circles. She shifted her glance to the right, the blade resting fractions of an inch away from her face.

Angrily she hissed, "Over my dead body."

Why'd she say that? She didn't mean that. Ashlee didn't want to kill herself. She just couldn't stand the pain, the heartaches, from knowing that Darius was happy without her. Happier with Fancy.

Forcing back tears, she thought, *My God, does anyone understand my pain?* Did anyone care?

For anyone who had a heart, anyone who'd been in love, whether they'd admit it or not, they'd have to understand her suicidal tendencies. She wasn't crazy. She had an obsession she couldn't deny. Darius Jones-Williams.

What would people think about sweet little innocent Ashlee if she killed herself? *But she was so nice, so polite, a good girl.* How would her obituary read? Survived by everyone except herself. Didn't matter. As long as no one knew what really happened. Dead or alive, Ashlee wanted her family and Darius to love, not hate, her. No one could hate a dead person. Could they?

Slumbering, Ashlee returned to the living room, sat on the sofa, placed the cold stainless steel beside her thigh, and then stared at the duplicate picture lying on the coffee table of their son cradled in Darius's arms the day of his birth. That was the only day Darius had seen or held little Darius. Leaning forward, she picked up the photo, kissing the glossy image. Her body tensed as she reflected on how her son, their son, little Darius, was almost taken away from her. So young. So fragile. So harmless.

Ashlee scooted back on the white leather cushion. The tip of the knife punctured her thigh. "Damn it!" she shouted, grabbing the handle. Lifting her hand above her head, she plunged the knife with a mighty force, lodging the blade into the sofa. The yellowish cushion burst through the tear.

Sitting on the sofa, she stared ahead, reflecting on how she didn't know how to be a mother. She had her own issues to deal with. And no one had prepared her for a baby's incessant crying. The more Ashlee had rocked her baby, the more little Darius cried. The more she'd walked him, the louder he cried. "What do you want from me!" Ashlee had yelled throughout her home in Dallas, that lonely night after being discharged prematurely from the hospital. But no one heard her, no one was there with her, except her baby . . . and he kept crying.

When Ashlee had put him in his crib, he screamed so loud her eardrums vibrated. Feeling like a failed and hopeless new mom, Ashlee had stood over his crib and begun crying too. Never having imagined being a single parent, she cried louder than her baby. The sight of little Darius faded into a visualization of Darius smiling, not at them, at Fancy, his lovely bride-to-be.

Ashlee sat on her sofa continuously drowning in bad memories. "Darius was supposed to be here for me. With me. With us. And I was stupid enough to let him fuck me again." Ashlee gripped the knife, then hurled it across the room while yelling, "I didn't fuck myself!" The knife stuck in the mauve-colored wallpaper as she countered, "But then again, maybe I did." She'd heard the saying "Once a player, always a player," but she didn't want to believe that Darius would play her every chance she'd given him.

"I hate him," Ashlee recalled whispering that oh-so-lonely night while gazing at little Darius.

That's when she did it.

Painfully, Ashlee relived the moment she'd covered little Darius's face with the soft baby-blue blanket, walked out of his room, and then quietly shut the door. Gradually little Darius's screaming quieted to wailing, turned into whimpering, then faded into silence. Even when she couldn't hear her baby—their baby—crying anymore, she didn't go to check on him. She'd figured he'd cried himself to sleep.

Since Darius was already gone, maybe if she went away, the baby would go away, and everyone would disappear. They were already invisible. Darius wouldn't see her, she couldn't see their baby, and their baby should've seen his father and mother standing side by side. Neither saw the other.

That night, depressed and lonely, Ashlee had cried herself to sleep. The next morning, when she went to check on little Darius, she entered his room, then lifted the blanket.

Nothing could've prepared her for what she saw.

Rocking back and forth on the leather sofa, staring at her baby's picture, Ashlee wondered if she'd ever see Darius again, then mumbled, "I don't deserve to live."

Why did men use her? Having Darius's baby should've been the happiest day of their lives. But before she'd given birth, Darius had already moved on. Nine months of carrying a child inside her womb and Darius, without a conscience, had abandoned them. If she didn't have a conscience, she would've aborted his child, but then she would've been the murderer. And she wouldn't have a reason to desperately cling to Darius. Either way, the way Ashlee saw it, one of them must die for the others to survive. Since she was the saddest, might as well be her.

No one ever blamed the runaway dad when a mother killed her child. Why couldn't she move on too? After all the wrong Darius had done, why did she still love him so much? Maybe Darius was right, she didn't love herself enough.

Don't do it.

Ashlee's fingers wrapped around the cellular. She needed to call Darius but phoned her father instead.

"Hi, Daddy. You busy?"

"Never too busy for you, sweetheart, but I do have a client coming in ten minutes. What's wrong? You sound sad."

"Of course I'm sad, Daddy. I'm a single parent. Mother won't babysit. You refuse to keep my baby overnight. I have no—"

Her father interrupted. "Not again. Well, we'll discuss this later.

I gotta go, sweetheart. And don't forget to take your medication. Bye."

"But—" Daddy had hung up. Ending the call, Ashlee whispered, "Good-bye, Daddy. I love you."

Ashlee screamed into midair as though someone was seated on the love seat facing her and listening. "I was the one who went with Darius to the hospital years ago when he thought he'd contracted HIV from his ex-fiancée, Maxine. I was the one who held his hand, saw him through his moments of despair, always there to pick his inconsiderate, sorry ass up, encouraging him that he could accomplish anything whenever he was down. No matter how low. And now he has the audacity to despise me!"

Ashlee cried, recalling her rendition of how the lies had started with one phone call. That evening when she'd dialed Darius's cell number, right before his wedding, she'd said to him, "I need to tell you something and, well, I didn't want you to think I was trying to ruin your wedding, but you need to know. And if you would've come to visit our son's grave, I would've told you then."

Truth was, if Darius would've come the first time she'd asked, he would've known that his son was still alive. But no, Darius got upset with her, like she was annoying or interrupting him, when all she wanted was for him to want her. Want them.

Instead Darius had replied, "Ashlee, stop playing games. I gotta go. Bye."

"Darius, wait," Ashlee had pleaded to Darius on his wedding day in a trembling voice. "Please don't hang up."

"What? Ashlee! What the fuck is it?"

Whoa, what the fuck is it? she'd repeated in her mind. For the first time Darius had cursed her, so Ashlee decided to curse him. She was calling to tell him the truth, but Darius didn't deserve to know the truth. "You remember how I never told you the cause of our son's death?"

It sounded like Darius had stopped breathing when he replied, "Ashlee, why? Why now? Why are you doing this to me?"

Doing this to him! Doing this to him! Wrong fucking answer! What about me? Ashlee thought as she'd replied, "I'm sorry. I never wanted to hurt you. And no matter what, I love you. But you need to know."

"Then tell me."

Ashlee vividly recalled crying. Knowing how important sex was to Darius, she'd told a lie on top of a lie. "Our son, Darius Junior, died from HIV complications."

"And you?" Darius had whispered.

Oh, now she had his undivided attention and Ashlee knew what he'd meant, but she was in too deep to tell the truth or give Darius a reason to doubt her, so she lied again. "Positive."

The next voice Ashlee heard was that home-wrecker Fancy. "What did you tell him?" Not knowing what to say next, and refusing to talk to Fancy, Ashlee had quietly hung up.

Tired of running away from her lie, from herself, Ashlee pried the knife from the wall, returned to the kitchen, slid the blade into the slot, swallowed two prescribed tablets, and then decided the time had come to tell Darius the truth. Little Darius shouldn't have to grow up without his father.

After all, Darius had risked his life to rescue her from his burning office building. Didn't that mean he loved her unconditionally?

Ashlee spoke softly to herself. "Call him now."

Returning to sit on the sofa, before she changed her mind, she dialed Darius's cell phone. No answer. She dialed his cellular again. Immediately she got his voice mail. Determined to tell Darius the truth, Ashlee would try every single number she had for him until he answered. Frantically, she dialed his Los Angeles home, and when he picked up she blurted out, "I lied! It's not true! Please forgive me! Our—"

"Ashlee?" a woman's voice responded quizzically. "What's wrong with you? I'm glad you called, because we need to talk. What did you tell my man on our supposed-to-be wedding day that *still* has him so upset he won't tell me?"

Narrowing her eyes, breathing heavily into the receiver, Ashlee asked what she already knew, "Fancy?"

"Yes, of course."

"I fucked him last night," Ashlee said, then screamed, "Bitch! I hate you!"

Raising her arm high in the air, with all the strength in her body . . . *slam*! The phone crashed to the snow-white carpet. The battery bounced one way, the phone another. Ashlee jumped up and down until her feet ached, just like her heart.

"Screw you, Darius!"

Darius didn't give a damn about anyone except himself. Little Darius was better off not knowing his father or his mother.

CHAPTER 12

Fancy

A man should never date a stupid woman; because not only did he not know what she was doing, she didn't know what the hell she was doing.

Maybe at one point in her life, people labeled Fancy a gold digger, a slut, a straight-up ho, but that just proved she was no man's fool, trophy, or easy lay. If he wanted to get laid, Fancy had to get paid; well, and in advance. No exceptions. Before Fancy fell in love with Darius, no man had captured her heart. Darius took her on a never-a-dull-moment, unpredictable, emotional ride so exhilarating she couldn't imagine being happier with anyone else.

Glancing around Darius's spacious bedroom, Fancy bounced up and down on the edge of his king-size bed. "I don't have anything to worry about. Darius loves me and that's all that matters."

The gold wedding gown she'd removed last night now hung in the closet, forever a memento. Fancy couldn't possibly wear the same gown twice, and if Darius didn't marry her in a few months, her pregnant belly wouldn't fit anyway. Even after catching Darius with other women in the same bed she was now rolling around in, she still loved him. Forgave him.

If infidelity was the worst she had to deal with, Fancy figured she was in the ninety-plus percentile with the majority of other women. Her difference was, Fancy was marrying a megamillionaire and she didn't lie to herself or try to psyche herself into believing Darius would never cheat again. As long as he didn't bring home any incurable life-threatening diseases, sex with those desperate women was what it was, sex. How many of those women could say their man would die for them? How could Fancy ever repay Darius for sacrificing his life to save hers? How many men could match Darius's good looks, supersized dick, or financial status?

Fancy paced, hugging her stomach. Lying on the floor, she began her daily morning routine of doing five hundred sit-ups. Unlike the men from her past, including Desmond Brown, who was just a friend, and Byron Van Lee, who still wanted to be more than just a friend, Fancy promised herself, no matter what happened between Darius and her, she'd never leave Darius. He was undoubtedly her soul mate. Her decision might not have been rational, but unlike Ashlee Anderson, Fancy Taylor wasn't stupid. Fancy walked to the nightstand, staring at the digital clock: 7:15 a.m. Darius hadn't come home yet, nor had he called.

How could Ashlee not know her phone number showed up on Darius's caller ID? Or maybe Ashlee was dumb enough to hope that Fancy wouldn't move in with Darius so the only person who'd answer the phone was Darius. Either way it didn't matter. What did matter was that Fancy found out from either Darius or Ashlee what the hell was going on. Darius had better not have left her home alone to go and fuck Ashlee. What was so secretive between them that Darius refused to make love and Ashlee had called her a bitch, then hung up in her face?

Briefly, Fancy reflected on when she'd phoned her ex Byron's house, calling his sister a bitch, assuming Byron was married when he wasn't. Whenever one woman called another woman a bitch, that made it clear that the woman doing the cursing wanted that man and was willing lie to break up the relationship. Fuck that. Ashlee needed to move on and find her own dick.

Reaching toward the black base, Fancy picked up the cordless and walked onto the balcony overlooking the houses descending downhill and the mountains ascending in the background. She inhaled the fresh air in an attempt to alleviate the tightness in her lower abdomen. Maybe she'd cut back from five hundred to four hundred, but there was no way Fancy was prematurely losing her figure to a bulging belly. Before Fancy dialed the first digit to Ashlee's number the phone rang. Looking at the caller ID, she saw SaVoy Edmonds.

Fancy sighed long into the receiver, answering, "Hey, girl. What's up?"

"I should be asking you. What the heck happened yesterday? Everybody was at your wedding except you and Darius. What's wrong with y'all?"

"Look, it's nothing we can't handle. You and Tyronne all set to jump the broom?"

"The question is," SaVoy replied with a high pitch, "are you all set to be in Oakland as my maid of honor? I don't want you faking on me like you did your guests."

Whatever. "Yeah, you know I'ma be there."

"My flight doesn't leave L.A. until tonight. You wanna have lunch with us?"

Hell no. The last thing Fancy wanted to do was sit across the table from SaVoy's manipulative fiancé, Tyronne. "I've got a lot of things going on today, but I wouldn't miss standing in your wedding, you know that, but I'ma pass on lunch. You're my best friend. And you know I love you because I can't stand your broke-ass from-the-hood fiancé."

"Well, at least my man is marrying me," SaVoy snapped.

"And Darius is out planning something special for me right now," Fancy countered, wondering why Darius hadn't called, then confessed, "I'm trippin' out, SaVoy . . . having doubts if Darius is really going to marry me before I have our baby." Fancy rubbed her stomach. "Ashlee called our house all upset and stuff, and, well, I don't want Darius to get comfortable with us living together. He—"

"Living what? Having who? What's wrong with you? You can't live in sin. You've got two houses of your own virtually sitting empty except for the Merry Maids that clean 'em every week. You don't need to live with Darius. And you can't move in when Ashlee just moved out. Better yet, got kicked out. But you know how I feel, it's best you don't marry Darius, because you and everybody else including God and Ashlee knows that Darius is a straight-up dog, he's a ho. Lord forgive me, but it's true. He's lying about marrying you, and now that he's signed that megamillion-dollar contract with Atlanta, get ready because you'll be spending a lot of nights alone. You're kidding yourself if you think he's going to be faithful to you with all the women waiting for an opportunity to lick and ride Slugger, as you say he calls his manhood, and then you go and get pregnant *before* he marries you. Don't you know that's so he can keep you at home while he's out dippin' his thing in only God knows who? I thought you were smarter than that, girlfriend. That's a sin and you ought to be ashamed . . . and—"

"And that's enough! Damn it, SaVoy! Can't you learn to listen *sometimes* and stop judging me! Your phony-Christian ass is not perfect! Good-bye!" Fancy yelled, hanging up the phone, continuing, "What is this? Fuck-with-Fancy day?"

Fancy walked inside, placing the handset on the base. Glancing at the digital clock, she said, "Oh, shit! I'm late for my eight o'clock client."

She shouldn't have scheduled an appointment the day after her wedding, but this was the only day her out-of-state client was available to do the final walk-through at his five-million-dollar home before closing. Fancy retrieved the handset and dialed his number.

After waiting several seconds for the phone to ring, Fancy glanced at the caller ID, knowing she'd dialed the right numbers, but why in hell were Ashlee's name and number on the display?

Annoyed, Fancy answered, "What?"

"Yeah, bitch," Ashlee's voice echoed in a weird white-trying-to-sound-black, too-black kinda way.

"What the fuck is it?" Fancy faintly yelled back.

"You need to stop seeing my man," Ashlee yelled louder, "that's what the fuck!"

Fancy gasped, breathing deeply, "Ashlee? What the hell are you trying to prove?"

"You heard me, bitch. You need to stop seeing my man."

"Reality check. Earth to Ashlee. Darius is not your man. He's your brother."

"Stepbrother and mind you he's not biologically related to me, so our relationship is no different from yours, and I had his baby."

"That's right. Had." Fancy paused, then said, "Well, I'm having his baby. And I don't have time to entertain your childish bullshit. Grow the hell up!"

"No, not had. Ha—"

Click! Fancy hung up the phone, showered, dressed, then dialed Darius's cell number.

"Hey, Ladycat. Good morning, baby."

"Don't good morning me. Darius, where are you?"

"My mom's. I didn't tell you?"

"No, you didn't. And if you're at your mom's, why didn't you answer my calls or phone me back?"

"I was asleep. You woke me up."

Fancy heard knocking or rocking or something in the background. "What's that?"

"Look, I've gotta go. I'll be home in a few hours," Darius said, then hung up.

A *few* hours. Yeah, right. Fancy redialed Darius's number. Immediately she heard, "You know who you've reached, don't leave a speech. Speak." *Beep.*

She knew who to call next. One, two, three, four, five, six, seven presses of the buttons on the phone. Fancy waited.

"Hello."

"Hi, Mrs. Tanner. May I speak to Darius please?"

"Fancy, Darius isn't here. Try him on his cell phone."

"Thanks," Fancy said, ending the call. "Lying bastard."

Pressing her middle fingers into her temples, Fancy reentered the bathroom, glancing at the red and white bottle on the counter. "Stop trippin' on all that crap SaVoy said to you earlier. Darius will explain when he gets home."

She redialed her client. When he answered, she asked, "Can we push your appointment back to this afternoon?" Fancy could've added, "I'm pregnant and I'm suffering from morning sickness," but businessmen discounted all female-related illnesses—menstrual cramps, PMS, kids—as excuses.

"Actually this afternoon works out fine. Say around two."

"I'll see you then. Thanks." Pausing, Fancy knew she was forgetting to do something. "Oh yeah."

Fancy phoned information. "Yes, I'd like the number to Child Protective Services." Jotting down the number, she dialed the agency. "Yes, I'd like to report a child abandonment." She reported all that she knew, the car, the 9-1-1 call, and the policeman's arrival, and the woman on the other and thanked her.

Ending her call, Fancy wanted to stop trippin' but couldn't. Her head pounded with all kinds of crazy visuals of Darius fucking Ashlee or some other woman. SaVoy was right. Darius was a pathological liar and it was time for Fancy to admit that he couldn't be trusted before they got married. Unsnapping the top, Fancy shook two tablets in her palm, went to the kitchen, opened the refrigerator, and said, "Damn! What happened to all the juice? Just like a bachelor to drink out of the container, then put it back empty. That's going to change."

Clenching the tablets in her hand, Fancy went into the storage area inside the garage and saw Darius's next-door neighbor, Michael, standing in the driveway.

"Well, good morning," Michael said, smiling wide. "You really shouldn't leave your garage door open all night. There's all sorts of wild animals lurking in the dark." Still smiling, Michael winked at her.

Although Michael was largely responsible for making her a millionaire, Fancy wasn't interested in flirting with him. "Thanks, I didn't realize it was open. I just came to get something to drink," she said, picking up a gallon of cranberry juice. On her way inside, she hit a button and the garage door lowered.

Fancy filled an empty goblet with ice cubes and juice. Shifting the pills to her fingertips, she tilted her head backward. The pain was so excruciating she closed her eyes.

CHAPTER 13

Jada

Life. What was the purpose? Her purpose? She'd lived, not a perfect, but a passionate life. She didn't sleepwalk, or half-ass do things. She didn't make excuses, or take the people she loved for granted. She didn't belittle anyone, or put herself down. The one thing she didn't do enough was put herself first. Fulfill her needs. Her desires. Her dreams. She was too busy for herself.

One of her dreams was to have a daughter. Grateful she regained her figure after having Darius, Jada wanted to adopt a little girl. What good was being a millionaire if she didn't give back to someone less fortunate? Give another female an opportunity to excel in life. One day, but not today.

Stop. Now that her life was closer to death, she was sure she wouldn't live as many years as she'd lived. She wished she would've put herself first more often. Twenty years she dedicated to her son. Another twenty-plus to her husband. Too many to count to her company, Black Diamonds.

If she could roll back the hands of time, what would've been different? She knew without hesitation. The lie. She wouldn't have lied to her son, her son's father, her husband, or herself. She didn't have yesterday and she wasn't guaranteed tomorrow, so from this

day forth, Jada Diamond Tanner promised herself she would live in the moment.

If she couldn't keep a commitment to herself, then who could she be honest with? Each moment she'd stand in her truth. No more lying to herself in order to spare others' feelings.

Why was it so hard to make decisions about remaining in her marriage and easy to make decisions about work? Why did Jada feel it was her responsibility to save everyone around her except herself? When was the last time she'd meditated? Pampered herself? Exercised?

Jada nestled into the arms of her husband as they lay across the sofa like dominos, one on top of the other, in front of the wood-burning fireplace. Wellington hugged her shoulders. The back of her head rested against his chest, her back on top of his stomach, her butt curved below his pelvis.

The past weekend was overwhelming. Neither Darius nor Fancy showed up for their own wedding. Both acted as though nothing went wrong. Jada was livid, having apologized to almost a thousand guests, wasting more than five hundred thousand dollars on caterers, florists, wedding planners, and as a courtesy, she insisted on reimbursing their guests, many of whom flew in from Atlanta, for travel expenses.

Glancing over her shoulder, she saw the flames reflected in Wellington's weary eyes. Wellington had postponed his surgery for the wedding but declined attending Darius's wedding. He refused to be admitted without her by his side. Wellington's I-told-you-sos weren't welcome and Jada demanded that he keep his comments to himself. Any reason would've sufficed for Wellington to put off his surgery, but this was his last day home before checking into the hospital.

Wellington squirmed. "Ba, I'm starting to get uncomfortable. I hate to ask you to move but . . ."

Cautiously, Jada sat up.

"No, don't get up. Just move down a little."

Jada scooted an inch or two and said, "Is this okay?"

"Yeah. That's better."

"You've been awfully quiet. What are you thinking?" Jada asked, leaning back, resuming her new position. She pressed the back of her head below Wellington's salt-and-pepper hairy chest.

Wellington whispered, "About life. About how grateful I am to have spent"—he sniffled, then continued—"most of my life in love with you. You know, ba, some folk spend all their lives searching. Searching for happiness. Searching for love or someone to love. Praying that the person they love loves them too. Searching for what's right in front of their faces. Or worse, taking the people who do love them for granted."

Wellington cupped Jada's breasts, squeezing gently.

This time it was okay for her husband to affectionately touch her breasts. He wasn't attempting to arouse her, and she realized he sought comfort feeling her body.

"Oh, Wellington," Jada said, interlocking her fingers atop his hand. "Remember the night we met?"

Why couldn't they have spent more moments like this before Wellington got sick? Cuddling. Caressing. Enjoying and appreciating one another. A simple caring touch of the human hand provided so much healing. Healing that no doctor could prescribe, nor medicine could cure.

Their jobs consumed them Monday through Friday from seven in the morning to well past nine at night. Almost every weekend was occupied by Wellington's son, Wellington the Second, running around while Wellington the Second's mother, Simone Smith, jet-setted all over the world with her single girlfriends.

Passionately squeezing her nipples, Wellington replied, "How could I ever forget? You were the hottest, sexiest, most sophisticated woman at Cityscape. Ba, you stood out in that crowded room the moment you stepped off that elevator with that leopard dress wearing you. The moon was full that night. The view from the forty-second floor was spectacular. But not nearly as spectacular as that dress or the woman in it. And I still love these." Wellington squeezed again.

The tingling sensation made Jada smile. Since Wellington couldn't make love to her, she didn't want to get overly excited. "Yeah, that dress was hot. Split from my ankles up to my privates in the front.

A dip," she said, tossing her head to the side, "all the way down my back to my ass. But what I remember most are the yellow roses and the one red rose too. You sent me a rose every—"

"They were all red, and one yellow," Wellington corrected, then continued, "every fifteen minutes until I asked you to dance with me. Thought I was gonna have to take a rain check the way Darryl tried to run interference."

Darryl did have bad timing, but Jada refused to dwell on Darryl during their beautiful moment of reflection. Darryl had his own agenda, then and now. Since his wife had recently become his ex-wife, Darryl had already convinced Darius to let him run Somebody's Gotta Be on Top. Now that Wellington was sick, Darryl was trying to find his way back into Jada's life.

"Yeah, Rachelle Farrell's 'Nothing Has Ever Felt like This' was the last song and our first dance and you continued sending me roses every week for over ten years, even after I married Lawrence." Jada smiled. She could've questioned Wellington about why he'd stopped sending her roses, but she appreciated the many years that her husband was a true gentleman. Wellington was good to her.

"I love you more than I could ever have imagined loving a woman. But you know what the best part is?"

"Tell me," Jada said, rubbing Wellington's thighs, knowing her loving touch helped lessen his pain.

"The best part is . . . no matter how bad I screwed up, you never stopped loving me." Wellington sniffled again, then continued, "Ba, I have to ask a question. Tell me the truth. Don't say what you think I want to hear. Now that I'm not the *man* you married, are you still in love with me?"

Looking over her shoulder again, Jada asked, "Are you serious? Why would you ask a stupid question like that?"

"I need to hear you say it. Like I said, I know I've done some dumb things lately. Things you didn't deserve. And I need to know you've forgiven me. Before I enter that operating room, in case I don't come out, I want to go knowing, not guessing, whether or not my soul mate is *in love* with me."

"Move, Wellington." Jada waited until Wellington sat up, and then she sat on the sofa beside him, laying his bald head onto the pillow in her lap. Tracing his eyebrows with her fingertip, Jada explained, "Wellington Jones, how could I ever repay you for raising Darius, being there for us, for me, even after you found out he wasn't your child? If anyone is guessing who loves whom, it should be me."

"True love never requires restitution. But it's beautiful when the person shows they appreciate you. As far as Darius is concerned, he resents me now that he knows his real father. That hurts like hell. I've always loved that boy like he was my own son. Still would do anything for him. I was hard on him because he needed, make that needs, to grow up, ba. You were too easy on him. That boy doesn't know nothing 'bout an honest day's work for an honest day's pay. Or how to respect women. Now he has Darryl as a role model. That's a joke, and Darius is foolish to let Darryl run his film company. The apple don't fall far from the tree. Think about Darryl's boys. What do I know? No one asked my opinion. But, ba, you . . . ya didn't answer my question."

Jada wanted to ask a question instead of answering one. What made Wellington interested when he'd taken over Somebody's Gotta Be on Top?

"I will, but let me ask, why did you have so much interest in taking over Darius's company?"

Wellington's eyes rolled to the top of his head. Looking at her, he said, "Are you serious? Do you know how much money that company is worth? Darius is a billionaire. And that's his net worth. Not gross. I didn't want him to screw that up like he'd done everything else. But if what you really want to know is if I've given back his third of the business legally, the answer is, no, I haven't. But I will. Darryl is the one to watch out for."

Wellington gave her a lot to think about. If anything happened to Wellington, the one thing he would do was will his share to them. His third would be divided equally between her and Darius. Jada wondered if Darius realized he had so much money.

"Yes, Wellington Jones, I am in love with you. Always have been. Always will be. And your surgery is going to go fine." Jada crossed

her fingers underneath the pillow, silently saying a quick prayer, then continued, "So stop worrying yourself."

"Well, this is it. I'm finally going under the knife. The next time y'all see me I'll be lighter, if you know what I mean."

Leaning over, Jada held Wellington's head close to her stomach, intentionally letting her breasts smother his face. "You'll always be a whole man in my eyes. I love you, baby."

"You say that now. We'll see . . ." Wellington's words trailed off.

Nervously Jada leaned closer to his face, and then she lowered her eyes to his chest, waiting for a sign that he was breathing. When his chest moved, she sighed.

"Ma," Darius whispered.

Jada jumped, placing her hand over her chest. "Darius, stop creeping up behind me like that."

"Sorry. Didn't mean to scare you. I need to go check on Fancy. I'll be back in a few hours to go with you to take Wellington to the hospital." Affectionately Darius kissed her forehead.

"Thank you, baby," Jada said, watching her son walk out the door. Something bothered her baby. She could see it. Feel it.

The phone rang, interrupting her thoughts. Hurriedly Jada placed a pillow under Wellington's head and sprinted three steps to the phone before it rang again.

Softly she answered, "Hello."

"Hi, Mrs. Tanner. Is Darius there?"

"No, Fancy, he's not. Call him on his cell." Jada hung up the phone. It rang again, so she quickly answered, annoyed, "Yeess?"

"Hey, how are you?"

"Oh, I'm fine. Wellington is trying to rest."

"I'm here for you if you need anything, you know that. What time did you say we're meeting at the hospital?"

Jada heard an announcement in the background. "Last boarding call for flight 332 to Los Angeles." "Where are you?"

"I had to make a quick run to Dallas, I'll be back in a few hours."

Jada frowned. "Dallas? I just saw you a few hours ago."

"Oh, I'll explain later. I gotta go."

"Candice, you've done enough. You don't have to make it to the hospital. Darius is going."

"Darius? Wonderful, then I'll make sure I head to the hospital as soon as I get in."

"Fine. Bye, Candice."

Jada appreciated her friend's support, but Candice was acting a bit odd. She'd already invaded Jada's life once, writing and selling a screenplay about the most personal aspects of her life. Fortunately Darius's company was controlling the production. Unfortunately Darius's ex-wife Ciara's casting company was hiring the actors, including Candice's ex-husband. Thanks to her best friend, Candice Jordan, everybody was making money. But Candice was also a true friend and wouldn't disappoint her again. How did Jada ever forgive Candice the first time? Maybe the same way she'd forgiven her husband. She didn't want to be one of those women who held a lifetime grudge against her girlfriend but easily forgave her man.

"I've gotta pee," Jada said, entering the downstairs bathroom. When Jada lifted the toilet seat, her mouth opened wide but she couldn't scream. Like the roses Wellington used to send, more red than yellow settled in the porcelain bowl. *Oh my God*, she thought, racing to the front door. Darius's car was gone. Jada ran to the phone and dialed 9-1-1.

When the operator answered, Jada frantically said, "Yes, I need an ambulance at . . . Hurry, it's an emergency. My husband's urine is full of blood."

CHAPTER 14

Darius

Driving home from his mother's, Darius contemplated telling Fancy the truth. She deserved to know. What if this time he weren't so fortunate? Would she stay? Leave? Darius couldn't imagine life without Fancy. She stayed after catching him with two women in his bed at the same time. She stayed after discovering why he couldn't marry her. She stayed after knowing three women could've been pregnant by him. Exhaling a sigh of relief, Darius thought, *Oh, sweet Fancy didn't have a choice.* She had to stay, she was carrying his child.

As soon as Darius powered on his cell to call Fancy in attempt to gauge her mood before walking through the door, his phone rang. Looking at his caller ID, Darius debated answering. On the fourth ring, he said, "Hey, coach. What's up?"

"You know what's up."

Darius nodded along with the coach's statement.

"You've got forty-eight hours. If you don't take your physical before then, you won't have a contract. We've already lined up your replacement."

"You can't replace me. Next to K'Nine, I'm your best player."

"Can and will. No player is bigger than our team."

Darius mumbled, "That's probably the problem." Wannabe head, merely assistant coach. At least Darius knew what to expect from this loser.

"What was that?"

"Nothing." Darius wasn't about to kiss his ass but to keep the peace until his contract was legit, he explained, "Look, coach. I'ma do my part and then some. You know this. But I meant to call and tell you my dad is having surgery and I'm grooming someone to run my multimillion-dollar business, you know, Somebody's Gotta Be on Top. Seriously, all I need is about four mo' days."

"You've had almost four months. A wedding that didn't happen. An arrest that did. A son you don't take care of. A pregnant fiancée. A mama who can't say no to your spoiled lying ass. A baby mama who, thanks to you, is one day away from checking into a mental institution. It's your stepfather who's having surgery. Your real dad has been running your company for months . . . Yada yada ya, you're full of shit! One sorry-ass excuse after another. You need to grow the fuck up! You weren't my recommendation and if it weren't for your father's great reputation and relationship with our head coach, he wouldn't have given you a chance to make millions that I'm positive you won't earn, obviously because you think like a dick with your dick. You'll be outta here in less than a year. You're one big failure, Williams. You hear me? You're nothing but a liar, a user, and a failure! Don't think I won't have you replaced, don't show up. Oh, and in the NBA, we don't give a damn about your mama or your billion-dollar company. We pay you to work your ass off for us. You've got forty-eight hours and your time starts right now," the assistant coach said, then hung up.

"Whoa." Darius paused, then screamed into a dead receiver, "Fuck you, man! You're just jealous. Everyone's fuckin' hatin' on a brotha." As he threw his cell in the passenger seat, tears filled Darius's eyes. A man had never spoken to him like that. No one had. Coach's fact was a lie. Darius had the paternity test to prove Ciara's baby wasn't his son. And it was millions, not billions. "You don't know me," Darius yelled, froze, then blinked repeatedly. "Nobody knows me."

Darius sat crying for a long time, reevaluating his life. "I'm sick of this hiding all the time, crying-like-a-baby shit." Darius wanted help. He didn't want to be disliked. The time had come to face his fears. Picking up his cell, he dialed Mandy's number.

"Mandy's office. How may I help you?"

"Yes, um, um, I'd like to schedule an appointment."

"Your name?"

"Williams. Darius Williams."

"Well, congratulations, Mr. Williams. I know getting that large contract must be stressful, people calling pretending they're related to you and stuff, huh?"

"Something like that. How soon can I get in?"

"Hold please."

Hopefully soon, Darius thought, still flaming about the coach's comments. What the fuck was he doing, an independent background check?

"Mandy has her first opening in three months."

"Forget it."

"Wait, Mr. Williams, don't hang up. I can call you if we have a cancellation."

"Whateva. That's fine," Darius said, hanging up. "Fuck!"

What the fuck?

No, Darius did not see his next-door neighbor tiptoeing out of his garage. Driving slower, Darius stopped and watched in disbelief. Michael sprinted. *No, he did not trample on the grass.* Before Darius could press the button on his remote to close the garage, the door lowered. "Oh, this had better be good." Darius didn't bother parking in the garage; he left his car diagonally in the driveway, then burst through the front door.

"Fancy!" he yelled out. "Fancy! Where the hell are you!"

"In here." Fancy's choppy voice crept echoing from his kitchen.

Rushing over to Fancy, he slapped her hand away from her mouth, and two small tablets fell to the iridescent marbled tiles. Shoving Fancy, Darius yelled, "Why the fuck was Michael coming out of my house? You know my rule. No men in my house unless I'm here!"

Setting the cranberry-filled goblet on the counter, Fancy whaled her arms through the air in front of Darius's face as she drew back a trembling hand, then yelled back, "What the hell do you think you're doing? You're the one who stayed out all night!" *Smack!* Her hand landed across his cheek.

Darius's jaw tightened as he clenched his back teeth. Oh, he desperately wanted to hit Fancy back. He stormed to the bedroom with Fancy stomping on his heels. Marching around the room, lifting the comforter, checking the trash cans, and sniffing the air, Darius faced Fancy. Shoving his pointing fingers fractions of an inch from her forehead, he yelled, "You tryna get even with me? In my house! In my bed! Oh, you fucked him, didn't you!" Grabbing Fancy's shoulders, Darius rattled her back and forth, then forced her onto the bed. He stood over Fancy, waiting for a response, and it'd better not be the wrong one.

Sitting up, Fancy countered, "Maybe you should go next door and thank Michael."

Darius's eyes narrowed; his heart raced. "Wha—what are you talking about? Thank him for what? Fucking my woman!" He bent over, picking up the soiled underwear that popped from under the sheet. As he inhaled the white lace suctioned into his nostrils. "Explain this nasty shit! He got you all wet and you were too turned on to move your crusty fuckin' drawers from underneath my cover!"

Fancy leaned toward Darius, snatching the panties from his grip. "Give me that! Darius, you've lost your damn mind!" Inspecting the material, she yelled, "This cheap-ass lace is not mine!" throwing them in Darius's face. "If you would fuck me, instead of dippin' your dick in half of L.A., I wouldn't have to fuck myself! But obviously you're not missing out on any pussy! Maybe I should fuck Michael!"

Exhaling, Darius stared at Fancy's heaving tits, her lips; she looked sexy as hell mad. His dick twitched. Maybe he should fuck her right now. Show her ass who was the boss. In the heat of the moment, he could flip this aggression into make-up sex. He knew the pussy would be ten times better than his session hours ago with Ashlee.

Panting, Fancy said, "Michael was nice enough to let me know the garage door was open. Whateva bitch you were in such a hurry to fuck last night must've been damn good."

Damn, her words had just registered. He couldn't sexually satisfy his woman? But he hadn't planned on fucking Ashlee. It just sorta, kinda happened. A man had two choices and he was taking option number one; Darius wasn't admitting a thing. Softening his tone, he said, "I'm sorry, baby, I did leave the garage door up. I've got a lot of stuff on my mind. I was at my mom's last night. She's not doing too well."

"Stop lying! I'm sick of your lies, Darius. I'm stressing. I'm the one who's not feeling well. I'm considering not having this baby."

Backing away from Fancy before he did something he'd regret, Darius said, "No way. No fuckin' way." Tears swelled in his eyes. Not again, he thought, unable to control Fancy's decision. Streams flowed down Darius's cheeks. He sat on the bed stroking Fancy's hair. "Ladycat, what are you stressed about?"

"You. Ashlee. Ciara. Us. Getting married. Not getting married. Everything. You're selfish. You always react before getting all the facts. It's your way or no way. When you don't want to talk about something, I'm supposed to forget about it. I called your mother's house. She said you weren't there."

Not hearing a word after Fancy said Ashlee, Darius nervously asked, "Why Ashlee?"

"She called today. Several times."

His eyes shifted to the corners away from Fancy. "And? Said what?"

"Right before she called me a bitch, she told me everything," Fancy said, then turned her back toward Darius. "I'm just disappointed that you didn't tell me. Darius, how could you!" Fancy yelled, balling into a fetal position, holding her stomach with one hand, her head with the other. "Now I know why you haven't made love to me."

Darius paced alongside the bed, then whispered, "I was going to tell you. I swear. I just didn't know how." He stopped in front the three-way mirror, staring at his reflection. Two times in a row, he felt like shit.

"So now what, mister, I've got all the answers? What are you going to do?" Fancy asked.

"I'll call my doctor and have him come to the house and test us. Or I can get that new home self-test kit, but I don't trust that shit. From what I hear, people who're negative are testing positive. Either way I need to know something *before* I take my physical for Atlanta. Coach just called, breathing down my neck and shit. But you have to promise me you won't leave me if my HIV test comes back positive or . . ." Darius paused, massaged Fancy's shoulder, then continued, "If you and the baby test positive."

As she sat in the center of the bed facing Darius, Fancy's eyes grew the size of golf balls. "Hold up! Wait one muthafuckin' minute! Darius Jones-Williams, please tell me you are *not* telling me that you might have AIDS? That I might have AIDS! And our baby! I will hurt you up in here!" Covering her mouth, Fancy continued, "Oh my God! You nasty son of a bitch! You came in my mouth knowing you might be . . ."

Darius stood looking at Fancy. One pillow after another flew in his face. When he didn't bother blocking the pillows, Fancy leaped catlike from the bed onto him, throwing punches like she was Laila Ali, to Darius's head, neck, face, and shoulders, screaming, "I hate you!"

"Stop punching me, you crazy bitch! You said you knew. Ashlee told you. Right? Fuck!" Darius yelled, thrusting Fancy onto the bed. "What did she tell you?"

Kicking in his direction, Fancy screamed, "Oh my God! My back!" scrambling out the opposite side of the bed. "My back is killing me! You always fuck up, Darius! You always manage to fuck up everything that's good! I hate you!" Heaving, holding her stomach, Fancy desperately tried to regurgitate but couldn't until she succeeded by forcing her middle finger down her throat.

His eyes froze, his body became numb, the woman he loved hated him. The contract he wanted he might not get. What would Darius do without basketball and Fancy?

He flashed back to the day he had shoved Ciara while she was pregnant, causing her to hit her head on the edge of the table. The gash in Ciara's head leaked a pillow of blood under her head. Darius became frightened that he might've hurt Fancy. The baby. But he wasn't going back to jail for nobody.

Ashlee's voice echoed in Darius's mind, "I have lots of scars, emotionally and physically, to remind me of you. How many scars do you have to remind you of me?" Darius didn't want to scar Fancy.

"Fancy, wait, don't. I'm sorry. Baby, please don't leave," Darius pleaded, watching Fancy stumble about the bedroom, hopping on one leg, trying to put on her pants. Darius shut the bedroom door from the outside, raced to the kitchen, grabbed Fancy's goblet, picked her pills up off the floor, blowing them off en route back to the bedroom. "Here, you were about to take these," he said, handing her the glass and pills.

"Get the hell out of my way!" Fancy screamed.

Swallowing both pills at once, she gulped down the juice, then hurled the crystal goblet at Darius's head. "Bastard!"

Darius ducked. The glass shattered against the wall. He stood nodding, grateful she'd missed.

She buttoned her blouse, the right side hanging lower. "Darius," she cried, "how could you keep something like this from me! You're still fucking Ashlee and God knows who else! And you're having unprotected sex! Why! Darius, why! I gave you all the pussy you wanted. Good pussy. Ass too! Lap dances. Everything. Wasn't I enough for you?" Fancy fell facefirst onto the bed, crying into the cover.

Falling to his knees beside Fancy, Darius cried too. "I'm sorry, Ladycat, but I swear on my grandmother's grave. I haven't been with Ashlee since she got pregnant or anyone else since, since . . ." *Ma Dear, please forgive me.* Darius placed his hand on Fancy's spine, promising himself he never wanted to hurt Fancy this way again.

"Since, since when! You can't even get your lie straight. Don't touch me! Get away from me! I can't bring a child into this madness." Rolling over, Fancy peered into Darius's eyes, crying harder. Her body moved in wavelike motions of convulsions as she layered her hands over her stomach. "I'm having an abortion and that's final."

Quietly Darius went to his closet and packed an overnight bag. As he angrily shoved T-shirts, pants, extra underwear, and socks inside, his jaw flinched. He couldn't stand the sight of Fancy, and he'd best leave before seriously hurting her.

"What difference does it make if I try to do right but you don't believe me? Fuck this shit!" Darius yelled, knocking the contents on the nightstand onto the floor. The lamp broke into halves. The framed picture of them together shattered. "I'll be at the hospital with my mom today and in Atlanta tonight." His cell phone beeped. The text message from his mother read *URGENT! Meet me at emergency. NOW!*

Staring down on Fancy, Darius whispered, "Ladycat, if you kill my child, I swear I hope you die too. If you don't, you'll wish you were dead." Turning away from Fancy's pitiful face, he ran out of the bedroom, jumped in his Bentley, and hurried to the hospital.

CHAPTER 15

Jada

Some said people who suffered on earth before dying were basically good folk paying for all of their earthly sins; one last chance to repent before entering the pearly gates of heaven. Although Wellington's condition was critical, Jada remained optimistic. Hopefully his pain was one of those unexplainable hardships that no one could understand the "why me?" but in retrospect the experience made them better. More grateful. Refusing to take life for granted ever again. That is, if they survived.

Sirens blared, zooming along the interstate as the ambulance zigzagged between SUVs, eighteen wheelers, sedans, and small hatchbacks. Mercedeses, BMWs, Porches, and throwbacks. Every car model built was on a highway, street, or backyard in L.A.

Jada squatted on a rectangular padded bench beside her husband's gurney, gently holding his hand. Silently she prayed, "Lord, I know Your will will be done. I pray that You spare my husband of unbearable pain and I pray it's in Your will to please, please let him be healthy again. No matter how imperfect, he makes me complete. If it's his time, I ask that You do not allow him to suffer."

A walnut-sized lump lodged in Jada's throat. Barely breathing, she turned her head, trying to swallow, but couldn't. Trying to shed tears but she didn't. Opening her mouth, Jada slowly inhaled. Wellington quietly stared at the roof. He didn't blink. Didn't move. His body was limp. Chest cold to her touch.

The paramedic beside her firmly said, "Ma'am, please don't touch him. Just hold his hand."

Jada's eyes narrowed, nearly closing. *That's my damn husband,* she thought. Doing what she felt was in Wellington's best interest, she didn't respond. Desperately she wanted to call her support group, Darius, Wellington's sister, Jazzmyne, Candice, Darryl, and Simone, so they could meet her at the hospital, but Jada didn't want to upset Wellington. Nor did she want to be alone. Instead, she text-messaged all of them the same note, *URGENT! Meet me at emergency. NOW!*

"Baby, everything's gonna be all right," Jada said, squeezing Wellington's hand.

Wellington's jaw flinched and his lips tightened while he continuously stared ahead. Tears glided into his ears. No response.

The paramedic gripped a pair of shears and began cutting Wellington's pajama pants down one leg, then up the other. Peeling away the plaid cotton material, Jada covered her mouth and gagged. "Oh my God." Heaving and holding her stomach, she fought to keep down the bile percolating up her esophagus.

Bloodstains showered the white boxers as Wellington began urinating on himself. Not yellow. Not white. Red blood secreted from his penis.

The paramedic looked at her, then asked, "Advanced prostate cancer?" covering Wellington's private area with a sheet.

Jada nodded. Prunelike, her face shrank as she forced back her tears. She wasn't trying to spare Wellington's feelings. She was trying so hard to be strong for her husband. There was a difference.

Exiting the freeway and running a few red lights, the driver parked in the hospital's reserved emergency space. Jada waited until the paramedics removed Wellington's gurney, rushing him inside. Stumbling out of the ambulance, Jada leaned against the side. If she would've eaten a salad, partially digested lettuce, tomatoes, and croutons would've splattered beside the rear tire instead of yellowish bile. Another day she'd forgotten to take care of herself.

Hurrying inside, Jada scanned, searching for Wellington. Grabbing the first medical assistant she saw, she asked, "Where'd they take my husband? They just brought him in."

"Eew, ma'am." The assistant covered his mouth, mumbling, "Visitors aren't allowed beyond this point." Pinching his nose, he continued in his froggy voice, "You'll have to wait in the seating area or the main lobby. But I'll see what I can find out for you." Stepping back, releasing his nostrils, he asked, "What's your husband's name?"

Covering her mouth, Jada answered, "Wellington Jones. He has a bald head. He's about—"

"If he just came in, the name is sufficient." Swiftly the medical assistant disappeared behind the swinging double doors.

Racing to the restroom, Jada cried the tears she couldn't shed in front of Wellington. She cupped her hands under the cold water, splattering her face. Filling her mouth with water, she swished, swished, then spat repeatedly into the trash can.

"What was I thinking?" A hospital, with all its contaminations, bacteria, and diseases, was the worst place to use water for anything except washing your hands.

Gnawing her nails, Jada paced from the towel dispenser to the stall and back, praying she hadn't contracted any germs. "Damn!" She'd exposed herself again, placing her fingers in her mouth. Dabbing her face with a paper towel, exiting the restroom, she thought, *What if they're looking for me?*

Scanning the room, Jada noticed that none of the medical professionals were looking for anyone. "Excuse me," Jada said, interrupting the take-in specialist, "can you please tell me where my husband is? Someone went to check on him. His name is Wellington Jones."

After a few taps on the keyboard, the lady asked, "When did he come in?"

"About fifteen minutes ago."

"It'll take time to get him in the system. First the doctors have to access his condition and determine where to send him. Check back in about a half hour."

"A half hour?"

Ignoring Jada, the take-in specialist announced, "Sylvia Carrington."

Jada walked to the lobby entrance in search of Darius and was relieved when she saw Jazzmyne looking around.

"Jazzmyne, I'm over here," Jada said, waving and then walking in Jazzmyne's direction.

"Everything's gonna be all right," Jazzmyne said reassuringly, wrapping her arms around Jada. "How's my brother?"

"I'm so glad you're here. I don't know yet." Jada's stomach churned with nervous energy. "They said it'll take about a half hour."

In circular motions, Jazzmyne rubbed Jada's back. "Well, Wellington will be happy to hear that Shelly and Brandon sent their prayers. And . . ." Retrieving a tiny frame from her handbag, Jazzmyne held a painted superhero of Wellington cloaked in a red cape.

Jada smiled, then nodded. "Shelly."

"You know his girl had to paint something for her favorite uncle," Jazzmyne said.

"He's her only uncle," Jada said.

The last time Jada had seen Jazzmyne's kids was a few days ago at the wedding. But Wellington hadn't seen his niece or nephew for months.

"Ma," Darius said, strolling into the lobby. His arms held Jada for what appeared to be a lifetime. Almost like he needed her as much as she needed him. "I'm here, Ma. I love you. You're my girl. Lean on me. I'ma be strong for you."

Jada cried on Darius's shoulder. "Thank you, sweetheart."

Letting go, Darius asked, "Where's Wellington?"

Jada stared at Darius.

"I mean, where's Dad?"

"They took him in the back."

How could she make Darius respect Wellington? She'd correct Darius until he corrected himself.

"Already. It only took me a few minutes to get here. I parked in the garage behind Jazzmyne."

Candice walked in and said, "Hey, girl. I got your text. Where's your husband?"

Exhaling, Jada said, "How long do y'all think it takes to get to the hospital in an ambulance? He's gone. I mean—"

Jazzmyne interrupted, "We know what you mean. What do you want me to do to help?"

Jada's phone rang. It was Wellington's baby's mama. "Hi, Simone. We're in the lobby."

"Oh, I'm not at the hospital," Simone replied. "I don't think it's a good idea to bring little Wellington to a hospital. He's too young and impressionable."

If there was ever a time for family to come together, the time was now. "Simone, this is not about you, that's Wellington's only son." Jada wished she could've taken back those words when she saw Darius turn away from her, but communication was irreversible, so she continued, "Wellington is in critical condition. Bring your son so Wellington can be with both of his sons. I'll call you back and tell you what's a good time."

"You might rule Wellington and his broken ruler, but you don't rule me. This is my child and I said he's not coming to the hospital. Call me when Wellington gets home."

"You are one self-centered jealous witch. As long as Wellington sends you ten times more money than what you deserve, pays for your vacations, and leaves your son with me on weekend visits, you don't give a damn about . . . whateva." Jada hung up noticing that Candice was staring in her mouth clinging to every word. Jazzmyne was talking to Darius.

Jada interrupted, "Candice, you can go home. To your house. Jazzmyne, you can leave too. Darius is staying with me."

In unison, Candice and Jazzmyne replied, "What?" then looked at Darius.

Watching Darius's lips disappear inside his mouth, Darius exhaled, then said, "Ma, I have to fly to Atlanta tonight, but I'll be back late tomorrow and I'll come straight from the airport to the hospital or wherever you are."

Candice said, "Uh-huh," rolling her eyes at Darius. "Sure you will."

Jazzmyne chimed in, "We know you have NBA obligations. It's okay, Darius. We'll take care of your mom until you get back."

Jada choked as her eyes watered. She didn't mind Jazzmyne, or anyone else, with the exception of Candice, being there for her. Jada couldn't tell what it was, but she'd gotten bad vibes from Candice lately. For whatever unexplainable reason, she needed Darius. "But, baby, you promised me you'd—"

Jazzmyne hugged Jada. "It's okay, Darius will be back before you know it. I'll stay with you until he returns."

"Me too," Candice hurriedly volunteered.

"See, Mom? You'll be okay. And I promise—"

"Don't promise me another thing as long as you live, Darius. You've hurt me for the last time. You're always my priority, but I'm never yours! Just go!" As she turned away from Darius, Jada's heart cried with disappointment.

The nurse entered the lobby with the medical assistant, pointing at Jada. Jada's heart skipped a beat when the nurse opened her mouth. "Mrs. Tanner, your husband wants to see you for a minute before he goes into the operating room."

"They're going to operate now?" Jada's knees weakened. She wanted to hug Darius but couldn't. All she could do was cry while saying, "Darius, I can't count on you for anything. But that's okay. I'll be all right. Just do me one favor." Jada dried her eyes.

"Anything, Ma, what is it?"

"Don't cry at my funeral, on my casket, or on my grave." Watching Darius blink repeatedly, Jada turned to the nurse, then said, "I can't let my husband see me like this. He'll think I'm crying because of his condition. Please, just tell him I've already left."

"I'll stay with Jada," a deep voice resonated from behind.

When everyone turned, Jada's ex, Darius's father, Darryl, dangled from her charm bracelet.

Exhaling, Jada allowed Darryl to wrap his arms around her shoulders. Although she felt better, Darryl wasn't Darius.

Passionately rocking her side to side, Darryl whispered, "I'm here for you. Whateva you need, I've got." Peering into Jada's eyes, he continued, "Now go in that restroom, dry your tears, and go see your husband. I know if it were me in there, I'd need to see you too."

Jazzmyne accompanied Jada to the ladies' room. When the door closed, Jada cried more. "Why does everyone love me, except the person I love most, my son?"

"Stop talking crazy. You mustn't have expectations of Darius. He can never give back to you what you've given him. Mark my words, Darius will be there for you the most when you least expect it. He has a good spirit. I can feel it. And you know Darius loves you. In his way, he loves you with all his heart. I can see that. Why can't you?" Jazzmyne said, wiping Jada's face.

"Thanks. I hope you're right. I'll be fine." Jada peacefully exited the restroom, ready to see her husband. "Where's Darius?"

The expressions and hunches said Darius was gone.

The nurse said, "I'm sorry. Your husband's condition has escalated. You'll have to wait until after his surgery."

"What happened? Is Wellington okay?" Jada asked, following the nurse.

Darryl followed Jada. Candice followed Darryl. Jazzmyne trailed Candice.

Turning around, the nurse said, "Stop," shaking her head. "You can't see him now. Obviously you're aware your husband hasn't been okay for quite some time. The doctors will do all they can. I suggest going home, getting some rest. Bring a change of clothes with you when you come back tomorrow. He'll need you to be strong for him after his operation."

Jada faintly said, "Tomorrow," then collapsed in Darryl's arms.

Catching Jada, Darryl said, "You can't be alone. Candice. Jazzmyne. I'll stay with Jada tonight and call you guys tomorrow."

Immediately, Candice replied, "I'll stay in my room at Jada's house. Just in case."

CHAPTER 16

Fancy

Love.
The most intense emotion known to mankind could make anyone simultaneously adore, worship, hate, and hurt their lover while self-imposing the same feelings upon themselves. Fancy hated herself for loving Darius so much and hated Darius for putting her and their baby at risk.

Was the pussy worth dying for? Why didn't Darius use protection?

There was nothing at Darius's home that Fancy couldn't live without or replace, except Darius. In time, she'd find someone new to love her and her unborn baby. One last tour through the bedroom. One last sniff of his cologne. One last kick, stump, on his sexy-ass lips onto a broken photo frame lying next to the lamp beside his bed. "I hate you!" She ground the heel of her shoe into his face, hoping she'd never see him again.

After all their drama, Fancy had barely made it to her appointment on time yesterday. She had to fake smiles, pretending she was happy all along, cursing Darius out in her head. No matter how upset, no man would make Fancy so depressed she didn't handle her business. Years of depending on men to take care of her every need thankfully was history. Fancy was comforted knowing she had property of her own, a thriving business, and enough financial investments to retire off of today if she wanted to.

Opening the top drawer, Fancy held a ripped bra in her hand. Digging deeper, she found several panties torn. Checking the remaining sets, Fancy shook her head. "Why?" What had she done to deserve this?

"When did Darius have time to . . . He didn't."

Player recognized game. Another bitch had ruined her shit. Probably the same one with the tainted pussy that had possibly ruined her future. "That's okay," Fancy whispered. "Just one more reason to leave his ass alone." Like she wasn't already convinced.

Picking up the cordless, Fancy dialed pound seventy-two, then dialed her cell phone number, answered her cell phone, then hung up. Forwarding Darius's home incoming calls to her cell phone would let her know if or when he'd called the house to check his messages, or to check on her.

Lying on her back, Fancy bent her knees, clamping her hands behind her head. "Ow," she moaned, crunching, sucking in her stomach.

"I am not going to let Darius drive me crazy. One, two, three . . ." Placing her hand below her abdomen, Fancy kept crunching. "Fifty-five. Damn, this hurts, ow, ow!" Determined to reach five hundred, she blocked out the physical pain mentally, thinking about life without Darius.

Under all of his lies, what was the truth? His? Hers? Forget the truth. Truths were manipulated by desires. If she still desired to marry him, she was a fool. But God protected babies and fools. Didn't He? If she stayed, the truth wouldn't matter because the horrible things Darius had done could never be undone. Fancy replaced trying to conclude truth with the facts.

Fact: no man would knowingly make love to her if she tested positive. Fact: Darius had become too aggressive and for unknown reasons, hostile. Fact: she couldn't solve Darius's problems. Fact: if she stayed, she'd be unhappy more than she'd be happy. Fact: despite all that had happened, Fancy hated Darius at the moment, but deep inside she couldn't understand why she still loved him.

"Four hundred ninety-eight, ninety-nine, whew! Five hundred! Yes!"

Rolling onto her hands and knees, Fancy stood slowly, then stepped out onto the deck, gulping the cool fresh air. On the second inhale, she doubled over in pain like a heavyweight champion had punched her below the belt. Fancy flopped over the balcony. Back to back, each cramp became more severe. Breathing deeply, she held on to the redwood rail, praying her spinning head wouldn't push her over the edge.

"Ow!" she yelled into the crisp air. Her eyes glazed over the trees below, meshing them into one big evergreen blur. Fancy closed her eyes, then opened them, focusing on Michael intensely watching her.

Circling his hands on opposite sides of his mouth, Michael stared at her from his deck, then yelled, "Are you okay, Fancy?"

"Oh my God," Fancy moaned repeatedly. Shaking her head, she dragged herself onto the deck's floor, then flopped to her knees. Weakly her hand wavered in the air. Not soliciting Michael's help but for him to stay away. He'd helped her relationship enough.

"I'll be right over!" Michael yelled, disappearing through his back patio door.

Michael Baines, regardless of the circumstances, was the last person Fancy wanted in Darius's house again. Michael, one of the best real estate brokers in California, had helped her become a millionaire and although she'd never fucked him—not because she hadn't considered lately—Darius wasn't convinced. What Darius was was insecure in attempting to keep her away from every man except himself.

Fancy wanted to yell back, but her syllables were muffled. "No, Michael. I'll be all right." What if Darius came home and started more unnecessary bullshit? Her plan was to leave before Darius arrived, but she was in too much pain to go anywhere.

"Feels like I'm gonna die." Dragging one foot after the other, Fancy crawled to the bathroom, hoisted herself up, and sat on the toilet. She ignored the constant ringing of the doorbell, her breasts touching her thighs, until her legs became numb. Well, she couldn't stay on the toilet forever and truly didn't want to die there. Wiping herself, Fancy looked at the tissue. Tiny bloody lumps and slimy pink mucus stained the tissue.

"Oh my God!" Her eyes closed. Opened. Turning to inspect the toilet, she saw a thin line of clumps of blood trailing the white porcelain bowl to the bottom. Fancy balled her fists, clamped her arms to her side, and squeezed her legs together, trying to hold in the contents.

Plop. Plop. Plop.

"God, no. Please, stop my baby from falling."

Tears poured one stream after another as the clumps kept splashing. Fancy's entire body tensed.

Pulling up her purple silk panties, Fancy grabbed the red and white bottle, faintly shaking it. Unscrewing the top, she thought, *Good, I have four more aspirins to take away the pain.*

Filling a small mouthwash cup with water, Fancy swallowed two pills. When the second round of blows struck, she hurried to the phone and dialed medical emergency. Continuing to ignore the doorbell, Fancy placed the phone next to her ear and said, "Hello. Hello."

"Bitch, you still up in my man's house!"

This time, pissed off and in pain, Fancy cried, "Ashlee, why? I haven't done anything to you."

Karma had a way of wreaking revenge. Fancy hadn't done anything to Ashlee, but she had shown up at Byron's sister's house a few years ago pretending to be a Realtor. That was before Fancy had gotten her license and before she discovered the woman was his sister, not his wife. Byron's sister was nice, invited her in, and when the woman's water bag broke, she'd pleaded with Fancy to stay with her. But Fancy couldn't, she had to escape before Byron saw her there. Scared, Fancy had deserted a pregnant woman in labor, and Byron had shown up before she'd driven away.

"Since you keep answering the damn phone, the phone I used to answer, give Darius a message from me. Tell Darius his son, I mean our son, is—"

Fancy hung up. "That bitch is c-r-a-z-y. Desperate and deranged. I see why Darius put her pathetic ass out. But she can have him!" Deniably, Fancy understood Ashlee's irrational behavior. Momentarily Fancy forgot about her pain, clenching the red and white bottle until an almost paralyzing fiery sensation darted up her spine, burning.

"Oh, shit!" Fancy yelled. "Oh, God, why me?"

Frantically, she peeped inside her panties. More blood flowed. Returning to the bathroom, thoroughly wiping one final time, she flushed the toilet, put on two panty liners, and a torn but clean pair of underwear. Fancy changed her clothes, grabbed her purse, tossed the bottle inside, then hopped in the new platinum S-type Jaguar Darius had bought her as a wedding or make-up gift. The huge red bow was neatly attached to the top. Backing out the driveway, Fancy stopped within inches of rolling over Michael.

Fancy pressed the button to lower her window. "I'm going to the hospital. I'll be okay."

"Not the way you're leaning over that steering wheel. Like it or not, I'm taking you. Get out." Michael helped Fancy into the passenger seat, snatched the bow off, tossing it on the lawn.

Unsuccessfully she tried to step one foot out of the car but doubled over in pain. The pain in Fancy's stomach left her no choice but to stay in the car. Driving along the freeway, zooming in and out of lanes, Michael arrived at the nearest hospital parking at the entrance.

Sliding her feet as Fancy entered the main lobby, she heard, "Fancy?"

Turning to witness the familiar voice, she saw Jada. "I can't talk right now. Would you please tell Darius where I am?" Fancy said, leaning on Michael.

"She doesn't have to."

Looking to her opposite side, Fancy saw Darius. Weakly she stretched her arms out to him. "Help me. I feel like I'm dying."

Swatting her hands away, Darius said, "So you decided to do it, huh? What'd I tell you? I hope you die, too."

"Darius, please," Fancy begged. "Listen—"

"What for? You with who you wanna be with. Stay with that nigga. All you bitches are just alike."

"Darius Jones!" Jada yelled, then sternly said, "You will not treat Fancy like your father treated me. Apologize right this minute."

Looking at Darryl, then at his mother, Darius replied, "Williams. My last name is Williams. Besides what do you care? I went to the restroom for two minutes and you and everybody else thought I'd left. Well, this time I am leaving." Then he stumped out of the lobby.

Michael ushered Fancy toward emergency, saying, "Let him go. He's not man enough for you. You can do a lot better, if you know what I mean."

Silence was best. Fancy couldn't believe, not knowing her condition, Darius abandoned her. "Oh my God! He thinks I'm having an abortion," Fancy cried, entering the emergency room filled with more people than seats. She could hardly breathe.

"This is ridiculous," Fancy mumbled, leaving Michael. Managing her way to the front of the line, she walked up to the triage nurse and placed her medical card on the counter.

Without looking up the nurse said, "Wait your turn. I'll be with you after I've helped the people in front of—"

Another clump of blood pushed through Fancy's vaginal canal. She collapsed to the floor. Her eyes fluttered, then shut. She couldn't move.

The nurse jumped up, staring over the counter, and yelled, "Oh my gosh! Patient down! I need a doctor over here quick! Patient down! Hurry!"

A few minutes later, Fancy lay on the gurney with Michael trailing behind the assistants rushing her through the hallway.

"Sir, you'll have to wait in the lobby," the assistant said to Michael.

"No, please." Reaching her arms toward Michael, Fancy said, "I'm scared. I want you to stay with me."

Moments later, Fancy was in a private room with a doctor sticking his fingers inside her pussy. After poking inside and pressing on her abdomen, he removed his bloody rubber gloves, tossing them into the trash bin marked *contaminated*.

"Well, your abortion process is under way. It won't take much longer."

Michael's brows rose, widening his eyes. "Abortion?"

Shaking her head, Fancy replied, "Doctor, what are you saying? Am I having a miscarriage?"

"Well, from the way you're bleeding, and I've seen this before, your abortion *pills* are working. This is perfectly normal. Who's your doctor? Have you inserted the vaginal tablets yet?"

"Please tell me you're confused," Fancy said, peeping under the sheet looking down at the fresh circle of blood on the blue pad underneath her butt. "Oh my God. Don't just stand there. Do something. Help me! Save my baby!"

Michael extended his hand for comfort. "Calm down. Let the doctor do his job."

"Stop stressing yourself out, Mrs. Taylor. Lots of women take the abortion pill and then when it's too late, wish they hadn't. What type of work do you do?"

"You have got to be insane. Okay, maybe your question is to help me in some sadistic kind of way. Maybe you really are a doctor. Look, I own a real estate firm and sell homes to celebrities and businesspeople with more money than time. I hate wasting my time. In fact I want you to stop wasting my time and quit lying or taking 'educated guesses' with me." Fancy glanced at the blood again, then continued. "Save my baby!"

Shaking his head, the doctor looked up at Michael and asked, "Are you her husband?"

"No, please don't say that. He's my neighbor. All I care about right now is saving my baby. That and I have to be in my best friend's wedding."

The doctor was now shaking his head again. "Mrs. Taylor, you don't realize how serious this is. You can't just take abortion pills and then pretend you didn't want to terminate your pregnancy."

"What do you keep talkin' about? I took four aspirins. Aspirins! Two yesterday and two today. Give me my purse, Michael. I'll show you."

Michael handed Fancy her purse.

"Whatever you say, Mrs. Taylor. Maybe you don't want your husband to know the truth. Let me reassure you. He doesn't have access to your *confidential* records. So if you don't tell him, or your friend standing here doesn't tell him, he'll never know."

"Here," Fancy said, handing the red and white bottle to the doctor.

Removing the top, the doctor shook the two remaining pills into his palm. Flipping them over, he showed them to Fancy. "See here? Just as I thought. RU. Abortion pills. You've stopped your pregnancy. But how did you get these? Only a doctor can administer these."

"I didn't get them!"

"Okay, calm down. Now back to your health. I have patients waiting. We can't keep you against your will, but my professional recommendation is that you check yourself in and let us take care of you. You'll probably get discharged tomorrow or the next day at the latest. However, if you leave, please let me be clear. You have stopped your pregnancy. If you choose not to complete the abortion process, there is a high risk of fetal deformities, you could miscarry, you could experience severe bleeding, or you could die. Oh yeah, *and* I strongly recommend you see a professional psychiatrist immediately upon your release. We can provide referrals if you'd like."

"Naw." Shaking her head, Fancy said, "I'm not crazy. I don't know what happened, but I do know Darius gave me those pills. It's best I stay here." She closed her eyes in disbelief.

How could she be so stupid?

CHAPTER 17

Candice

Everyone in Hollywood was a star.

Los Angeles. The land of milk and honeys, where women knew how to pay the rent by sweet-talking, fucking, or charming a man. In Southern California, everything had a price, and to yield a return on an investment was like winning the Mega lottery. The average person's looks could easily win a Mr. or Miss Universe contest, and visitors got whiplash from lusting over the abundance of booty and bodybuilders dressed in thongs on Venice Beach or the ladies of the night strolling along Sunset Boulevard.

Northern California, where Candice once lived, was the complete opposite. The average Bay Area migrant was overweight and the women were underlaid and underpaid, upholding that equal rights crap. Cohabiting women foolishly split the bills: restaurant and household. The beaches were dried up, the weather was too chilly most of the time, especially during summer, and the men were blander than seasonless chicken.

L.A. The land of opportunities and opportunists. Every second, good or bad, someone was taken advantage of, and it was a matter of when, not if, she'd get hers. Until then, Candice's motto was that of the majority of the county's residents, vagabonds, and transients, "Do unto others before they do unto you." When had she become such a devious diva that at her best friend's weakest moment she'd prey? Candice had more than enough money, and in L.A. money could buy a stunt double.

The night was young yet old. Warm and cold-blooded. Darius deserved every bad thing that could happen to him, Candice thought, after listening to how he degraded Fancy in front of all of them and left Ashlee stranded at that hotel in Beverly Hills.

En route to Jada's via Darius's house, darkness visited around 6:00 p.m. A lot had transpired since sunrise, with very few sprinkles of sunshine in between. Candice's visual of Wellington's dick lying in a chop shop waiting to be stripped was gloomy. Exactly what were the doctors cutting? How could she get a copy of Wellington's report?

Honk, honk.

It only took one driver to start a band of horn blowers. Most of the working-class people surrounding her in rush-hour traffic were impatiently in transit from their nine-to-fives to their postwork destinations. Home. A bar. Happy hour. Preschool. A second job. Eight-plus hours of routine servitude, without gratitude. Oblivious of their surroundings, they probably hadn't noticed anything new along the way. Rat-racing to earn a dollar or a dime that was already spent.

Having money had its advantages. No two days were the same in Candice's life. One day in Dallas. The next in Los Angeles. Tomorrow she'd be back in Dallas. Every day she had to look over her shoulder, never forgetting her motto.

Darryl had eagerly escorted Jada home. At Jada's request, Candice had agreed to give them a few hours alone. Hopefully her girlfriend would go on and get her some dick. Life was what it was and the reality was Jada could benefit from a couple of big orgasms.

Parking in his driveway, Candice got excited using her duplicate key to enter Darius's home. This time she didn't have to hurry. Fancy was admitted to the hospital. Darius was on his way to the airport. Ashlee was in Dallas. Candice would have at least eighteen hours before her departure back to Texas.

"Now, where does Mr. Lover store his recording devices?" Candice scanned the baseboards, ceilings, tried following the direction of the infrared beam. She was clueless.

What about fingerprints? Candice shook her head. Gloves. She hadn't bother with those. She wasn't a burglar. She was their die-hard friend to the end. Carefully she placed her laptop on the living room table, plugged in the cord, pressed the Power button, tossed the ten memory cards from Jada's house next to the laptop, then went upstairs.

Twisting a knob to a closed door, she found the room locked. Jiggle. Wiggle. She'd figure out how to manipulate the latch later. Entering the weight room, Candice doubted much action had taken place there. Never know. She replaced the blue memory card, then shut the door. Not saving the best for last, she went to Darius's bedroom next. Candice paused in the doorway, then entered. "My God. What happened here?"

Nasty bloodstains on the toilet seat, broken glass on the floor. Removing her hidden camera, Candice slid out the memory card, placing it in her pocket. Easing a new card into the camera, she pushed the device into its hiding place.

"Oh yes. Another button. Should I? I wouldn't be a great detective if I didn't." Her finger curled, applying pressure. Candice listened to objects moving.

This time the three mirrors in Darius's bedroom rotated halfway, then stopped. She peeped inside. Shallow breaths barely inflated her lungs. She couldn't believe there was a room inside his bedroom. "Who would think of all this?" Turning sideways, she stepped inside the well-lit area. There were twelve TV screens monitoring outdoors and every room in the house, and . . . *bingo!* The tapes she'd been looking for.

"Hot damn! I'm good!"

Eager to see what was on them, Candice sat on the edge of the burgundy computer chair pressing buttons.

"So that's what Ashlee was doing. She's crazy. Okay, Fancy can't decide if she wants to masturbate or not. Darius!" Candice replayed the tape several times. "No, he did not shove Fancy like that. What if he's responsible for Fancy losing the baby? If his mama saw this, she'd, she'd make excuses for his reckless behavior. That was Darius's problem. He's gotten away with everything, including murder."

Realizing she'd gone too far, Candice had second thoughts on exposing Jada and Darius. Exhaling, she said, "This could turn out all bad. Hell, all of us could end up behind bars." A lot of emotional events had happened in their lives. But Candice could change the names, maybe alter the scenes—a little. What if Jada was spying on her?

"I wonder what would happen if I . . ." Curious, Candice flipped a red switch.

Zurp. Zurp. The monitors shut down. The mirror doors slammed, then locked. Power off. Lights out.

Alone, Candice sat wishing she was by the bay window.

CHAPTER 18

Ashlee

Was the dick that good?

Emotionally, Ashlee had multiple orgasms, absorbing Darius's sexual energy. Whenever she replayed their last intimate moment, she came again. Darius's presence sensuously overwhelmed her. His body was so strong, perfectly shaped, and irresistibly sexy. What made her love him? Laying her head against Darius's chest made Ashlee believe Darius cared for her too. His fingers strummed her strands of hair musically, reassuring his feelings. Instantly she'd dozed off. Dream. Fantasy? Fairy tale. Myth?

Nervous, lonely, and back in Dallas, she found the melodies embedded in her memory. Ashlee sat in a rocking chair with little Darius in her arms. "You light up my life, you . . ." She paused, then exhaled, watching her son. "Not this again," she complained, watching his sniffles escalate. His lips opened wide for her to see his fluttering tonsils.

"*Waaa! Waaa!*"

"Hush, baby, please," she sang. "You give me strength to carry, baby, please, Mommy's here."

"*Waaa! Waaa!*"

Standing, Ashlee laid his head on her shoulder, pacing in his room. Light blue walls, accented with Spiderman borders, and a crib filled with dozens of stuffed animals. Little Darius no longer slept in his room at night. Her bed was his bed but not during the day.

Ashlee patted his back. "Please, go to sleep for Mommy."

"Buurrrpppp."

"Oh, Mommy sorry. I forgot to burp you." Ashlee slid her fingers under his diaper, bumping a mushy lump of waste. "Okay. Now I see. I forgot to do that too . . . You light up my life, you give me strength to carry on . . . hum, hum," Ashlee sang changing little Darius's diaper, then placed him in his playpen.

She rocked, waiting until his crying quieted into a peaceful sleep. When was the last time she'd given him a bath? Before the wedding? Ashlee couldn't remember that either. She'd give little Darius a bath in the Jacuzzi with her after he woke up. Ashlee picked up the white handheld room monitor, then dimmed his light.

Lounging on the living room sofa, Ashlee flipped through hundreds of cable channels, trying to find one program worth watching. Cathy Hughes was interviewing Terrance on *TV One*.

"Wow, and I thought my life was jacked up," Ashlee commented, listening to Terrance. In a matter of minutes, his entire family was devastated.

Closing her eyes, Ashlee thought, *What in the world was I thinking leaving my baby alone in the car overnight? He could've suffocated, choked, fallen off the seat. Someone could've taken him.* "All for what!" she angrily yelled.

Living alone had benefits, like no one to answer or witness her outbreaks, but gave Ashlee a lot of time to do nothing or too much time to think. Over the past year her life had drastically changed. Always having to take her baby everywhere she went while Darius kicked it with whomever doing whatever. Seemed like the day her son was born, a part of her died. Darius's lifestyle wasn't affected at all. A one-day turnaround visit and that was the last time she'd seen him until yesterday, but Darius had taken their photo out of her purse. That meant he still wanted her—them. Hopefully one day soon they'd be a family.

Ashlee picked up the phone. Seven beeping buttons later her mother answered, "Hello, honey."

"Hi, Mommy. How are you?"

"Fine, headed to the gym, to keep my hot figure," her mother replied.

"Mommy, I desperately need a break. I feel like I'm going crazy. Can you skip class and watch your grandson, please? One day. That's all."

"I told you. I raised you. I'm not raising your son too. That's your job. Maybe next time you'll keep your legs closed or at least pick a better man to have a baby with. If only by example, I know I taught you better. Then you fly out to L.A. for Darius's wedding. You haven't learned a thing. Keep on following him around, you'll end up with another baby he won't take care of. I'm late for my aerobics class. Bye, honey."

Ashlee's mom's memory wasn't that great. She gave herself more credit than she deserved because Ashlee was partly raised by her father and Darius's mother.

What was her mother talking about? Her mom and dad barely got along. Ashlee smiled. She was a daddy's girl. Her father took better care of her, the best he could.

Ashlee's father, Lawrence, was a workaholic, which was the main reason her mother divorced him and Darius's mom married her dad for ten years before they divorced. Easily Lawrence spent twelve to sixteen hours a day at his law office or with clients. Like most kids, Ashlee dearly loved both of her dysfunctional parents.

Flipping to the *Tyra Banks Show*, Ashlee said, "See, Tyra, that's what I'm talkin' 'bout. I need a break, a nanny, day care, something."

Tyra had given the single mom on her show three months of paid babysitting for twelve straight weekends. "I'd never be that lucky or that trusting," Ashlee said, walking into little Darius's room. Good. He was asleep. Ashlee slipped her fingers inside his diaper. The liner was dry. Bored, she returned to the living room and resumed watching television.

Being alone wasn't bad, being a loner was horrible. Ashlee realized that, aside from Darius, she didn't have any close friends. During college she'd met some nice guys and a few girls who were cool to hang out with, but once she graduated and started working for Darius, Darius became her life again. Somehow Kevin had slipped between her legs too. Another bad decision influenced by a man. Why did she have sex with Kevin? She didn't even like him. He was too short, ugly, conniving, available, and insanely jealous of Darius, wanting everything Darius had.

After the last phone call to Fancy, Fancy seemed like she was breaking down emotionally. That was good. Maybe she'd move out of Darius's house and then Ashlee could move back in. Replacing the aspirin with abortion pills was a bad idea. What if Fancy found out? Would she press charges? Could she? Had Ashlee committed a crime?

Lying on her new sofa cover, Ashlee picked up the cordless phone and dialed Darius's number. Indirectly she'd question him, then convince him to throw away the tablets. Moving the phone, Ashlee stretched her ear toward little Darius's room and listened, then placed the phone back to her ear.

Beep, was all she'd heard.

"Hi, Darius. You know who this is. I, I, I forgot something, um, my medication, at your house and, well, I'd like to get my pills back. I'm glad we made love on your should-have-been wedding night because I'm gonna be your wife. I love you, too. Bye. Call me. Wait a minute. I called to be honest. Truth is, the reason I'm calling is to confess, I replaced your aspirins with abortion pills. Please, throw them away before—"

Not wanting to say Fancy's name, Ashlee ended the call. She did have spare keys to their home. "Our home." Ashlee could go back and throw the pills out. She knew what would happen to Fancy, but what would happen to Darius if he took the pills?

Hearing her front door squeak, Ashlee yelled, "Daddy, is that you?"

"Yeah, sweetheart."

Greeting him at the entry, Ashlee said, "Hey, Papa. How was your day?" Yippee! She had a visitor, an adult capable of speaking in complete sentences. She wasn't alone anymore. Ashlee hugged, then kissed her father on the cheek. Maybe he'd keep her baby.

"Fine, sweetheart. Did you—"

"Yes, I took my meds," Ashlee replied, rolling her eyes.

"I'm sorry. I don't mean to upset you. But you know how you get when you don't."

"I know." Depressed. Too late for that.

Her father smiled at her.

"What? What is it?"

"I'm just proud of you. You're really handling being a single parent well."

Ashlee's mouth hung open. No, she wasn't. "Can you keep the baby just one night for me? Please, Daddy."

"I can't. In fact, I can't stay long, where's DJ?"

Ashlee's dad refused to call his grandson Darius. "Asleep."

"I have a client to meet in a few, I'll come back tomorrow, though."

"Promise?"

As she was escorting her dad out the front door, they noticed a stranger standing in front of the house comparing the address on the siding to that on a notepad.

"Can we help you?" Lawrence asked.

"Yes, I'm looking for an Ashlee Anderson."

"That's me."

Flashing her identification badge, the woman said, "I'm Ms. Benson with Child Protective Services. We received a complaint about child abuse and I'm here to investigate the matter. May I come in?"

"Obviously you have the wrong person. No, you may not come in," Lawrence answered in Ashlee's defense, partially closing the door.

"Well, consider this your courtesy twenty-four-hour notice. I'll be back tomorrow with the authorities."

"So will I. I'll be back too. I'm her counsel," Lawrence answered, then said, "Wait, what's the basis?"

"What's your name?"

"Lawrence Anderson, her father."

Ms. Benson sternly replied, "Abandonment."

"That's nonsense," Lawrence said.

"Then you have nothing to worry about. Do you, Ms. Anderson?" Ms. Benson said, walking away.

Speechless, Ashlee felt like killing herself.

CHAPTER 19

Darius

Unlike love, hate had no expectations.

Darius's fear of falling in love, with Ashlee or Fancy, and loving his mother unconditionally, made him want to distance himself from all of them. Easier to start over. Meet a new woman. Women. Criteria this time: more attractive than Fancy, something to lose, financially independent, no kids, highly skilled in pleasing him sexually—mediocre low-libido, missionary-style-preferred females who didn't move their ass need not apply—willing to relocate to Atlanta but not live with him.

Darius glanced at the overweight woman with glossy, cherry, succulent lips seated across from him.

"I bet she can suck the cum out of my dick like . . . a vein out of a neck bone."

"We'll begin our preboarding to Chicago in a few minutes," the gate attendant at LAX announced.

Good. Hopefully the woman across from him was on that flight and not on his, because if she was down for blowin' him, he'd let her do her thang. Shit! With so many things happening, he'd forgotten to make that call. Scrolling his phone book, Darius dialed the locksmith for his company, Somebody's Gotta Be on Top. Surprised he'd answered at eight o'clock at night, Darius said, "Man, what's up?"

"Apparently an emergency," he replied. "I haven't heard from you in months."

"Yeah, it is. I need *all* the locks at my house changed."

"Tonight, I take it."

"Hell yeah, tonight."

"A woman, I take it."

"Damn straight."

"I thought you were sharper than that, playa," he said, laughing. "I'm on my way. Where do you want me to leave your new keys?"

"My mom's house is cool. Just drop them in the mail slot. Thanks, man. Later."

"No problem, D. Be at *peace.*"

Darius sat at the gate two hours early for his ten o'clock red-eye flight to Atlanta, analyzing his mistakes. Lots of memories surfaced. Some good. Some bad.

Like the day he was supposed to fly out of LAX to meet his mother's executive, Zen, on one of his all-expenses-paid fuckfeasts. That Asian chick used to stroke his dick better than any sista. Small, strong, soft, skilled hands. Whoever taught her how to jerk off a man, better than a man could do himself, should hold class.

"Um, um, um."

Later Darius discovered Ginger, his mother's other executive, had canceled his confirmations, his flights, his limos, and his hotels to meet Zen in Chicago and Miranda in Canada. Women. Ginger had transferred all his Palm Pilot appointments, confirmations, and reservations to her PDA, including his address book. Ginger followed him all the way to New Orleans on his leisure trip with Heather, coincidentally showed up at The House of Blues in the French Quarters, and slipped her room key into his hand. Being the dawg he was then, Darius showed up at Ginger's hotel. Thank God for sperm reproduction because Ginger fucked every single X and Y chromosome out of his nuts. That greedy sista was serious about leaving his dick on limp.

Those were the good old days. No attachments. Free-flowing pussy.

Women jockeying for position to ride Slugger. Kimberly Stokes. Her fine ass was now working for his wife, Ciara, starring in his movie production of *Soul Mates Dissipate*. The West Coast was too damn small and Darius was eager to move to the East and explore new territory.

"Hey, man," a familiar voice from the past echoed from behind. "Feet chilled on ya, huh, or what, nigga?" K'Nine said, sitting next to Darius. "It's been a long time. I knew you'd make it pro." K'Nine slapped hands with Darius. "Welcome to the club."

Which club was that? Darius wondered.

K'Nine was Darius's high school teammate and the closest male friend Darius ever had until that day. In high school they were ballin' out of control on and off the court. Young. Wild. Adventurous. When K'Nine got recruited to the University of Maryland, Darius got a scholarship to Georgetown. But once his boy went pro, Darius felt like a failure because Darius had lost his college spot to a white boy, and almost lost his virginity to K'Nine.

"Naw, man, that's not it. I didn't get cold feet but I'm glad as a muthafucka I didn't say 'I do.'"

Darius wasn't gay. He was young, in college, and adventurous. Almost doing K'Nine felt as dirty as being done. Bisexuality wasn't a trend Darius wanted to perpetuate. His first time considering doing that shit was his last time. But he couldn't lie to himself, he'd fantasized about it. A woman's finger up his ass made Darius cum his hardest . . . so he could only imagine. Why could women get away with doing other women with men cheering them on jockeying for the chance to join in?

"What? Like that. I heard yo' stuff is tight, D."

Darius knew what K'Nine meant, but it was the way he'd said "tight" that fucked up Darius's heads. *Yeah, and it's gonna stay that way.* Darius smiled, nodding.

"Yeah, she is mesmerizing. Make a *man* stop dead in his tracks. I had to play it off like she wasn't all that when I first saw her, 'cause she was kickin' it with a dude I knew. Only woman I've ever loved.

Got too close to falling, man, and that fucked me up bad. Plus, I been going through it. My firstborn, a boy, man, he died. My second child, his crazy mama, I guess because we didn't get married, just killed him today. Walked in the hospital with another man to abort my kid." Darius pressed his thumb and middle fingers into his eye sockets.

"Damn, man. Maybe it wasn't yours. Look at it this way, at least you don't have baby mama drama like me. I got six people driving me nuts," K'Nine said, holding his balls.

Darius leaned back. "Damn! Six?"

"Naw, not the kids, yo. Three and three. Mamas plus kids. I have two knuckleheads and a two-year-old baby girl who gets any and every fuckin' thang she wants and then some, so when she's old enough to date, any man who steps to my daughter, he has no choice but to treat her right."

What if Darius had a little girl? He'd be hard on her and every dude who thought too loud about fucking his daughter. Like K'Nine, Darius knew how men really thought about women. That was why no man treated his woman the way he expected another man to treat his daughter.

Nudging Darius's thigh, K'Nine asked, "How'd your boy die?"

Uncomfortable with K'Nine's touch, Darius moved his legs. "I don't know," he lied, then became quiet.

"Chill, man. Sorry I asked. Here's my numba. I'ma throw one back befo' last call. Join me."

"I'm *straight*," Darius said, looking away, refusing to cry in front of his boy. The last thing Darius needed was alcohol to exacerbate his depression.

"I'm glad yo' ass is runnin' with us. Sho nuff wouldn't wanna have to work that hard to push up on you," K'Nine said, walking away.

Darius frowned, shaking his head. Until now, he hadn't noticed that the woman across from him was gone. What if K'Nine found out if Darius failed his physical? Would he wanna run with him then? Darius could go back to operating his company and forget about playing for Atlanta. Wasn't like he needed the money. The competition got him off.

Darius's cell phone rang. Looking at the caller ID, he answered, "Hey, what's up? Something wrong?"

His locksmith replied, "I'm done. Your laptop is on, D."

"Man, do your job and get out of my house. What you doin' snoopin' in my study?"

"Man, yo' shit is on the coffee table. Thought it kinda strange for what I saw."

"Leave it. And leave the keys under the mat. I'm on my way."

"I'll drop an extra set off at your mom's. Be at peace."

Ending the call, Darius picked up his carry-on bag, then strolled down the concourse. K'Nine was talking to some pretty lil' thang barely twenty-one. An undercover way for a baller to check a woman's age: buy her a drink and let the bartender do the job. Darius paused in front of the bar. "They're boarding, man."

"Hey, thanks, but aren't you headed the wrong way?"

"I'll take a flight out tomorrow. Got some unfinished business."

K'Nine smiled at the woman beside him. "Me too. Might see ya. Gimme a holla."

"For sho," Darius said, resuming his stroll to the garage.

Starting up his car, Darius drove to his house, removed the keys from underneath the mat, and walked through the front door. Sure enough, a laptop was on his coffee table. Darius sat on the sofa, rotated his middle finger on the mouse pad, then hit PLAY.

"What the fuck? Fancy been spying on my mother? Wait a minute." Darius opened My Computer, clicked on View System Information. Glancing at General, Registered to . . . Candice Jordan. "That bitch is still flippin' tricks, spying on my mother. I got something for her ass when I see her."

Glancing up at his ceiling, he saw that the red-dot indicator for his camera was off. Darius packed up the laptop, placed the bag on the sofa, then toured every room. All of the red lights were off, which meant one thing. Someone was locked inside the room inside his bedroom. Picking up the phone, Darius dialed 9-1-1 and waited downstairs for the police.

In his neighborhood a cop was always patrolling. Before the doorbell rang, Darius opened the door.

"Hey, Nero."

"What's up, Williams? Another crazy groupie?"

"Someone broke into my house and the idiot locked themselves in."

"My kinda work," Nero said, drawing his gun and following Darius upstairs.

Darius opened a concealed panel inside his closet, pressed a button, and waited.

Nero shouted, "Come out with your hands up! Make one false move and you're dead! Keep your hands where I can see them!"

Darius watched in disbelief as she stepped into the light. "What the fuck are you doing in my house? Forget that, I already know. I have your little memory cards," he said, twirling the blue chip between his fingers.

"You," Officer Nero said. "You were the one crawling in the bushes looking for a puppy."

"Darius, I'm sorry. I can explain."

Officer Nero looked at Darius. "It's your call."

Darius looked at Candice and said, "Lock her ass up."

"No! Darius! Don't do this!" Candice cried as Officer Nero handcuffed her. "I'ma expose your trifling ass, Darius!" she shouted as Nero escorted her out of the house.

His mother was dealing with enough stress that she didn't need some two-timing, backstabbing girlfriend in her house. Darius knew the only way Candice would post bail was to call his mother. Candice would tell the truth, fearing Darius had told his mom, but Darius wasn't saying anything. That is, unless Candice lied. That would be all bad because if she lied, her ass was doing time. Serious time.

Darius drove to his mother's house. Parking alongside his father's car, Darius felt there was no easy way for him to do anything anymore. Dragging his issues like a ball and chain around his ankle, he cried. How could he tell his mother that he couldn't do the one thing he'd promised and he'd had her best friend arrested? Neither was his fault. Darius sat in his car outside his mother's home, this time listening to the breeze whistle around his Bentley.

Closing his eyes, Darius pressed his thumb and middle finger into his sockets and massaged his eyeballs. Exhaling slowly, he opened the door. *Thump.* This time his soul greeted the asphalt. *Click.*

Quietly opening the door, Darius saw his father cuddled on the sofa into a spoon position with his mother wrapped in his embrace. Darius picked up a blanket, kissed his mom's forehead, then covered her up.

Sleepily his mother said, "Hey, baby. I thought you were on your way—"

Kissing his mother again, Darius said, "I was but I changed my mind. I've hurt you enough. I don't want to fail you anymore, Ma. I love you. Go back to sleep. We'll talk in the morning."

Entering his bedroom, Darius admired his trophies. Seeing his parents together made Darius more confused about relationships. Over the years, his dad certainly hadn't been a friend to his mother. Hadn't stepped up to raise him. Now that all the hard work was done, his dad easily lay with his mom, probably sexually too, while his stepdad was in the hospital. His dad had divorced his wife, in Darius's opinion to be with his mother. But why?

Turning off the light, Darius lay in his bed praying that his dad wouldn't break his mother's heart again.

Staring into darkness, Darius wondered why he flashed on Ashlee. He'd already said he was sorry. There was nothing else to mention. A visual of Fancy at the hospital with Michael going to have an abortion made him angry.

"Why? Why would Ladycat do that to me? To us?" Maybe she could explain. He needed to hear her say something, if it was only to hear her voice. Fumbling, Darius dialed his home number, hoping she'd left a voice mail message, and heard. "You've reached Fancy Taylor's Realty. Leave us a message with your name, number, and a brief message." *Beep.*

"That was weird." Why'd Fancy change his message? Maybe she was expecting a business call. If she came back to him, what would he do? Hug her and never let go. Put her out and never take her back. Or make love to her like never before. Darius hung up. He closed his eyes as the tears streamed into his ears.

Was this God's way of teaching him life lessons?

CHAPTER 20

Fancy

A pleasant voice chimed in her ear, "Ms. Taylor, your procedure was a success. It's time for your breakfast."

Rolling onto her back, Fancy thought, *No, it wasn't. I'm never getting pregnant again.*

What kind of man murders his baby? *A murderer*, whispered in her mind. In a way, Fancy regretted that Darius had killed her father. She knew he'd done it to save her life, but what if she'd never lied to the police when she was a child, claiming Thaddeus had raped her? Fancy had to protect her mother from Thaddeus's brutal beatings. If he hadn't abused her mother, Thaddeus wouldn't have gone to jail. If her mother had told her that Thaddeus was her father before Fancy had lied, maybe Fancy wouldn't have called the police, or if she'd known the truth while Thaddeus was in jail, maybe their reunion after he'd gotten out would've been different.

Watching the nurse prepare her meal, Fancy realized she'd never had the chance to say, "Daddy, I'm sorry. Please forgive me."

"Make sure we give you after-care instructions. No foreign objects inside your vagina for one week. That means no sex, no tampons, nothing. You may experience some bleeding for the next few days, so make sure you wear a pad. And if you take contraceptives, start them this Sunday. You can read the rest on your own."

Fancy heard what the nurse said, and would read the instructions carefully. For some unknown reason, losing her father weighed on her mind. An innocent man had lost over ten years of his freedom, brutally lost his virginity for rape charges, and lost his sanity after he'd gotten out of jail, all because of her one lie. Truth, no fact. Fancy wasn't any better than Darius. She didn't pull the trigger but she'd taken a man's life.

Darius wasn't man enough to face her in the hospital's lobby. Easier to walk away from her in her moment of need. At least he was consistent, never helping anyone other than himself. Fancy had to overcome the most challenging obstacle of her life. Alone. Where was everybody?

The nurse rolled the tray stand in front of Fancy. "There, sweetie, you're all set. If you need me, you know how to buzz."

Admissions. Michael was there, but he was gone by the time they rolled her to the operating room. With surgery, understandably she couldn't have visitors. In recovery, no one was waiting. Didn't her loved ones know she was terrified?

The nurse opened the door to exit.

"Wait, please. Can I ask you a question?"

Releasing the handle, the nurse returned.

Exhaling, Fancy asked, "Was it a boy or a girl?"

"What did you want?"

"A healthy baby," Fancy answered, waiting for a response.

"A girl."

Crying, Fancy asked, "Did I receive any calls? Any messages?"

"No. We're discharging you today. Do you have someone who can pick you up?" the nurse asked.

Between the sniffles, Fancy said, "No, I don't."

Didn't anyone check their voice mail? Where was her mother? *Oh, that's right.* Her mother's graduation was today. Fancy smiled. A little. Picturing her mother walking down the aisle. Where was SaVoy? Damn, her wedding was yesterday. Where was Darius?

Somebody could've phoned. After all she'd been through, Fancy realized no one cared enough to take care of her. Immediately after the doctor recommended she visit a psychiatrist, Michael had left, claiming, "I'll call you later." The diversion of Michael's eye contact and the disappointed flat tone in his voice implied the opposite.

Elevating her bed, Fancy solemnly continued, "When it's time to leave, I'll take a taxi home."

Home, a once familiar word, was now a foreign place. Sure she had a house, but Fancy didn't have a home. Pinching her muffin, Fancy ate, and ate, and ate, until she'd consumed everything on her tray. Foods she'd never eaten or didn't eat anymore, soupy oatmeal with raisins, white toast, banana, coffee, tea, and milk, disappeared in minutes.

Fancy powered on her cell phone. One notch of battery life remained. The voice-mail indicator red light flashed. Pressing her Message button, Fancy entered her password and listened.

"Hi, Darius." *Beep, beep.*

With so much happening, Fancy had forgotten she'd forwarded Darius's messages.

"You know who this is. I, I, I forgot something . . ."*Beep, beep . . .* "Um, my medication at your house, and, well, I'd like to get my pills back. I'm glad we made love on your should-have-been wedding night because I'm gonna be your wife. I love you, too. Bye. Call me. Wait a minute. I called to be honest. Truth is, the reason I'm calling is to confess . . ."*Beep, beep, beep, beep.*

"Damn it!" Fancy tossed the phone on the cluttered stand beside her bed.

Too upset to cry, she dialed Darius's cellular from the hospital phone.

"At the sound of the beep, do you—" *Beep.*

Fancy slammed the handset on the base.

The nurse's head peeped inside the room. "Excuse me, Ms. Taylor, you have a visitor."

Frowning, Fancy hadn't noticed she'd left. She leaned forward. Her body was numb. "I don't want to see anyone right now." But wait until she saw that bitch Ashlee.

"Okay. I'll let him know."

Him? "Wait." Why should Fancy allow Ashlee to dictate her emotions? "Who is it?"

"A Mr. Desmond Brown. Should I send him in?"

Fancy's lips spread wide. Her spirit lightened. "Dez? Came all the way here to see me? Yes, please, send him in."

When Desmond entered the room, Fancy's jaw dropped. His hair was cropped low and neat. No more untamed Afro. Designer casual dress clothes: slacks, nice button-up shirt, polished shoes. His inviting cologne greeted her well before he stood next to her.

Standing at her bedside, Desmond said, "Hey, you. How are you?" Gently rubbing her uncombed hair, Desmond held her hand.

A manicure? Wow. Fancy was impressed. This was not the same pitiful man she'd dropped off at the airport the last time he'd visited.

Her hand trembled in his palm. "I'm fine, I guess."

Squeezing her fingers, Desmond sat, his hip touching hers. Gazing into her eyes, he said, "You don't always have to be a superwoman. I can tell you're hurting. You wanna talk about it? I'm a good listener, remember?"

"Dez, I don't know what to think. I'm just happy you're here."

"Excuse me. Ms. Taylor, you have another visitor."

Frowning, Fancy thought, *Oh no,* then asked, "Who is it?"

"Your mother."

Whew! Fancy thought, nodding, relieved and disappointed it wasn't Darius.

Caroline stood at the doorway wearing a blue gown and a blue cap. The blue and gold tassel dangled over the left side. A burgundy folder with gold engraving was clutched under her left arm. Glancing around the room, Caroline walked to the opposite side of the bed from Desmond. "I have something for you," she said proudly, placing the diploma in Fancy's hands.

"No, Mama, I can't take this."

"Well, baby, I wouldn't have it if it weren't for you. I wanted to give you something that was special to me. Oh, hello, Desmond."

"Hello, Ms. Taylor. Congratulations."

Silent tears rolled down Fancy's cheeks.

Desmond kissed her lips. "I'll be outside."

Fancy squeezed his hand.

Caroline said, "Desmond, you don't have to leave on my account."

"It's okay, Dez. Stay." Fancy was overjoyed with having so much love around her, she wanted it all.

Caroline opened the drawer beside Fancy's bed, removed a comb, and began untangling Fancy's weave. "What happened, sweetheart?"

Sweetheart. Her mother never called her sweetheart. The tightness in Fancy's throat choked her. "I'm not sure. Darius acted like he was excited about having a baby, and then I get a message from Ashlee saying she made love to Darius and left her pills in his house."

"Whoa," Desmond said, widening his eyes.

"Are you on sedation medication, baby?" Caroline asked. "Darius was excited about you having his baby and Ashlee doesn't live with him."

"Obviously, I'm confused. Pissed. Angry. I don't want to talk about him, or them, anymore. What's done is done. The people who truly love me are here with me now. Will you guys take me home? I'm ready to go."

"Excuse me. Ms. Taylor, you have another visitor."

"Who is it this time?"

"SaVoy Edmonds."

Fancy watched Desmond's eyes light up as he mouthed, "SaVoy's here."

Glad SaVoy wasn't with Tyronne, Fancy extended her arms, saying, "Move, Dez."

SaVoy's embrace was warm and loving. There was no need to exchange apologies for their last parting words. Fancy knew SaVoy was her best friend.

"Sorry I'm late. I had to use the restroom," Tyronne said, walking up, standing between SaVoy and Desmond.

Tyronne kissed SaVoy, then rubbed the small of her back before holding her hand. Then Tyronne gently grasped Fancy's hand.

"Hey, lady. How are you? You know whatever you need, we're only a phone call away." Then Tyronne kissed Fancy's forehead.

Fancy couldn't believe Tyronne's kindness. They'd fought since the day Tyronne and SaVoy started dating. "Thanks."

"I can't bash on you while you down. I'm saving my insults for the wedding reception."

Fancy laughed.

"Ty-ronne," SaVoy said. "We talked about this."

"I know. I'm kidding. But you know that's how Fancy and I communicate. We're not happy unless we're insulting one another."

Desmond moved between Caroline and SaVoy, so Tyronne moved to the other side of SaVoy.

SaVoy's hand wrapped around Fancy's. "Tyronne, Desmond, Ms. Taylor, hold hands and let's bow our heads in prayer. . . . Oh Heavenly Father, we gather here today to celebrate the homegoing of Fancy's unborn child. Heavenly Father, lift his spirit—"

"Her. I was having a girl."

"*Her* spirit into Your house. We know that You know best. We ask that You bless Fancy. Give her strength, Lord, to aid in a healthy and speedy recovery. Give her peace, Lord, to make it through the times when her family and friends aren't near. In Jesus' name, amen."

In unison Fancy said, "Amen," relieved that SaVoy didn't judge her. True friendship was about loving, not judging, and everyone, especially Tyronne, had proven that to Fancy. "How was the wedding?"

"The wedding is this weekend coming up," SaVoy answered.

Desmond grinned like a kid. So that's why Dez was in town.

"Sorry, with so much happening, I forgot," Fancy said, ignoring Desmond's overt attention toward SaVoy.

"Man, you better stop cheezin' so hard," Tyronne said, staring at Desmond.

"Baby, don't. Not with your friend. It's just Desmond."

There was something about the way SaVoy said "Just Desmond," that made Dez's smile vanish.

Kissing Fancy's forehead, SaVoy continued "Just don't forget. But if you can't make it, I'll understand. I see you're in good hands. We've got a few stops to make. I'll see you at your house."

Hugging SaVoy, Fancy said, "Thanks. You don't know how much this means to me."

"No thanks is necessary. We'll see you later."

"Don't I get a hug too?" Desmond pleaded.

SaVoy said, "This isn't about you. It's about Fancy," then walked out with Tyronne.

Caroline looked at Desmond and said, "Can we have a moment alone?"

"Sure, I'll be back." Desmond squared his shoulders, then abruptly left the room.

Caroline resumed combing Fancy's hair. "You know life is filled with challenges. Having us here right now I know is helping you. But we're not the father of your baby. That's who you really want to see. What Mama wants to know is, how do you feel about Darius?"

"Confused."

"Well, don't be like your mama. Forty-something and just figuring out how to deal with men. The best advice I can give you that I should've taken from my mother when I was your age but didn't is, love with your head, think with your heart."

"That's backward," Fancy countered.

"No, most people are backward. That's the truth."

"Then what are you saying?"

"My mother's response was, 'Caroline, when you love with your heart, you can't think straight. That's why you're confused.'"

"So I should move on and forget about Darius?" There were too many unanswered questions to walk away.

"No, sweetheart. That's not what Mama's telling you. You don't have to decide right now. Have a talk with Darius, then take time to make up your mind. But don't go to him. If Darius truly loves and wants you, he'll be a man about it and come to you."

CHAPTER 21

Ashlee

Shortly after sunrise, Ashlee grabbed little Darius's red, blue, and green toddler's suitcase, opened his drawers, and selected three changes of clothing. The basics of what she'd need for their impromptu getaway. Where? Anywhere outside of Texas's ridiculous laws. "D.C. That's a busy place where no one would recognize us." With Chocolate City's shortage of men, Ashlee would fair well on her own, not worrying about getting a man.

The diapers, stroller, and baby food were already in the car. One pair of shoes would do until they were out of town. Ashlee hoisted little Darius onto her hip, grabbed her purse, and locked the door. She put her son in his car seat, started the engine. "Oh, damn, I forgot my medication." Fumbling through her purse, Ashlee removed her house keys. "Baby, Mama'll be right back."

Leaving the car running, quickly, Ashlee ran inside. As she was wrapping her fingers around the yellow bottle on the end table, her phone rang. "Should I?" *At least check the caller ID.* Picking up the handset, whoa, she saw it was Darius.

Softly, Ashlee answered, "Hey, I'm glad you called. I need to tell you something."

Darius interrupted. "I can't talk long. I just called to say I'm sorry for all the wrong I've done you."

"Darius, do you mean it? I miss you so much. I want you to meet someone. Before I say who, do you love me?"

"Yes, I really am sorry. You've been good to me, Ashlee. I don't want to hurt you again. I mean that. Thanks. I gotta go—"

"Darius, don't hang—"

Click.

"—up," Ashlee whispered. She wanted to ask Darius if they could stay with him. CPS couldn't label her unfit if she was . . . if they were with Darius. Knowing he still loved her, he wouldn't refuse them when she showed up at his front door. Ashlee decided to drive west instead of east.

Oh my God, not again, Ashlee thought, running out the door to her car. Settling into the driver's seat, she exhaled. "Mommy sor—" Looking in the car seat, she screamed, "Aaaahhhhh!" Frantically she got out, opened the back door, and checked the floor. "Oh my God. Baby. Baby!" Ashlee leaned over as far as she could, checking under the seat. She swiped her hand deep under the passenger seat.

"Hello, Ms. Anderson. Looking for something, or shall we say someone?"

"You! You took my son! Where is he?" Facing Ms. Benson, Ashlee began wringing her hands to refrain from strangling that wicked witch of a caseworker.

Ms. Benson calmly said, "Ashlee, we need to talk. Let's go inside."

"Wait just one minute, you, you thief," Ashlee said, turning off her engine. "I want my son back! I'm going to call my father and have you arrested for kidnapping. You can't go around taking people's children!" Walking to Ms. Benson's car, Ashlee peeped inside the window. Little Darius wasn't there.

Calmly Ms. Benson, said, "What if I told you I didn't take your son?"

Breathing in Ms. Benson's face, Ashlee yelled, "Liar! Liar! Who else would've taken him?"

"We can go inside. Or I can leave and wait for you to come to my office or to court, but I'm not going to stand out here entertaining your outbursts."

Ashlee scanned her neighborhood. She was so consumed she hadn't noticed the neighborhood wives across the street watching. Ashlee narrowed her eyes toward them, pointing in their direction. "Get a day job! If I find out either one of you reported me, I'll make sure you get yours!"

Entering Ashlee's home, Ms. Benson said, "Ms. Anderson, your eruptive behavior and threats aren't helping your case any."

Marching inside three feet behind Ms. Benson, Ashlee yelled, "What case!" then slammed the door, rattling the pictures on the wall.

Ms. Benson didn't wait for an invitation to sit on the love seat. "Where's your husband?"

"You so smart, you tell me."

Ms. Benson stood. "I'll issue my report to my supervisor and we'll see you in court."

"Okay, please don't leave. I don't have one, satisfied?"

"How was your weekend?" she asked.

"Weekend? What are you talking about?"

"I'm starting from the beginning of our investigation. You rented an SUV in Los Angeles over the weekend. Reportedly you left your son alone in the car overnight. Tell me your side about your weekend."

She would bring that up. "That's a lie. I went for a wedding that didn't happen, so I came back home, but I did not leave my son in a car overnight."

Raising her brows, Ms. Benson asked, "Whose wedding? And before you answer, let me say, lying will hurt your chances of getting your son back."

"So you do have my son?" Ashlee became silent. When Ms. Benson didn't answer, Ashlee answered, "Darius Williams."

"Same name as your son's. The NBA player? Is he the father? Of your child?"

"What's it to you?" Ashlee thought about her brief conversation with Darius moments ago. Love was a hurting thing. Status was worthless if Darius didn't want them. Couldn't Ms. Benson see her pain? "What I'd like to know is, where is my baby and who reported me?"

"That's the least of your worries right now and both are confidential."

"So just because someone reports me, you can show up at my house and take my baby? Just like that?"

"Ms. Anderson, accept responsibility for your actions. You were the one who left your son in a running vehicle. Alone. We're placing him in protective custody."

"I'm not negligent. All new mothers make mistakes."

"Ms. Anderson, a mistake is forgetting to pack an extra change of clothing, or leaving the stroller at home. CSP doesn't remove children from their homes for parental mistakes."

"Okay, so it was an accident. I only came in to get my . . . It won't happen again. Please, I need my son," Ashlee pleaded, wringing her hands.

"Ms. Anderson, this is serious. You endangered your infant son. And my report shows Darius Williams Junior was taken to emergency shortly after he was born and diagnosed with oxygen deprivation. You'd better thank God your son doesn't have permanent brain damage. I read that the hospital kept your baby a few days for observation, but I don't know how that incident went unreported to us, so I'll have to investigate that as well, and I've already requested copies of your mental health records."

Ashlee feared the suicide attempts she'd shared in private with her therapist would be in the reports, along with the abortion pills incident, and how she hated Fancy. Salty tears burned her eyes. "He wrapped himself in the blanket one night. All babies wiggle in their sleep. How's that endangerment?"

Pressing her lips flatly together, Ms. Benson said, "Hmm, let me guess. Probably another accident, I suppose. You didn't check on him?"

"Whatever. I did check on him, but no one stays awake all night watching their baby."

"Let me explain a few things that'll perhaps help you understand my role."

"Fine," Ashlee said, leaning back on the sofa. The torn cushion pressing underneath the decorative cover began hurting her thighs.

Better for Ashlee to endure the pain than for Ms. Nosy to ask more questions.

"I'm not here to break up your family. It's the law that if someone suspects child abuse of any kind, sexual, physical, in your case, abandonment, whatever, they are obligated to report it to Child Protective Services or another authority who can properly investigate the matter. The reporter's identity is private and protected by law. All of your records you thought were secured become accessible to CSP. Now, I was considering allowing you supervised visitation, but from what I've heard here today, you're not quite ready."

"Considering. Allowing. Supervised visitation? Of my own son! How would you like it if somebody told you I was gonna let you see your child but I changed my mind!"

Standing, Ms. Benson, said, "Ms. Anderson, this case is far more serious than you realize. When we found your son, I asked my supervisor not to have you arrested. The jails are filled with mothers who are capable but unable to take care of their children, all because of the law and how it works. Ms. Anderson, I didn't want to add you to the list."

Flexing back one finger at the time, Ms. Benson continued. "Your son was in a running car. He could've died from carbon monoxide poisoning. The car could've shifted into gear. Someone could've driven off with your car not knowing, or worse, not caring that your child was inside. And I believe you did leave your son in that SUV overnight. You deserve to go to jail, but I found out that your father is a well-respected attorney in the community, so I'm giving you a break, but I'm not giving you back your son. I'm recommending you get medical help and I'll reevaluate your mental state in thirty days."

Leaping from the sofa like she'd been ejected, Ashlee yelled, "Thirty what?"

"I'm filing my case plan with the court, which will be reviewed at the hearing. Also, think about who you want to keep your son. We try to place the children with family. Does Mr. Williams live in Los Angeles?"

"No."

"Would he be interested in custody?"

"Hell no."

"Well, he does have parental rights too and he'll have to tell us no himself. We will contact him, and another relative like a sister or your mother can have temporary custody." Ms. Benson pulled out a business card, placed it on the coffee table, then concluded, "Good-bye."

"You can't leave me like this. I need my son!"

Not looking back, shaking her head, Ms. Benson left the door open.

Locking the door, Ashlee ran to her bedroom and dialed Darius's cell phone number.

Darius answered, "What are you, crazy? Stop fuckin' calling me and you'd better not call my fiancée again. And if you ever call her a bitch again, or come near her, I swear I'ma hurt you if you come near me or Fancy." Darius paused, then said, "Ashlee, whatever we had is over. You hear me, it's over!" Then he hung up.

"No, no, that's not true," Ashlee whispered into the receiver. What happened to make Darius angry again? Ashlee squeezed the phone so tight the blood rushed to her fingertips. "You've got to see your son before you marry Fancy. Better yet, I know what I'll do. I'll get my baby back, and just like the first time we'll wait until the wedding."

Ashlee had no real way to prove to Darius his son was alive, since she didn't know where CPS had placed him. She had to get little Darius before they contacted Darius. Ms. Benson was going to tell her where her son was today or somebody was going to get hurt.

CHAPTER 22

Jada

Lying in Darryl's arms, Jada was reassured she'd made the best decision. Living on a planet where men fulfilled their sexist desires, why shouldn't a woman have the best of both worlds too?

"Yes," she moaned, grinding her lips into Darryl's. "That feels so good you just don't know. Mmmmmmm."

Darryl's vibrations trembled on her clit as he said, "You still taste like chocolate."

Slowly, the ridges on his tongue massaged the folds of her pussy. The tip of his tongue explored her inside walls.

Felling her clit disappear between soft, succulent lips, Jada whispered, "Ohhhhh yessss."

Darryl suctioned a little faster, sticking his finger inside her wet pussy.

"Ummmm, yeesss," Jada grunted into the pillow.

In and out. Farther in, then out. Deeper and faster, Darryl's finger slid from her pussy into her asshole. His cottony lips sucked in rhythm with two fingers stroking her pussy and her ass at the same time.

Jada's body rose up from the bed, as she yelled the loudest "Yeessss!" repeatedly. From head to toe her body exploded in one orgasm after another until she collapsed back onto the guest bed.

"That's enough. Please stop," she begged, trying to catch her breath.

Darryl asked, "Are you finished?"

"For now, yes." Jada's breasts rose and fell continuously.

At one point she questioned whether she should've divorced Wellington when she discovered after years of marriage he was still having an affair with the same damn woman he'd fucked during their engagement more than twenty years ago. Why hadn't she signed the divorce papers when she had a chance? Before she'd learned her husband had prostate cancer? The papers were already drawn, in her hands, and all she had to do was scribble across the bottom line in permanent ink and she would've been a free woman. Naw, not free, fifty-plus and single. But she wouldn't have been an adulteress.

Until the doctor's report Wellington acted like he didn't need her. Now he not only needed her but professed he couldn't survive without her. Where was his Ms. Home-wrecker Thang, Melanie Thompson, now that Wellington was hospitalized? Maybe that was a question Jada shouldn't ask. Melanie had a way of showing up when least expected, like at the repast at Jada's mother's house after Jada's mother's funeral. Melanie was a bold, inconsiderate bitch.

Dressed in black from head to toe: purse, shoes, hat, veil, gloves. Melanie had steeped foot into Jada's mother's house. "Jada, I'm so sorry you've lost someone close to you again. My condolences."

Again? Jada had reached back. That bitch must have forgotten whom she was playing with. Maybe the first time Jada had knocked Melanie across the room hadn't been enough.

"Tell Wellington his wife said hello. If you need anything, just let us know." Melanie waved bye as though she'd won a Miss Universe contest. "Ciao."

Jada continued questioning herself as she wiggled from Darryl's embrace. Maybe the only reason she doubted her intentions was she felt somewhat guilty that Wellington was in the hospital and she'd had sex with Darryl several times, allowing him to practically move into their home. He was there every night, every morning. Darryl had clothes in the closet and draws in the drawers.

Darryl's body felt good. Natural. Jada couldn't remember how many years had gone by since she was sexed really good every night. She'd continued cheating on Wellington. With Darryl's hard erection buried in her pulsating pussy, she had one total-body orgasm after another in her dreams too. Emotional infidelity didn't count. If only for the moment, Jada felt like a new woman.

"Hey, where're you going?" Darryl asked, reaching out to her.

"To wash you off of me."

"To do what?" he asked with a half smile.

"Shower. I have to stop at the office before going to the hospital."

A man could smell another man on his woman. Jada didn't want Wellington inhaling Darryl's aroma.

"Yeah, me too. That boy of ours has the most successful, well-operated business I've seen. You taught him well. Makes my job easy, but I have to stay on top of things."

"We taught him well. Wellington and I, not you. Don't go claiming credit where it's not due. I don't want you to go to the hospital with us."

"Us?"

"Yeah, Darius came back last night."

Darryl smiled. "He did? And you was screaming like we were home alone, woman?"

"Nothing he hasn't heard before, I'm sure. Besides, I'm just glad he came back."

"That's my boy. Question, do you think Darius will approve of me giving Kevin a job at the company when he gets out next week?"

Jada's eyebrows reached for her hairline while her neck jerked back.

Darryl said, "Never mind, before you get all heated. I'll ask him myself. Well, I'ma hit the guest shower. Call me when you get to your office."

"Your office is only down the hall. I'll stop by on my way out."

When the home phone rang, Darryl picked up the cordless.

"Oh no, you don't. Give me that," Jada said, answering, "Hello."

"Hi, Mrs. Tanner?"

"Yes."

"I won't keep you long. This is Fancy's mother, Caroline. Could you give Darius a message from me?"

"He's here. You can—"

"No, just give him this message. . . ."

Jada listened until Caroline finished explaining what had happened to Fancy, then hung up the phone. Jada tapped on Darius's door. He didn't answer. Slowly she turned the knob.

"Yeah, Mom?" Darius said, lifting his head off the pillow.

"I have to go to the office for an hour or so. You can meet me at the hospital."

The telephone rang. Hastily, Darius answered, "Hello." He paused, then repeated, "Collect call from Candice who?"

Taking the phone from Darius, Jada said, "Darius, stop playing. Hello?"

"Collect call from Los Angeles County Jail from Candice Jordan. Will you accept?"

"Of course I'll accept."

"Hey, girlfriend," Candice said.

"What in the world are you doing calling from jail? That's why I haven't been able to reach you."

"Darius didn't tell you?"

Jada squinted at Darius. "Darius didn't tell me what?"

Darius hunched, tossed back the covers, and entered his bathroom.

"He had me arrested. I'm in jail."

"What! Darius Jones, what's wrong with you?"

Peeping through the door, Darius asked, "With me? Obviously she's withholding information so you'll get her trespassing ass out."

"Darius, stop it! Candice, I'm on my way, where are you? County? I know exactly where that is," Jada said, staring at Darius with his toothbrush in his hand.

"Ma. Don't leave me. I'm going with you."

"Then you need to get ready fast."

Jada closed Darius's door. Stepping into her bedroom, Jada stood in the middle of the floor glancing around. She had so many years of good memories with Wellington. Wellington was the only man who had slept, or would sleep, in their bed. That's why Darryl was relegated to the living room and guest bedroom. Jada showered, dressed. Darius was in the living room waiting for her.

"What's that?" she asked, looking at the envelope in his hand.

"Oh, I had the locks changed at my house. I told the locksmith to drop a set here. You ready?"

"Yeah," Jada said, exhaling.

Darius wrapped his arms around her shoulders. "I love you, Ma."

"I love you too." Jada embraced her son, appreciating his expression of love. She had things to do, places to go, but nothing was more important than living in the moment.

When Darius let go, he opened the front door for her. Opening his car door, he waited until she got in. Driving along the highway, Jada said, "Candice wasn't trespassing. I asked Candice to go to your house and collect the wedding gifts so I could return them. Why did you have to have her arrested?"

"I think Candice should be the one to tell you. Trust me, Ma, you know how she is and you're in no hurry to find out, so let's stop at the office first."

Exhaling, Jada said, "Fine, whatever. I don't have the energy or strength to argue. How's Fancy?"

"Ma, I don't want to talk about her. We're not getting married."

"No, baby. Why not? What—"

"Life. Murder. She killed my baby." Darius blinked repeatedly. "I can't marry a woman who doesn't care about my feelings."

"Darius, Fancy loves you. And if you loved her back, you would know that. Fancy's mother said she didn't kill your baby."

"Mom, don't side with them. Of course her mother is going to take her side."

"I'm not taking sides. Honey, Caroline called me this morning. She told me Fancy said the pills you gave her were abortion pills."

"What! That lying—"

"Darius, stop it right now! Before you go getting all upset you need to listen. I mean really listen to Fancy. Don't be like me.

Drawing conclusions and making decisions on your own, only to find out years later you made the worst decision of your life. That girl loves you."

"Ma, why didn't you tell me she'd called?"

"Darius, I've got enough to worry about with Wellington, Candice, and Darryl, I don't need to get caught up in your drama. For once, can you just be a man and handle your business?"

"Be a man about it," Darius repeated. "Drama?" He became silent. Parking in front of her office building, he said, "I'll be up in a minute."

Jada quietly closed the passenger door. None of what Caroline had told her made sense, but she'd learned a long time ago that a lot of things in life that were true didn't make sense.

"Good morning, Ms. Tanner," Jada's secretary said, hurrying from behind the desk to give her hug.

"Good morning. And thanks for working the long hours."

"Don't mention it. Jazzmyne takes excellent care of everyone. She brings or orders breakfast, lunch, and she even orders dinner when we work late. She's so nice."

Jada nodded and smiled. Jazzmyne was the kind of employee, woman, and friend who didn't ask what needed to be done, she'd just do it.

Entering her office, she saw that everything looked the same except the dozen fresh red roses with one yellow one in a vase by the window.

"Here's a cup of coffee, Ms. Tanner," her secretary said setting the cup on her desk and turning on her computer. "The flowers were delivered this morning from your husband."

"Thanks," Jada said. "Close my door behind you."

As she sat at her desk admiring the roses, tears splattered into her coffee cup. The screen saver on her computer vanished, turning black.

Somberly shifting her eyes back to her cup, Jada sipped, then inhaled the fresh-roasted coffee. No one was inside her office. No one was listening to her but God. Today, other than trying to center her spirit, get in touch with her inner peace, and trying not to cross that fine line from sanity into insanity, nothing else mattered.

Jada was more than a businesswoman. In addition to owning and operating her company, she was a mother, a wife, and a best friend to Candice and Jazzmyne. But none of those people could help heal Jada's heart.

Jada couldn't force Darius to get married, but she knew Fancy was the only woman her son ever loved, and if Darius let Fancy get away, like his father, he'd add himself to a long list of men who regretfully married the wrong woman, someone other than their soul mate.

"Huuuhhh, I can't leave Wellington in his time of need. I just can't do it. I know he'd stay with me if I were the one diagnosed with cancer. I did marry him for better or worse. Damn it! Why am I having doubts now?" Jada screamed, plunking the silver spoon into the china cup. Pushing away from her desk, she grabbed her head, pressing her palms into her temples. Pacing from one end of her office to the other, Jada suddenly dropped to her knees and cried aloud, "God, why me! Haven't I suffered enough? Haven't I given enough? My father! My mother! Dead! My selfish son! Is this Your way of testing me? Why me, Lord!"

A faint tap on her door was followed by the whispering voice of her secretary. "Ms. Tanner. Are you okay?"

Oh my gosh! How much did she hear?

Crawling into her swivel chair, Jada propped her elbow on the desk, pressed her forehead into her palm, and then closed her watery eyes. *Okay, focus on your breathing.* "Calm down," Jada whispered. Refusing to suppress her emotions, she yelled, "No, go away!"

Ring, ring.

Jada retrieved her cell phone from her purse. Looking at the caller ID, she sniffled, then half smiled, answering, "Hello," trying to disguise the sadness in her voice.

"Hey, you. I know you're not over there moping over what to do about your husband," Darryl said.

"You know me too well, and I've told you too much and allowed you to get too close."

"Actually, you haven't told me enough. I didn't want to say this last night, but I know you're not happy in your marriage. You're stuck between doing what's best for him and doing what's right for you. And you have such a big heart, you'd never leave anyone while they were down."

"You know, you're right. I thought no one understood. But the bottom line is, like it or not, I am a married woman."

"And you know I've been in your life since we were kids. I am the father of our son. And I know you better than you know yourself. Right now you need to stop pacing around your office and you need someone to listen to all that stuff going on in your head instead of talking to yourself."

"Maybe it's just karma. I haven't exactly been a saint myself, you know."

"And neither have I. Who has? But that doesn't mean you should . . . Look, just let me go to the hospital with you. Bye."

Dropping her cell phone into her purse, Jada entered her private restroom, washed her face, and reapplied her makeup. "Thank God I look better than I feel."

When she walked into the lobby, Darius and Darryl were waiting.

"Hey, you," Darryl said, smiling as he embraced Jada.

"Hi. Thanks," Jada replied, allowing Darryl to hold her in his arms. His grip was affectionate. Her sexual desires intensified. Why should she feel guilty? Wellington had fucked Melanie on several occasions. Jada's pussy quivered as she eased out of Darryl's arms.

Sarcastically, Darius said, "Mom, not in the office in front of your selfish son. You're embarrassing me."

Jada looked at them and said, "You're so vain, you're right. For the first time, my life isn't about you. Let's go and get Candice. Then we'll go to the hospital to see Wellington."

"Mmmmm, yeessss," Darius mimicked. "I take after you."

CHAPTER 23

Fancy

Fancy lounged at her quaint three-bedroom home along Malibu Beach. Easing out of bed, she entered her office, locked the door, then sat at her desk with pen and paper. Every single word was personal, intentional, and purposeful. Typing a letter wouldn't have sent him the same message.

Dear Darius,

First, I've enclosed all of your keys: homes and cars. I don't understand why you pretended you were excited about us having a baby, then you give me abortion pills and kill our daughter. For that, I will never forgive you. A part of me hates you and wishes I'd never met you, while the other part still loves the Darius I used to know. Your lies and deceit are more than I care to deal with. I thought about pressing charges to teach you a lesson, but I can't. Even though you've wronged me. I can't find it in my heart to hurt you. So I'm letting go. Darius, you were never there for me when I needed you. I take that back, yes, you were. You saved my life, then took life away from me. Darius, you've changed, and as a result, you've changed me. My heart can never love or trust you the same. This is no way to start a marriage, so to finalize everything, I'm mending my broken heart and I'm giving you back your ring.

Love,

Ladycat

Sliding the five-carat platinum solitaire off her finger, Fancy placed the princess cut in a small white box. Her heart was heavy, her spirit lighter. Her heart ached but there were no tears. Why should she be sad or depressed over a man who couldn't love her back? That was his loss. Maybe he'd learn how to love the next woman. Fancy would remember the good times, and unlike Ashlee, she'd move on.

Fancy bundled the letter, keys, and ring into a large envelope, walked into the kitchen, and said, "Good morning, Mama."

"Hey, baby. How you feelin'?"

"I'm good." Handing her mother the envelope, Fancy continued, "I need for you to drop this off at Darius's house for me today."

Caroline shook the contents. "What's in it?"

"His ring and things."

Intensely shaking her head, Caroline gasped "Baby, you never give back the ring. You earned that gorgeous rock. It's yours."

"Some things aren't worth holding on to. Mama, you keep the ring when you want to keep the man; otherwise, the ring is meaningless."

"Chile, you know I disagree, but if you insist, I'll drop off the package after breakfast."

"Mama, I'm trying to love Darius with my head. And I'm sorry I missed your graduation."

Caroline smiled, then hugged Fancy. "You're a fast learner. But, sweetheart, you didn't miss a thang at the ceremony. Those folk were all half my age."

"Then I missed a lot. I love you too, Ma." Fancy kissed her mother on the cheek and returned to her bedroom. Opening the patio doors, she joined Desmond and SaVoy on the white wooden deck.

"Good morning," Fancy said, occupying the surprisingly empty seat between them.

"How you feel?" Desmond asked.

"Fine, physically." Looking at SaVoy, Fancy continued. "Emotionally, don't ask."

Desmond held Fancy's hand. "When SaVoy called me, I got on the first plane headin' out of Atlanta."

Fancy said, "And I appreciate you two so much."

Desmond probably changed his reservation to depart a few days early. Fancy couldn't express how loved she felt seeing them at the hospital.

"Where's your mom?" Desmond asked. "She said she was going to join us out here." He inhaled, stretched his arms wide, and said, "I could do this every day. This is living. On the beach!"

Maybe he could, at a different house. After that brief stay with Darius, unless Fancy was married first, she wasn't cohabiting at his place or hers.

Fancy answered, "In the kitchen cooking breakfast. She'll bring breakfast to us."

SaVoy said, "You know your mom changed her mind about you raising her baby. She doesn't want to tell you because she doesn't want to upset you."

Exhaling, trying not to become annoyed, Fancy calmly replied, "That's cool either way. I promised my mom so she can change her mind again."

"After all you've been through, I thought you'd be relieved. That's very Christian-like. God challenges us when we don't praise Him. Give your life to God, girlfriend. He is blessing you to bless others. Don't be bitter toward men. Keep your heart open," SaVoy said with a smile.

There went SaVoy throwing out the baby with the bathwater. Obviously she'd wanted to approach this topic before she returned to Oakland. What was her point?

Fancy eyed her girlfriend, then said, "SaVoy, everyone does not praise God the way you do. I'm not the type of person who's going to go to church every Sunday morning, then become hypocritical like some of you so-called Christians talking bad about your church members and friends on Sunday evening. I know you talk about me behind my back, SaVoy, because you're always judging me to my face. I'm not going to sit around listening to some preacher who makes me feel guilty about everything I do. I relate to God in my own special way and I honestly try my best to help people and treat them right. If I'm going to hell for living by the Golden Rule, then so be it. But you are not my Savior. As far as my mother is concerned, my mom and I finally have a mother-daughter relationship. You don't have to feel like it's your duty to report back to me what my mother confides in you. She'll talk to me when she's ready."

Desmond interrupted. "We're all just glad that you're okay. Especially me."

Since SaVoy didn't counter her comment about talking behind her back, her silence confirmed Fancy's beliefs. Fancy asked SaVoy, "How long are you here?"

"My flight leaves tomorrow. Gotta finish planning for the wedding."

"I'm still your maid of honor. And I will be there."

Desmond followed with, "We'll be there."

Fancy looked at her two best friends and said, "I hate to admit it but I was jealous watching how you looked at SaVoy when she walked into my hospital room."

"Fancy, you never have to be jealous of any woman when it comes to me. I was just happy to see SaVoy. And I was messing with Tyronne because he's so paranoid and doesn't want any man, including me, close to SaVoy. Now, I can admit that at one time I was interested in SaVoy. When she first started dating my boy."

SaVoy's head snapped in Desmond's direction. "What? I never knew that."

"Honestly, what I was attracted to wasn't you, SaVoy, but what you represent. You're every man's dream for an ideal wife and mother. Good-looking. Mixed features, more white than black. Nice. Educated. Independent."

"And still a virgin," SaVoy added.

"I was getting to that. That too. But the truth is I'm in love with Fancy. She's sexy. Smart. And if I can say, sexually experienced. Definitely more black than white. Fancy is a challenge. But a good challenge. Good girls become boring after a while. It's like once you know them, you know them. There's nothing new or exciting about them. Whereas womanly women always keep a man on his toes because he never knows what the, excuse my expression, fuck she's going to do next."

Fancy didn't respond. She drifted with the waves washing the sand onto, then away from, the beach, wondering how Darius felt about not being with her. Was he lonely? Did he miss her? Did he care?

"Well, Tyronne will never grow tired of me. We're saved. I'm going to see if your mom needs help," SaVoy said. She kissed Desmond on the cheek, then patted Fancy on the head. "When love calls, you better choose right this time, girlfriend."

Fancy replied, "I chose right with Darius Williams. Darius wasn't a mistake. God doesn't make any mistakes. And I don't have any regrets. Everything happens for a reason."

SaVoy said, "You know what, you're right," then disappeared through the patio doors into Fancy's bedroom, mumbling, "Lord, help her, for she knows not what she says."

SaVoy had better not get too comfortable with Tyronne. Fancy didn't care how saved Tyronne was, he was from the streets of Oakland and chasing women was in his blood. Game recognized game, was the reason Fancy clashed with Tyronne. Street sense came with benefits, like next week Tyronne would have full access to SaVoy's father's commercial property to start his business. SaVoy couldn't see it but she was Tyronne's hopefully one-way ticket out of the ghetto. If marrying SaVoy and worshiping her God was all he had to do, "Let the church say, amen."

Fancy waited until SaVoy was out of sight. "Dez, thanks for coming. I mean that," she said, gripping his hand.

Kneeling on one knee, never letting go of Fancy's hand, Desmond removed a small black box from his pocket.

Fancy cried. Shaking her head, she covered her mouth. "Dez, no. Please, don't. This isn't right."

Flashing back, Fancy recalled the first time Desmond proposed.

Cupping her hand over her mouth, Fancy had choked. That little-bitty-ass stone could hardly be considered a diamond. Some jeweler must have discovered a way to fuse two granules of sugar together and make them sparkle. Then that loser must have used the world's smallest tweezers to set it in sterling silver. Fancy had turned away, shaking her head in disbelief.

Would she coldheartedly reject Desmond a second time? The answer partially remained unrevealed inside the white box.

"Fancy, yes. I have to ask one last time. I need to know that you love me the way that I love you. Fancy Taylor, will you marry me?"

Fancy swallowed hard. She was happy that the doctor reported her HIV test was nonreactive. What about Darius? Had her heart dissolved their relationship? Soon as she got away from Desmond, Fancy was calling Mandy to beg for an appointment and she wasn't accepting no for an answer.

Fancy lovingly gazed into Desmond's eyes, thinking about what her mother had told her, and replied, "My head says yes. My heart says . . ."

CHAPTER 24

Darius

Darius watched as his mom narrowed her eyes at him. Her lips crunched into an O. Darius grabbed his keys quietly, waiting for his mom to leave her office. Avoiding an unwanted confrontation, he felt it was best not to say anything. Following his parents out of Black Diamonds, he'd heard them making love on several occasions. What he actually heard was his mother moaning, which let him know, like father, like son, his old man had his woman screaming so loud her echoes of ecstasy traveled across three rooms into Darius's bedroom.

Darius drove to the hospital staring straight ahead, avoiding eye contact with his mom, who was shifting restlessly in her seat. Guess his dad also saw his mom was upset, 'cause he hadn't said a word.

The car was silent until his mother spoke. "Darius, you should say hello to Wellington when we get to the hospital. After all, he did raise you."

"Sure, Mom. Anything for you," Darius replied, looking in his rearview mirror at his dad, who was reclining across the backseat.

"I don't know how I'm going to work all of this out. I need to pick up Candice too. Darius, honey, could you—"

"No, Mom. Don't ask."

"Son, that's not the way to talk to your mother."

"Sorry, Ma. If you seriously want me to go and get her out, I will." When? was the question his mother should ask.

Darryl commented, "Out from where?"

"I didn't tell you. Candice is locked up because of Darius."

"Because of me? She's the one snooping in our houses. Ma, I have X-rated videos of you and my dad that Candice recorded."

"Stop your damn lies, Darius!" his mother screamed, slapping his arm. "You don't have to make up stories. If you don't want to get her out, just say so."

"Wait a minute," Darryl said, grabbing Jada's shoulder. "Darius needs to go to Atlanta to take his physical. I tell you what, I'll bail Candice out. Baby, you go see Wellington and I'll meet you at the hospital later. Son, you go home and get ready for your trip."

Why did she have to lay hands on him? All he did was tell the truth. Women. Staring ahead, Darius said, "Fine by me." After his mother's episode, he would never have gotten Candice out.

Darius imagined what his mother would say after Candice told the truth. "Oh, I'm sorry, sweetie, it's just that you lie so much, I didn't believe you." And he was the one who didn't accept responsibility for his actions. Yeah, right.

"That's fine," Jada agreed.

Gladly, Darius dropped his mom off at the hospital first, drove his dad back to his mom's house, then headed home. Cruising into his driveway, he spotted Ciara parking in front of his house. "Damn, I forgot she was coming over with lil' man today."

Approaching her car, he said, "Hey, you're looking good."

Ciara sported a slappin' new, at least new to him, hairstyle, slicked on the sides, loosely curled on top, cut close along her neckline. She'd lost a few pounds too.

"Hi, Darius. This is my son, Solomon."

That kid was definitely breast-feeding. Ciara's double-Ds had enlarged to a triple. Man, was that what having a kid did for a woman? If his HIV test was negative, he was tearing Ciara's pussy up the first chance she'd give him. Darius didn't care if he was married, fucking his wife on the regular. He couldn't say no to his ex-wife. Darius vowed never to jam his Johnson raw again. Fucking familiar pussy wasn't cheating. Ciara's pussy had his name stamped on it and he had unlimited access. At least he'd hope so.

Holding Solomon, Darius tickled his stomach. "Hey, lil' man. What's up?"

Solomon smiled, drooling on Darius's new shirt.

Darius looked at Ciara. "I only stopped home to pack."

"You're leaving?" Ciara asked, drying Solomon's lips with his bib.

"Yeah, but I'll be back. Gotta go to ATL to take my NBA physical. Got a lot on my mind these days." Especially the fact that his forty-eight hours expired tonight.

"I can just about imagine. Well, I can help," Ciara said, handing Darius a white letter-sized envelope.

Grasping the edge, Darius quizzically stared at Ciara. "You sure this is gonna help? What is it?"

Ciara smiled, then said, "Your divorce papers."

One eyebrow lifted, the other lowered. "Are you serious?" Darius said, grinning and inserting his finger into the opening. Unfolding the certified document, he kissed Ciara on her succulent lips. Those were his lips. "Whoa. You have no idea how much this means to me," he said, kissing her again.

"Yes, I do. Now get to Atlanta," Ciara said, reaching for Solomon, "You can hang out with Solomon another time. Call me and let me know what your doctor says. If you need me to do anything, let me know."

Darius's spirit filled with appreciation. Why the sudden change of heart with Ciara? He would definitely call her when he returned and, as promised, hang out with Solomon. Maybe Ciara would let him be Solomon's godfather. When Ciara drove off, the mailman drove up, handing Darius several envelopes. Sitting in his car, he selected the letter from Texas Superior Court, then placed the others in the passenger seat. "What's this?" Hopefully not another woman claiming he was the father of her child. "I'll open this piece later."

Looking up the driveway, he saw an unfamiliar car entering, parking where Ciara's car once was. Darius peeped through his windshield. The woman got out of the car, wobbling up to his window.

"Caroline?" he asked, already knowing but not believing his eyes.

"Who else?" Caroline said, handing him an envelope. "Fancy asked me to hand-deliver this to you."

Reaching for the package, Darius said, "Can you come inside for a moment?"

"Sure. For a moment. I've got things to do."

Frowning, Darius asked, "How soon before your delivery? Is Fancy still going to adopt your baby?" Darius escorted Caroline through the front door. He wanted to know Fancy's decision because he didn't want an instant family unless the kid was his. Darius sat on the sofa beside Caroline, placing the envelope on the table.

"No, I might not be the perfect mother but I'm a better person than when I raised Fancy."

"Ms. Taylor, I want you to know that I never meant to hurt your daughter. I love Fancy."

"Men never mean to hurt us but somehow always do. Fancy loves you. In many ways you've opened her heart. And sometimes we make people better persons, not for ourselves but for others."

Swallowing hard, Darius asked, "What are you saying?"

"For the first time, my daughter and I have a real relationship. I saw how happy she was with you and thought, why can't I make my daughter happy? Not like you. Like a mother should. All she ever wanted was for me to love her back. So when you hurt her the most, I loved her the most."

"Wow." Darius blinked repeatedly. "So how is she? I wanted to call her—"

Caroline interrupted. "But. Real men never have buts. Other men always have a but. An excuse. Or some sort of distorted justification for their lame attempts to explain what they *were* gonna do. Problem is, the but never ends up with them accepting responsibility for their actions, so as far as I'm concerned, you can save your buts for someone else. Not my daughter. If you love my daughter, show her, let her know. If you don't, no buts, let her go." Caroline paused, stood, then said, "You might want to open that envelope first, then listen, don't talk at her, or counter everything she says or cut her off when she's trying to explain. Call her, before it's too late. I've gotta go. Take care of yourself, Mr. Williams. Oh yeah. One more thing. Money buys opportunities, not happiness. And damn sure nuff not my daughter."

Darius was speechless, watching Fancy's mother leave. She'd gained a lot of weight but looked really healthy. Her self-esteem was high and Darius could feel the love Caroline displayed for Fancy. Staring at the package, he debated on opening it, or calling Fancy. Either could make him love Fancy more or less.

Picking up his cell phone, Darius dialed Fancy's number.

"Hi, I take it you've read my letter," she answered.

"Naw, not yet. Ladycat, before you say anything else, I need to see you."

"Didn't you get my package?"

"Yes, but I mean, I need to hear what happened at the hospital."

"Darius, it doesn't matter. All you care about is yourself."

"Don't say that. Ladycat, please give me another chance."

"To do what? Use me? The way you used Ashlee? Look, I've got to go. I wish you well. And press star seventy-three on your home phone. I'm tired of getting your crazy messages from Ashlee. I saved the most important one on my phone in case I decide to . . . since you didn't believe me, maybe you'll believe her. Oh, and I want to thank you for helping me find my true love. Bye, Darius."

Darius remained silent but hopeful as the *da-doop* resonated from his blue-tooth headset, ending their conversation.

Hopefully, not showing up in Atlanta hadn't squashed his deal. Darius decided to enlist his parents for help. Opening the envelope, he read *Dear Darius . . . First, I've enclosed all of your keys: homes and cars . . . This is no way to start a marriage, so to finalize everything, I'm taking back my heart and I'm giving you back your ring.*

Rolling the diamond between his thumb and fingers, Darius wasn't giving up that easily. The letter was Fancy's way of venting while pleading to get back together. True love didn't end with words on paper. Fancy would have to prove to Darius that she didn't love him the way he loved her.

CHAPTER 25

Darryl

If every breathing body didn't have a personal agenda, shame on them for being live bait, suckered, used. Second chances didn't always come. Best to make relationships work the first time around if one was genuinely interested. Twenty-plus years had passed since Darryl felt his dick inside Jada.

Often, months, years, lifetimes divided lovers: coast-to-coast marriages, unwanted spouses, commitments to the kids, careers, family values, new homes, and the list went on. Regardless of the circumstances, distant lovers were doomed. No man would abstain from having sex simply because he was in love. A woman was different. She could go without riding, rubbing, or sniffing a dick for a whole year if she believed her man was monogamous too. But if the lovers were in close proximity, no more than a few cities or miles apart, close enough to get it on, on the regular, they could maintain some sorta relationship.

Glad his only obstacle was getting Jada to say yes, Darryl decided to reunite with the only woman he'd loved. Jada was beautiful, wealthy, and on the verge of becoming a widow. Darryl had respected his body. Easily he could subtract ten years off his age. He was happily divorced; unfortunately broke.

Broke to a millionaire wasn't the same as to a nine-to-five employee living paycheck to paycheck. What Darryl disliked most, his lifestyle had diminished. Working for Darius significantly improved his bottom line. Not nearly enough. Thankfully, Darryl a plan. An agenda.

Once Darius signed his NBA contract, Darryl would become his agent, traveling around the country during basketball season. Darryl would groom Kevin to take over his position at Somebody's Gotta Be on Top, and together they could focus on creating their own empire. God blessed the child who had his own.

Any man could see there was something special about Jada. A few decades ago, if he weren't young, cold, callous, careless, arrogant, inconsiderate, and selfish, he would've married her then instead of acting a fool, running away from his obligations only to settle with a woman who didn't have a pot to piss in or a window to throw it out of until the judge awarded her a huge settlement. It was easier for Darryl to play the reverse psychology game, piss Jada off by saying Darius wasn't his child, then move on with his life, never calling her again and hoping she'd do the same.

Like father, like son. When it came to women, Darius was his clone. Darryl knew it when he'd shown up at one of Darius's elementary school basketball games. Darryl was married. Jada was married to Lawrence. Wellington was at the game sitting beside Jada. Darryl felt useless that Jada didn't need him, so he signed Darius's autograph, then pretended he didn't know that Darius was his son. Darryl especially knew Darius was his when he'd heard his son tell Fancy, "All you bitches are just alike." Verbatim, those were the regrettable words Darryl had spoken to Jada when she'd said, "I called to tell you I'm pregnant."

"And?" he had questioned, knowing damn well he could've been the father. But another baby didn't fit into his paycheck. That would've cramped his leisure trips around the world with new pussy on every layover.

"And what?" Jada had defensively asked.

"So who's the father? Not me. I know because I pulled my snake out of your pussy the last time we fucked."

Fucked. Naw, Darryl never fucked Jada. Every time they were together he made love to her. Last night was beautiful as he prayed for many more nights of holding her in his arms. Darryl was patient, passionate, and attentive to her every desire. Basically that was all women wanted. Attention. Appreciation. Affection. But it was Jada who fucked up back then when she decided she couldn't wait for him to make a commitment. Darryl had lived for the day his perks would roll in, showering him with groupies riding his dick, two, three, four, the more the merrier, dippers in his bed at a time taking turns. Darryl was happy as hell back then. Jada would've been miserable like his ex-wife, who still complained about giving him the best years of her life. Whose fault was that? She could afford to start all over. He couldn't.

"Well, I'm not one hundred percent sure it isn't yours."

That meant Jada had been double-dippin' between Wellington and him. What man wanted to lay claims to a maybe baby and risk finding out nine months later it wasn't his?

"Well, look-a-here. Call me when you're ninety-nine point ninety-nine percent sure. I know the routine all too well. I thought you were different, but all you bitches are just alike . . . You'd better call Wellington—Mr. lover-boy, financial adviser—Jones and let him foot the bill. I don't believe this bullshit. Pregnant?"

Darryl couldn't undue what he'd done, but he'd straight-up punked out. Voluntarily allowed another man to raise his son until all the hard work was done. The foundation was laid. The house was built. Wellington had raised Darius from day one. All Darryl had done was exterior decorating, making his fatherly roll pleasing to the eye while his son was still fucked up on the inside.

Darryl sat in the waiting room with Jada and Darius. He felt like he'd died and gone to heaven. Jada was still as beautiful as the day he'd met her. She shouldn't have had to raise Darius without him. Nodding, Darryl thought, she did it all. Without him. Never complained. And she'd done a hell of a job. If he could do it all over again, things would be different. Yesterday was gone, but he had today, and hopefully tomorrow, if Jada and Darius would allow him full-time involvement in their lives, irrespective of Wellington's outcome.

Interrupting his thoughts, Darius said, "Hey, Dad?"

"Yes, Son."

"I need your help."

"Anything, Son." After all these years he still had a chance to make a difference.

The nurse entered, saying, "Mrs. Tanner, your husband is asking for you."

Jada stood slowly. No smile accompanied her underlying glow.

"Ma, you want me to go with you?" Darius asked, springing to his feet. "This is why I came back. To be here for you."

"No, baby," Jada softly replied, "I'll be all right. But you can come in later and talk to Wellington."

While Darius gave Jada a long embrace, Darryl wanted to ask Jada to ask Wellington if it was okay for a quick visit. Darryl had never thanked Wellington for raising his son, but he wanted to. Maybe this wasn't a good time.

"No matter how long, Ma, I'll be right here when you come back. If you need me, send the nurse. I love you."

Darryl felt the love-filled tears between Jada's and Darius's eyes, making his eyes watery too.

After Jada departed with the nurse, Darryl asked, "What is it, Son?"

"What's what? Oh, my assistant coach said I had to be back in Atlanta for my physical with the team doctor by tonight."

"Or?"

"Or I'm losing my contract."

"Nonsense." Nothing was lost in faith. Darryl had to protect his interest. Darryl never believed in speaking with anyone who wasn't in a position to make a final decision, so he bypassed the assistant and went straight to the head coach. If necessary, Darryl would call the manager and the owner. He pulled out his cell phone, scrolled through his phone book, and placed a call to an associate who happened to be the head coach.

"Yeah, hey, what's up?" Darryl nodded.

"Everything's great," the head coach replied. "What's up with you, Williams?"

"At the hospital with my son. We have a family emergency and it'd be appreciated if he could have another week or two to take his physical."

"Sure thing. I believe in family values. You know that. I'll tell my assistant, but we can't give Darius more than one week."

"He'll be there. Thanks," Darryl said, hanging up. Looking at Darius he said, "You have one week."

"Straight up? How'd you do that?"

"People respect me. It's not what you do. It's how you do it. That's what I keep trying to teach you. You divorce Ciara yet?"

Darius nodded. "She handed me my papers today. I'm a free man."

Once less item on Darryl's to-do list. "Let me see," Darryl demanded.

Frowning, Darius said, "I left them at home. You don't trust me either?"

"I trust you. I don't trust her. Speaking of trust, how do you feel about Kevin working for me?"

Shaking his head, Darius answered, "Hell no, end of conversation. Changing the subject, Fancy had an abortion."

"Son, pro-choice does not apply to men. Abortion is a woman's prerogative as well as everything else she does. There's nothing on earth more complex than a woman. She wants you to figure her out. You can't control her. That was Fancy's choice. But I will say that you must've done something to make her feel you wouldn't be there for them. No woman wants to raise a kid alone."

"But Mom said Fancy is claiming I gave her abortion pills."

"Did you?"

Shaking his head, Darius said, "No, all I gave her was the same two aspirins that she was getting ready to take when I walked into the kitchen."

Darryl drilled Darius with, "If she was getting ready to take the pills, then why did you have to give them to her? Start from the beginning."

"It all started when I didn't change my locks, and Ashlee was in my house when Fancy and I returned, but Fancy never knew Ashlee was there . . ."

Darryl laughed.

"What's funny, Dad? This is serious."

"You're right. This is serious. You need to grow up. I'm surprised that to be a so-called playa, you know nothing about women. Son, Ashlee put the abortion pills in the aspirin bottle."

CHAPTER 26

Darius

"Come on, baby, move your ass," Darius said.
Midafternoon traffic was bumper-to-bumper on the loop.
Abruptly hitting her brakes every few seconds, the woman in front
of him couldn't keep up with the flow. "I bet she's a bad fuck,"
Darius said, tuning the radio to 102.5. Rush hour was not his pre-
ferred bump-'n-grind.

"This is Michael Baisden. The Bad Boy of Radio coming at you.
Today's topic is Sex 101. Ladies, does your man know what he's
doing in the bedroom? Call me now at 1-866 . . ."

Although Michael said "Ladies," Darius couldn't resist dialing
in. Waiting for someone to answer, he said, "Hell no. That's why I
get so much pussy."

"Caller, you're on, who is this?"

"Slugger," Darius arrogantly said.

"So I take it you know what you're doing in your bedroom."

"Man, I don't need a bedroom. All I require is a female volun-
teer. Mike, check this out. Male or female, you can spot a bad lover
a mile away. I'll give you three examples. First, observe everything
about how they eat. While not preferred, sloppy can be a good
thing, but what you're looking for is patience and passion. Pay attention to the rhythm of their walk. Slouchy, lazy, or sluggish is all
bad and if they use their hands to get up from a chair, their legs

are weak and you'll end up doing all the work. Then, ask 'em their wildest sexual fantasy. Pay attention to the details. If a man says he wants to do a ménage à trois and stop there, he's clueless and has zero imagination."

"I heard that, Slugger. Listeners, y'all got that lesson down? This is the Bad Boy of Radio, Michael Baisden. Next caller, who's this?"

Darius happily exited downtown, navigating his way along in search of, was it Peachtree Lane, Road, Boulevard, Street, Circle, Drive, or Avenue? Boulevard, that was it.

Yes, the land of the Georgia peaches. Darius's mouth watered as he thought about all the naturally sweet pussy. He'd have bushels with pussies spilling over the rims, if what he'd heard was true about the high population of gay brothas in the ATL. One he could name personally. K'Nine had better not try that shit again.

Darius sat in his rental car outside the doctor's office. After his father broke down the details to his mother about the physical, she'd pleaded for Darius not to jeopardize his contract. Mom insisted he immediately go to Atlanta, take his exam, and then return directly to L.A. "No detours," she'd emphatically said, shaking her finger. When had his mother become so frustrated? Pointing. Slapping. Yelling. Darius wanted to stay an extra day and get busy, but he'd do the right thing for his mom now and rake in the honeys like leaves later.

"Okay, dawg. This is it." Darius tapped his forehead, chest, then left and right shoulders. Remotely locking the door, he straightened his black slacks and button-down long-sleeve shirt. Smoothing his locks into a ponytail, he glanced at his image in the window.

"You look almost as good as me, brotha," a fine-ass sista said, strutting by.

What was that supposed to mean?

Darius scratched his hairless chin, wanting to bark at her to prove he was all man, but he didn't. He watched her humongous, bodacious booty juggle a sheer yellow dress that divided her cheeks into two phat cantaloupes.

"Whew! Focus, dawg, focus."

Entering the doctor's office, Darius checked in with the receptionist, took a seat, and waited, thinking about what he'd do if the results were positive. If Fancy stayed with him, there was nothing he couldn't do. He'd get his woman back. But how?

Darius's cell phone rang, interrupting his thoughts. Blocked ID. What the hell? He couldn't talk long anyway. He answered, "Hello."

"Hi, Mr. Williams?"

"Yes."

"Mandy has an opening late tomorrow. Six p.m. Would you like to come in?"

"Your timing couldn't be better. I'll be there. Thanks. Later."

"Darius Williams," the assistant announced, walking toward him with a chart. "Dr. Chase is ready for you."

Quietly, Darius stood, followed the assistant into the doctor's office. Glancing around, he noticed a black leather bed with a white tissue lining, a medicine cabinet, and supplies on the countertop: needles, swabs, and six empty tubes.

"Hello, Mr. Williams."

"Hey, Dr. Chase." Relieved to see a woman, nervous about the unknown, Darius give her a half smile.

"Relax, this is a thorough but relatively painless exam. Have a seat," the doctor said, pointing to the bed. "How's everything?"

Legs shaking, voice trembling, Darius lied, "Good," knowing things couldn't get much worse. He was terrified to take the exam.

"I like to know as much as possible before doing an exam. Is there anything you'd like to share with me? Any stress, medical concerns, or family-related illnesses?"

"Nope. Everything's cool." Darius silently prayed to his Ma Dear. *I know you're watching over me. Please put in a good word with the Man upstairs, I need Him right now.*

"Give me your arm."

The doctor tightly tied a yellowish rubber band around his biceps, swabbed the fold above his elbow with alcohol, and inserted a needle. One glass tube after another she filled with blood until all six were full. Placing a cold stethoscope against the left side of his chest, the doctor said, "Nice. Strong," then placed the metal against his abs and his back. She checked his ears. "Open wide and say aaahhhhh."

"Aaaahhhhh."

"So far everything looks good. Now I need for you to drop your pants and underwear to the floor, but you don't have to take them off. You can lean over the table or hold your ankles."

Proud of what he exhibited, Darius smiled. Leaning over the table, out of the corner of his eyes, Darius watched the doctor put on one rubber glove. She squirted K-Y jelly onto her fingers. The doctor's hand disappeared behind his back.

"Oh, shit!" Darius yelled as the doctor's finger slid all the way inside his ass. "Damn! You need to warn a brotha about that shit."

"You're done," she said, smiling.

Standing tall, Darius said, "Damn straight." He'd cum all over the white tissue he'd been holding. A release was a release and he felt great afterward. The best orgasms he'd had were when something was up his ass. Preferably a woman's finger. Dicks were off-limits.

Cleaning Slugger, Darius pulled up his pants. "How long before I get my results?"

"A day or two at the most. I'll call you if there's any concerns, but these types of physicals are routine, generally with good results. Every once in a while an athlete will have kidney problems, heart trouble, or high blood pressure, but that's rare," Dr. Chase said, washing her hands.

"Thanks," Darius said, buckling his pants.

Darius left, thinking two days max and he'd know. Sitting behind the steering wheel, he headed back to the airport. At the ticket counter he changed his arrival city from Los Angeles to Oakland. Just as he was getting ready to turn off his cell phone, it rang.

"Texas?" Darius wanted to treat her kinder. "Ashlee, I apologize. I shouldn't have made you upset. Forgive me."

"Mr. Williams?"

"Yes?"

"This is Ms. Benson with Child Protective Services. We've placed your son in protective custody."

"Who is this?" Darius asked, settling into his first-class seat.

Ms. Benson continued, "The mother has endangered your son. We've placed your son under protective custody."

Staring out the window at workers loading the luggage, Darius said, "You have the wrong number, lady. My son died almost a year ago."

"Are you Darius Williams?"

"Yes."

The flight attendant interrupted. "Sir, you're going to have to turn off your phone."

Listening attentively to Ms. Benson, Darius held up his pointing finger at the attendant.

"Is the mother of your child Ashlee Anderson?"

Darius gasped for air, then nodded.

Ms. Benson repeated the question.

"Oh, I thought I answered, Yes."

"Is your son named Darius Williams Junior?"

Darius's voice trembled. "Yes."

"Sir, we can't leave until you turn off your phone. Please."

The passenger seated across the aisle said, "Man, turn off the damn phone."

Darius's jaw flinched as he continued listening.

"Then we have your son in protective custody. The reason I'm calling is we try to place the child with family first. Your son's mother is emotionally unstable. Are you interested in having temporary custody of your son? If not he may end up in the foster care system."

"No."

"No, you're not interested?"

"No, yes, yes, of course. I want my son. Permanently. Yes. What do I have to do?"

Standing in front of him, the flight attendant folded her arms.

"I know. One more minute."

Ms. Benson asked, "What's the earliest you can attend a court hearing in Dallas, Texas?"

"I can be wherever you want me, whenever you need me."

Powering off his phone, Darius yelled, "Yes! Hell yes!" His son was alive and that meant another thing. Darius Jones-Williams did not have HIV!

CHAPTER 27

Ashlee

Nobody had the right to take her child away. Not the state of Texas, the court, and surely not some old-ass caseworker who had one foot in the grave playing Russian roulette with people's lives. Ashlee was one step away from homicide, suicide, or both.

Dialing Darius's number, Ashlee hoped he hadn't listened to her message.

Darius answered, "Why you lied to me, huh? You said my son was dead. Had me trippin' and shit. What's wrong with you? You truly are crazy. God don't like ugly, Ash. I'ma take you to court and take my son away from your crazy ass."

Before she could respond "What!" Darius hung up. He was the insane one, playing his reverse psychology games. Once the judge found out all the women Darius had fucked, there was no way he'd get custody. But how could Ashlee prove Darius was a dog? No need to call him back. Ashlee's eyes shifted as she contemplated what to do next.

Snatching her purse and keys, she slammed the front door behind her, praying the address on the business card was where Ms. Benson had taken her son. Hopefully Ms. Benson hadn't placed her baby with some stranger.

Ashlee had heard the horror stories about how foster parents beat, sexually abused, and starved the kids while using the kids' money to buy houses and cars. And the government paid those people while penalizing the parents. Then when something devastating was exposed, like sodomy or murder, the state wanted to launch an investigation. If they weren't so damn impulsive and gung ho in the beginning, kidnapping people's babies and shit, maybe those things wouldn't happen.

"I'm going to get my baby!" Ashlee yelled to her father.

Quickly Lawrence got out of the car and hurried over to Ashlee.

No, she wasn't the best parent, and maybe she'd made a few bad decisions but no one loved her baby more than she did. Not even Darius.

"Hey, sweetheart. Whoa, slow down," her father said, grasping her arm as Ashlee brushed by him.

"Let me go, Daddy! I've gotta go get my son!"

"From where?"

"Ms. Benson."

"Wait, sweetheart. You're going about this the wrong way. What are you talking about?"

"Ms. Benson took DJ from me. He's gone. And she's trying to keep him," Ashlee said, struggling to take steps toward her car. "She called Darius." She jerked her arm. "Ow! Let go! You're hurting me!"

Lawrence held her firmer. "Wait. Why didn't you call me?"

"I didn't have time. Plus, you're always with a client, Daddy. You don't really have time for *me*. You stop by for a few minutes, play with DJ, ask me the same questions every visit, 'Sweetheart, did you take your medication? Where's DJ?' If he's asleep, you leave right away. If he's awake, you play with him for ten minutes and then you're gone. Besides, all of this happened so fast."

Ashlee's head spun; her vision blurred. Crying hysterically, she recapped the events and conversation for her father, conveniently omitting a few details here and there.

Lawrence shook his head, rubbing his palm atop his hair. "Honey, this is serious. I can call your mother. See if she'll keep DJ for a few days until we can straighten out this misunderstanding. Ms. Benson had to ask you for a relative who was willing to keep DJ? Didn't she?"

Ashlee's neighbors gathered outside again. "You're next!" Ashlee shouted, running toward them. "I'ma get all y'all nosy bitches!"

Stopping in the middle of the street, Ashlee watched the women scatter.

"Honey, look out!" her dad yelled.

Screeeecchhh . . . bam! A red convertible Mercedes crashed into Ashlee's neighbor's parked car. If Ashlee had taken one step in the wrong direction, she could be dead. Satisfied, Ashlee smiled at the women, then frowned, walking toward the driver.

"Candice? What are you doing here?"

"Help me, Ashlee," Candice pleaded.

Blood streamed from a gash in Candice's head. Before Ashlee or Lawrence could dial emergency, an ambulance raced to the scene. The paramedics rolled the gurney to the driver's side.

Not knowing what to do, Ashlee stood in the middle of the street.

"Lady, move before you cause another accident," the paramedic said.

Candice lay on the gurney, the black belt latched across her waist.

"Ashlee, please go to the hospital with me," Candice begged.

The paramedic interjected, "Sorry, ma'am, we're not allow to transport passengers, only patients."

"Where are you taking her?" Ashlee questioned.

"County." The paramedic slammed the door.

Sirens blared.

Hugging Ashlee's waist, Lawrence said, "We can't afford to have them fault you for this accident. Let the paramedics do their job."

"Wait," Ashlee said, reaching into Candice's car, grabbing her purse and tote bag. "But, Daddy, we know her."

"No, we don't. We'll get the details later." Lawrence unlocked the front door, motioning for Ashlee to go inside.

Sirens blared again as the police arrived at the scene.

Oh well. Sitting on the sofa, Ashlee resumed their conversation. "No, Daddy, Ms. Benson didn't ask me for a relative. Once she found out Darius played professional basketball, all she wanted was Darius's information. And she said, 'You better not lie to me.' So I gave her what she wanted. For all I know, she might be trying to take Darius away from me."

Lawrence exhaled. "That can't be the truth or the whole story, sweetheart. Let me contact her." Tugging the business card from Ashlee's grip, he glanced at the number, then dialed six digits.

Sadly Ashlee said, "You don't believe me either. Nobody believes me. That's okay."

"It's not you, sweetheart. It's the medication. You're not back to normal yet."

"Then I refuse to take another pill until I am."

Lawrence pressed the last number, then placed his pointing finger over his lip. "Hello, Ms. Benson." He paused, then continued. "This is Lawrence Anderson. Could you please explain to me what happened and where is my grandson?" He nodded. "Confidential? I see. Then we will see you in court."

"Let me go and see her rusty butt," Ashlee said.

"Sit down," Lawrence said, terminating the call. "You have to take this matter seriously. I refuse to let Darius gain custody. You will get DJ back. I promise."

Staring at Candice's bags, somehow Ashlee believed her father was trying to convince himself.

Ashlee thought, *I wonder what's inside.* As soon as her father left, she'd find out.

CHAPTER 28

Wellington

Wellington's life would never be the same. What had he done to deserve cancer? Why had he waited so long to get professional help? If he had to do it over, he would've had the surgery years ago instead of secretly going to Mexico, taking alternative medicine, fooling himself that his body was in remission.

"Mr. Jones. Can you hear me?" the doctor asked, sitting on a stool beside the bed.

Opening his eyes, Wellington nodded.

"Can you speak?"

Wellington nodded again.

"We want to make you as comfortable as possible."

"Just give it to me straight, Doc. I can handle it."

"We can operate again, immediately. We can provide treatment, radiation and chemo. Or we can recommend hospice. Do you want us to sustain you on life support if—"

"Hospice?" Shaking his head, Wellington tried to smile but couldn't. "I wanna be the one to tell my wife. How long do I have?"

"Not very." Squeezing Wellington's hand, the doctor said, "A Ms. Thompson is waiting to see you."

Wellington nodded, glad that Melanie had come. He knew she would.

"Hi ya, handsome," Melanie said, kissing his hand. "How you feel?"

"Better now."

"Well, we can do better than that," Melanie said, closing the door.

Unbuttoning her blouse, unfastening her bra, Melanie sat topless, keeping him company. "Remember that threesome we did? Jada was such a prude. But girlfriend didn't have a problem with me eating her pussy." Melanie laughed aloud.

Admiring Melanie, Wellington felt guilty for misleading her. Melanie knew he'd never divorce Jada, but she had high hopes even after they divorced. Lots of men dreamed of having a mistress. Wellington had one point five. Simone was happy, make that content, with Wellington supplying her every need. Financial, that is. Simone wasn't emotionally strong like Melanie. Melanie could handle Jada being number one as long as she got her fair share of his dick and his money. The one time Wellington made love to Simone she cried the entire time, asking, "What does she have that I don't have? What can she give you that I can't?"

Wellington wasn't perfect and he didn't try to be. But he couldn't stand seeing Simone cry.

Holding Melanie's hand, Wellington said, "I spoke with my lawyer. He's revising my trust to include you and Morgan. Did you bring your papers?"

Melanie handed him the document. "Sign here. You don't know how much this means to us."

Yes, he did. Wellington nodded in order to suppress his emotions and pain. "I want you to have my share of Darius's business."

Bouncing her titties, Melanie kissed him. "Are you serious?"

"Yes. Neither Jada nor Darius needs the money. Now put on your clothes and leave. Jada'll be here soon. We don't want to piss her off. Everything should be finalized in a few days. I'll call you. Take care of my girl."

"I love you," Melanie said, pressing and holding her lips to his.

"I love you, too."

Wellington didn't have to ask Melanie twice. Neatly dressing, she quietly closed the door.

"I know you have womanly needs. I know I haven't been able to sexually satisfy you for a long time. But why did you have to fuck that nigga in my house!" His yell was barely above a normal tone because that was all the energy he could force out of his body. "Why did you have to kick me while I'm down? While I'm helpless and incapacitated? You don't have to answer me. I can look at you and tell you're glowing." Wellington's fingers curled into a ball. "If I don't survive, my other request is that you have my blessing to re-marry. But, ba, whateva you do, don't marry Darryl. What has he ever done to help you? Or Darius? He's only trying to move me out to get his hands on your money and Darius's money."

Jada moved closer to kiss Wellington's lips, but before her lips touched his, he turned away. "Be quiet, baby. I only have one soul mate."

Wellington closed his eyes, then said, "Don't be so sure. And my last request is the most difficult of all, but I thought you should know, Melanie came by."

Jada remained silent. She stood and said, "They must've re-moved half your brain."

Wellington continued. "I agreed to sign the papers, leaving her my third interest in Somebody's Gotta Be on Top plus five million dollars cash and I signed the birth certificate acknowledging that Morgan is my daughter."

Jada slapped Wellington's face so hard the breathing tube slipped from his nose. "So this is how you want to sabotage every-thing we've built. Just divide your money up and tell me all of this shit! What if you weren't sick? When were you going to tell me the truth?"

"Ba, wait," Wellington said, putting the tube back in his nose. "There's no easy way to tell you any of this, but I can't leave you with my conscience being guilty."

"Well, as long as you're clearing your conscience, do you love Melanie? Is she your soul mate too?" Jada sarcastically asked.

Wellington closed his eyes, then replied, "Yes, and yes."

CHAPTER 29

Darius

Familiarity?
"You can know a person most of your life and still not know them at all."

Ignoring the warning signs of her emotional attachment cost him time, money, and the freedom to walk the streets without looking over his shoulder. The phone calls, the *I love yous,* entering his home without his permission. How could a man control a woman's feelings toward him? More importantly, how could he control her behavior?

Darius's Oakland home felt strange. Weeks had passed since he was there. Anxiously Darius awaited his departure to Mandy's office. "I sure hope Mandy is ready for me, 'cause I gotta lotta shit to get off my chest." After his appointment he'd head straight for the next flight to L.A. to be with his mother. Maybe Mandy could help Ashlee. More good than bad memories of Ashlee surfaced.

Sitting on his king-size circular bed, Darius reminisced on the time they'd plotted to run away, protesting their parents' marriage.

One summer day, after fifth grade, going into the sixth, Darius had said, "Honestly, I don't want my mom to marry your dad."

"You too? I wanted my parents to get back together, but my mom keeps saying I'm dreaming."

"I've got a plan," Darius had said. "We can run away from home."

"Yeah, and divorce our parents," Ashlee agreed. "Maybe then they'll take us serious."

Darius spoke firmly. "Make sure you pack a toothbrush, and lots of clean underwear and socks."

"Is that all?" Ashlee had asked. "What about food?"

"I don't know. My mom always says, 'Darius, you got your toothbrush? And extra underwear and socks?' so I guess that stuff must be pretty important. She never mentions food because we always have money, I guess."

"Okay. Let's run away right before the wedding," Ashlee had suggested.

"Great idea!"

Bad idea. Both of them got their asses whupped. Ashlee by her dad. Darius by Wellington. Those were the days simple things were fun. Like the caricature Ashlee had drawn of him with a basketball head. The days before Darius understood what sex was or how great cumming felt. Ashlee was cute. Bright. Talented. Innocent. Funny. Back then they didn't have to do much to make one another laugh. A silly expression. A tickle. A pillow fight. The one thing Darius had with Ashlee that he didn't have with Fancy was way-back history. Now everything Ashlee did pissed him off. Ashlee had, in his opinion, done the unforgivable. In time, he'd forget both Ashlee and her random acts of jealousy.

Love?

Darius had thought he loved Ashlee. Not anymore. She'd failed him. Why would the woman who supported him the most try to force him to marry her? Make him be her lover? Make him be in love with her? Knowing she'd fabricated the worst lie a man could imagine? If Ashlee had a slither of a chance, she'd blown her opportunity.

Guilt.

Darius's conscience was attached to Ashlee, not his heart. He felt bad for treating her wrong. Using her. Manipulating her. But Ashlee had encouraged his behavior by accepting him regardless of his actions.

Deception.

Darius feared what his dad had said could've been true. The Ashlee Darius knew would never kill his child, sneaking abortion pills into his house. But then again, she'd never break into his home, deface his property, hide in his car, or lie to him, all of which she'd done in the past few days.

Closing the front door behind him, Darius stood in front of his Oakland home remembering the time he and Kimberly had fucked on the lawn. Stepping out of the limo that day, all Kimberly wore was the mink coat he'd bought her and a necklace of pearls around her waist. "Man, oh, man." Shaking his head, he felt his dick getting hard. "If Kimberly was here right now, I'd tear that pussy up!"

Frantically searching for his ringing cell phone before he missed the call, he saw it was his doctor. A happy finger pressed the Talk key as Darius answered, "Hey, Doc."

"Mr. Williams, where are you?"

No return hello. Straight to business. Damn. Darius's heart skipped a beat. "Oakland. Why? What's up?"

"Based on your results, the head coach disapproved your physical. We need to have you retested right away."

His legs weakened, collapsing him onto the bottom step. "What's the problem? You make it sound like I'm dying or something," Darius said, fearing the unthinkable.

"You could be. Your WBC is extremely high. Unsafe. Possibly life-threatening."

"WBC?"

"White blood count."

"What's the problem?"

"We don't know yet. Could be as simple as a foreign substance in your body, a cold or a bladder infection, all of which are treatable with antibiotics. You may have kidney problems."

"Or?" Darius asked.

"Worst-case scenario, you could be HIV-positive. Next time we'll check your T-cell count."

"But you're not sure."

"No, that's why we have to retest you right away. Everything else is fine. When I call you back, you must go straight to our recommended doctor's office in Oakland. You'll be in and out fairly quick. They're only going to draw blood."

Great, he'd have to spend another night in Oakland. "Thanks, Doc. I'll be waiting by my phone for your call."

Stumbling to his car, Darius drove to Mandy's office. He parked on University Avenue, then hurried upstairs. Entering the lobby, he approached the receptionist, then said, "Darius Williams."

"You can have a seat, Mr. Williams. Mandy is running a little over with her client."

Darius sat thumbing through a *Sports Illustrated* magazine. Yeah, soon he'd be on the cover flashing a championship ring. Then Dr. Chase's phone call hit him hard. If he weren't so promiscuous he wouldn't have to worry. Leaning into the swimsuit issue, he gagged. When Darius looked up, he couldn't believe his eyes.

"Ladycat?" he said, tossing the magazine into the trash.

"Mr. William, Mandy will see you now," the receptionist said.

Fancy's eyes were red and brown. "How could you fuck her, then let her kill our daughter and act like nothing happened?"

Darius hugged Fancy. "What are you talking about?"

Fancy's arms looped inside his embrace, forcefully lowering his arms, severing his touch. Damn. Clearly she was no match for him, but Fancy was stronger than he'd realized. "Where'd you learn how to do that?"

"Let me go! I hate you!" Fancy screamed, dialing her cell phone. "Here, you listen to this, then look me in my eyes and tell me she's lying."

Darius became quiet. He took Fancy's phone and listened to Ashlee's voice in his ear.

"Hi, Darius. You know who this is. I, I, I forgot something, um, my medication, at your house and, well, I'd like to get my pills back. I'm glad we made love on your should-have-been wedding night because I'm gonna be your wife. I love you, too. Bye. Call me. Wait a minute. I called to be honest. Truth is, the reason I'm calling is to confess, I replaced your aspirins with abortion pills. Please, throw them away before—"

Dropping his hand to his thigh, Darius clenched his teeth, flinching his jaw. Fuck! He'd taken abortion pills? That's why he started throwing up that night and couldn't stop.

"I'm so sorry. I forgot to get my keys back and she did this before we got back from Oakland, I mean Berkeley. She also lied to me. My son is alive."

Blankly Fancy stared at him. Wasn't Ladycat happy for him?

Flatly she said, "Well, excuse me if I can't rejoice in your happiness, 'cause my baby is dead. Darius, did you or did you not fuck Ashlee that night?"

"I swear, I did not."

The sting of Fancy's hand burned his face.

"Darius, you will lie till you die. That woman is not acting crazy for no reason. I'm glad you're trying to get help. God knows you need all you can get."

"Fancy, please, stay here until I finish my appointment. I need to talk to you. Please, I'm begging you. Wait," Darius said, nudging Fancy into the chair.

"Mr. Williams, Mandy will see you now," the receptionist repeated.

"Please, I love you," Darius begged one last time before entering Mandy's office.

"Well, hello, Darius. Congratulations are in order," Mandy said, giving him a hug.

Lightly he patted her back, then sat on the sofa. "Thanks."

"I apologize to cut your hour short, but I went over with my last client. We have forty-five minutes." Sitting in her swivel high-back chair, Mandy slid her eyeglasses to the tip of her nose, then scooted over to Darius.

Cushioning his elbows into his thighs inches above his knees, Darius stared at the carpet while clasping his hands. His teeth clenched; jaw flinched.

"My goodness. You are seriously stressing. What's going on in your life?"

Mandy had to know his situation with Fancy. "Damn, where do I start?"

"Wherever you'd like."

Focusing from his knees to his feet, Darius said, "Let's see, I'm worried about my mother because my stepfather is dying. She spends most of her time at the hospital, she's lost a lot of weight too. My fiancée, Fancy, who was in your office a few minutes ago, just lost our baby. I might have HIV but I don't think so."

"For the record, everything Fancy told me is confidential. Now, did you say you're worried about your mother?"

"Of course."

"Why?" Mandy asked, reaching for her yellow legal-sized notepad.

"Because I love her."

"Keep going."

Darius had given lots of thought to that question before now. The answer remained unchanged. "I don't know what I'd do without her."

"So are your feelings for your mother based on your fear of losing her?"

Darius nodded, then answered, "They say spouses sometimes die close together. If Wellington dies . . . yes, I am scared."

"How do you feel about Fancy?"

"She's the only woman I've ever loved—"

"Loved or love?"

"Love—"

"But."

Lowering his head, Darius said, "There is no but. I'm in love with Fancy and that scares me too. What if she rejects me?"

"So your fear is rejection or falling in love?"

"Both."

"What about abandonment?" Mandy asked.

"That too."

"Darius, were you there for Fancy when she lost the baby?"

No need to lie on this one. Darius was certain Mandy knew the answer. "No, I wasn't."

"Why not?"

"At first I thought she had an abortion. Then I thought she was fucking my next-door neighbor."

"You didn't talk with her?"

"No."

"Why not?" Mandy urged.

"Stupid, I guess."

"Don't cop out, Mr. Williams. You're smarter than that. Tell me."

"I was angry, okay."

"Angry or feeling guilty?"

"Both."

"Why both?"

"Because I had sex with Ashlee, then lied to Fancy. I wanted something to be Fancy's fault too. But her only fault was loving me."

"Don't cop out, Darius. This is not a pity party. I have zero sympathy for you. You're capable, but are you willing to be honest with yourself and Fancy?"

"Yes."

"Have you been tested for HIV?"

"Yes."

"Did you receive your results?"

"Not yet," Darius said, looking at his phone. "I'm waiting for a call back to take another test."

"Stop worrying about things you can not control. Accept responsibility for actions. Learn to overcome your fears. And make better decisions."

"How do I do that?"

"You can start by stopping lying to yourself and learning how to be honest with others. You are your own worst enemy. The average person would welcome your troubles. You have the power to change your way of thinking. About your life. About how you treat the people in your life."

Honesty wasn't always the best policy. "What if I lose out?"

"What if, Mr. Williams, you try? Tell my receptionist to set up another appointment for next week, if you'd like. Mandy folded a white piece of paper in half, then handed it to him. "To whom much is given, much is required. Take care of yourself, Mr. Williams." Mandy turned her back to him and began closing her laptop.

Darius folded the paper again and again until it was small enough to slide into his pocket as his phone rang. "Yeah, Doc," he answered.

"Here's the address. Go to the lab now . . . I've expedited your tests and will call you first thing in the morning with the results."

"Thanks."

Mandy hadn't turned around, so Darius exited into the lobby. Fancy was gone. Darius decided not to set up his next appointment. His shoes thumped several blocks up to Cal Berkeley's campus. Sitting on a tree stump, Darius removed Mandy's paper from his pocket. The handwriting wasn't Mandy's, it was Fancy's.

Darius read *I do love you . . . still.*

To whom much is given, much is required. What if he tried to love Fancy back?

CHAPTER 30

Fancy

Closure. Her head said forget about him. Her heart disagreed. The last flight back to L.A. had departed without them. Fancy had agreed to visit Darius.

"You're going to see him. Aren't you?" Desmond asked, lying across the bed in Fancy's Oakland Hills penthouse.

"No, I'm not," Fancy lied. "I have to consult with SaVoy on her wedding. It'll only take about an hour."

The last time Fancy left Desmond alone in their room in Los Angeles, she returned to the hotel from Michael Baines's house at the break of dawn. Kissing Desmond's lips, Fancy said, "I love you, Dez. I'll be right back."

Grabbing his jacket, Desmond insisted, "Then I'll ride with you. I can hang out with my boy Tyronne while you talk to SaVoy."

All Fancy thought about on her way home from her appointment with Mandy was Darius. Fancy confided in Mandy the things that had happened. Mandy's advice was, "You can create your own truth, you can ask Darius to tell you the truth, or you can simply let him go, move on, and marry a man you know won't make you happy."

Mandy was right. Desmond was what he was, just a friend. But Dez was a great friend. A true friend. Fancy hated lying to him.

Stepping out of her penthouse directly into the elevator, Fancy exhaled, refusing to tell the truth. "When I return, we can go for a late dinner at Kincaid's in Jack London Square. Now stay here."

"Wait a second," Desmond said, disappearing, then returning. "You forgot your ring."

No, she hadn't. "Thanks," Fancy said. Watching Desmond toss his jacket on the sofa, she knew what she had to do. Hopefully after she spoke with Darius, Fancy could define her relationship with Desmond.

The ride to Darius's house was a blur. Fancy recalled the first time she had stepped foot in Darius's Oakland house was with her ex, Byron. If Fancy could've ditched Byron for Darius that night, she would have. The same way she met Byron at the New Year's Eve gala Desmond had taken her to. Fancy was definitely an opportunist, and every date was an opportunity for her to upgrade until she hit the jackpot. Miss Kitty had earned them free rent, a Mercedes, and lots of cash. If Darius didn't act right, she could marry one of his wealthy teammates.

Parking in Darius's driveway, Fancy sat for a moment preparing for the worst. If their relationship was over, she still couldn't marry Dez. Slowly walking up three white steps, Fancy thought, *Why does Darius have a house this big collecting dust?* Maybe she could convince him to let her sell it. The house was beautiful. Rolling green hillside adorned the large white columns. On a clear night from the upstairs balcony one could see the sparkling lights on the Oakland/San Francisco Bay Bridge and the city's skyline. The moon was full. So was her heart, filled with love.

Ding-dong.

The melody of the doorbell rang in her ears. She could hear Darius scrambling, scratching to open his door. There he stood. He opened the door wider as she gracefully stepped inside.

"How are you?" he asked.

"Fine, I guess. I can't stay long. I came to hear why." That and to think with her heart.

Caressing her hand, Darius said, "Let's go upstairs."

"Let's not," Fancy countered. "I'm not interested in being intimate with you." At least not tonight, she thought, standing still in the foyer.

"Okay, whateva you say. Whatever you want, Ladycat. I'm just glad you came. The living room is okay?"

Fancy knew her way around his houses well. Darius followed her, then sat beside her on the sofa.

"If it's too cold in here, I can turn on the heater."

She shook her head in response. Silence lingered as Fancy pretended she didn't care about him at all.

She stood, then said, "Well, you invited me over, so if you don't have anything to say, I guess I'll be—"

"Please, don't leave. I was waiting because I wanted to listen to what you have to say."

Sitting, Fancy said, "You've got ten seconds."

"You don't have to talk to me this way." Darius exhaled, then continued. "Look, I'm sorry. I never meant to hurt you. I lied about not fucking Ashlee, but . . ." He paused, then said, "No buts. I was wrong. I apologize for not believing you, for leaving you at the hospital, for not being there for you . . . You can stop me at any time."

Looking into his watery eyes, Fancy asked, "Darius, what do you want from me?"

His eyes shifted to the corners, then swiftly back to her. "I'm scared, Ladycat. I'm afraid that if I love you too much I'll lose you. I thought being a man was being hard, never saying sorry, and shit like that." Darius's hand grazed his locks. His side profile was sexy as hell.

Focus, Fancy, focus. "You know what I want from you, Darius."

"Tell me. Anything you want I'll provide."

"I want you to stop lying to me. I want you to hold me in your arms. Protect me. Make me your priority. Show me that you love me too."

Wrapping his arms around her, Darius didn't hold back his tears. This was the first time that Fancy felt his pain. He was scared. She was too. He cried. She cried. They cried together.

CHAPTER 31

Jada

Meanings were in people, not words.

People had a way of saying things they didn't mean. Or meaning things they didn't say.

Wellington had a lot of nerve, dropping all his skeletons in her lap at once. If he weren't sick, Jada would've, she should've, hell, she didn't know what she could've done. She sat quietly in their bedroom. Wellington didn't have to become a jerk because he was ill. Melanie was his soul mate too? Throwing her hands up, Jada yelled, "Bullshit! My gosh. When did he realize that? Liar." Surely that was his justification for wanting to give Melanie the business and money she'd never get.

Jada flopped backward onto her bed in disgust, staring at the ceiling. No wife wanted to be the other woman. But if Jada had to be the other woman, Wellington was overdue for being the other man. Men could dish out infidelity, but their egos couldn't handle their wives fucking another man.

"Yeah, since you're Mr. Big and Bad, I got one for your ass," Jada said, then thought, *Maybe I should let Darryl say his good-byes to Wellington.* That would kill Wellington for sure.

"Um, um, um." All of Melanie's pathetic life she'd spent chasing Wellington. Maybe if Melanie weren't so preoccupied with Wellington, she could've found her own damn husband. The lie she'd told Wellington about being pregnant wasn't enough to make him stay married to her after she miscarried another man's triplets, so she had to find another way to get Wellington. "Here, doggie, doggie, doggie, dog." Throwing her old bag of bones at him. And just like a mutt, he lapped her up. Well, now that Wellington was dying, Melanie could find somebody else's husband to screw.

Jazzmyne sat in a chair across from Jada's bed and said, "Everything will be all right. You know Wellington was heavily sedated when he said those things to you."

"Heavily sedated? That's like excusing infidelity on drinking too much alcohol. Wellington had said what he'd meant. He also knew enough to know about my affair with Darryl. How's that?" Jada knew Jazzmyne was reporting back to Wellington. How else would he know?

Jazzmyne continued. "If you're insinuating it was me, maybe you're feeling guilty. I'm sure my brother will explain when he's coherent. But you know, when it comes to matters of the heart, love is about as illogical as one can imagine. You of all people know that." Jazzmyne kept talking, but Jada wasn't listening.

Jada's eyes narrowed, she thought, *How dare he leave me like this? Well, God knows best. Maybe He was on vacation or break or something, because where was He when Wellington was doing all his madness?* She'd better not think too loud. What about what she'd done?

"Whether we accept the truth or not, each person is so special, so unique, it is possible to be in love with more than one person at the same time. It's possible to have more than one soul mate. And one's heart is often torn between what is right for family and what is right for self. We can constantly struggle to get all of it right and never please anybody. Not even ourselves. I've seen this situation over and over while counseling battered women who go back time and time again to their abusive husbands. And I see it in you. You love Darryl."

Jada realized Jazzmyne wanted to help, but all Jazzmyne did was irritate the hell out of her. Sitting up on the edge of the bed, Jada asked, barely above a whisper, "Where's Darius?"

"In his room. Asleep. He came straight from the airport after he got back from his doctor's appointment in Oakland."

"Appointment? Oakland? I thought he went to Atlanta."

"He said the team doctor ordered a retest of his blood."

"Is he okay? I want to see my baby," Jada said, moving to the dresser, farther away from Jazzmyne. She ruffled the clothes in the top drawer, removing a canary-colored bra she hadn't worn in months. Inspecting the sheer material, Jada stuffed the bra back inside.

Jazzmyne left the room. Moments later, Darius entered.

"Hey, Ma. How are you?"

Opening her arms wide, Jada said, "Tired. Come here, honey."

"What time you wanna go to the hospital?"

"Not sure that I wanna go back at all."

Staring at her, Darius hugged, then rocked her in his arms. "Go to sleep, Ma. Take a nap. You need to rest. You'll feel better when you wake up."

Jazzmyne entered the room, holding the cordless phone. "Jada, it's the hospital."

"Darius, honey, talk to them for me."

"This is Darius Williams." He paused, then said, "Uh-huh. I see. Okay, I'll tell my mom." Darius placed the cordless on the night-stand. "Ma—"

Jada whispered, "I know. Wellington is dead."

"No, Ma. But they don't expect him to make it till tomorrow." Grasping her biceps, Darius insisted, "We gotta go now."

Jada sat on their bed, lay atop the covers, and curled into a fetal position. What more could Wellington say? Her entire body ached with more disappointment than sadness.

Darius sat on the edge of the bed beside her. His side touched her spine as he lovingly stroked her hair. "Ma, what is it? Tell me."

Exhaling Jada cried, "There's nothing I can do."

"I'm here for you, Ma. Whatever you need. Whatever you want. I'll do. Nothing is more important to me than you, and I'm not going anywhere until you say it's okay, Ma, and mean it."

Regrets.

Jada didn't understand why her mind said go; her body said stay. She didn't want to be angry at her husband as he took his last breath. Nor did she want to abandon him on his deathbed. Seeing Wellington die was not the way she wanted to remember her husband.

"Lord, forgive me," Jada whispered as she closed her watery eyes.

CHAPTER 32

Darius

Out of sight wasn't good when she weighed heavily on his mind. Kissing his mother's forehead, Darius softly said, "Ma, I'm going home for a sec and I'll be right back."

Stretching her legs toward the foot of her bed, turning onto her stomach, his mother said, "Uh-huh. Okay, sweetie. Hurry."

What happened to Candice? Where was his dad?

Entering the living room, Darius asked, "Auntie Jazzmyne, have you seen my dad? Or Candice?"

"Your dad mentioned something about giving your mom space, that and he had to train his new employee."

Flinching his jaw, Darius asked, "Who?"

"You know who. And Candice was in a car accident in Dallas. She'll be here tonight to pick up her things."

Shaking his head, Darius said, "Thanks, Auntie."

What if Candice was back early? Darius drove toward his house. *But what if Kevin is stealing my money?* Darius thought, making a detour to Somebody's Gotta Be on Top. Parking at a meter, he dropped in eight quarters for fifty minutes. "Man, this is wild." Shouldn't take more than a half hour, but he wasn't sure. Darius dropped in fifty cents more.

Entering his office, Darius said, "Hello," bypassing the secretary.

"Excuse me, sir. Who are you here to see?"

No, she did not question him.

"Another fuckup like that and you're fired!" Darius said, entering his dad's office.

Who else but Kevin's short ass, thieving ass, Williams was in his office, behind his desk, on his phone.

"One minute, brother," Kevin said, holding up his finger. "I'm negotiating a big deal here for us."

"For us, my ass! Nigga, if you don't," Darius said, leaping across the glass top, "get your ass out of here before I—"

Backing away, Kevin tossed the phone to the floor, shielding his face. "Dad didn't tell you?"

"Tell me what! Nigga, what!"

Darius picked up the receiver slamming it onto the base.

"He made me executive vice president so I could help out in the office while he traveled with you to Atlanta. Now that he's your agent—"

"My what? Get your lying ass out of my office."

"It's true, D. I'm straight now. No more stealing from you, my brother. I ain't going back to that hellhole for nobody. But you know I'm good at this movie business shit. I can wheel and deal with the best of 'em. I was just sealing a one-hundred-million-dollar package."

"Kev, man, I don't wanna hurt you. You'd better leave now. I'll talk with Dad later. Sorry, I just don't trust someone who's stolen a million dollars from me."

Kevin exhaled, lowering his shoulders.

"Move, nigga, move, this ain't no joke."

Standing face-to-face with Darius, Kevin said, "If that's how you want it, *my perfect brother,* your loss."

Covering Kevin's face with his hand, Darius pushed his brother away. "Don't make me ask again."

Thankfully Kevin left, because Darius didn't feel like fighting. Picking up an incoming fax, he read the dollar amount on the contract. One hundred million dollars. Maybe he could find forgiveness in his heart, but not today.

Darius exited into the lobby area. "Come on, baby doll. Pack your shit and get out too."

"I don't work for you."

"But you do. Get out!" Darius yelled, pounding on her desk. "And give me your keys."

As he locked the door, Darius realized he had forgotten to get Kevin's keys.

Sitting in his Bentley, he dialed the locksmith. "Yeah, man, can you change my locks at Somebody's right away and leave the keys at my mom's house?"

"You got it, D. Be at peace," the locksmith said, hanging up.

Darius drove home, pissed off the entire trip. Parking in his driveway, he clenched his teeth. His cell phone rang as soon as he entered his front door. Blocked ID. Darius started not to answer, but assuming it was his dad calling on behalf of his brother, he answered, "What?"

"Mr. Williams?"

"Who's this?"

"Dr. Chase."

Darius's anger melted into fear. "Yes?"

"I have good and bad news. Which would you like first?"

His lips disappeared inside his mouth. Silent for a moment, Darius finally said, "Give me the bad news. Wait, yeah." Might as well.

"You, Mr. Williams, have a bladder infection," Dr. Chase said.

Air escaped Darius's lungs. "What? That's it?"

"What did you expect?"

"Yes!" Darius danced in the middle of his living room floor.

"And the good news is, you passed your physical. You can fly back to sign your contract. I'll phone in a prescription for you to pick up at your local pharmacy. Have a good day."

"Thank you, Jesus! Thank you, Ma Dear! Boy, I'm one lucky mutherfucka."

Jumping on, then off his couch, high into the air, Darius tapped his forehead, heart, then left and right shoulders. His fist pounded three times against his chest. He'd never been happier to have a bladder infection. He thought that was for women only. A few antibiotics and he'd be a healthy man again.

Gripping his dick, Darius yanked up and down.

"You lucky too, dawg. We gotta celebrate!" Darius thrust his fist high above his head. "Yes! Yes!"

Darius dialed Mandy's number. "Yes, this is Mr. Williams. Put me through to Mandy."

"She's with a client. Would you like her voice mail?"

"Sure," Darius replied, smiling. When he heard the beep, he said, "Mandy, this is Mr. Williams calling to ecstatically inform you my report is clear. Bye."

Darius was so elated he wasn't mad at anyone anymore. Not Ashlee. Not Fancy. Not Kevin. Not his dad. Not Candice. Not even his new teammate, K'Nine.

God only knew what Candice was plotting next. Darius was certain she didn't accidentally end up in Dallas.

Changing into a pair of oversize denims, Jordans, and a tall T-shirt, Darius rocked his Bentley all the way to his mom's house.

Entering his mother's front door, Darius stopped when he saw Candice on the sofa. Her face was long, her head was wrapped in bandages. A white brace covered her neck.

"Where's my mom?" Darius asked, sitting across from Candice.

"She's upstairs. In her bed. Won't get out."

"So, you told her the truth?"

"I don't think this is a good time, considering Wellington is dying. She's dealing with enough, don't you think?"

"If it were up to me, I woulda left your ass behind bars."

"Why is it that everyone can bail your sorry ass out but you're so damn righteous that you can't forgive anybody else? Huh, Darius? Your little test came back negative and now you're shittin' on top of the world."

How'd she know that? Clenching his teeth, Darius thought about the message he'd left for Mandy. Closing in two inches from Candice's face, he said, "I don't know how you found out, but if you publicize anything about me, my mother, or my family, I'll make sure you dry-rot in prison. You hear me?"

"A fine role model you'll make for your son," Candice said. "You better be glad I got my purse and tote bag back from Ashlee or your ass would be six, ten, and midnight news!"

Grabbing Candice's blouse, Darius French-kissed her square in her mouth, thrusting his tongue down her throat. "You know you want me." Breathing in her face he said, "You know too much about me not to. You're curious. I can tell."

Trotting upstairs to his mother's room, Darius knocked on the door.

"Who is it?"

"It's me, Ma."

"Come in."

Entering his mother's room, Darius sat on her bed. "How are you?"

His mother was quiet.

"Wanna talk?"

She didn't respond.

"Where's my dad?"

Silence.

Darius knew she could say something, because she told him to come in. "You want me to leave?"

His mother shook her head.

Darius grabbed a pillow, laid his head at the foot of his mother's bed, then gently rubbed her feet. No one knew better than Darius Williams the power of the human touch. He'd call Fancy later to share his great news. Hopefully, after he'd finish taking care of his mom, Ladycat would pack her bags and move with him to Atlanta.

CHAPTER 33

Fancy

Two wrongs didn't make them right.

What woman wouldn't want a man who'd drop everything in his life to be at her side when she needed him?

No distance too far to travel. No mountain too high to climb. No pain too great to endure. Fancy had broken Desmond's heart countless times. Or perhaps Desmond was to blame for having a foolish heart. Irrespective of her analysis, if she used him again, he'd leave her for good.

God only knew how much Desmond had sacrificed to pay for her diamond solitaire. Should Fancy care? What if Desmond had more student loans and credit card debt than Fancy was willing to marry into? Perhaps she should give Desmond back his ring. But he was so excited. Fancy hadn't worked hard to become wealthy, to give her money away to bill collectors that didn't care who settled the account. What if Desmond's credit score was below seven hundred? Fancy didn't have that much love for him. One thing for sure, Fancy never had financially related concerns with Darius.

Prepping in the pastor's study for SaVoy's special day, Fancy stared at her reflection in the mirror, unsure if she'd accepted Desmond's proposal because she sincerely wanted to marry Dez, or because she loved the way he loved her. Why couldn't Darius love her the way Dez did?

Lavishly layering her skin with retinol vitamin A cream mixed with vitamin E oil, Fancy massaged her feet, then covered them with cotton socks, then massaged her legs, knees, thighs, butt, all the way up to her neck, continuing to her face. Admiring her body, she saw she had no cellulite, no stretch marks, no blemishes. Everything happened for a reason. Seeing how much weight her mother gained, maybe she should be grateful she wasn't carrying Darius's baby, especially since she wasn't a hundred percent sure she wanted Darius back in her life.

Careful not to graze her false eyelashes, Fancy meticulously applied her waterproof foundation. Tracing her eyes, then her lips with separate pencils, she blended sexy shades of brown eye shadow and mocha lipstick to perfection. Releasing the pins from her fresh Top Notch Salon weave, Fancy fingered the loose curls, tossing them over her shoulders. Stepping into her maid-of-honor dress, she removed her socks, easing on her open-toe shoes. Last and least desired, Fancy slipped on her engagement ring, knowing that would be the first thing Desmond would look for.

Feeling more like a bride, not a maid of anything, Fancy sashayed to the choir fitting room to join Tanya and the two bridesmaids Fancy hadn't met. It'd been a long time since Fancy had seen or spoken with Tanya, a friend she'd befriended in high school exclusively because of SaVoy.

Tanya was not sophisticated enough to hang out on or off campus with Fancy. Tanya was overweight, unattractive, and shy. SaVoy, with her tree-hugging personality, had insisted on welcoming Tanya to join them.

"Fancy, you're still so beautiful," Tanya said, smiling. "I'm so happy for our girl."

Suctioning in her stomach superflat, Fancy thought she had to hit the gym first thing in the morning to work off the two remaining pounds she'd gained from drowning her Darius sorrows in junk food. No man could make Fancy so depressed that she'd ruin her perfect body.

"I'm happy for SaVoy too," Fancy said, looking at Tanya's appearance. "You're looking good, but the way you hooked up that ensemble is killing me. Let me help you out."

Fancy should've helped Tanya when they were in high school, but Fancy hadn't matured beyond peer pressure. Looking good at all times, being best dressed, and most congenial was essential for Fancy's reputation. No one, except SaVoy, witnessed what Fancy had to endure at home. Cleaning up behind a drunken mother who threw up every weekend only scratched the surface of her childhood problems.

Tanya moved closer to Fancy. "I'm still trying to get myself together. I ended up leaving William. Marriage made him worse. He had the same old controlling, abusive ways. Somehow after I said, 'I do,' he thought signing the license gave him the right to beat me. But when he started acting a fool in front of our son, I knew my son and I had to go. Funny how I couldn't find the courage to protect myself, but I had the strength to protect my son."

"Well, good for you." Fancy removed, then reapplied Tanya's makeup. "Girl, you've got to make your twins comfortable. You can't just snap on a bra and you're done. Look at your titties all smashed under the wire." Fancy lifted each breast high into the cup, pulled the back comfortably across Tanya's shoulders, then reshaped Tanya's breasts until they touched, to show cleavage. Then Fancy went to work on Tanya's hair. "You definitely made the right decision to leave him. What are you doing now?"

"I'm just a stay-at-home mom for now." Lowering her head, Tanya continued. "On welfare."

Placing her hand under Tanya's chin, Fancy looked into Tanya's eyes, and said, "Honey, raising kids is a full-time job. Trust me, no mom is *just* a stay-at-home mom."

For a brief moment, Fancy wondered, what if her little girl hadn't been taken away?

"But I need a break. It's hard trying to find a job that pays enough to take care of our expenses, plus pay for day care. I can't afford either."

"Turn around. Look at yourself in the mirror."

"Wow." Tanya smiled, then covered her mouth. "Is that me?"

"A little attention to details goes a long way. From now on I want you to make time for Tanya. You're beautiful. You don't think I get this way by rushing out the door, or slapping on lipstick straight from a tube, do you?"

Hugging Fancy, Tanya said, "Thanks."

Fancy held Tanya's hand. "Welfare is a temporary solution to your future success. You have to visualize being wealthy, then commit to working hard to make it happen. I can help you. If I told you I grossed ten million last year, I know you wouldn't believe me. But it's true. If you want to make some real money, I need a dependable office assistant to operate my Oakland office. Nothing too demanding, but you have to be efficient and timely because in my business time is money. I'll cover your day-care expenses for six months. And if you find you love and have a passion for real estate, I'll pay for your classes, hire you as an agent, and we can both make money."

"For real?" Tanya became teary.

"None of that. Not today. You'll ruin my fabulous makeup job. Enjoy this weekend and call me Monday."

The flower girl raced into the room saying, "She's here. The limo just pulled up."

This was the moment Fancy had wished a long time for herself. She was happy for SaVoy and glad that Desmond was there. But in her heart, she truly wished she was the one marrying Darius.

CHAPTER 34

SaVoy

True love wasn't easy to find.

Marrying Tyronne Davis was a blessing. If SaVoy had listened to Fancy, she might have suffered Fancy's faith of being manless and confused, questioning if she wanted a husband, a relationship, or neither.

Yes, Tyronne knew the streets well. Was that a bad thing? He didn't hide his Sidekick. He always answered his phone. And the one time SaVoy caught him with a woman on his lap—after dumping the woman on the floor—Tyronne raced out of the club after SaVoy, then admitted the truth. Tyronne knew how to sweet-talk the ladies, but he wasn't a dog.

SaVoy's daddy once said, "A man who has something to hide will always get caught in a lie."

What SaVoy loved about Tyronne was, unlike Darius, Tyronne respected, loved, and protected her. And unlike Desmond, Tyronne didn't try to be somebody he wasn't. Tyronne wanted a good woman, but similar to finding a good man, a good woman was hard to find too. The one thing SaVoy had asked of Tyronne before they married, he had done. Tyronne had committed his life to God.

SaVoy gave thanks first unto the Lord, then to Vanessa, her father's girlfriend, for teaching her invaluable life lessons. Before SaVoy married Tyronne, Vanessa instructed her on how to masturbate and enjoy orgasms without losing her virginity. Then after the wedding reception, Vanessa had said, "Rule number one. Discuss your relationship issues with your man, not with your girlfriends. Number two, never, ever tell your friends, males and females, how good your man is in bed. That'll make them curious enough to fuck him behind your back." She added, "You never know. And three, don't sweat the small stuff. Not everything is worth arguing over." That was wise advice from a woman who refused to remarry.

Closing the door to their Hawaii honeymoon suite, SaVoy began preparing her body for her husband. She borrowed a few tips from Fancy, like the milk and honey bath and stretching before sex. SaVoy styled her hair, allowing a few curls to dangle. Then she put on a thin layer of pink lip gloss, her white sheer nightgown with matching robe, and clear high heels. Double-checking to ensure that the right CD was in the player, SaVoy unlocked the door and said, "Honey, I'm ready for you."

The music played as Tyronne strolled into the bedroom dressed in white linen. "Every time I close my eyes I thank the Lord that I've got you. And you've got me too . . ." Tyronne had dedicated Babyface's song as their special song when they first started dating.

"You look so beautiful, I almost don't want to touch you."

SaVoy smiled. "You'd better touch me soon before I explode."

Slowly, Tyronne untied, then peeled away her robe, letting it fall to the floor. He kissed her fingers, one at a time, trailing his moist lip prints over her wrist, to the arch in her elbow. He French-kissed her, moving to her triceps, and then he licked her armpit.

"Uh," SaVoy said, smirking.

"Uh, nothing, woman. No parts of you are off-limits to me ever again."

SaVoy unbuttoned his shirt, then touched Tyronne's muscular chest and began kissing him as he continued loving her. His lips patted through the material around her nipple, making her hotter.

Her tongue fluttered in his ear.

Softly he sucked her breast, soaking her gown. "So beautiful," he said, kissing the other breast.

Easing her hands to his waist, she untied his pants, shoving them toward his ankles. Tyronne stepped, leaving two circles where his feet were once planted.

He slid the thin straps off her shoulders, releasing the gown to the floor. With one hand cradled around her back and the other underneath her knees, Tyronne carried, then laid her in the middle of their king-size bed atop the soft white sheets.

"Let me see her," he whispered, removing his linen jacket and tossing it to the floor.

Spreading her legs wide, SaVoy closed her eyes. Tyronne kissed her lips as his saliva rolled between her cheeks over her asshole.

"Mmmmm," she moaned with pleasure.

He placed his finger against her hymen, pressing gently. "That's what we're going to work getting past." He poked. "This outer layer of tissue right here."

As Tyronne crawled on top of her, SaVoy lifted her legs, wondering if his dick was too big. What if it didn't fit? Sliding the tip of his head in, Tyronne gently moved in and out, stretching her hymen— the membranous fold of tissue. Soon her pearly gate would finally unlock.

That wasn't so bad, SaVoy thought. In fact, it felt good.

Tyronne's lips covered hers as his tongue invaded her mouth.

"I love you, SaVoy," he said, gazing deep into her eyes.

"I love you, Tyronne."

"I'm gonna go a little deeper. If you're ever too uncomfortable, let me know."

"Okay," SaVoy said, closing her eyes. Bracing her arms and hands against his back, she held him tight.

"Relax," he said, kissing her again.

Tyronne's shaft pressed firm against her cherry, pushing in and out. With each thrust he probed a little deeper.

"Ow," SaVoy moaned.

"You want me to stop?"

"No, don't stop," SaVoy said, burying her face in his chest. With every thrust, SaVoy held Tyronne closer.

"Ow." She paused, breathed, then repeated, "Ow," a little louder. "Ba-beee! Ba-bee! Owwww!" SaVoy screamed like never before as the excruciating pain darted throughout her entire body.

"I'm in. Relax. She's open. You're not a virgin anymore. We can stop here and continue in the morning or I can go down on you if you'd like."

Shaking her head, SaVoy cried tears of pain and joy as her husband continued loving her.

SaVoy Edmonds-Davis knew neither of them was perfect, but they both believed in God and that was a blessed foundation to build their marriage.

CHAPTER 35

Simone

He was worth more to her dead than alive.
Who does that bitch think she is, telling me what she's not going to do? Simone thought, exiting the freeway en route to Jada's house. Her nostrils flared, her chest rose and fell with each breath, while her fingers wrapped snug at ten and two on the steering wheel. *She didn't have the decency to phone and say my son's father was dead.*

Bitch. I hate her, Simone thought, desperately wanting to curse aloud. "Uuuhhhh!" she screamed, squirming in her seat.

Leaning forward from the backseat, her son frowned. "Mommy, you gotta use the bathroom?"

Simone should've used the restroom when she stopped for gas, but she was too anxious to hear Jada's excuse. Simone was livid and didn't mind taking out her frustrations on that "I got my own business, don't need a man, but I'll take yours" Hollywood whore.

The thought of kicking Jada's ass and going to the bathroom brought back bad memories of the night Wellington had ended their relationship, all casual and shit.

Simone had gone to the bathroom and returned with a smoking-hot wet towel. Cleaning Wellington off, she asked, "Is everything okay? Why'd you stop?"

"Yeah, give me a minute," Wellington had said, rubbing his head.

"Just seems like you're tensed. Almost like you forced that orgasm out." Simone tried reviving The Ruler, but he only shriveled up more.

She knew him too well. He might as well tell her the truth.

"Diamond asked me to marry her."

What the hell? The towel smacked against his privates like Silly Putty sticking to the wall.

"Ouch! Goddamn, Simone. What did you do that for?" Wellington had asked, covering his dick.

"How could you make love to me without telling me this first! And what did you tell her?"

"I said yes."

"Fuck you, Wellington Jones. And fuck that Hollywood whore. I hate her ass too!"

But why did Simone hate Jada? She didn't. Simone was possessed with envy, the green-eyed monster that had turned her into a raging beast. Jada hadn't done anything to her. She was always polite. Friendly. Treated her son well. There was no justifiable explanation for why Simone loved Wellington but still hated Jada.

"Mommy, you okay?"

"No, baby. I'm not okay." Who was going to pay their mortgage?

"We're going to see Daddy!" Wellington the second said, bouncing on the backseat.

"Calm down, baby."

The father of her son, the love of her life, the keeper of her lifestyle, and the source of her happiness was gone, forever.

Why hadn't Simone come to L.A. earlier? She couldn't ask Wellington for money while he was sick. If she had tried, Jada would've intervened. Jada was the reason Simone didn't visit Wellington at the hospital. Simone didn't want Jada telling her what to do. Jazzmyne could've asked. Wellington could've asked. Darius could've asked and she would've come. But not that Hollywood whore.

Huffing, Simone took her last turn into Jada's driveway. The spinning tires skidded to a smoky stop. "Over five hundred miles I had to drive to handle my business. Oh, she'd better not piss me off ta-day! Get out, Wellington." Simone's wide hips swung hard as she marched to Jada's front door.

Ding-dong. Ding-dong. Ding-dong. Ding-dong.

Yanking the door open, Jazzmyne complained, "Hey, lean off the doorbell. We heard you the first fifty times."

"Hmph." Just because she was Wellington's only sibling didn't mean Simone wouldn't whup her ass. Simone stormed into the house, tugging Wellington the Second along. "Where is she?"

Scanning the living room, Simone decided she was going to get Wellington's framed jazz pictures, his decorative jazz rug with Billy Holiday on it. Wellington the Second wanted his daddy's pictures of them together.

"Well, hello, Simone. Is there a problem?" Jazzmyne asked, closing the door.

"Baby, cover your ears," Simone told her son, then said, "Ya damn right there's a problem. I wanna know, why did I have to call the hospital to find out about my son's father's situation? And to find out where his remains were sent? Huh, why?"

Placing both hands on her hips, Jazzmyne said, "Look, sit your ass down. You're not running anything up in here. Now if you had come when Jada called you, you would've known like everybody else. You come marchin' in here like a madwoman—"

Madwoman wasn't the proper word. Demon was more like what Simone had turned into, holding an invisible pitchfork, waiting to stick the first person that made the wrong move.

"I don't have to kiss her ass! That's my baby's daddy. Wellington's only biological child. At least I didn't go around lying to him for twenty years. Jada, Jada, Jada. Every other word out of his mouth was Jada. Wellington thought that bitch could walk on water and do no wrong until she surprised his ass. Then he still forgave her. Hmph."

What was up with men overlooking women who treated them wrong, marrying these women, and at the same time trying to hold onto the women who treated them right? Who was at the top of love triangles?

Shaking her head, Jazzmyne asked, "Simone, what does that have to do with anything? My brother is dead."

Wellington the Second ran toward Simone, screaming, "My daddy is dead?"

Opening her arms, Simone picked up her son. "No, baby. He's okay."

"Where is he?"

"Mommy's talking right now. Be quiet."

Tilting her head sideways, Jazzmyne frowned at Simone, deliberately saying, "Jada isn't feeling well. You need to show some respect. Maybe Jada will talk to you tomorrow or the next day."

"Oh, hell no." Lowering her son to his feet, Simone hollered, "She's going to talk to me today. Right here! Right now! Jada! Oh, Jada!"

Darius stood at the top of the stairs. "What's your damn problem?" Almost skiing down the steps, he stopped two inches from Simone's face, staring down at her. "What's your problem, disrespecting my mother's house?"

Damn, he was fine. Simone's heart raced as she said, "News flash. This is just as much Wellington the Second's home as it is yours. Even more so if you ask me. What I need to know is, when is yo' mama going to make the funeral arrangements? And I want a copy of my son's father's will."

Shunning Simone, Darius nodded. "So that's the real reason you're here, trick. Well, you'll have to wait until my mother is ready to deal with this. You'll get what's yours. And not a penny more."

"Jada!" Simone yelled over Darius's head.

Darius covered Simone's mouth, then harshly said, pointing, "You have three choices. You walk out that door, get carried out the door, or crawl your fat ass out the door, but whichever way, you got to get the hell out of here." He steered Simone toward the door Jazzmyne held open.

"Don't you talk to my mama like that," Wellington the Second shouted, kicking Darius in the shin.

"You little . . ." Darius swung, grazing his behind.

As hard as she could, Simone slapped Darius's face while he was bent to her level. "Stay away from my baby, you murderer."

Darius's hand rose high into space above her head, descending inches from Simone's face. "Oh, I oughtta," he grunted, balling his fist.

Jazzmyne yelled, "Darius, don't! She's not worth it."

Darryl walked through the door, looked at Darius, then raced and grabbed Darius's arm, pulling his fist to his side. "Son, what the hell are you doing?"

Launching her face forward, Simone said, "Oh, let him hit me so I can get more money. He'll be signing those NBA checks over to me."

"What's going on here?" Darryl asked, looking at Simone, Jazzmyne, and finally Darius.

Grinding his teeth, Darius said, "I'm going upstairs to check on my mother, and all I know is she'd"—Darius pointed his finger in Simone's face—"better be gone when I come back or I'm calling the police."

Darryl motioned for Darius to go upstairs. "I'll handle this. Simone, have a seat."

Darius stood at the top of the stairs listening as Simone sat with Darryl and Jazzmyne. "What's the problem?"

"All I wanna know is, what's taking Jada so long to make the funeral arrangements?" Simone answered, staring at the top of the stairs. Darius had taken a seat on the steps, intensely watching her.

"Wellington, baby, come with me," Jazzmyne said, escorting the child out of the room. "He doesn't need to hear this."

"Simone, have you ever lost a loved one?" Darryl asked.

"Yes, Wellington. Don't you think I loved him too? But what does that have to do with what I'm talking about?"

"Jada is grieving the death of *her husband.*"

"Yeah, I can see. Is that why you're here? To console her? Or are you trying to steal the money Wellington left for me and my son, huh? How clever, lover man. You can have her ass, and I mean that literally, but you ain't taking shit that's mine."

Simone wasn't stupid. She could tell Darryl was plotting to be Jada's next husband. Where was his ass the twenty-plus years Wellington raised his son? If Jada did turn around and marry Darryl she was a bigger whore than Simone imagined.

"Simone, I'm not here to argue, or debate, or see who can yell the loudest. Jada is depressed. She's not mentally ready to deal with anything. Funeral arrangements, work, probate, nothing. So you'll have to wait until she is. We'll notify you."

Simone mimicked, "'We'll notify you.' You ain't got shit to do with this. This is between me and Jada. If it weren't for her, Wellington would've been married to me. Why does everyone always protect and take up for her triflin' ass?"

Darryl politely replied, "Because we love her."

Darius echoed from the top of the stairs, "Yeah, *we* love her, not you."

Simone stared at Darius, then at Darryl, wishing she had someone to feel that way about her. Jada had one man dead less than a week and another man obviously waiting to take his place. What did Jada have that Simone didn't? What made some women so lucky at love and others so unlucky?

"Well, I'm not gonna wait for her to get better. I'll have my attorney proceed and I'll make my son's father's funeral arrangements myself."

"There's no getting through to you." Darryl called out, "Jazzmyne, bring Simone her son. They're leaving."

"No, we're not. I'll be right here in L.A. until everything's settled."

"Good luck. But I wouldn't waste money on a lawyer just yet. Only Wellington's wife can legally make any decisions, and I've seen the will and unless there's another one that I haven't seen, you're not getting as much as you probably think."

Narrowing her eyes to a sliver, Simone said, "We'll see about that. Come on, Wellington."

Driving directly to the funeral home, Simone requested, "I'd like to view my son's father's body."

A man dressed in a suit and tie replied, "Sorry, but we'll have to contact Mrs. Tanner for approval."

Simone drove to Wellington's attorney's office and demanded a copy of the will.

"Sorry, but that's confidential. You'll have to wait for the probate hearing. Maybe Mrs. Tanner can give you a copy," the petite secretary suggested.

Simone drove to Wellington's bank. He'd wired her money on countless occasions. "Yes, I'd like to know if my son is the beneficiary on his father's account."

"You have identification for your son?" the teller asked.

Simone exhaled, then handed the woman Wellington the Second's passport.

The clerk asked a few more questions, tapped on several keys, and replied, "Yes, he sure is."

"Great, I'd like to close this account."

"I'm sorry, we can't do that."

Simone whispered, "His father is dead. I'm his mother. And I'd like to close this account right now. How much is in it?"

"We can't disclose that information to you. Nor can you close this account. First we have to wait until the bank receives a death certificate. And your son is not the only beneficiary on this account."

"Who else is on the account?"

"We can't disclose that information to you either. You'll have to wait until probate settles, and depending on how fast the primary beneficiary closes this account, if she closes the account, that could take a while. Sorry." The clerk looked at the line and said, "Next."

Simone repeated in her mind, *If she closes the account.* That bitch had control of everything.

Simone had problems that only money could solve. The IRS had placed a tax lien against her house, threatening a forced sale, and they'd already repossessed her cars. And did the government care how much they got in exchange for her personal property? Hell no. She would've been better off selling the car, but she couldn't diminish her image. Compound interest, penalties, and fees were multiplying daily.

Simone should've allowed Wellington's accountant to do her taxes when Wellington offered years ago, but she didn't want Jada in her business. Figured Wellington would stop giving her money if Jada saw how frivolously she'd spent his generous child support, traveling around the world with her girlfriends.

Her lifestyle went from driving two expensive foreign cars, to leasing a midsize rental. Simone deserved to live the life Jada and Wellington had, even if she was single. Unless Simone got her hands on thirty-five grand quick, they'd have to move in with her mother. Maybe she should've visited her baby's daddy while he was alive.

Why did Wellington have to be the one who died?

CHAPTER 36

Melanie

Money. The root of all evil.

People who hadn't spoken in years traveled miles praying that their old rich relative, distant friend, ex or estranged lover was generous enough to leave something in the will for them. Not a pet, or a stamp collection; most people wanted what they hadn't earned and probably didn't deserve, OPM, other people's money.

Melanie had nothing to lose and everything to gain. Wellington had died, making her the multimillionaire she'd dreamt of being all her life. Morgan wasn't his biological daughter, but Melanie had convinced Wellington that since he'd taken care of Darius for more than twenty years and Darius wasn't his, the least he could do, since they were lovers and in love, was financially provide for her and Morgan.

Any woman could open her legs to fuck or open her mouth to suck a dick for free, but not Melanie Marie Thompson. She knew her self-worth. Knew what she wanted and exactly how to get it. Wellington was her security blanket and now that he was dead, she was getting paid.

Ringing Jada's doorbell, Melanie fussed with a few out-of-place strands of hair on Morgan's head. "Keep still."

"That's enough, Mama, I look pretty. Can't I be a tad messy sometimes?"

"No, you cannot. The best-kept ladies get the richest men. Remember that."

Morgan shook her head, singing, "I ain't sayin' I'm a gold digger, but I ain't messin' with no broke niggas."

Melanie scolded, "Didn't I tell you to take the word nigga out of our theme song?"

Morgan rebutted, "But it's in the song and it sounds better."

"I don't care what sounds better. You are forbidden to use that word."

Shaking her head, Melanie thought, *My God, why does my child have to have the last word every single time?*

"Okay, if it makes you feel better, I won't use it in your presence."

Melanie was thankful the double door opened on one side, because it took all the strength she had not to pop Morgan in the mouth.

"May I help you?" the man asked.

"Yes, I'm looking for Jada Tanner," Melanie said, admiring the handsome hunk of a man standing before her.

"And you are?" he questioned.

She knew exactly who he was, and answered, "Melanie Marie Thompson, and you?"

Darius slammed the door in her face.

Melanie rang the doorbell repeatedly. This time an older but similar-looking man opened the door. "Yes?"

"Before you slam the door in my face too, this is Wellington's daughter, Morgan, and I'm her mother, Melanie Marie Thompson."

"I'm Darryl Williams, the man of this house, and Wellington doesn't have a daughter."

"Yes, he does," an old familiar voice resonated in the background. Jada still sounded the same, but she looked despicable.

Darryl responded to Jada, "Sweetheart, you should be in bed. I can handle this for us. Go back upstairs."

"Yeah, Ma. You don't know what you're saying. Wellington didn't have any other children. All of these leeches are trying to get paid and I ain't havin' it. Especially not from her nasty ass—"

"Darius Jones," Jada said.

Both Darryl and Darius stared at Jada.

"Whateva," Jada said, squeezing between them.

Sweetheart? What was this? Wellington was barely dead and Darryl was being ultrafriendly with Jada and awfully comfortable like they were one big happy family.

Morgan pinched her nose. "Mommy, she looks and smells funny."

Ignoring Morgan's truth, Melanie guessed girlfriend had her thang going on too. Melanie said, "We're not leaving," trying to muscle her way between them.

Darius was the first to grab her arm, shoving her three steps back.

"Mommy, you can't intimidate everybody. He's stronger than you."

Jada stood face-to-face with Melanie.

Yeah, Jada was big and bad because she had backup. If her stank booty was home alone, she probably wouldn't have opened the door 'cause Jada knew who was more dominant.

"At least the child has common sense. Melanie, you have a lot of nerve knocking on my front door."

"I didn't knock. I rang the bell."

"I don't have the energy to argue. If you want to know if Wellington left you and Morgan anything, he didn't." Jada disappeared inside.

"Wait, that's a lie! You liar! I know he did because he told me he had his attorney revise his will to include us before he died."

Reappearing, Jada coldly said, "The papers were never signed."

"Mama, why are you bothering this woman?" Morgan asked, then pointed behind them. "What are you talking about? My daddy isn't dead. He's waiting for us in the car."

Raising her eyebrows, Jada slammed the door.

Melanie covered Morgan's mouth, pushing her toward the car.

"Didn't I tell you not to say anything? You'd better hope you haven't ruined my chances of getting that money."

"Or?" Morgan asked, being shoved into the backseat.

"You don't wanna find out the answer to that question."

"Why not?"

"Sit your smart ass down and shut up!"

"If you say so."

CHAPTER 37

Fancy

There was no place like home.

Fancy could've stayed in her Oakland penthouse, but it didn't compare to waking up to an ocean view's sunrise. In time, she'd spend more time in Oakland, but only if her mother refused to stay with her in Malibu after having the baby.

SaVoy's wedding was beautiful, and by now SaVoy should be in Honolulu in her honeymoon suite sharing her sacred virginity with her husband, Tyronne. Fancy cared not to count the times or number of men she'd sexed, including Desmond, who was eagerly waiting naked in her bed. Being with Dez was okay because Fancy needed to know if she was making the right decision. Gradually, Fancy understood what Caroline meant by thinking with your heart. Marriage was easy to get into, hard to get out of, especially when the relationship wasn't equally yoked and equally stroked.

Sex was one thing. Making love was another. As estranged as her relationship was with Darius their chemistry blended like the milk and honey she'd just added to her bathwater. The Jacuzzi was filled with ultrawarm water to blend the sweetness and softness into her skin.

The loofa sponge lightly rotated in tiny circular motions from her foot, up her leg, pausing, giving her knee special attention. Moving up her thigh, Fancy abandoned the loofa, watching it float as she caressed her body. It'd been too long since she'd shared herself with anyone. Tonight, she'd try her best to give her all to Desmond: mind, body, and soul.

Closing her eyes, Fancy moaned, "Ummm," touching her breasts, her lips, her neck. Every nerve ending tingled with aliveness, reminding her she'd survived. Fancy whispered, "Thank you, Lord," grateful she wasn't pregnant by a man she wasn't with. Her head lay on the white inflated pillow.

Who was Darius loving? Fucking? Why was he so unforgettable?

"Love yourself first." Fancy reminded herself of what was most important. She was. That's why Desmond was in her bed and not Darius. Michael Baines had phoned, inviting her to partner on a REIT, Real Estate Investment Trust. The deal was too lucrative to say no to. But would she end up fucking Michael? He was a good catch. Tall, dark, handsome, wealthy, sparkling white teeth, the brightest smile, and Michael was always happy. Never spoke negative about anyone.

Would Desmond move to California or would she move to Atlanta? Fancy didn't want Darius to think she was following behind him. Was she? Would she? If that was as close as she could get, maybe.

"Mind if I join you?" Desmond asked.

Opening her eyes, Fancy admired Desmond's sexy physique. Unlike most men, Dez was so sincere. Genuine. Gullible. Henpecked, as the older generation would say.

"Sure, I'd like that," she answered. She welcomed a distraction from the marathon of thoughts racing in her head.

Desmond stepped into the Jacuzzi. "Dang, this water feels soft. What's in here?"

"My secret ingredients. Come here. Lay your head on my pillow. Relax."

Fancy reached for the softer sponge. Dipping it into the water, she washed Desmond's neck, shoulders, chest, and back, ever so gently.

"Umm, that feels so good. I never had a woman bathe me before."

Why didn't that surprise Fancy?

"Consider this my way of saying thanks for taking care of me."

The sponge traveled under the water, dipping in the waves of Desmond's abs, around his sides, to his lower back. Fancy swiped the sponge between his cheeks, massaging his asshole.

"Hey, whoa, not too deep."

"Relax," Fancy said, swishing Desmond's balls.

Her hand wrapped around his shaft. Slowly she moved her hand up and down, over his head, then back down, delving into the deepest part of the base. "You know, Dez, if you start exercising this part"—she squeezed the muscles hiding at the base of his pubic hairs—"your erection can become ten times stronger. If you do what I tell you your dick will be superhard and amazingly strong. Just contract and relax. Contract, yeah, like that, now relax. Move your dick up and down without touching it. Now hold it down with your hand and apply upward resistance. See if you can make your hand move."

"How do you know so much about a man's dick?"

Fancy smiled, then answered, "I read a lot."

Straddling Desmond in the Jacuzzi, Fancy squatted on his head. "Umm, I'd forgotten how good you feel, Dez."

Lowering her hips a little at a time, Fancy rolled back and forth, teasing her G-spot.

"I love you, Fancy."

"Uh-huh. I know, Dez." She moaned his name, riding him halfway down, then back up.

Her pussy was hot, wet from the inside out. Quickening her stride, Fancy kissed Dez, then leaned her head back, placing his hands over her breasts. Dipping into her pot of honey, Fancy stroked her clit.

"I'm cumming, Dez. I'm cumming so hard."

"Me too," Dez grunted, forcing her hips lower.

Slowly Fancy closed her eyes, moaning, "Fuck me, Darius. Fuck me, Daddy!" She yelled, then swallowed a gulp of water.

Breaking through the layer of water covering her body, Fancy swiped her face, gasping for air. "Huuuh. Huuuuh. What's the hell wrong with you?"

Silently, Desmond stepped out, dragging bubbles and milky water over the side.

Puzzled, Fancy said, "O-*kay*, then let's get out, why don't we? Dez, what is it?"

Drying herself off, she watched Desmond do the same. She wanted so badly to finish making love, but what was Dez's problem? Lying on her back beside him, Fancy stared at the ceiling.

Desmond's hands cupped his dick like he was hiding it from her.

Fancy kissed Desmond, then rolled over. "I'm exhausted and sleepy. We can continue this in the morning," she lied, knowing she'd be out of the bed well before Desmond woke up.

CHAPTER 38

Darius

When Darius returned from Atlanta, he was putting his dad out of his mom's house. Darius carried his packed suitcase into the hallway, setting the brown designer bag by the rail. The first day of training camp was tomorrow.

Knock, knock.

"Yes," Candice answered.

"Can I come in?"

"Sure, it's open."

Turning the knob, Darius entered. "Got a minute?" he asked, sitting on the bench.

Surrounded by pillows, Candice sandwiched one between her thighs, sat in the center of the bed, folded her legs, and listened. The head bandage was gone, but a small scar remained.

"I guess that means yes. Look, I've been thinking about what you said the other day and just wanted to say, you're right."

"I'm right?" Candice repeated.

"Yes, and wrong, but I know beneath all your snooping, you have my mother's best interest at heart. Please look after her until I get back."

Candice had known his mom before he was born. Considering his dad was being kicked out soon, Darius feared that if he ostracized Candice and if Auntie Jazzmyne left, his mom would be all alone. Darius was moving too far away to personally take care of his mother.

Candice chuckled. "Your dad's got that covered. Besides, I'm perfectly content staying out of the way. The less I know the better. I'm here in case she needs me, but after the funeral, I'm gone." A tear fell from her eye.

"There'll be none of that," Darius said, extending his hands. "Don't leave my mom. She needs you."

Candice gently placed her palms atop his. "Give me a hug." As she moved closer, Candice's breasts pressed hard against his chest. "Good luck in Atlanta." Her face nestled into his collarbone as she kissed him softly. "You know you want me too."

If this ain't the realest. "I gotta go." Darius stood so fast, Candice fell over the bench onto the floor. He didn't look back. Darius loved pussy. Ten, maybe fifteen years his senior was cool as long as there were no gray hairs, which he was almost certain Candice had a few. The first time he saw one he threw up between the woman's legs, slapping her thighs together. Darius couldn't remember her name, but he'd said, "Shave that nasty shit off!" then left. Candice was fine. Not that fine. The thought of being with a woman more than twice his age was downright nauseating.

Darius closed Candice's door. Standing in the hallway, he thought, *Go on, get it out of the way, dawg.*

His mother was better but not her normal self. Darius got her to do things others couldn't, like she'd finally agreed to make Wellington's arrangements.

Darryl felt Darius was infringing upon his time and invading his space, so Darryl eagerly encouraged him to go, saying, "The assistant coach doesn't need a reason to act a fool. Leave. Now."

Knock, knock.

"Yes," his dad's voice resonated from inside his mother's bedroom.

"Ma."

"Come in, sweetie."

Afraid he'd see more than he desired, Darius opened the door six inches, standing outside. "Ma, I'm headin' out to Atlanta for a few days. I'll be back when you set a date for the services."

"No, come here. Why are you leaving me?"

Darryl interrupted. "He'll be back, honey. I'll be here with you. Darius has to go."

There was something chilling about the way his dad said "Darius has to go" that made him angry. *That's my mom*, Darius thought, entering her room.

"How long? Why, Darius?"

"Not long, Ma. I promise. You my girl, remember that," he said, kissing his mother's forehead, then her cheek. "I love you. I'll call as soon as I get in. Now give me a kiss." Darius leaned his cheek beside his mother's lips as she puckered.

"Okay, sweetie."

Emphatically, Darryl said, "Good-bye, Son."

Flatly, Darius replied, "Bye, Dad. And do not let Kevin step foot in my office."

Damn, Darius wished he had time to hire new staff and fire his dad.

"Don't forget who helped you get that NBA contract. One phone call and you'll never see your first game."

"Don't you forget who owns my multimillion-dollar company," Darius returned, fire fueling his words.

"Billion-dollar company sweetie," his mom said, slapping Darryl repeatedly. "Don't you dare talk to my baby like that, like *he* owes *you* something. Darius has done more for you than you've ever done for him."

Good. Sucking his teeth, Darius closed his mom's door. *So that's why he was eager to step in.* Darius was clear on what he had to do but had no idea before today that he was a billionaire.

Tapping on Candice's door, Darius peeped inside. Candice sat beside the bay window staring outside. "Do me a favor. Let me know if my brother Kevin conducts any business for my company while I'm away."

"What? You're asking me to spy for you?"

"It's what you do best. Yes. Thank you and good-bye."

Exhaling, Darius raced downstairs with his suitcase. "Should I fire my dad, demote him, or leave him alone?" Being a family for the first time felt more strange than natural. Darius exited the front door, tossing his luggage in the trunk.

"You don't have to worry about that right now, baby. He'll give you the answer," his auntie Jazzmyne said, sitting on the sofa. She never turned around.

Kissing her cheek, Darius said, "Keep an eye on him for me."

"I'll keep two. Now you get out of here."

Opening his car door, Darius stopped and smiled as a familiar car drove up. He mouthed, "Ladycat." His heart began beating fast but damn near stopped when saw a man in the passenger seat.

Fancy parked beside his car. When she got out, dude got out too.

"Hi, Darius. Desmond, can you get the sympathy card and flowers out of the car for me please?"

"Sure, baby," Desmond answered.

Darius thought about the conversation he'd had with Fancy's mother. "Hey, Ladycat," he said, holding her close. "I'm so sorry I didn't listen to you. I hope you've forgiven me."

What was Fancy doing with that loser who damn near broke his neck getting back to her?

"I have forgiven you."

But not the way Darius wanted her to. "Can we talk? I mean can I listen to what you have to say?"

Desmond shook his head.

Fancy replied, "This is not a good time."

"For me either. I'm on my way to NBA camp." *Compete with that, you little unemployed runt.*

"Besides, I'm not sure you heard my side objectively the first time."

Great! Fancy had given Darius the perfect opportunity. "Oh, you mean when we spent the night together at my house in Oakland last week? Baby, don't. Don't do this to us. Please, I've been dying inside without you."

Desmond rattled the flowers. "You lied to me. Again. Let's go."

Darius's eyes locked into Fancy's. He could feel she'd give him another chance if he didn't fuck it up before she decided.

"Darius, this is my fiancé, Desmond Brown. Dez, this is my ex-fiancé, Darius Williams."

That was a jacked-up introduction.

"What's up, man?" Desmond said, squaring his shoulders, then extending his hand to Darius.

Staring down into Desmond's eyes, Darius shook his hand. "Congratulations, man."

Desmond smiled. "Thanks."

Darius thought *Thanks, my ass, with that punk-ass handshake,* then boldly said, "On finding your own woman. Fancy is mine."

Hugging Fancy for what seemed like forever, Darius was pleased when she didn't pull away from his embrace. His lips pressed against her ear as he whispered, "I love you, Ladycat. Please. Come back home."

CHAPTER 39

Jada

Once an adult, three times a child.

Infancy to childhood, teens to late twenties, and after fifty, men were like kids. Immature. Selfish. Know-it-alls.

Jada stood in Wellington's study. His bookshelves spilled over with nonfiction, accounting, investing, and, kneeling to the bottom row, Jada scanned a series of subjects on anticancer diets based on whole foods; and vitamins, minerals, enzymes, and herbs used to strengthen the body's ability to eliminate cancer cells. Hypnosis. How to boost your immune system to combat and destroy cancer cells.

"My God," she said, sitting at Wellington's desk. "That silly, silly man."

Jada fumbled through Wellington's personal items and newspaper clippings. The last time she'd snooped through his personal items his PDA schedule had Melanie on the calendar. When Jada made that discovery, she'd flown all the way to San Francisco to confront Wellington while he dined at the Cheesecake Factory atop Macy's with Melanie. The entire ordeal was ludicrous. Jada couldn't keep a grown man from fucking even if he was her husband. From that day forward, Jada promised herself never to invade Wellington's privacy.

Jada's curiosity was an intrusion of sorts because Wellington had hid so much from her. Didn't he trust her to have his best interest at heart? He'd saved the articles on Coretta Scott King's death. Well, she too sought alternative cancer treatments. There had to be some theory behind the vast options, but where was the proof?

"Goddamn greedy Americans can spend billions of dollars to put a man on the moon, but with all the money we've donated to cancer research they can't find a cure." When was the last time researchers found a cure for any disease? "All these new medications with more side effects that keep people sick . . . You bastards helped kill my husband!" Jada yelled, flinging recyclable paper into the trash. "This isn't news, this is propaganda."

Cleaning out Wellington's safe, Jada wasn't surprised as she picked up one of dozens of bottles that fell out. She read the label, "Detox pills; chemo replacement enzymes." Shaking every bottle, she saw they were all empty and had expired over a year ago.

"That childish man tried to treat his cancer naturally only to find out the disease had spread rapidly throughout his body."

Alternative medicine. He had to have gotten it from Mexico or Melanie. Either way it hadn't worked. Jada really didn't know enough about the treatments, but why didn't he tell her? Early surgery could've prolonged his life. Maybe he could've done both. Well, it was too late now.

Closing the safe, Jada opened the file cabinet. She thumbed through the Ls once, twice, three times. The file labeled *Living Trust* was gone. No telling what Wellington had advised his attorney or who removed the file and why. Jada could speculate forever and not find the answer. Wellington would be her first guess, then Darius, Darryl, Jazzmyne, Candice, everyone who had access.

Exiting Wellington's office, Jada sat in the living room for the first time since Wellington's death. She held Darryl's hand, thankful she didn't have to manage on her own. That sneaky husband of hers.

Exhaling, Jada said, "At least he was consistent."

Jazzmyne sat quietly watching. Jada was sure Jazzmyne didn't approve of Darryl being in the house but hadn't commented.

"I'm ready," Jada whispered. "It's time."

"What?" Jazzmyne said softly.

"I'm ready to handle all of Wellington's affairs. I have to find the copy of his living trust, but we can proceed without it. I must've misplaced it and can't remember." Jada paused, hoping Jazzmyne or Darryl would speak up. Neither of them spoke a word. "Where's the phone?"

Darryl asked, "Are you sure? Sure you're ready to handle this? So soon?"

Jazzmyne frowned. "Don't you think it's time? My brother's body is lying cold in a morgue. He deserves better."

That was debatable, Jada thought. But no one except her knew the whole truth. She was kidding herself if she believed Wellington had told her everything, but Jada prayed she knew more than Melanie and Simone.

"Give me the phone, the number to the funeral home, and Wellington's attorney's." Jada couldn't remember to eat, let alone recall details.

Jazzmyne offered, "I can do this for you."

"No, I have to do this myself. I'm ready to bring closure to this part of my life." Jada looked at Darryl. "And start anew."

Dialing the number to Wellington's attorney first, Jada said, "I'd like to arrange a preliminary probate hearing in two days. Messenger me Wellington's latest living trust." She needed to see what the attorney would present.

"That's incredibly short notice, Mrs. Tanner. Can we do it next week?"

"Next week is fine. A few more days won't matter. But make sure I receive a copy of the trust today."

"But—"

"No buts." Jada hung up, then dialed her pastor. "Yes, Pastor."

"Hello, Sister Tanner. Praise God, you're finally ready?"

"Yes."

"I know you don't want to delay Brother Jones's services. I'm available tomorrow. Or the next day."

"Tomorrow is fine."

Jazzmyne moved to the edge of her seat, shaking her head.

"Tomorrow is not fine. You can't just put this off, then all of a sudden bury my brother without giving his out-of-town clients and friends an opportunity to attend."

Jada looked at Jazzmyne and said, "He was my husband. Not yours. I don't mean to sound rude or insensitive, but I have to let go. The sooner the better. He's gone. My soul mate is gone."

Darryl wrapped his arm around Jada's shoulder, reminding her of what Wellington had said.

"So, probate is next week?" Darryl asked.

"Yes, I need to call Simone and Melanie. Did either of them go into Wellington's study?"

Suddenly avoiding eye contact, Jazzmyne said, "Not that I know of, but I can text them if you want."

"I'll do it. I prefer to call."

Jada dialed Simone's number first.

"Simone, probate is next week. The funeral is tomorrow. Did you go into Wellington's study?"

"Tomorrow," Simone said. "We can't make it tomorrow. I need more time."

"What you need to do is make up your mind. I'll call you back with the details. Services are tomorrow at three with the burial immediately following."

Hanging up, Jada phoned Melanie with the same information.

"Where's Darius?"

"He went to Atlanta, remember?"

"Oh, that's right." Jada dialed Darius's number. "Honey, the services are tomorrow at three."

"Ma, can you do it next week? I have an appointment I have to attend tomorrow morning in Dallas. But once I'm done, I'm on my way, Ma. I'll be on the next flight out. I'll see you tomorrow *night*."

Jada looked at Jazzmyne. "Can you call everyone and reschedule the funeral for next week?"

"Oh, because Darius asked, you'll change everything, but not for me after all I've done for you?"

"Please, don't take any of this personally. You know I love you."

Extending her hand, Jazzmyne pressed her lips together, then replied, "Give me the damn phone, I'll handle my brother's services the right way."

Jada added, "Oh, and please call Fancy and give her the details. I'm going back upstairs. Wake me when Darius arrives."

"I'll go with," Darryl said, escorting Jada toward the staircase.

Peering over her shoulder, Jada caught a glimpse of Jazzmyne staring before suddenly looking away. Whatever Jazzmyne was attempting to do Jada would eventually find out.

Peeling back the covers, Jada crawled into bed fully dressed. Removing her shoes, Darryl sat beside her.

"Ba, are you all right?"

"Please don't ever call me ba again," Jada said.

"What can I call you?"

"Anything except ba."

"Do you want to do a weekend hideaway before the hearing?"

"Darryl?"

"Yes, b—honey."

"Why are you really here with me? Wasn't it enough taking over Darius's company?"

Darryl rubbed her back. "I'm here because I've got a second chance. I'm not going to blow it. And I've always loved you."

"Always?"

"Yes, always. And I still do."

"Wellington believed you only came back into our lives, Darius's and mine, because you saw a financial opportunity for security. Is that why you hired Kevin to work at Darius's firm after Kevin stole over a million dollars from Darius?"

"Look, I want all of my kids to do well. And if we as a family can keep Kevin off the streets and out of jail, then this is bigger than Darius, we're obligated."

"We?" Jada whispered. "Darryl, have you noticed the only child you gave life to that's successful is the only one you didn't raise? I'm never going to remarry. You or anyone else," she said, pulling the covers up to her neck. "I'm exhausted. When Darius gets home, wake me."

"Look, I love you. It's not about the money."

"Then find another job. You're fired."

CHAPTER 40

Fancy

Who was Fancy kidding? Darius might have not been the man for her, but Desmond truly wasn't. Michael Baines was rich, but they'd never make a good couple. Michael was single for a reason, and Fancy didn't want to find out.

"Mama, I'll be back. I'm taking Dez to the airport."

"Okay, I'll be right here. Too fat to fit behind a steering wheel and too uncomfortable to ride anywhere if I don't have to," Caroline said, rubbing her stomach.

"Bye, Ms. Taylor," Desmond said, kissing her cheek.

"Bye, baby. Fancy, come back here. Desmond, excuse us for a minute."

"Yes, Mama?"

Caroline patted the bed. "Sit here."

"What is it this time?" Fancy said, becoming annoyed.

"Tell him the truth. Don't let Desmond leave here believing you're going to marry him."

"But the truth is, I don't know what to do."

"Do you love him?"

"Yes, I do."

"Are you in love with him?"

"People fall in and out of love all the time. You know that."

"You're right. I do. I also know that Desmond is not the man for you. We'll talk later. But, baby, please, you'll break his heart if you tell him now, you'll break his loving spirit if you wait."

Fancy exhaled, kissed her mother's forehead, then said, "I'll be back."

Dez was waiting in her car.

"Your mom all right?"

"Yeah, she's fine."

Barely turning out of her driveway onto Highway 1, Desmond asked, "So how soon you want to set a date?"

"Huh?" Fancy stared at the hillside to her left and then the ocean to her right.

"A date? When?"

No matter how hard she tried, Fancy just couldn't do it. She couldn't tell Desmond she wasn't going to marry him.

Her cell phone chimed. Nosy Desmond had glanced at the caller ID before she had. It was Darius.

"What does he want?" Desmond questioned like he was the police and she was telepathic.

Fancy answered, "Hi, Darius. Is your mom okay?"

"Better, not okay. At least she scheduled the services."

"When?"

"Next week. I called to ask a favor."

"I'm listening," Fancy said.

"Tell him you're engaged and whatever he needs get it from someone else."

Fancy exhaled. That was the immature Desmond she'd known for years and one of several reasons why she couldn't marry him. No man was controlling her. Ignoring Dez, Fancy replied, "What is it?"

"Can you meet me in Dallas tomorrow? I have to attend a custody hearing."

"A what?"

"You remember I told you my son was alive?"

"And?"

"The hearing is tomorrow."

"Let me call you back in a few minutes."

"Please, Fancy. I need you. I'll be waiting for your call."

"What the hell you got to call him back for? After the way he treated you, you shouldn't ever speak to that jerk again."

Fancy remained silent, parking curbside at departures. She got out of the car, waited for Desmond to unload his luggage. Her arms wrapped around his shoulders.

"I love you, Dez."

"I love you too. But—"

Fancy interrupted. "But I can't marry you."

She pressed her thumb and middle finger on opposite sides of Desmond's engagement ring, eased the platinum and diamond ensemble over her nail, enclosed it in Desmond's hand, got in her car, and drove away knowing that would be their last time together as a couple.

Picking up her cell phone, Fancy text-messaged Darius, *Make my arrangements. I'll be there.* She had her own motive for wanting to confront Ashlee Anderson face-to-face.

CHAPTER 41

Darius

Dressed in his single buttoned-down black suit with thin beige stripes, white-collared shirt, and a black, brown, and beige tie, Darius humbly entered the courtroom with his attorney on one side and Fancy on the other.

Fancy had packed three outfits, deciding to wear the caramel-colored skirt suit that matched his attire. Her snakeskin open-toe slip-ons showed off her curvaceous legs. Darius proudly sat next to Fancy on the last row closest to the exit while his attorney approached the bench.

Holding Fancy's French-manicured hand, Darius whispered, "I just want this to be over with. I sure hope they call us first."

"She looks pretty bad, don't you think? Like she's here physically but not mentally."

"She should look bad. How can she live with herself? Liar."

Squeezing Darius's hand, Fancy said, "You have no right to judge her. But I do."

All righty then. Darius would let that conversation ride solo. He wasn't surprised that Ashlee was accompanied by her father, but he was shocked to see Ashlee's mother.

"Anderson versus Jones. Will all parties rise and come forward," the judge announced, reaching for two manila folders the clerk handed her.

Looking at Fancy, Darius said, "Come with me."

Fancy stared at Ashlee staring at her. Darius knew the tension was thick, and they all knew exactly why.

"Raise your right hands. You swear to tell the truth and nothing but the truth? Respond by saying 'I do.'"

Almost everyone said, "I do."

The judge looked at Ashlee and said, "Excuse me, Ms. Anderson, I didn't hear you."

Ashlee whispered, "I do."

"The purpose of this trial is to determine temporary custody so that the child may be placed with family until Child Protective Services completes its investigation. Looks like all interested parties are here. Ms. Anderson, we'll hear your testimony first. Then we'll hear from you, Mr. Williams."

Lawrence stood. "Your Honor, I'm representing Ms. Anderson. Darius Williams Jr. was prematurely removed from Ms. Anderson's custody before a full and impartial investigation was initiated. She is taking medication for postpartum depression because Mr. Williams abandoned Ms. Anderson the day Darius Williams Jr. was born."

Darius stood, and yelled, "That's a lie!"

"Mr. Williams, sit down. You'll get your opportunity to respond."

Darius's attorney grabbed his forearm, pulling him into his seat.

"Like I was saying, Mr. Williams has not seen his son, nor has he tried to contact his son, since his son was born, nor has he paid a dime in child support to Ms. Anderson. Ms. Anderson, a single mother, is the only parent the child knows. She's fully capable of continuing her motherly duties. She's done so all this time by herself. I'd like to call Darius Williams Sr. to the stand."

The judge scanned the file. "Mr. Williams, please take the stand. And remember you are under oath."

Darius sat to the judge's left, focusing on Fancy, glad she'd come. Win or lose, his heart was overwhelmed with the joy that Fancy had officially fired that loser.

Lawrence evilly stared at Darius, then asked, "Mr. Williams, how much time would you say you've spent with your son?"

"I can explain—"

Interrupting his response, the judge said, "Just answer the question."

"Approximately one hour."

Ashlee smiled, poking her tongue at him.

Lawrence asked, "Mr. Williams, when is your son's birthday?"

"I can tell you the day he supposedly died."

The judge said, "That's not the concern. Your son is alive. Answer the question."

Ashlee smiled again.

"He was born eight months ago."

"Seven. No further questions, Your Honor," Lawrence said, sitting next to Ashlee, holding her hand under the table.

Darius's lawyer interjected, "I'd like to question my client."

"You may proceed," the judge said, tapping her pen on the folder.

"Mr. Williams, did you or did you not receive a phone call from Ms. Anderson saying your son was dead?"

Darius's heart smiled with relief. "I did."

"And what did Ms. Anderson tell you the cause of death was?"

"HIV complications."

"Did Ms. Anderson ever call to confess she'd lied?"

"Yes, she left a message on my voice mail."

"Did Ms. Anderson trespass on your property, enter your home, and . . ." The attorney paused, looked at Ashlee, then continued. "Replace your aspirins with abortion pills, knowing that your then fiancée was impregnated with your child?"

Lawrence stood. "This is ridiculous! My daughter, I mean, my client did not do such things."

The judge said, "Answer the questions, Mr. Williams."

Darius whispered, "Yes, yes, and yes. And correction, Fancy *is* my fiancée."

"As a result of Ms. Anderson's actions, did your fiancée's fetus abort?"

Pressing his thumb and middle fingers into his eyes, Darius lowered his head and answered, "Yes."

"No further questions, Your Honor."

The judge looked at Darius and said, "You may step down. I'll take into consideration the voice mail only if it's dated and available. Ms. Anderson, please take the stand."

Slowly, Ashlee sat where Darius once was.

Darius's attorney continued questioning. "Ms. Anderson, did you tell Mr. Williams his son was dead?"

Holding her head down, Ashlee answered, "Yes."

"Your Honor—"

"Not now, Mr. Anderson. Have a seat."

"Ms. Anderson, did you trespass on Mr. Williams's property?"

"Yes."

"And before you answer my next question, I want you to know if true, you face time in prison if my client presses charges. Did you replace the aspirins in Mr. Williams's home with abortion pills?"

Ashlee looked in Fancy's eyes and replied, "No, I did not."

"Liar!" Fancy yelled. "She's a damn liar! You left that voice-mail message on my phone, confessing. And I know the time on the message matches the time of the outgoing call on your cell phone bill."

Tears streamed down Ashlee's face.

Darius looked at his attorney, then lied loud enough for the judge to hear, "I deleted the message."

"Ms. Anderson, I'm going to ask you one more time. Did you replace the aspirins in Mr. Williams's home with abortion pills?"

This time Ashlee remorsefully stared at Darius and replied, "No. I did not."

The judge said, "I've heard enough testimonies. I'll take a fifteen-minute recess and return with my decision."

Darius hugged Fancy and said, "Please forgive me, Ladycat. We know the truth, but I don't want my son's visitations with his mother to be behind bars. Thanks for coming." Darius kissed Fancy's face from one cheek across her nose to the other side. "I love you. I love you. I need you."

The judge reentered the room.

The bailiff announced, "All rise."

The clerk said, "Court is back in session. You may be seated."

"Based on the caseworker's recommendation and the testimony given today, the court awards full custody to"—the judge's eyes scanned from Fancy, to Darius, to Darius's attorney, to Lawrence, and finally to Ashlee, stopped, then continued—"Mr. Darius Williams."

Darius leaped from his seat, hugged his attorney, picked up Fancy, spun her around.

The judge continued, "With supervised visitation to Ms. Ashlee Anderson."

Quietly Ashlee asked, "Judge, may I say something?"

"Sure, Ms. Anderson. I've rendered my decision, so be brief."

"Why isn't that man"—Ashlee's voice trembled as she pointed at Darius—"held accountable for his heartless actions? How can he one day say he loves me? Wants to marry me? Make love to me? Get me pregnant? Then despise me? Why can't the system recognize I'm a woman in pain? I was a mother on the verge of losing my sanity. I carried our son. Alone and lonely. All because that man"—she said, pointing again—"who once loved me, doesn't love me anymore. Now he shows up, and because he's a big-time NBA player, he can walk out of this courtroom with custody of our son, when he's only seen our son once since he was born, and all I get is more pain accompanied by some stranger supervising my visits. What about me? I'm dying inside. And now he's going to leave here with *her*"—Ashlee pointed at Fancy—"and he's going to marry *her*. And my son is going to grow up calling *her* Mommy. Judge, I've already lost my best friend. If I don't get custody of my son, I have absolutely no reason to live."

Darius covered his face with his palms. His once-upon-a-time best friend was hurting and he was so busy with his own conquests, Fancy and his son, that he hadn't felt her pain. At what point did Ashlee stop being his friend? Why did he hate her? Maybe she reminded him of what his mother had done. Ashlee hadn't been sure he was the father until after the paternity test. Why should he have wasted time with waiting to find out? If she hadn't cheated on him, she wouldn't have needed a test. What if he tried to make things right between them?

The judge said, "I'm concurring on a psychiatric evaluation for you, Ms. Anderson. I empathize with you, but"—the judged looked at Fancy, then continued—"when are women going to stop allowing manipulative men to control and destroy your lives?" Then she turned to Ashlee. "Unfortunately for you, Ms. Anderson, Mr. Williams has proven himself a fit parent. The court has no grounds for denying him his parental rights. However, if in twelve months you're emotionally stable, the court will, if you file, reconsider your case for custody. Choose a better man next time, Ms. Anderson."

Lawrence interrupted. "Your Honor, what about back child support?"

"Child support was not requested in the filing. If you file, the court will review the case. Court will reconvene in fifteen minutes." The judge banged her gavel one final time before she left.

Lawrence sat shaking his head. What was the point of Ashlee's mother coming to court? She hadn't spoken one word.

Darius stood, escorted Ashlee out of the courtroom, hugged her head to his chest, and said, "I'm sorry. Ashlee, I'm so sorry. You are my best friend. And I do love you. We'll get through this. Together."

By the time Darius stopped hugging Ashlee and turned around, Fancy quietly stood next to them. "Ashlee, I need to know the truth. Why did you put those abortion pills in the medicine bottle?"

Ashlee looked at Fancy, then at Darius, and back at Fancy and said, "I'm so sorry I did that."

"Thank you for being honest." Fancy slapped Ashlee as hard as she could, then watched Ashlee fall to the floor.

Darius grabbed Fancy's arm. "Stop, Ladycat, she's sick. I'm partially to blame that her mind is messed up," he explained, helping Ashlee to her feet. "Look at it this way. She took our child. But God gave us hers. And no matter what happens, I cannot change the fact that Ashlee is the mother of my son."

CHAPTER 42

Jada

With the exception of going to the bathroom, Jada stayed in bed. Restless. Seldom sleeping. Time went by, incapacitating her emotions. It was like she'd been sucked into the belly of a whale, waiting for life to digest her spirit. The spirit that once moved her was the only thing sustaining her. If it weren't for Darius, Jada didn't know what she'd do.

Her limp flesh sank into the sheets. The same sheets Wellington last slept on. No desire to escape the mammal's stomach, Jada felt infantlike. Inside she knew what she wanted to say, but she couldn't effectively communicate. If she stayed in bed until the sun set again, Wellington's services would be over.

"Honey, try to drink this broth Jazzmyne made for you while it's warm. You need something on your stomach," Darryl said, trying to raise her into a sitting position.

Jada backhanded the cup. "Uh-uh."

Setting the cup on the nightstand, Darryl pleaded, "But you have to eat something. You haven't eaten in days."

"I'll feed her," Darius said, entering the room.

"Son, when did you get back?"

"Does it matter?"

"It won't help. She's been like this since she realized you left."

"Then why didn't you call me?"

"Why didn't you call?" Darryl countered.

"Move," Darius said angrily.

"Make me," Darryl said.

"Darius?" Jada uttered, lifting her head. "Sweetie, is that you?"

"Yeah, Ma. It's me. I told you I'd be back." Darius eased his arm under her waist, sliding her back against the pillows, then picked up the cup. "Ma, open your mouth. For your sweetie. Come on. Come on, Ma."

Weakly Jada separated her lips as wide as she could, enough for him to set the cup on her bottom lip and pour the liquid inside. Slowly she swallowed. The salty juices streamed down her throat. "Uh-uh."

"I need you to finish it, Ma." Darius paused, then said, "That's my girl." Looking at Darryl, Darius said, "I got her, Dad. Give us some time alone. I'll help her get dressed for the funeral."

Jada allowed and wanted Darius to be the one to take care of her. In a way, she'd waited for his return. Darius uncovered her body.

"Ma, you're fully dressed." Sniffing, he said, "Aw, Ma. These are the same clothes you had on when I left."

Placing her feet on the floor, Darius said, "On three, I want you to stand up. One. Two. Three." He lifted his mother, supporting her with his upper body.

Jada took tiny steps to the bathroom as Darius sat her on the toilet with her clothes on, then began drawing her bathwater.

"I look a mess, don't I?" Jada said, looking at her reflection in the ceiling-to-floor mirror.

"Naw, Ma. You look beautiful."

"You're just saying that."

"No. I mean that. You're beautiful. Inside and out. Now we have to get you cleaned up. The funeral is today."

Darius undressed her, helped her into the tub, then gently washed her body.

"Okay, Ma. I need you to wash the lower half. I'm not going down there. Here's the towel. Make sure you wash *really* good."

Helping her out of the Jacuzzi, Darius dried his mother off, wrapped a dry towel around her body, then sat her on the side of the bed. He went to the closet, selected a black dress, shoes, and underwear, then placed them at her side.

"Ma, I'm going to take a quick shower and change and then I'll be right back. I need you to be my girl and dress yourself, okay?"

"He's here, sweetheart."

"Who?" Darius asked, looking around the room.

"Wellington. He's here. I can feel him. He's proud of you."

"Okay, then you talk to him while you're getting dressed, Ma. I'll be right back."

When Darius closed the door, Jada had a private conversation with her husband. Death hadn't ended their relationship.

"I know you're listening. I want you to know that no man can ever take your place. You're my angel now. And what's done is done. Can't say I understand, but it'd do me no good to become bitter or hold on to anger and jealousy when you're not here. Now it's my turn. And regardless of how you feel about Darryl, you'll have to get used to him being around. You've done your thing. You were a sneak about it, but you damn sure nuff lived as you damn well pleased and I'm going to do the same until we meet again. I'm not going to be alone or lonely. I don't want to meet somebody new. And I'm surely not going to be celibate. But what I will do, for me and you, is I will never remarry."

CHAPTER 43

Ashlee

Hopelessly devoted.

If she couldn't move on, she could move away in hopes to one day stop loving Darius. Ashlee intended to board a direct flight. She had no idea where she was going when she arrived at Dallas/Ft. Worth Airport.

"This is fine," she said to the taxi driver. Leaning forward to see the meter, Ashlee got out, waited for him to unload her two roll-a-way suitcases, then handed him exact change. Thirty-five dollars. Never again would she tip a man.

Bypassing curbside, Ashlee approached the ticket counter, scanned the departing flights, then said, "One way. Washington, Dulles International."

"Did you make a reservation?" the agent asked, holding Ashlee's driver's license.

"No, I didn't." Momentarily those words haunted Ashlee as she'd recalled lying under oath to the judge.

Ashlee was thankful, certain that Fancy's slap didn't hurt nearly as much as handcuffs. She deserved worse. Darius or Fancy could've pressed charges but didn't. Fancy had forwarded the message to Ashlee after their court session to prove Darius had lied. Once more Darius had protected her. Why?

As she was fumbling through her purse for her credit card, Ashlee's phone rang.

"Excuse me one moment," she said to the agent, then answered, "Hi, Daddy."

"Sweetheart, where are you? I came by, your car is here, but you're not."

"At the airport."

"Airport? Where're you going?"

Without hesitation, Ashlee said, "I'm not sure." She had gotten better at lying.

"Miss, could you step aside until you're ready?"

"Bye, Daddy. Sorry, here's my credit card."

After she'd received her boarding pass and cleared security, her flight was preboarding. Ashlee reclined in first class. Waiting for the remaining passengers to take their seats, she closed her eyes.

The last time Ashlee laid eyes on her son was a few days ago. Darius was nice enough to let her hold him for a few minutes before their flight departed to Los Angeles. They'd met her at a small coffee shop near Dallas/Ft. Worth Airport. Fancy was looking gorgeous, the same way she stepped into the courtroom, fashionable. She was quiet but had already begun exhibiting motherly instincts, holding, feeding, and changing little Darius's diaper.

Then Fancy held Ashlee's hand and said, "Ashlee, I forgive you. I want you to take care of yourself so we can all take care of this little man. And I don't care what that judge said, this is your son, you are his mother, and you don't need a court order granting you permission to see him. Our home is your home." Fancy's palm was still incredibly soft.

Ashlee's heart skipped a beat, but when Fancy tickled little Darius's chin and his two bottom teeth joyfully smiled at Fancy, Ashlee's heart stopped. Her eyes filled with tears, she finding it difficult to hate someone who had every right to hate her but didn't.

Would Ashlee have to befriend Fancy to have a relationship with her own son? Hopefully not. Clearly Ashlee was better off not being a full-time mother. Fancy had forgiven her for what she'd done, but Ashlee hadn't forgiven herself. For giving so much to

Darius. None of those bad things would've happened if Ashlee had only loved herself more than she loved Darius. Ashlee promised herself never to love anyone more than she loved herself.

The trip to D.C. was a blur. Hailing a taxi, Ashlee instructed the driver, "Take me to the Mall."

"Lady, unless you're talking about Tyson's Corner, the Mall isn't one specific destination. It's a huge area spanning from the Capitol to the Washington Monument."

"Just drive. I'll tell you where to stop."

"It's your money," he said, starting his meter and merging onto the freeway.

When the driver stopped at a red light near the Smithsonian, Ashlee pointed upward. "What's that?"

"The Grand Hyatt Hotel."

"Take me there."

Checking into a suite, Ashlee had the doorman deliver her bags. "Where's a good place for a lady to go out alone?"

"Depends on what you like but you can't go wrong with Zanzibar on the Waterfront."

Ashlee showered, changed into something sexy but conservative, and headed to the bar for a much-needed drink.

The woman in the booth said, "Ten dollars please."

The man at the door signaled to her, then said to Ashlee, "As fine as you are, I'm personally escorting you to our V.I.P. section," seating her at a table near the window.

Scanning the room, Ashlee noticed a sexy chocolate man across the room checking her out. "If he knew what was best for him, he'd keep his tongue in his mouth." The sight of him made her hot. When was the last time she'd been with a man?

Trying to ignore him, Ashlee was through with men. For a while anyway. This time she was focusing on her needs and her needs only.

CHAPTER 44

Jada

Jada rechecked Wellington's office in search of a copy of his living will. The file was mysteriously there. "That's odd," she said. She sat at Wellington's desk, flipping and scanning the heirs and assets. Maybe she'd overlooked it before.

Melanie Marie Thompson, *fifty* million dollars! Wellington the Second, Jazzmyne Jones, and Simone Smith, Wellington Jones and Associates. Melanie Marie Thompson, a third ownership in Somebody's Gotta Be on Top. Jazzmyne Jones, four million dollars, Shelly and Brandon, one million dollars each, from his investment fund. Melanie Marie Thompson, the house in Half Moon Bay.

Jada slammed the documents on the desk, picked up the phone, and dialed Wellington's attorney. "Now I see why the messenger never delivered the will. What the hell is this?"

"Your husband signed the papers before he died. It's what he wanted."

"That is a lie! I'll sue you and whomever you're in cahoots with. Namely Melanie Marie Thompson."

"Mrs. Tanner, there's no need for threats. I'll talk with you when you arrive."

Jada hung up the phone, and called Darius.

"Hi, Ma. I'm pulling up in the driveway."

"Don't turn off your engine, I'm on my way out." Storming by Darryl, Jada said, "I'll be back."

"Wait, I'm going with you."

"No, you're not. In fact, you need to leave. Get out."

Love or no love, there was no way Darryl would have access or knowledge of her personal worth. And until Jada found out the truth, no one was welcome in her home, including Candice, who was upstairs in the bedroom.

Darius opened the passenger door and waited until she was seated before closing the door.

"Ma, what's wrong?"

"I can't believe this shit! This will states that Wellington . . ." Jada reiterated the details.

"Ma, let me see," Darius said, parking in the emergency lane on the freeway. He handed the papers back to her, then merged into traffic. "That's not Wellington's signature."

"What?"

"Look at it. I've seen his signature many times on my company's documents. That's not his signature. Someone else signed that will."

"Maybe it looks different because he was sick."

"He wasn't that sick, he pulled his own breathing tube, remember?"

Jada studied the Ls. One was higher than the other. The W and J were higher than all the other letters. Wellington, being an accountant, aligned everything, including the underwear in his drawer.

Calmly entering the lawyer's conference room, Jada walked up to Melanie and said, "When did you sign this? How did you get the document from and back into my house? And I'm not giving you a dime."

"You don't have to. Wellington already has."

Darius walked over to Melanie, grabbed her key chain, then stepped back.

"Give me that!" Melanie yelled, leaning backward over her chair.

Aligning the key on Melanie's key ring with the key to his mother's house on his key chain, Darius said, "Bingo!"

"Give me my damn keys!"

"Correction, this key is not yours," Darius said, removing the key. "Ma, you got your keys to the other houses on you?"

Jada handed her keys to Darius. After matching up keys to every residence, Darius removed all except two keys from Melanie's ring.

Simone interrupted. "I don't give a damn about her, what did my son's father leave us?"

The attorney interrupted. "First we have to determine which trust is valid. Then we have to reschedule a hearing. Today, no one gets anything!"

"My son needs his tuition paid and my mortgage payments are late, no thanks to y'all! Wellington never would've allowed this." Simone stood, heaving.

Jada looked at Simone and said, "I don't owe you anything. Wellington has generously given you more than you deserve and you've pissed it off trying to keep up with the Joneses, flying all over the world with your man. Where's he at? Why can't he pay your bills for a few months until this is settled?"

Simone sat in her chair and said, "Because Wellington was my man."

"What!" Jada screamed.

"I mean he was our sole provider. He didn't mind taking care of us, so I didn't need another man in my life to take care of us financially. Wellington made sure we never wanted for anything."

At that moment, Jada knew her soul mate might not have been perfect, but he had lived his life trying to treat others right.

Appealing to the attorney, Jada said, "Grant Simone a million-dollar advance against ownership of Wellington Jones and Associates, which will be given in trust to Wellington Jones the Second, Jazzmyne Jones, and Simone Smith, equally."

Melanie protested, "What!"

"Jazzmyne, you can have an advance as well for you and your children."

Melanie waved her arms. "Wait a minute!"

Ignoring Melanie, Jada continued. "Give Melanie Marie Thompson two dollars. On second thought." Jada reached into her purse and handed Melanie a five-dollar bill.

Melanie objected, "You crazy bitch!"

"And place in a trust account one million dollars for Morgan Thompson when she turns twenty-one."

"Oh, hell no!" Melanie yelled.

Darius shouted at Melanie, "Shut up and sit down. Ma, are you sure you want to do this?"

Calmly Jada said, "No, I'm not sure. I'm positive. This was part of my husband's last request. I'm honoring some"—Jada looked at Melanie, then continued—"not all of his wishes. Besides, keeping the money won't make me richer. I'm already rich. I've loved you all of my life, Son. And for you to finally love me back, no amount of money could replace that."

Looking at Melanie, Jada said, "Oh yeah, I'm not stupid. I know Wellington loved Morgan because he loved you, but I knew before Morgan said her daddy was in the car that she wasn't Wellington's child. I suggest you take your five dollars and move on. You don't have enough money to fight with me. If you challenge me, someone else will have to raise your child because I will file forgery charges."

Melanie looked at Simone. "I know she did not just threaten me."

"I'm getting paid. You're on your own. Shouldn't have fucked up."

"Oh, don't act like Wellington wasn't fucking you too," Melanie said.

Jada motioned for Darius to accompany her. "Son, let's go."

Driving her home, Darius said, "Ma, that was so generous of you."

"Sweetie, money brings opportunities, not happiness."

"Whoa, speaking of happiness, I have someone I want you to meet."

"Who?"

"You'll see."

CHAPTER 45

Darius

The first shall become last and the last shall become first.
Ashlee was his first love, and now she was his last. Darius still loved her because she would forever be the mother of his son. Fancy never again would be last. Fancy was his first lady, and for the first time in his life, everything was perfect.

Darius had grown up. More than he'd imagined. Realizing that it wasn't the women in life that he didn't trust. He didn't trust himself. But because of the women in his life—Fancy, his mother, and Ashlee, in a very special kind of way—he found the spirit of true love.

Reflecting on his life, he wouldn't change a thing. Everything that happened to him, good and bad, finally made Darius Jones-Williams a man.

His mother was not to blame for him not knowing his father. His father was to blame for not being man enough to accept responsibility for his actions. Zen, Miranda, Heather, and Ginger, his mother's executives, taught Darius that women could be equally as devious as men.

Maxine. Maxine wasn't his first true love, she was his first heartbreak, when he discovered she'd cheated on him. But his out-of-control teenage hormones, which didn't have a clue about marriage or commitment, were to blame for him randomly fucking Kimberly Stokes and other women.

Society was to blame for his distorted view of relationships. It was okay for a man to marry a good take-home-to-Mama woman while he fucked freaky women on the side. And as long as his wife didn't find out, he was just, well, being a man. A man with backed-up cum freely donating sperm, but a man who had no balls.

Darius was happy that Kimberly finally found a career she loved, and that Ciara wasn't too bitter to help Kimberly or him to grow. Ciara was no saint, but her well-wishes for him were sincere. Darius would keep his word and help Ciara raise Solomon.

Caroline might have had a rough upbringing, but in the end, he'd somehow helped her to love Fancy, and in return Fancy had given him another chance. Why? Darius didn't know, but thanking God, he was grateful.

His mother was his foundation and his grandmother was his rock. They loved him when he didn't love himself. They supported him at his lowest points and raised him to his highest heights.

Darryl, his biological dad, made a huge difference in Darius's life. But no man grounded him like Wellington Jones. Darryl made him realize any man could father a child, but it took a special man to be a daddy. Wellington was his daddy. Darryl was his father. Darius didn't resent Wellington. Darius resented that he wasn't man enough to tell Wellington "Thanks" before he died.

In the end, Wellington was no different from Darryl and Darryl was no different from his mother. His mother was no different from Fancy, Fancy was no different from Ashlee, and Darius Williams was no different from all of them.

They were all sinners. They were all God's children. They were all infallible. They were all human. And each of them had a heart longing to be loved.

Everybody plays the fool. Darius refused to remain foolish.

Because of what he'd done wrong, not because of what he'd done right, Darius Jones-Williams would forever be a better man, and his strong black woman would never have to do it all by herself.

EPILOGUE

Darius fussed over little Darius, pulling up his pants. Straightening his shirt. "You have to look good for Grandma. She'll be here in a minute."

"He looks fine," Fancy said, kissing Darius's lips, then little Darius's forehead.

When the doorbell rang, Darius sat his son on his forearm, then leaned him against his chest. "She's here, lil' man."

Opening the door, Darius kissed his mom and said, "Here he is."

"Oh my. And who's this?"

"Your grandson," Darius said, handing him to his mom.

"Well, where have you been? You look like you're almost one. How old is he?"

"Close. Seven and a half months, Ma."

"And who's your mother?" Jada asked as if he could answer.

Darius said, "Ashlee."

"I thought she said—"

"She lied, Ma. That's the first lie that I was grateful wasn't the truth."

Darius kissed his son. Little Darius smacked Darius in the face.

"Boy," Darius said, raising his hand to tap his son's butt.

His mom shielded his son, then said, "Don't hit Nana's baby."

Darius smiled knowing that his mother was now the grand-

mother that would protect little Darius the same way his Ma Dear
protected him.

"I love you, Fancy. I love you, Ma," Darius said and from this
point forward he'd show them.

Darius married Fancy, then relocated to Atlanta to play professional basketball. During the off-season he lived in Los Angeles so
they could be near his mother.

Fancy found motherhood enjoyable but missed being a daughter. After marrying Darius, she moved back to Los Angeles until
her mother gave birth to a beautiful baby girl. Caroline named her
daughter Diamond. Months later, Fancy convinced her mother to
move to Atlanta.

Jada found comfort in having Darryl around. She kept her
promise and never remarried.

Melanie miserably searched for someone else's rich husband
while Morgan's sassy behavior constantly reminded her not to
have any more kids.

Ashlee eventually moved to D.C. but hadn't moved on. She was
still hopelessly in love with Darius and jealous of Fancy.

SaVoy and Tyrone, having made their commitment to God before taking their vows before Him, lived a virtually happy life.
Tyronne started his business. SaVoy balanced his checkbook.

Desmond graduated from law school, married Trina, and gave
Trina the two kids she'd always wanted. Although Desmond had
moved on, he'd always love Fancy.

Tanya was a fast learner, quickly earning her real estate license
and later her broker's license. Not wanting to own a company, she
remained loyal to Fancy, and as Fancy had promised, Tanya made
lots of money.

Jazzmyne Jones operated her brother's company. Jazzmyne
started teaching Wellington the Second about investments in
hopes that one day, in another twelve years or so, he'd take over
his father's business. As long as Simone received quarterly dis-
bursements, she was happy.

Darryl Williams realized he wasn't getting any younger and having Jada meant more to him than having Jada's money.

Kevin Williams returned to his roots in New York City, working for a janitorial company.

Homeless Lady continued to share her gift of sight but not with Darius or Fancy. Psychics aren't meant to be in anyone's life for an extended period of time. That's why she wasn't in this book. She's traveling the world and who knows, the psychic lady might read you next.

Lagniappe Section

Since we're wrapping up this series, and I say "we" because I'm grateful that you've been on this journey with me, I'd like to give you a little lagniappe, as we say in New Orleans, meaning a little extra somethin', somethin'.

First a simple thank-you.

It's not easy doing a series of six books that fans like you continue to love, support, and rave about. One day I'll write book number seven, but for now it's time for us to move on to my next series, *Sweeter than Honey*. *Sweeter than Honey* is a lifestyle change for abused women and women with low self-esteem. Abuse comes in several forms, and failure to change unhealthy situations translates into self-imposed abuse and mental and physical illness. If my writing has helped you before, I want to help you a whole lot more because over the years, you've helped me to grow. I thank you.

I read your e-mails of encouragement, your prayers, and whether you realize it or not, that is truly, straight from my heart, the main reason I keep on writing, asking God to never let me pen a book that doesn't have a purpose and I ask Him to help me to make a positive difference in somebody's life. I listen to my spirit when writing and hope that you won't mind that this book isn't as sexually explicit.

When Somebody Loves You Back displays the various ways we love one another even when we don't know how to show it. How love makes us feel. And the things love, or the lack thereof, makes us do. Whether it's a wife begging her husband not to continue having an affair or a husband not having anyone to tell that he's hurting because his wife is leaving him. This story line solicits your appreciation of the love exhibited on so many important levels. I hope you didn't miss my points and that you will judge less and love more.

One day soon, I'd like to diversify into having my books adapted into movies, starting with *Soul Mates Dissipate,* so keep me in your prayers. I've written the screenplay for *Soul Mates Dissipate.* In numbers we can make a difference. I'd like for you to e-mail Oprah one important line, "Oprah, please option *Soul Mates Dissipate* by Mary B. Morrison." Thanks in advance.

Honey B., that's me.

Honey B. is my new pen name and my tag line is "You are what you eat . . . so stay sweet." The word "eat" is used as a parable. Life is all about making healthy personal choices. Check out *www.Sweeter ThanHoney.net* for more info.

The Honey Bee is my new online monthly newsletter geared toward female sexual empowerment and women helping empower women. For more info visit me online at *www.SweeterThanHoney.net.*

What's My Name is a short story included at the end for some steamy sex. And after reading *What's My Name* I hope you'll live out one of your sexual fantasies. If you get arrested for indecent exposure, as we say in Nawlins, "It ain't my fault."

The Average Black Man is written simply because I'm calling it how I see it. Now, everyone is entitled to disagree, especially the fellas, but, brothas, all I say is get real with yourself before you get defensive with me. And if you're not "average," well then, I'm not talking about you, am I? My current and future focus is on "Female Empowerment." Women are dealing with a lot, and our men are not fully supporting us as they could or should so women need to support one another because no woman should have to do it all by herself.

Tip.

I want all women to stop tipping men. Never again tip a man for pouring your drink, opening your door, parking your car, rubbing your feet, massaging your body, serving your meal, etc. For every dollar you would've tipped a man, either save it in a jar somewhere at home (tip yourself for doing a damn good job) or tip a woman. And don't feel guilty for not tipping men. Tip the working waitress at the coffee shop, the cleaning woman in the restroom, the baby-sitter, etc. I want women to start supporting women. Compliment your sister, your coworker, a stranger. Smile at one another. Be friendly. Be honest with one another and stop lying to other women to cover up for a man. Women will make this world a much better place when we start loving and appreciating one another. What will you do today to make a woman's life better tomorrow?

WHAT'S MY NAME

by Honey B.

A casual glance ignited her wildest fantasy.

She'd always wanted to fuck a fine-ass, strong, healthy, sexy, mouthwatering man she didn't know. Like the brotha standing less than six feet away.

His biceps were chiseled beneath perfect shoulders that were squared, rounding off at the edges. Easily he could hoist her pussy up to his face, then grind his lips into her clit. His well-defined chest, sculpted abs, dented-on-each-side ass, sliced back that was cut with the depth of his sunken spine, glorified the definition of King.

Traveling below his waist, she admired the panoramic view of his lethal python companion that took her breath away. The snake folded behind his zipper would slowly and deliberately explore her pipelines the moment she bit him. Oh yes, she was definitely going to bite him in all the right, and a couple of wrong, places.

Her pussy panted to the rhythm of her favorite song, "Wait'll you see my dick . . . I'ma beat that pussy up like bam, bam, bam . . . Damn, he's got a thick-ass salami!" Her subconscious whispered, "What are you waiting for?" Her body jerked at the thought of holding his dick next to her cheek, kissing its praises while singing, "You. I would die for you." Well, she might not die for him but truly she'd risk getting a divorce.

"He's definitely the one," she decided, not caring that she'd had sex last night with her husband. Her freakish desires didn't include him. Things at home were falling apart outside the bedroom, and the only reason she'd spread her legs for her husband was that the dick was g-double-o-d. That, and the fact that she was a nymphomaniac.

Her husband couldn't outlast her multiorgasmic battery-operated "Fuckin' Rabbit" that had become so addictive like a drug habit that she carried it in her purse everywhere she went. Sometimes she'd sit in her car, prop her feet on the windshield, and fuck herself while the sunshine warmed her pussy. Sad but true, her husband had become robotic. She could set her watch to the tick of his dick. Worst of all he'd never licked her pussy. Not even once.

That was okay only because her pussy-licking-loving friend waxed her shit so good she couldn't walk straight for two days without cumming in public after fucking with him. He lived next door to her girlfriend. But her husband wasn't down with going down, so she slipped away to her girlfriend's every chance she got. His hot lips would kiss hers. Slowly his tongue explored her walls like he was cleaning windows and wanted them to squeak.

"Oh yes," she moaned, seducing the zucchinis. Her juices saturated the tip of her vagina. Thanks to her pussy-licker, she knew how to mentally masturbate without touching herself, but she was saving herself for the brotha standing near the nectarines.

Breaking her high, she thought about her husband.

Warm up, missionary style. Lick his dick a little while. Hit it from back, smack, smack. Squeeze his balls, he liked that. Get on top, hump, hump, hump, stop. "Damn, baby, I'm cumming, cum with me," was all he needed to explode inside her. But routine sex wasn't enough to make her faithful. If she had to do all the work anyway, she didn't believe in half-ass doing any job. So someone else could finish what her husband wouldn't. Couldn't. His repressive hangups sure as hell weren't her problem.

Lustfully admiring the sexy-chocolate-melt-in-her-panties brotha loading his shopping cart up with vegetables made her cum. She shivered. No one knew but her. Like no one knew she wasn't wearing any panties under her free-flowing leopard-print summer dress. It was too damn hot outside and watching that fine-ass man made her hotter. Rubbing against the silk, her nipples tingled, making her cum again. Damn, they'd better get to fucking soon. She was two orgasms ahead of him and he didn't even know it. Make that three.

Her pussy sizzled, but didn't make her as hot as the times she fantasized about licking another woman's pussy while her husband fucked their lover doggie-style. She'd please them both at same time. Easing her husband's balls into her mouth, she'd stick her finger up his ass, while he fucked their lover. Not wanting the pussy to feel abandoned, she'd slip their lover's clit under the tip of her tongue; flutter and hum, flutter and hum, all along easing her finger in and out of her husband's ass while he fucked their lover. Best not to give him too much to do at the same time. He was good, but multitasking was not his forte. Her pleasure would cum when they came all at the same time. Damn, her husband was fine, but she wished he wasn't such a prude.

Observing Sexy Chocolate's long thick fingers grazing the ridges of the broccoli spears, she knew the attention he gave to those vegetables meant he was a muthafucka' who took sex seriously. Yeah, he'd fuck her hot percolating pussy real good, she knew, nodding. Tweaking.

He put that bunch back, then carefully inspected another. This time she imagined him teasing her nipples. Glancing down below her spaghetti straps, she saw her nipples pointed at him.

Not noticing her, he moved on to the cucumbers. Wrapping his fingers around the green bulging mass from tip to tip, he slid his hand up and down, again and again. She shivered, envisioning how in-touch he was with masturbation.

Quietly she approached him from behind, tapping the mound of his shoulder. "Excuse me, but I couldn't help but notice"—she thrust her breasts closer to him—"your selection of foods. Are you a vege—"

"Vegan, I'm a vegan. You?"

Swaying her head, she replied, "Naw, I'm a meat lover," glancing below his waist.

Exposing his pearly whites set behind succulent lips, he said, "Well, you should try giving *it* up."

"I don't bite," she lied, cupping her hand under the misty water showering the red leaf lettuce. She slid her fingertips under her dress, then massaged her pubic hairs. "Um," she moaned, fanning the flap, airing her pussy scent in his direction. "It must be a hundred degrees."

"A hundred and one." His eyes settled on her tits as he whiffed, nodded, then smiled. "Oh, but I do. Bite that, is. Um, um, um." He backed her ass into the peaches, teetering her nipples until they leaked milk. "Sweet," he moaned.

"Exactly how adventurous are you?" she asked.

"Depends. What's on your mind?"

"You. Care to shop later?"

He hunched, then abandoned his grocery cart. "Where to?"

Her eyes signaled for him to follow her. He did. Straight to the cherry tomatoes.

"Here?" he asked, eyeing the shoppers.

"Right here," she said, posing in the most public section of the supermarket. She lowered her straps beneath her tits and fed him. The thought of strangers watching excited the hell out of her. Sexy Chocolate was more gentle than she'd imagined.

Licking his full lips, he suctioned her nipples into pointier points. Squatting to his knees, he lifted her skirt, and kissed her kitty. Then he licked, long solid strokes, again and again until she purred. Pushing her under the mist that showered the vegetables, he layered his body atop hers.

A nice and slow *zzzziiiiippppp*, followed.

She felt his head, smooth, big, and hard, unfold between her thighs. As he eased his dick inside her, she inhaled, squeezing him, trying hard not to have the big orgasm spreading throughout her entire body.

"Wait. Don't move. Give me a minute."

"You sure you want this right here?"

If he moved an inch she was gonna scream like never before. "Yes, but don't move. Talk dirty to me."

"Not a problem," he said with a half smile. Pulling out, grabbing his dick, he said, "Drop to your goddamn knees and suck my dick."

Her husband would never talk to her that way. Sexy Chocolate's dick was pleasantly huge, thick, and the head so beautifully shiny she popped it in her mouth, then sucked him like her favorite juicy watermelon Blow-Pop. The big one. Moaning she glanced up. His head tilted back.

"Damn, that feels good, girl. Your juicy lips on this big-ass dick. You are heaven-sent. Suck my dick harder," he begged, gripping the back of her head.

"Umm, delicious. Must be all those vegetables." Tilting her head, she opened her throat, allowing his dick to glide until his balls smacked her chin. He was only halfway in. That was the most she could devour. Her hand stroked the lower part of his shaft as she bobbed again and again, giving him free rein and complete control to delve to her desire.

Oh, fuck! she screamed in her mind when his dick hit the g-spot at the back of throat, making her cum.

Her pussy felt left out. Pushing her vibrator aside, she removed a condom from her purse. Quickly she glided the latex down his shaft, turned around, spread her ass, and led his head to her back door. She never had to worry about her husband doing a "pussy inspection" because he always checked the wrong hole. Always thought he could tell when she was giving away, as he'd say, "his pussy." She moaned as Sexy Chocolate eased his dick in her asshole.

Glancing in the misty mirror, she saw he was handsome. Sexy. Beautiful. They looked good having sex. "You're a passionate lover," she complimented, watching them fuck like the free-spirited animals they were.

"Not passionate. Attentive. I'm attentive to everything I decide to do. Like doing you."

"Umm," she moaned, as he pushed the first inch inside. "Slow down, I'm gonna cum too fast!" she yelled just as he pushed in another inch.

A store clerk walked over and said, "Y'all can't do this here."

270   *Mary B. Morrison*

Her lover kept stroking as if no one had spoken. "Passion requires attachment. I don't like attachments."

Thrusting her ass into his pelvis, she'd definitely picked the right man. Men. The clerk was a hot and sexy mocha man. "Give me your dick," she insisted.

"Who?" he asked, looking around.

"Give it to her, man, before it's too late, 'cause I'ma about to bust a nut," Sexy Chocolate grunted.

Easing his dick from under his apron, he said, "Here," placing his erection in her hand.

"Nice. Stand right here in front of me. Better yet, hand me that can of whipped cream." Lubing her hand with cream, she rhythmically stroked the clerk while Sexy Chocolate penetrated deep inside her. "Yes! Fuck me!" she yelled to Sexy Chocolate, stroking the clerk's dick harder.

"Oh my. I don't believe this is happening," Sexy Chocolate said. "I'm gonna explode in your ass." Reaching between her thighs, he grabbed her pussy and massaged her clit.

Faintly she said, "Not yet."

The clerk's large hands cupped both her titties firmly then pinched her nipples.

"Oh yeah. I'm cumming!" she screamed as Sexy Chocolate pumped and pumped. Her pussy juices flowed onto his fingers as he stroked faster. "Don't stop. Fuck me! Harder!"

Every time he penetrated her, she stroked the clerk faster. Looping her other hand between the clerk's thighs, she bypassed his nuts, frantically finger-fucking him. His dick was nice and plump. Thick white cum flowed out of his hole down his shaft, and onto her hand.

"Oh, shit!" Sexy Chocolate yelled.

"Oh, shit," she echoed in unison with the clerk.

Repeatedly, they took turns yelling while cumming together. Her body orgasm shot from her toes to her head, then deep inside her rectum.

Sexy Chocolate massaged her back. "Whew! I gotta shop here more often."

"I gotta get back to work. Thanks for, whew!" the clerk said, walking away.

Standing, she tilted her head back, breasts forward, her hair flowing back, and her eyes rolling to the top of her lids. Mr. Attentive slung the best dick she'd ever had. Her pussy spasms continued as she kept cumming after he'd eased his dick out.

Sexy Chocolate moaned, "I feel you. I'm still leaking."

The clerk returned, waving several paper towels under the mist, then handed them to her and waved. She dabbed her pussy, then patted Sexy Chocolate's face. Fanning the flap of her dress in his direction, she kissed him on the cheek. "Thanks. I needed that." Shaking her hair behind her shoulders, she walked away slowly, swaggering her hips.

Sexy Chocolate yelled, "Hey, wait a minute! What's your name?"

Slowly turning around, she smiled, winked, then disappeared into the sunshine.

THE AVERAGE BLACK MAN

by Honey B.

The *average* black man is an underachiever.

Although the average black man possesses intellect and talent beyond measure to excel at whatever he commits to, he won't fully apply himself. He expects his woman to treat him like his mother.

"My mama used to work, clean the house, and cook dinner every day."

I ask, "Is that something for a black man to be proud of?" perpetuating a system that denounces his manhood.

The average black man has expectations of everyone except himself. He wants his money like his women, fast, easy, and sometimes sleazy, so he's willing to get his hustle on—have a kid or two, somebody else's wife will do—as long as he's not required to break a sweat or pay a debt like child support because he's too worried about the black woman getting ahead of him.

'"I don't know what she's doing with my money."

"Try being a man and raising your own kids, honey."

He doesn't realize the black woman was ahead of him well before she met him. Now because of his setback, she's working overtime to get back what she had before she met him.

The average black man will do more for the white man than he'll ever do for the black woman, all along despising both because neither respects him, primarily because he doesn't respect himself. A lie is easier to tell than the truth. Abusing his woman is the fastest way to raise his self-esteem. It's easy for the black man to become a user, using his mother, wife, family, friends, women, and strangers for one common purpose, all to meet his needs.

When the truth is the average black man doesn't know what he needs, let alone wants. "I want her, and her, and her, and her, but I don't want her to find out about her so I'll lie to them all because I love my wife."

The average black man substitutes his needs with greed to by any means necessary buy a fancy car to get classy women who are foolish enough to pay the note in order to let some other woman take the ride, all along kidding herself into believing that she's his prize until she's "surprised!"

The average black man cultivates his own demise. "I'm the king of my castle," he might say when his name is nowhere indeed on the deed. "I'm the king of my throne," he may shout, but if the black woman puts his ass out, he's gone, alone, and has no home. So what he does is uses another black woman to have his back.

"If I need a place to stay, can we shack?"

When what he's really saying is, "Just in case the one I've got finds out about you, you'll have to do until I find somebody new."

The average black man has got to, like Spike Lee said in *School Daze*, "Wake up! Wake up! Wake up!" And since the average black man won't read this message because he's sleepwalking through his life, I have to speak to the sistas and say it's time that you find "a man" who will love, cherish, and respect you, but you must first respect yourself. You see, when the black woman stops settling, the average black man will rise above minimum wage, denounce his minimalist attitude, stand tall, proud, and take center stage.

The average black man is a king . . . king . . . king . . . king. But he doesn't act like royalty.

I wish I could write a play about the average black man, but this is all too real. I sincerely hate the way I feel when I tell the average black man he's not good enough. No, no, no, in no way am I stuck up, but I refuse to let him fuck up or fuck me. For free. They say shit comes in threes, and if dissolution, more like disillusion, of marriage can dissolve before my eyes, to Halle, to Terry, then I know it can happen to any woman.

You see, I refuse to settle for the sour milk in the average black man's cheddar. I don't need to repeat someone else's mistakes because I know I can do better, or shall I say the average black man can do better? But he won't, if we don't require him to.

These days, I'm hella direct, almost to a fault. I don't like wasting my time, so I'll look a man in his eyes and say up front, "If you're not paying for our dates, don't ask me out." If he can't afford the meal, he can't enjoy the thrill.

I'll also say, "Drop your drawers, I need to do a dick check." I'm checking for a few things: length, thickness, responsiveness, and ultimately, cleanliness. Three out of four won't do. I am going to do the sniff test, place my hand directly in front of my face, and inhale. No sour balls allowed. He might say what the heck? but like it or not I gets my respect. He'll come correct or he won't cum at all. It's not what you do, it's how you do it. I love having fun so I am quite comical, at times.

Ladies, before that first date, get a few questions off your plate:
What's your vision for life?
You got a wife?
Cohabiting?
Involved in a relationship?
Live with your mama?
Got any baby mama drama?
How many kids do you have?
Have you ever let a man fuck you in your ass?

Girlfriends, don't be afraid to question men. Chances are, the average black man has more excuses, justifications, hesitations, and falsifications than direct answers. So, I say unto my sistas, stop lying for the black man because we are partially to blame for enabling them. And if you're like me, you're handling all the responsibilities, financial and otherwise, on your own, so don't take on any additional liabilities.

The average black man will abandon his woman, then say it was her fault that he left. Sistas, be smart about your money. Please do *not* share bank accounts with your man, never again put your money in his hand, do *not* freely hand him the keys to your car, and please *do* make sure you get paid before he gets laid.

The average black man is quick to lay claim to all your material things and he'll gladly lend you his name if you buy the rings. But let him get a dollar and all you'll hear is, "Holla at a playa when you see me on the street," on his way out the door. Why deal with infidelity and insecurity, then turn around and get married? There are too many married women housing *Single Husbands,* but that's a whole book I'm working on.

As for right now, my sistas, it's time for women to become empowered. Don't hesitate to overlook the average black man, because the average black man doesn't give a damn about you. Think I'm lying? File for divorce. Ask for child support without taking him to court. It's time to cross over to a *real* man (black or other) who will love you for you. From this day forward, quit digesting bullshit.

I say unto all my sisters, irrespective of race . . . because a man sees no color when he hates (or dislikes) himself, find and keep at least three good men and call them all friends. Then do what I do. Tell them all, "I love you, too."

Last but not least, starting from the inside out, be outrageously great to yourself. A man should never have to treat a woman better than she treats herself.

Until the *Honey Bee* stings again, remember, "You are what you eat . . . so stay sweet."

POETRY CORNER

by Honey B.

Dear God

Since You gave Your only son
To wash away our sins
Then where does purgatory fit in

Dear God
Since You are the only perfect One
And You sacrificed Your son to forgive our sins
Then where does the guilt trip begin

If you don't tithe ten percent
If you fornicate
If you don't honor your mother and father
Sin, sin, sin

Some of Your soldiers
Christians if You may
Believe they're going to heaven
Yet they sin every day

Their justifications seem so odd
When they sternly point their finger
Yes, I know that I'm a sinner
But surely you must see
That I'm a Christian and I'm saved
So regardless God loves me

Why does the leader, the pastor
Who's suppose to deliver Your word
Doesn't hear his own preaching
Doesn't practice his own teaching

If God is the only true Savior
Why do Allah, Jehovah, and Buddha exist
Why do men pray one day
Slay the next
Then after they've done their dirty work
They wash their hands for You

In light of all the failed marriages God
What happens to the woman who decides not to be a wife
Not to procreate
Rear a child by herself
Yet her sex life
Is great

Why does man easily yield to temptation
Overwhelming enjoying the sensation
Screams Your name during orgasms
Oh my God
Oh my God
Oh my God
Is that a sin
What if he repents
Then does it again

Dear God
If no one can ever be perfect
Why do we strive for perfection
If everyone sins
And nobody ever wins
Does that mean close enough is good enough
To enter the gates of heaven

Back to the guilt trip, Lord
Why should anyone worry
If all one has to do
Is confess with their mouth
And believe in their heart
Then wait for the day they'll see You

Is there a back door for atheists to creep through

We're taught to believe
That because of our sins
One day the world will come to an end
If that's true

Dear God
The last question is
Why did life ever begin

DAMN YOU

My hormones are escalating
As I watch the imprint of your dick
Growing down your thigh
Penetrating
Your denims
Wishing I was in 'em

My eyes linger imagining
How would it feel to hit it

Lick it
Kiss it
Suck it
The truth is
I want to fuck it
Fuck you

But our relationship is new
Right?

I exhale
Two inches from your lips
My hips
Curl into your dick
And I feel your throbbing head
Pressing against my clit

Shit!
My tits
Are tingling
Co-mingling
With my libido
This is a conspiracy
I'm sure you know
Your theory
Is working

Softly I exhale
Not remembering if I ever inhaled
But what the hell
Your smell
Is making me cum
Closer
To you
But I can't submit to my appetite

Because our relationship is new
Right?

Your tongue emerges
Filling the gap between our lips
Pulling me closer
You sit
Instinctively I straddle your lap
We're face-to-face
Our rapid breaths chasing one another
While my pussy secretly keeps the pace
Quietly
I want to be your lover

You ease my dress over my hips
Over my head
Then toss it next to us
On your bed
Your lips caress my nipples
At the same time
Your head presses against my clit
And my pussy dribbles
Onto your denims
Wising I was in 'em

I exhale
Not remembering if I ever inhaled
But what the hell
I'm feeling you
Damn
What should I do

Our relationship is new
Right?

I lose focus
My pussy is tight

I can't wait another minute
To hit it
Lick it
Kiss it
Suck it

It's time
Aw, yeah
It's time for me to
For me to
Fuck you
All right?
I'm taking your dick out of your pants
And into my hands
I want you so bad, man

My hips curl you
Into
My vagina
I exhale
Aw
Yes
Um-hum
Not remembering if I ever inhaled

Your dick is the best
I say taking control
Leading you way down inside my soul
I fuck you nice and slow
Then ride you hard-core
Squeezing teasing and pleasing
Until you explode like a rocket
Deep inside my pulsating pussy pocket

Seems like we cum forever
Together

We whisper together
Damn you
Damn you
Damn you
Is all we can say
As we lay

I inhale
In a matter of moments
Our relationship grew
But if I would've known
Your dick was that good
I would've fucked you
On date number two

Goddamn you

WHEN SOMEBODY LOVES YOU BACK

Hopeless
Helpless
Your stomach churns

Restless
Sleepless
You toss and turn

Angry
Depressed
Your soul burns

When one gives more than one receives
Incomprehensible
Indispensable
Often unmentioned

There is no
Democracy of reciprocity
Nor meeting point that's halfway

Love with your head
Think with your heart
Every single day
Believing everyone will be
Okay

I AM EVERYBODY

I am everybody
But everybody is not me
Violated by the master
I am Jewish, you see

Born in Louisiana
So there is French in me
I am Irish
Am I European
Definitely

It's a Black thing
So I do not expect for you to understand
But if you wonder why I understand all of you so well

. . . it is because
I am everybody
But everybody is not me

MY UNMARRIED HUSBAND

Your smile is so beautiful
I want to smile too
Mesmerized by your charm
The incredible strength in your arms

Dancing eyes that dance especially for me
Visible affection that others cannot see
In a special way you are my husband
Although you already have another life
Although you already have another wife

But I love you none the less
When you kiss and caress my breasts
The breasts that feed our child
As she gently gives us a smile

Although you must leave
You are never gone
Because she is your wife
But this is your home

WHEN SOMEBODY LOVES YOU BACK

Mary B. Morrison

ABOUT THIS GUIDE

The suggested questions are intended to enhance
your group's reading of
WHEN SOMEBODY LOVES YOU BACK
by Mary B. Morrison.

DISCUSSION QUESTIONS

1. Do you think African-American women (single and married) have more family responsibility than women of other nationalities? Experience more obstacles with communicating and sustaining a relationship? Are more sexually inhibited? Before answering, how many cultures are you familiar with?

2. Thinking about your previous and current relationship(s), do you base your expectations more on your beliefs, your frame of reference, society's standards, your mate's desires? For example, sex on the first date. Your parents convince you this is not right, not because they've never had sex on the first date, but they were taught not to. Then your friends say they're fucking on the first day. Society labels you a whore or a dog if you give it up so easily. But your mate desires sexual intercourse on the first date. This is just an example. Choose a different topic to explore why you think the way you think.

3. What is your opinion of Darius Jones-Williams? Would you marry a man like Darius? Do you believe people change or they basically remain the same? Do you think Darius will be faithful to Fancy? Why or why not?

4. Who's your favorite character in the Soul Mates Dissipate series? Why?

5. Do you believe Wellington should've confessed to Jada on his deathbed? Do you feel people who know they're dying view life differently from those who don't know when they're going to die? Why or why not? Assuming you're Jada, how would you have responded to Wellington's request to generously will his assets to Melanie and Simone? How much money would you have given Wellington's ex-lovers?

6. What's your favorite sex scene in the Soul Mates Dissipate series?

7. Why did Fancy forgive Ashlee? Should Fancy have pressed charges against Ashlee for planting the abortion pills? What about Darius? Why or why not?

8. Who was more Christian-like, SaVoy or Fancy?

9. Who was responsible for Ashlee's mental state? On a percentage basis, how much is a man responsible when he intentionally manipulates a woman?

10. Do you feel any portion of this novel was unrealistic? Why or why not?

11. Why do you believe many of the main characters found it difficult to move on with their lives? Have you ever loved someone so much that, although they've hurt you, you simply couldn't leave them? Why?

12. Do you love yourself? Before you answer, think openly and objectively. Meaning, if you have an illness (i.e., diabetes, high blood pressure, obesity, etc.) but don't take your medication, or make healthier food choices, then you're not truly loving yourself. Love is spiritual, mental, physical, and emotional. Now answer the question.

13. For God so loved the world, He gave His only begotten son . . . If you believe in God or in a higher power, the question is, how do you show Him that you love Him?

Until we meet again, "You are so special and beautiful. Live in the moment, loving yourself, and my prayer for you is, 'May all your dreams come true.' Peace."